P9-CCK-720

The Nameless Ones

Also by John Connolly

The Charlie Parker Stories
Every Dead Thing
Dark Hollow
The Killing Kind
The White Road
The Reflecting Eye (*novella in the* Nocturnes *collection*)
The Black Angel
The Unquiet
The Reapers
The Lovers
The Whisperers
The Burning Soul
The Wrath of Angels
The Wolf in Winter
A Song of Shadows
A Time of Torment
A Game of Ghosts
The Woman in the Woods
A Book of Bones
The Dirty South

Other Works
Bad Men
The Book of Lost Things
he: A Novel

Short Stories
Nocturnes
Night Music: Nocturnes Volume II

The Samuel Johnson Stories (for Young Adults)
The Gates
Hell's Bells
The Creeps

The Chronicles of the Invaders (with Jennifer Ridyard)
Conquest
Empire
Dominion

Non-Fiction
Books to Die For: The World's Greatest Mystery Writers on the
World's Greatest Mystery Novels (as editor, with Declan Burke)
Parker: A Miscellany
Midnight Movie Monographs: Horror Express

John Connolly

The Nameless Ones

HODDER &
STOUGHTON

First published in Great Britain in 2021 by Hodder & Stoughton
An Hachette UK company

1

Copyright © Bad Dog Books Limited 2021

The right of John Connolly to be identified as the
Author of the Work has been asserted by him in accordance
with the Copyright, Designs and Patents Act 1988.

All rights reserved. No part of this publication may be reproduced, stored in
a retrieval system, or transmitted, in any form or by any means without the
prior written permission of the publisher, nor be otherwise circulated in any
form of binding or cover other than that in which it is published and without
a similar condition being imposed on the subsequent purchaser.

All characters in this publication are fictitious and any resemblance
to real persons, living or dead, is purely coincidental.

A CIP catalogue record for this title is available from the British Library

Hardback ISBN 978 1 529 39834 2
Trade Paperback ISBN 978 1 529 39835 9
eBook ISBN 978 1 529 39837 3

Typeset in Sabon LT by
Palimpsest Book Production Limited, Falkirk, Stirlingshire

Printed and bound in Great Britain by Clays Ltd, Elcograf S.p.A.

Hodder & Stoughton policy is to use papers that are natural, renewable
and recyclable products and made from wood grown in sustainable forests.
The logging and manufacturing processes are expected to conform
to the environmental regulations of the country of origin.

Hodder & Stoughton Ltd
Carmelite House
50 Victoria Embankment
London EC4Y 0DZ

www.hodder.co.uk

For Jack Dennison

Author's Note

For those who may be too young to remember, or who have chosen to forget, a series of conflicts took place in the Balkans between 1991 and 1999 following the disintegration of the former Yugoslavia. That communist state was an uneasy federation of six republics, comprising Serbs, Croats, Bosnian Muslims (known as Bosniaks), Slovenes, Albanians, and other smaller ethnic groupings, all held together by the will of Yugoslavia's ruler, Josip Broz Tito.

Following Tito's death in 1980, the old tensions – some of them dating back to World War II, when the Catholic Croatian Ustasha had sided with the Nazis – began to manifest themselves once again, exacerbated by the fall of the Berlin Wall and the collapse of communism. Croatia and Slovenia declared independence in 1991, and immediately found themselves under attack by the Yugoslav People's Army (JNA) – which was dominated by Serbs – and Serbian paramilitary groups, leading to the death and displacement of thousands before a cease-fire was brokered by the United Nations in 1992.

Meanwhile, Bosnia was also seeking independence, but the Serbian minority in the territory resisted. Once again, elements of the Yugoslav army – operating as the Army of Republika Srpska, or VRS, commonly referred to as the Bosnian Serb Army – intervened, commencing a program of ethnic cleansing against Muslims and Croats in an effort to create a Serbian stronghold. UN intervention failed, and the death toll rose, most infamously at Srebrenica, where more than eight thousand Muslim men and boys were tortured and executed after the town surrendered to Serbian forces led by General Ratko Mladić. Finally, NATO resorted to bombing the Bosnian Serbs, enabling Muslim and

Croat forces to mount a counteroffensive. A peace agreement resulted in an independence referendum in 1992, and the subsequent international recognition of Bosnia and Herzegovina as an independent state. (The Bosnian Serbs, meanwhile, also declared their own version of independence, calling their region the Republika Srpska.)

But conflicts in the former Yugoslavia continued. In 1995, Croatian forces took control of previously Serb-dominated areas of Croatia, and in 1999 ethnic Albanians in Kosovo won a bloody war against Serb forces to obtain their independence. By then Slovenia, Macedonia, and Montenegro had also either severed ties with Belgrade or declared independence, and Serbian ambitions of creating a new Balkan empire from the ruins of the former Yugoslavia lay in tatters.

At least 130,000 people died in the wars, more than a million were displaced by ethnic cleansing, and up to fifty thousand women and children, mainly Bosniaks, were raped, with Serbian armed forces and militias bearing overwhelming responsibility for these atrocities. As one Serb put it during my research, 'A lot of bad things happened, and most of them were our fault. Most,' he emphasized, 'but not all.'

I

Home is the sailor, home from the sea,
And the hunter home from the hill.

Robert Louis Stevenson, 'Requiem'

Chapter I

The two figures were by now a familiar sight, if only to a select few, for even ones such as these, who guarded their privacy so assiduously, must inevitably become known to some of their neighbors. For a time, they had not been seen out together, and only the black man, generally believed to be the younger, was noticeable on the street and the surrounding blocks. It was rumored that the other, the older (marginally) and less elegant (by a more considerable degree), was ill, or perhaps recovering from illness, although questions directed, however discreetly, to Mrs Evelyn Bondarchuk, the woman who occupied the first floor apartment in their building, were met with a stony silence from the lady herself, and the disapproving yaps of her assorted Pomeranians.

According to local lore, it was Mrs Bondarchuk herself who owned the property, although she carefully concealed her interest through the use of shelf companies, a series of lawyers at least as tight-lipped as she, and a Dickensian amount of paperwork – not that anyone was unduly troubled by this minor act of deception, which had long ago mutated from suspicion into fact. After all, this was New York City, and more specifically Manhattan, where various levels of eccentricity, reinvention, and even downright criminality were, if not a given, then at least quotidian.

But the truth of the matter was that Mrs Bondarchuk was merely a tenant, albeit one who functioned also as a watchdog, since her chair by the bay window of her apartment offered a clear view of the street in two directions. (Mrs Bondarchuk's bark, it might have been said, was probably worse than her Pomeranians' bite, although it was a close-run thing, and none of the neighbors were in any hurry to test the hypothesis. The Pomeranians were nippy little beasts when the mood took them, but Mrs Bondarchuk possessed an undeniable solidity, and all her own teeth.)

A few years earlier, there had been some unpleasantness at the property involving a man with a gun, but it, and he, had been taken care of. Since then, Mrs Bondarchuk had committed with even greater acuity to her role as first line of defense. She now understood it was more than a sop from her landlords, a pointless task offered out of pity to an old woman, or a well-intended effort to endow her twilight years with a sense of purpose. No, Mrs Bondarchuk was essential to them, and she loved them for making her so. She had even inquired about the possibility of being given a gun, although this suggestion was politely rebuffed. Mrs Bondarchuk's feelings were not hurt, though. She had asked more out of interest than actual desire. She did not wish to own a gun. In her youth, her father had retained a seven-shot Nagant M1895 revolver from his period of service in the Soviet military. He had kept it clean, well-oiled, and concealed beneath a floorboard in the bedroom. Mrs Bondarchuk had used it only once, when a vagrant entered the house and attempted to rape her mother. Mrs Bondarchuk – or Elena Tikhonov as she was formerly known, before the changes to her name wrought by emigration, anglicization, and marriage – shot him in the chest, and later helped her father and mother to bury the remains in the forest. She was twelve years old.

Then, as now, she was untroubled by what she had done. The vagrant was bad, and had she not acted as she did, he would undoubtedly have hurt or murdered her mother, and possibly Elena, too, before going on to commit further degenerate acts. And, yes, the sixth commandment declared 'Thou shalt not kill', but Mrs Bondarchuk had always believed that Moses, in returning from Mount Sinai, had neglected to bring with him a final tablet, the one containing all the fine print, possibly because his arms were already full.

Mrs Bondarchuk had never shared with another soul outside her immediate family the details of the killing: not with her late husband, whom she had loved dearly, and not even with the two men who owned the building in which she lived, although she was certain that they, at least, would have understood. There was, she felt, no particular benefit to be gained from raising the subject. The vagrant, after all, was dead, and a confession was unlikely to alter that fact. Mrs Bondarchuk was also in possession of a clear conscience on the matter, and while she might, in the years that followed, have occasionally contemplated shooting someone else – certain politicians, for example, or particularly patronizing shopgirls – she had managed to resist the temptation, helped in large part by not being in possession of a suitable weapon. All in all, it was probably for the best that her landlords had not agreed to provide her with a gun. Shooting someone in extremis might be forgivable, but one shouldn't make a habit of it, regardless of provocation.

And here they came now, Mr Louis and Mr Angel, these two men whom she adored like errant sons, the first tall and black, the second short and, well, white*ish*. He had lately been so ill, her Mr Angel, and he had already suffered so much; this, Mrs Bondarchuk had always intuited from his face and eyes. He was recovering, though, even if he was now slower than before. His partner, too, regarded him differently, as if the sickness had reminded him that, in no time at all, one of them must inevitably be parted from the other, and whatever days remained to them were better spent in accord.

But at least they were not alone. They had friends. There was the private detective, Mr Parker, who brought her candy from Maine; and the two brothers, Tony and Paulie Fulci, who were so gentle for such big men, and whom she could not imagine hurting a fly – other people possibly, perhaps even probably, but not a fly.

And they in turn had Mrs Bondarchuk, who prayed for Mr Louis and Mr Angel every night. She prayed that they might have a good death, one marked by ritual and a proper burial, and therefore the salvation of the soul; and not a bad death, an interment in some pit without a blessing or a marker, in the manner of a wandering rapist. Death was the inescapable path. One's thoughts were over the mountains, but death was always behind one's shoulder. Death was an old woman who slept in hell, and took her instructions from God. She was inevitable, but not implacable. She could be spoken to, and negotiated with. Amuse her, interest her, and she might move on.

Mr Louis and Mr Angel, Mrs Bondarchuk believed, greatly amused Death.

Angel waved to Mrs Bondarchuk as they approached the stairs leading to the door of their building.

'Do you think Mrs Bondarchuk has ever killed anyone?' he said.

'Definitely,' said Louis.

'No doubt in your mind?'

'None at all.'

'I thought it was just me.'

'No, she's killed someone for sure. Shot them, is my guess. Remember that time she suggested we give her a gun?'

'Yeah,' said Angel. 'She was kind of matter-of-fact about it.'

'Maybe we should have let her have one.'

'We could always give her one for Christmas, if her heart is still set on it.'

'She's Orthodox. We'd have to wait until January.'

'On the other hand,' said Angel, 'might be best to stick with candy and a Macy's gift card.'

'Still, it's something to keep in reserve in case she gets bored of candy.'

Angel paused to watch a crow alight on a nearby tree.

'That's sorrow, right?' he said. 'One for sorrow, like in the rhyme.'

'I don't think it counts where we're concerned,' said Louis.

'No,' said Angel, 'I guess not.'

Mrs Bondarchuk had also noticed the crow. She crossed herself before offering up a brief prayer of protection. She remained constantly heedful of auguries – the appearance of owls, ravens, and crows, the births of twins and triplets – and kept note of her dreams, waking up in the night to add the details of them to the little writing pad by her bedside, leery always of visions of bread and bees, of teeth falling from gums, of church processions. She had yet to give a watch as a gift, eat from a knife, or mark a fortieth anniversary. She sat down before going on a journey, even if only to the store, in order to confuse any evil spirits that might be lurking, and never put out the garbage after sunset. On the wall by her front door hung a cross of aspen, the cursed wood, which possessed a talismanic power against evil, just as the potency of a vaccine relies upon the element it contains of its target disease.

But perhaps more than any of this, Mrs Bondarchuk believed that death, rather than marking an end, represented only an alteration, if a fundamental one, in the nature of existence. The dead and the living coexisted, each world feeding into the other, and the next realm was a mirror of this one. The dead remained in contact with the living, and spoke to them through dreams and portents.

One had to learn to listen.

And one had to be prepared.

Angel fumbled for his keys. Louis appeared distracted, even weary.

'You look tired,' said Angel.

'You say.'

'I have an excuse. Cancer beats all hands.'

'I didn't sleep so well last night,' said Louis. 'Comes with getting old.'

'You're sure that's all it is?'

'Yes,' Louis lied.

He had been dreaming again, the same dream. It had been coming to him more often in recent months. In his dream he stood by a lake and watched the dead immerse themselves in its waters, wading deeper and deeper, farther and farther, until finally they were lost to the great sea. Beside him stood a little girl: Jennifer, the dead child of the detective Charlie Parker, whom Louis had watched being buried. She held his hand. Her touch was warm against the coldness of his skin. In life, he had known her only from a distance. Now death had made intimates of them.

why are we here?

His voice seemed no longer his own. He heard it as a faded

whisper. Only the girl spoke without distortion, for this was her dominion.

'We're waiting,' she said.

for what?

'For the others to join us.'

and then?

She laughed.

'We shall set black flags in the firmament.'

And he would wake to the memory of her touch.

None of this he chose to share with Angel. They had few secrets from each other, but those they had, they kept close. Had Louis spoken of his dream to Mrs Bondarchuk, she might have advised him to be very wary, and gifted him a cross of aspen. But he had no intention of discussing his recurring dream with her, just as he had elected not to mention it to Angel.

Which was unfortunate, because Angel had been having a very similar dream.

Chapter II

The old man walking the quiet, dark stretch of the Herengracht in Amsterdam no longer dreamed; or perhaps, given his knowledge of the peculiarities of the human consciousness, both waking and sleeping, it would have been more correct to say that he did not recall his dreams. Maybe, he thought, he simply preferred not to do so, and had managed to communicate this to his psyche during the accumulated decades of his time on earth. By this stage of his life, he was happy just to enjoy some semblance of a night's sleep, even one destined to be disturbed by the call of his poor, failing bladder.

His name was De Jaager. He had a first name, although it was rarely used even by close friends, of which he had few. De Jaager was his actual patronym, and translated as 'The Hunter'. It was only partly accurate as a descriptor. For the most part, De Jaager was a *regelaar*, a fixer, but that lacked a certain dignity and authority; and he had, when necessary, assumed the role of hunter, although he typically left the final bloodletting to others, and resorted to such extremes only as a last resort. He was also, it had to be admitted, a criminal – by action, nature, inclination, and association – but he had always behaved with honor in his dealings with his own kind, because there was nothing worse than a felon who could not be trusted, and even malefactors required a code of conduct.

But that was all in the past. He was currently in the final stages of leaving behind this condition of malfeasance, just as he would soon surely retire from life itself. He had shed his business interests, both legitimate and otherwise. He had rid himself of warehouses and manufactories, and paid off those who had remained loyal to him over the years, so that most would never

9

have to work hard again. He was a man preparing for the end, discarding the base matter of this world until all that remained were flesh and memories, and death would ultimately take care of those, too. When he was done with his unburdening, he intended to retire to his small cottage in Amersfoort, where he would live in solitude and anonymity, surrounded by books and the remembrance of those he had lost.

Only one extraneous property remained to be sold: the safe house on the Herengracht, which had been used by only a handful of individuals over the years because it was the most secret and secure of his outposts. Most recently it had been occupied by three men who had come to Amsterdam seeking a book. They had left bodies in their wake, along with a legal mess that had required De Jaager to expend considerable effort and funds to clean up. He had also lost one of his own people, a young woman named Eva Meertens, of whom he had been most fond. Her death, in turn, had necessitated arranging the killing of her murderer, an employee of the US government named Armitage. It had all been very complicated and unsatisfactory, not to mention risky, and confirmed De Jaager in his belief that retirement was now the only reasonable option for a man of his advanced years.

The safe house had been stripped of all but the most inexpensive of furnishings, and De Jaager's lawyer alerted to his client's desire for a quick sale. Already the lawyer had interested parties eager to view the property, even though its precise location had not yet been shared with them. The starting price was five million euros, but De Jaager expected the final offer to exceed that by ten or twenty percent. It would assure him of a great deal of comfort in the winter of his years. He might even travel a little, if the mood took him, although he found airports wearying and people more wearying still. There were many countries he had not yet seen, but the effort of reaching them would almost certainly be greater than the rewards they promised. Possibly he would remain in Amersfoort, and walk each day to Café Onder de Linde for soup and coffee, and a glass of *genever* to keep out the cold. Eva used to say that he would be lost without her, and she also would therefore be required to relocate from Amsterdam to

Amersfoort in order to keep an eye on him. She made it sound like a joke, but De Jaager knew it was more than that. He had become a father to her following the death of her parents, steering her through grief and her rebellious late teens. She had not wanted to be without him, nor he without her. But he had failed to protect her, and her life had come to an end in the waters of an Amsterdam canal. Now, in the time that was left to him, he would mourn her, and have discourse with her ghost in Amersfoort.

He arrived at the safe house. A light burned behind the shutters in the kitchen. Anouk would be there with her son, Paulus; and Liesl, who had survived while her friend Eva had not, and would always feel guilty for it. In his right hand De Jaager held a bottle of champagne: a 1959 Dom Pérignon, one of only 306 ever produced, none of which was ever officially offered for sale. It was probably worth fourteen or fifteen thousand euros, and De Jaager could think of no better company with whom to share it.

For the last time, he placed his key in the lock of the door, entered the hallway of the late seventeenth-century dwelling, and waited for the living and the dead to greet him, each in their own way.

'*Ik ben hier, Ik ben hier,*' he announced, and noticed how different his voice sounded now that the building had been emptied of much of its contents. '*Et Ik bring rijkdom!*'

He walked to the kitchen and glanced inside. A man was seated against the wall beside the fireplace, his hands lying by his sides, palms up. He stared straight ahead, but saw nothing. On the wall behind him was a smear of blood, bone, and gray matter.

'Paulus,' said De Jaager softly, as though he might yet summon him back from the place to which his soul had fled, but the voice that answered was not that of his driver, his aide, his nephew. Instead it spoke with a pronounced Eastern European accent, even after all those years away from Serbia.

'You'll soon speak with him again,' it said. 'In the meantime, rest assured that he'll be able to hear you screaming.'

Chapter III

In New York, SAC Edgar Ross of the Federal Bureau of Investigation was seated before his immediate superior, Conrad Holt, in the bar of the White Horse Tavern on Bridge Street. They were at an isolated table, not a booth, because that way they could be sure they would not be overheard. Holt was drinking a beer, Ross a coffee. The two men often met in private conclave at the White Horse, because it was unwise to discuss subjects of importance or delicacy in a building full of snoops. Ross never even read a newspaper at 26 Federal Plaza, for fear someone might take note of a headline and decide to pass judgment accordingly.

Ross and Holt were going over the recent death of the federal legat, Armitage, in the Netherlands. Officially, her death was being described as a suicide. In the days before her body was discovered, Armitage had been absent from her desk at the US Embassy in The Hague due to some unspecified illness, and her colleagues had become concerned for her health, psychological as well as physical. Her remains were subsequently discovered in the shower of her apartment, her arms slit from elbow to wrist. These were incontestable facts.

More problematical, in terms of this narrative, were the absence of a blade and the presence in the shower of an Arabic word, written in red on the tiles – or more precisely, hacked into the ceramic, the implement used first having been dipped in Armitage's vital essence in the manner of a nib being plunged into an inkwell. Clearly, therefore, Armitage had not met her end by her own hand but by that of another: an Islamic terrorist, quite possibly, given the origin of the word on the tiles: نجل, or djinni.

Yet no group had come forward to claim credit for the killing, which was unusual. In addition, the CIA had struggled to find any terrorist operating under the nom de guerre of Djinni or Genie, or any reason, beyond her nationality, for Islamists to have targeted Armitage in particular. Another complicating factor was that Ross now believed Armitage had been involved in a criminal conspiracy, thanks to evidence gleaned from a burner phone discovered in her apartment after her death. It appeared that the legat had been dirty in ways her superiors did not yet understand, which was the worst kind of dirt because it was so hard to expunge.

It had been decided, therefore, that it would be better for all concerned if Armitage's death were ascribed to suicide, thus obviating the necessity of a formal investigation. Two of the numbers on Armitage's burner had proved untraceable, but others had since been identified, one of them as recently as the day before, when it had been used to send and receive text messages in the Netherlands. This was why Holt and Ross were currently meeting in the White Horse Tavern, away from any listening ears at Federal Plaza, because the Armitage situation was about as toxic as a situation could get without calling in FEMA.

'A Serb?' said Holt. 'Why the fuck was Armitage calling a Serbian gangster?'

'I don't know,' said Ross.

'Is there any chance at all that this was part of some unsanctioned operation?'

'None whatsoever.'

'What do we know about this Zippo, Zeppo, whatever?'

'Zivco Ilić,' said Ross.

'Yeah, him.'

'He works for the Vuksan crime syndicate.'

'And who are the Vuksans?'

'Very bad people.'

'How bad is "very bad"?'

'On a scale of one to ten,' said Ross, 'about a twelve.'

De Jaager stood in the kitchen of the canal house. Before him was Zivco Ilić, who had uncorked the bottle of Dom Pérignon and was drinking it straight from the neck. Ilić was of average

13

height, average build, and was averagely good looking. The only aspects of him that were not average were his native intelligence and his capacity for violence. The Vuksans did not employ dullards, and displayed a marked preference for sadists.

'This tastes like shit,' said Ilić, waving the bottle in the air.

'That's because you have no class,' said De Jaager.

Ilić spat a stream of champagne directly at De Jaager. It struck him in the face.

'May I reach for a handkerchief?' De Jaager asked, but the question was directed not at Ilić but at a second, older man leaning against the doorframe.

'Of course,' came the reply. 'We're not animals, or not all of us.'

This was Radovan Vuksan, brother of Spiridon, the head of the Vuksan syndicate. Radovan was in his sixties, and balding in the manner of a tonsured monk. He weighed 140 pounds soaking wet, most of it in the form of a distended potbelly that resembled a tumor. His eyes were shiny but lifeless, as though constructed from flawed glass, and if he had ever smiled, he had done so only in the privacy of his own company. He was the ice to his brother's fire, but each burned with equal ferocity.

De Jaager retrieved a handkerchief from his coat pocket and used it to wipe his face. When he was finished, Ilić spat another burst of champagne at him, this one heavier with saliva.

'Zivco,' warned Radovan Vuksan. 'No more.'

Ilić offered the bottle to Radovan, who declined.

'Such a waste,' said De Jaager, staring at Ilić.

'Of champagne?' said Radovan.

'Of oxygen. You should review your recruitment policy. I perceive flaws in your criteria.'

Radovan didn't rush to disagree, a fact that Ilić could not fail to notice. As far as Radovan was concerned, Ilić was his brother's acolyte, so it was for Spiridon to defend him, should he be bothered to do so. If nothing else, Radovan thought, De Jaager was a good judge of character.

'Are you worried about your women?' said Radovan.

De Jaager had not asked after them, just in case Anouk and

Liesl had been absent when the Vuksans arrived at the safe house. Now, with his worst fears confirmed, his eyes briefly fluttered closed.

'Yes,' he said.

'They're being looked after,' said Radovan.

'Don't hurt them,' said De Jaager.

Radovan Vuksan shrugged. 'That's out of my hands. Spiridon will decide what's to be done with them once he gets here.'

'I have money.'

'I know,' said Radovan. 'So do we. So do lots of people.'

'One can always have more,' said De Jaager.

'This isn't about money. This is about blood.'

'Really?' said De Jaager. 'I thought you'd be sick of it by now.'

'I am,' said Radovan. 'Others, not so much.'

Flies buzzed around the body of Paulus. Ilić emptied the remainder of the champagne over Paulus's head, dispersing some of the insects, even drowning one or two before the rest returned with a vengeance. From the street outside came the sound of a woman's laughter. A van pulled up. A door opened and closed. De Jaager heard footsteps coming down the stairs, and a figure passed behind Radovan to admit the new arrival.

'Now,' said Radovan, 'we can begin.'

Chapter IV

Angel was still removing his jacket when Mrs Bondarchuk opened the door of her apartment to peer at him. In her left arm she held one of the Pomeranians – Angel had no idea which one, since they all looked the same to him – while the head of a second manifested itself from somewhere around the level of her ankles.

'How far did you walk today?' said Mrs Bondarchuk.

'To Fifty-sixth and back,' said Angel.

'That's too far.'

'I walked to Sixtieth yesterday and you told me it wasn't far enough.'

'It wasn't, but Fifty-sixth is too far for today,' said Mrs Bondarchuk. 'You should have stopped at Fifty-eighth.'

The Pomeranian crouching in the crook of her arm yapped its agreement. Everyone, it seemed to Angel, was an expert on his health except him. The only consolation was that the chemo was over. He'd endured four cycles of it and now just had to accommodate himself to being monitored for the rest of his life, an endless pattern of worrying, testing, and relief – if he remained clear – before the worrying commenced again.

If, or when, they told him the cancer had returned, Angel thought he might kill himself. He'd asked Jennifer Parker about it, in one of his dreams. He'd been raised Catholic, and a fear of damnation persisted. Suicides, he recalled, received scant mercy in the next world. But in his dream, Jennifer had told him not to worry.

'In whatever manner you find your way here,' she said, 'I'll be waiting. I won't let anything bad happen to you.'

Angel had wanted to point out that, since he would be dead, something bad would already have happened to him. He'd resisted

16

the impulse, though, because a bad state of affairs could always be made worse. Also, it seemed imprudent to crack wise with a ghost, even in a dream.

Louis, who had proceeded upstairs ahead of him, called his name and instructed him to stop bothering Mrs Bondarchuk.

'Go on up,' said Mrs Bondarchuk. 'Rest awhile.'

Angel did as he was told. He would never have admitted it aloud, but he felt that Mrs Bondarchuk might have been right about those two extra blocks each way. His insides hurt, and he felt the urge to lie down and close his eyes. He was already on the fourth step when Mrs Bondarchuk said, 'You think maybe the Fulci boys will come visit again soon?'

Angel sighed. Yes, a bad state of affairs *could* always be made worse. Had the Fulci brothers been younger, and without a mother of their own, Mrs Bondarchuk might have adopted them, in which case even the rats would have moved out.

'God, I hope not,' he said softly, but Mrs Bondarchuk misheard, or decided to give the impression of it.

'I hope so, too,' she said.

And smiling, she closed the door.

Downtown, Conrad Holt ordered another drink, and SAC Ross consented to a refill of coffee. They had to tread carefully in their unraveling of Armitage's activities in the Netherlands. The legat program was the responsibility of the International Operations Division at FBI headquarters in Washington, and only the application of significant amounts of pressure from the State Department and the Department of Justice, as well as from within the Bureau itself, had persuaded the IOD to shelve any official investigation into her death. Ross had become involved because Armitage, on his instructions, had been in contact with the unusual private investigator named Charlie Parker during his time in the Netherlands. There was no suggestion that Parker might have been involved in Armitage's demise, as he had already left the country by then. Neither was he in the habit of hewing Arabic lettering into shower tiles or killing women by slitting their wrists. But Parker and his colleagues, the career criminals Angel and

Louis, had received financial, informational, and legal assistance from Ross while they were in Europe. Naturally enough, the deputy director in charge of the IOD was curious to know why, just in case the Parker connection might have led, directly or indirectly, to Armitage's death. Ross's answers had been unsatisfactory in that regard, but Holt's intervention had protected him from falling victim to the kind of intra-agency conflict that destroyed careers, while also ensuring that Ross continued to remain privy to the information gleaned from Armitage's burner phone.

As if the situation were not already sufficiently complex and fraught with risk for Holt and Ross, both men were career feds. Ross was marginally older, with more years of service, but Holt had risen faster and higher through the ranks. The latter had so far avoided scandal, opprobrium, and anything more threatening than the most routine of inquiries. Holt spoke the language of congressional committees and had a memory that was both comprehensive and selective. He was a survivor in the big pond, and like all survivors, he had sharp teeth.

Ross, on the other hand, would always be tainted by association with the Traveling Man investigation, specifically the lengthy and painful revelation of the Bureau's failings in the case. Because the Traveling Man had been responsible for the deaths of Susan and Jennifer Parker, respectively Charlie Parker's wife and young daughter, Ross had developed a relationship with the PI that was, in Holt's view, potentially compromising. That relationship, in turn, extended to Angel and Louis. For the present, the advantages of retaining links with Parker outweighed the disadvantages, which was why Holt had been willing to protect Ross from enemies both internal and external. Lately, though, Holt had begun seriously reconsidering the wisdom of that support.

'You still haven't told me why Armitage was in touch with the Vuksans,' said Holt.

'You're assuming I know,' said Ross, 'which flatters my intelligence.'

'It was entirely unintentional. Well, don't you have an answer?'

'No, but I have a theory. It won't make you happy.'

'I haven't been happy since Reagan was president,' said Holt, 'and I wasn't even very happy then.'

Ross pushed his coffee cup aside and laid his hands flat on the table, like a man steeling himself to speak, or perhaps to rise and depart, never to return.

'It's the timing of the contact that concerns me,' he said. 'Perhaps Armitage was in regular communication with the Vuksans, but my instinct is that she was not. It would have been too perilous, and I can't see any significant benefit accruing to her. But Armitage's disintegration – her absence from work, her illness, psychosomatic or otherwise – appears to have commenced with the arrival in the Netherlands of Parker and his colleagues.'

'So?'

'So,' said Ross, 'some years ago a Serb named Andrej Buha was murdered in Amsterdam. Buha was also known as Timmerman – the "Timber Man", or Carpenter, in Dutch – because of his fondness for crucifying Muslims and Croats during the Balkan conflicts. After the war, Buha signed on as an enforcer for elements within the Zemun crime syndicate, which by then had set up a base of operations in the Netherlands. The Zemuns were most upset when Buha was shot – not out of any great fondness for him, but because it made them appear vulnerable, and marked the beginning of a decline in their fortunes in that part of Europe which not even a great deal of bloodshed ever fully arrested.

'Out of that wreckage emerged the Vuksans: two brothers, Spiridon and Radovan, supported by a cadre of loyal disciples. The Zemun clan is dangerous, but the Vuksans are much worse. The rumor is that for years they'd been working from within to assume control of the Zemun syndicate's Dutch wing, and its dissolution was less a spontaneous collapse than a controlled explosion planned by the Vuksans and their allies.

'The three principal Zemun figures in the Netherlands have all since been neutralized in one manner or another. One died of a heart attack in 2010 while awaiting trial on money laundering charges, a second was shot dead in Rotterdam in 2013 by an unknown assassin, and the third vanished in Serbia shortly before the ascent of the Vuksans, and is now assumed to be getting in touch with nature from six feet below ground. Whatever the Vuksans' degree of involvement in any or all of these misfortunes, it left the way clear for them to consolidate a base of operations in Amsterdam.

'Meanwhile, the Zemun clan – it's named after a district in Belgrade, not a family – continues to function, but the Dutch share and all European territory to the west of the Netherlands were effectively ceded to the Vuksans, probably on orders from politicians in Belgrade, on the grounds that the bloodshed was making them look bad in front of their fancy European friends. The Zemun name stuck, though, because you can choose to call a wolf whatever you like, but it remains a wolf. It might also be argued that the Zemun brand had a certain market value, even a cachet.'

In truth, Holt's interest in Serbian gangsters was minimal and didn't extend much farther than Glendale, Ridgewood, and Astoria, the Serb enclaves in Queens, New York. But back in the late eighties and early nineties, the Bureau had briefly been forced to reckon with Boško 'The Yugo' Radonjić, who, thanks to his connections with the mobster Jimmy Coonan, had managed to gain control of the Irish-American Westies crime gang after most of its leadership was imprisoned. But Radonjić was dead now, and Jimmy Coonan was serving seventy-five years for racketeering, without the possibility of parole. As far as Holt was concerned, the Serbs were someone else's problem, and they could do what they liked as long as they did it outside the United States. Armitage's involvement with them was an unwelcome complication.

'Since their takeover of the Dutch operation,' said Ross, 'the Vuksans have renewed efforts to establish who might have killed Andrej Buha. He was their cousin, a Vuksan loyalist within the syndicate, and had served under Spiridon in the military, so his murder has always rankled. A Muslim group claimed responsibility for Buha's assassination as revenge for his activities during the war, but the Vuksans were never entirely convinced. A clean kill – two shots to the chest, and a double tap to the head – wasn't their style, and the Vuksans' own inquiries, which mostly involved torturing Muslim captives, seemed to confirm their suspicions.'

'Then who killed Buha?' said Holt.

'I think Louis did,' said Ross, 'as a favor to an old friend called De Jaager. Buha had murdered a man named Jos, the husband of De Jaager's sister-in-law, Anouk. De Jaager felt, not unreasonably, that a reprisal was in order, and tasked Louis with carrying it out. My understanding is that Louis did it for free.'

'And you believe Armitage discovered this?'

'There had long been rumors of an outside contractor for the hit on Buha, and Armitage had good contacts in IPOL, the Dutch police intelligence service. When Louis returned to the Netherlands with Parker, and made contact with De Jaager's people, Armitage might have started digging deeper and come up with gold.'

'But why feed this information to the Vuksans?' said Holt.

'Money. Or because she was told to.'

'Told by whom?'

'I don't know,' said Ross, 'but Armitage killed two people before she died, both of them connected to Parker's investigation, and also to some of our own interests. She didn't do that on a whim.'

Holt thought about finishing his drink and ordering yet another, but decided not to. If he kept on drinking, he might not stop until oblivion took him. Every time he heard the names of Parker and his friends, it seemed to trigger an ulcer.

'On the other hand,' said Holt, 'Armitage's call to this Zivco Ilić might have had nothing to do with the death of Buha.'

'No, it might not,' Ross admitted, 'but a warning to Louis may be in order nonetheless.'

'We're the FBI,' said Holt. 'We don't notify assassins that past sins could have returned to haunt them. We're supposed to put them behind bars.'

'Even the ones we've used to further our own ends?'

Any residual good nature seeped from Holt's face as he stared at Ross. Holt wondered when he would have to cast him adrift, and how he could ensure that Ross drowned immediately after.

'Not for the first time,' said Holt, 'it strikes me that you may be developing an affection for individuals who are unworthy of it.'

'Respect, not affection.'

'That's a distinction that might not be appreciated in a court of law.'

'Let's hope it never comes to that.'

'From your mouth to God's ear, although it would be preferable for all concerned if God wasn't listening to any of this.'

'Are you ordering me not to share our information with Louis?' said Ross.

'I'm not ordering you to do anything, because our conversation never happened.' Holt dropped cash on the table to cover the tab. He wasn't about to put this on his credit card. 'For now,' he added, 'the Vuksans aren't our concern, and it would be better for both of us if Armitage's reasons for being in contact with them remained a mystery.'

'I've seen an intelligence memorandum that says otherwise,' said Ross.

Holt removed a couple of dollar bills from the tip. He was a government employee, and his pension would only stretch so far.

'Go on,' he said.

'The Vuksans are people smugglers, of both high- and low-value cargo, and they don't perform background checks.'

'Terrorists?'

'That's the supposition.'

'Unless they're on US soil, or targeting American citizens, it's not an issue for the Bureau.'

'Not yet.'

'It's still no reason for pursuing unnecessary and unwise contacts with a known killer.'

'Suspected killer,' Ross corrected. 'And it may be a little late for us to begin keeping our distance.'

For you, perhaps, thought Holt, *but I still have some deniability.*

Yet the mention of a memorandum worried him. After 9/11, promising careers had been torpedoed by evidence of unwillingness to act on intelligence leads. His head would roll as easily as any other.

'I don't want to know about it,' said Holt at last. 'Officially, I've warned you against disseminating this information either within the Bureau or beyond it. Understood?'

'Perfectly,' said Ross, without resentment. He knew how the game was played, and had long ago resigned himself to the fact that the cards were almost irredeemably stacked against him. Under such circumstances, a man had three choices. He could fold; he could continue to play the hand that was dealt, relying on bluff and the hope of an improbable reversal of fortune; or he could cheat, and in Ross's dictionary, cheating was just another word for pragmatism. Holt knew this, too, hence his use of the word 'officially', which implied that, unofficially, Ross had latitude.

'But if what you believe is true,' said Holt, 'and Armitage sold Louis out to the Vuksans, wouldn't they have made their move by now?'

'I suppose so,' said Ross, 'but some men prefer to wait.'

'For what?' said Holt.

'For the perfect moment.'

Chapter V

It had been whispered of Spiridon Vuksan that he was in poor health, although he showed no signs of this as he entered the kitchen of the safe house, and the rumor could more correctly have been ascribed to wishful thinking. He was shorter than his brother, stocky and muscular where Radovan was thin and bird-like, paunch apart. Spiridon had also retained all of his hair, which was short and mostly gray, although patches of dark remained like the speckling on an egg. Just as Radovan had never been seen to smile, Spiridon had never been heard to raise his voice in anger: his speech rarely exceeded a murmur, as of one offering prayers in humility to his god. His aspect was entirely gentle, and every act of violence he had committed, every rape, mutilation, and murder, had been accompanied by an air of regret, as though some force outside and above Spiridon – whether an unknown deity, an unnamed superior, or even the victims themselves – had forced him to act against his better nature.

Spiridon had kindness in his eyes, but – as with his brother – it was painted on glass, and whatever reality lay behind them was revealed in the work of his hands. Had it been possible to excise the orbs, leaving only the ocular hollows, one might have discerned a cloudy blackness resembling ink in water, a mass that occasionally assumed the form of something ancient and predatory, an entity that would feed even when untroubled by hunger, for the pleasure of tearing another living creature apart. Spiridon Vuksan operated in a realm beyond reason, and his madness was all the more terrifying for its equanimity.

Spiridon removed his coat and handed it to his brother. He pulled up a chair and sat before De Jaager, so close that their knees almost touched. He intertwined his fingers and gazed upon the man before him, those clement eyes carefully taking in each of De Jaager's features in the manner of a physiognomist tasked with establishing the evidence of grave moral degeneracy in another. Finally, he spoke.

'I am sorry it has come to this,' he said.

De Jaager did not reply. This man was unworthy of it, and no words would make any difference to what was to come.

'You understand why you and I are sitting here, don't you?' said Spiridon. 'Please don't tell me you're about to die in ignorance.'

'Timmerman,' said De Jaager.

'Bravo,' said Spiridon, and gave a slow, sad clap. 'Although Andrej never cared for that appellation, and I didn't either. I had always wondered if you might have been responsible for his death, but then there were so many others who had cause to hate him. I was surprised that we didn't have a queue of candidates claiming credit for his execution, but perhaps caution caused them to remain silent. That was wise, given what is about to happen to you.'

He stared at his hands and De Jaager tensed, for it seemed to him that this might be the moment of his death, one in which Spiridon would descend upon him with nails like talons and tear him apart. But the Serb, having waited for so long, was now disinclined to hurry.

'Do you know,' he said, 'I once asked Andrej if he'd kept count of how many men he'd killed. I was genuinely curious, and he took the question to heart. He came to me some days later and told me he believed it was between two hundred and fifty and three hundred individuals. He regretted that he could not be more precise, but memory always betrays us. Still, it was impressive that he could recall so many, although I was told that he entered names in a notebook for many years until it became unwise to retain it. He said the wars against the Turks and Croats were the crowning glories of his life, and his only regret was that they had ever ended. He once killed thirty people in a single day, mostly men. They were brought to him from the camp at Omarska. They were forced to kneel before the stump of a tree, and then Andrej shattered their skulls with a mallet made of lignum vitae. He stopped when his arms grew heavy and he could no longer dispatch his victims with a single blow. The women, though, he raped first. Spoils of war.'

Behind his brother, Radovan Vuksan exhaled loudly through his nose. He objected as a matter of principle to the manner of Andrej Buha's death and the long failure to punish those responsible. He did not, however, regard the world as a poorer place for Buha's absence; the man's savagery had only increased as the years went by, and humanity could afford to lose a sadist or two without ever being in danger of running short. But then Radovan was no killer, although he had profited from the deaths of others. Spiridon liked to taunt him about this when Radovan counseled against acts of violence unless absolutely necessary. Radovan, in turn, would invariably counter that, while Spiridon's actions might have contributed to the fear in which the Vuksans were held, it was he, Radovan, who was responsible for their wealth. Fear brought power, but money secured it.

Spiridon turned to scowl at his brother.

'Is this too strong for your stomach?' he said.

'Not at all,' said Radovan. 'Indulge yourself.'

Spiridon returned his attention to De Jaager.

'Then,' Spiridon continued, 'after we took Srebrenica, Andrej became curious about the mechanics of crucifixion and its potency as an instrument of terror. He discovered that a man crucified with his arms fixed above his head will survive for half an hour at most, but often for as little as ten minutes. I think his interest in crucifixion was partly a consequence of his spiritual convictions. Andrej was intensely religious, with a particular devotion to Saint Joankije of Devič. I don't suppose you knew that. You probably think of us all as beasts.'

'I've tried,' said De Jaager, 'not to think of you at all. But I was unaware of a patron saint of rapists. I can only suppose that my spirituality is of a different aspect to your own.'

Spiridon tapped De Jaager on the knee.

'That's very clever,' he said. 'Of course, everyone acquainted with you says that you're a clever man. I've been hearing that for years. But if they could see you now, what would they say?'

26

'We will never know.'

'You won't, but I'll be sure to listen in your absence.'

There came a clicking from nearby. Radovan was tapping his watch.

'I'm almost done,' said Spiridon. 'De Jaager's history lesson is nearing its end. When the Shiptars' – Spiridon, like many of his generation, always used the derogatory Serbian term when talking of Albanians – 'attacked the Serbian Orthodox monastery at Devič in 2004, Andrej requested permission to go back to the region to punish those responsible. I refused. Had he gone, I doubt he would ever have returned. He would have signed up to hunt the guerillas of the Kosovo Liberation Army. But I needed him: He was my gauntlet, my mace, so I allowed him instead to gorge himself on the Albanians who had settled here in the Netherlands. It was, in retrospect, a mistake. I believe he tipped over into madness, and proved increasingly difficult to control in the aftermath. The killing of your brother-in-law, Jos, was an unfortunate consequence. That, in turn, led to Andrej's murder on your orders, which is why you and I have come to this pass. On one level, I bear responsibility for what occurred. I thought I could tame Andrej, but I was mistaken.'

Spiridon leaned forward.

'I genuinely do not understand why you stopped at Andrej,' he said. 'It was foolish of you. He was only the instrument of another's will. You might as well have taken out your anger on the hammer used to punch the nails through Jos's wrists and ankles, or the nails themselves. Were the positions reversed, I would have come for you.'

'But we are not alike,' said De Jaager.

'And perhaps you did not want a war, one that you could not hope to win?'

'Perhaps.'

'Yet the end result is the same,' said Spiridon. 'Your destruction, and the annihilation of all you hold dear.'

Spiridon produced a gun from his belt. He flipped the safety catch, positioned the muzzle under De Jaager's chin, and forced him to place a finger on the trigger.

'Not everything they say about me is true,' said Spiridon. 'I am capable of mercy, and I have always respected you. I don't want you to suffer, so I will settle for your life – as long as you are the one to take it. I want you to die a suicide. There is one bullet in the chamber. Apply the necessary pressure to the trigger, and this will all be over. If you don't, I guarantee that your passing from this world will be more painful than you could ever have imagined.'

De Jaager heard a noise from above. It sounded like a woman whimpering. Now he knew where at least one of them was being held.

'Who is up there?' he asked.

It was Radovan who answered.

'The old woman, Anouk, and a younger girl, Liesl.'

'What will happen to them?'

'Pull the trigger,' said Spiridon.

De Jaager's eyes moved frantically between the two brothers.

'Please,' he said. 'Let them go. They have nothing to do with this.'

'I give you my word,' said Spiridon, 'on this relic.' He removed a very old Serbian cross from under his shirt, the links of its chain damp with his sweat. 'If you kill yourself, I will let them go. I want to see you take your own life. I want to watch you dishonor yourself in this world and damn yourself in the next.'

De Jaager swallowed once, closed his eyes, and pulled the trigger.

The hammer fell. The gun clicked emptily.

For a moment there was silence, and then Spiridon Vuksan began to laugh. He was joined only by Zivco Ilić, for Radovan Vuksan had already left the room. The only people not laughing were Paulus, who was dead, and De Jaager, who soon would be.

'That was a good joke, eh?' said Spiridon.

He slapped De Jaager on the back and removed the gun from his hand. De Jaager did not resist. He did not even look up. His eyes were already fixed on the afterlife. There would be pain, but he was an old man and pain was not unfamiliar to him. He wished only that he could have spared others their agonies and, like Christ, added their sufferings to his own.

28

'I am a man of my word,' said Spiridon. 'You failed to kill yourself, so I don't have to let your women go. Come, come.' He took one of De Jaager's arms, and Ilić grabbed the other. Together they lifted the old man to his feet. 'Let's go upstairs. I have something I want you to see . . .'

Chapter VI

Angel and Louis ordered from Saiguette on Columbus Avenue. They got extra for Mrs Bondarchuk, although they did not invite her to join them and she did not ask. They ate grilled lemongrass pork shoulder banh mi and crispy shrimp, accompanied by half a bottle of German Riesling. When they were done, Louis washed up while Angel sat in his favorite armchair and read a book entitled *I Await the Devil's Coming*. Parker had originally recommended it to Louis, but he set it aside after two pages on the grounds that he had no interest in the affairs of nineteen-year-old girls; never had, never would. The book dated from 1902 and had been written by Mary MacLane, the nineteen-year-old girl in question, a native of Butte, Montana. Angel hadn't yet journeyed very far with MacLane, but he liked her already. She was a thief, but one with a coherent criminal philosophy.

'It has been suggested to me that I am a kleptomaniac,' she wrote. 'But I am sure my mind is perfectly sane. I have no such excuse. I am a plain, downright thief. This is only one of my many peculations. I steal money, or anything that I want, whenever I can, nearly always. It amuses me – and one must be amused. I have only two stipulations: that the person to whom it belongs does not need it pressingly, and that there is not the smallest chance of being found out. (And of course, I could not think of stealing from my one friend.) It would be extremely inconvenient to be known as a thief, merely.'

Angel thought that, had he ever been fortunate enough to have a daughter, he would have wanted her to turn out like Mary MacLane.

Louis appeared from the kitchen.

'You still reading that book?'

'You should give it another try,' said Angel. 'She was a singular young woman. Listen to this: "I am not trying to justify myself for stealing. I do not consider it a thing that needs to be justified, any more than walking or eating or going to bed."'

'You ever consider telling that to a judge?' said Louis.

'It never crossed my mind.'

'If it ever does, I recommend that you bite your tongue.'

Angel looked at him from over the top of his spectacles.

'You seem distracted,' he said.

'I've got a feeling, like something scratching at my brain.'

Angel let the book close, but used a finger to mark his page. He knew better than to utter some platitude in reply. When Louis was disturbed like this – and such instances were rare – clouds were gathering. It was not a psychic ability, or any form of sixth sense. It was simply a function of Louis's instinct for self-preservation, and linked to his predatory capacities. It was an atavistic response that had, in recent years, extended itself to encompass all those under his protection.

'Are we in trouble?' said Angel.

'No,' said Louis. He thought for a moment. 'But someone is.'

Chapter VII

De Jaager was seated in another hardbacked chair, this time in the larger of the upper bedrooms. His hands were restrained behind his back. The room contained two iron-frame beds. Anouk was tied to one, Liesl to the other. Both women were gagged and both were naked. Two men that De Jaager had not seen before now, and whom he did not recognize, were standing beside the beds. Each had a knife in his hand. There were marks on the throats of the women, probably where the blades had been held to keep them quiet.

Radovan Vuksan had declined to remain in the room, returning instead to the kitchen. Music was coming from below. Radovan had turned the radio up loud and De Jaager could hear a late Schumann song, one of the lieder for children, rising through the floor. Perhaps Radovan had even chosen it deliberately, playing it through the Bluetooth system via his phone, as though an idyll of childhood might permit him to evade the reality of what was happening above his head.

Now Spiridon spoke in Serbian and one of the men by the beds began to remove his clothing, because skin was easier to clean than fabric. The other, younger, hesitated before arguing with Spiridon, who scowled in response but appeared to assent, however grudgingly. The younger man remained clothed and stepped back. Ilić displayed no similar reluctance and was already stripping.

Spiridon stood over De Jaager. In his right hand he held a sharp pair of meat scissors.

'You're going to watch this,' Spiridon told De Jaager. 'You're going to watch every minute, because you caused it to happen. If you turn away, or close your eyes, I'll cut off your eyelids.'

De Jaager looked into the faces of each woman and tried to

32

communicate feelings that would have been beyond the power of speech even had he tried to use words. Both were terrified, but Anouk displayed defiance alongside fear. She had not asked him to avenge her husband's death at the hands of Andrej Buha, but when informed by De Jaager of what he planned to do, she had held him tightly and blessed his name.

'There may be repercussions,' he had told her. 'For all of us.'

'I understand,' she had replied. 'But if it were in my power, I would kill them all, just to be certain.'

I should have listened to her, De Jaager thought. *We should not have stopped at Buha.*

The men moved onto the beds. Against their gags, the women began to scream.

Chapter VIII

Angel woke in the night to discover Louis seated by the window. He had an ancient flip phone in his right hand, one of many he kept as throwaways, and was opening and closing it repeatedly. It was this noise that had roused Angel.

'What time is it?' he said.

'After midnight.'

'Who were you going to call?'

'I don't know,' said Louis. 'Everyone?'

Angel got out of bed and stood beside his partner. He ran a hand through Louis's graying hair.

'Whatever it is, we'll find out soon enough.'

'Yes, I suppose we will.'

It was strange, Angel thought, how many people they had come to care about. It had not always been this way. He blamed Charlie Parker. Who knew that a conscience could be contagious?

'Maybe we should try Parker,' said Angel. After all, he reasoned, if anyone was likely to be in difficulties, it was the private detective. The man could attract trouble in a vacuum.

'I did,' said Louis, 'while you were asleep. He's safe; his daughter, too.'

Angel watched a police car pass. Ordinary people could turn to the law in times of need – well, as long as they weren't minorities living in the wrong neighborhood, but nobody claimed the law was perfect, and even justice wasn't colorblind. Men like Angel and Louis, on the other hand, were required to make their own justice, forging it in their image.

'Could you be mistaken about this?' said Angel.

'No.'

Angel rubbed his eyes. He felt a lassitude that no sleep could relieve. Sometimes a man just became enervated by suffering. There seemed to be no end to it.

'You need to rest,' he said. 'You'll have to be fresh when it comes.'

'I'll be there shortly,' said Louis.

Angel returned to bed. When he woke again in the night, he was alone. He heard music playing softly from downstairs, but did not move. He closed his eyes, and waited for death's inevitable approach.

Chapter IX

I t was said that the Gestapo in Lyon, under their repellent chief Klaus Barbie, finally grew so frenzied in their torture and execution of prisoners that the floor of their headquarters at the École de Sainte Militaire could no longer accommodate the by-products of the butchery, and the very ceilings of the building began to bleed. Radovan Vuksan had thought it an exaggeration until he retreated to the kitchen of De Jaager's safe house in the hope of avoiding what was taking place upstairs, only to find droplets of blood exploding upon his bare head and redness pooling on the table. He looked up in time to see fluids leaking through the floorboards and stepped aside to avoid any further misfortune. He lit a cigarette, and saw that his hands were shaking.

Unlike his brother and the rest of the Vuksan clan, Radovan had not fought directly in the Balkan conflicts – or principally the 'War in Croatia', as it was known to Serbs – although arguably his role had been more important, and lethal, than those of his comrades who had taken lives. Radovan had worked as a 'senior advisor' at the MUP, the Serbian Ministry of Internal Affairs, his role and title being deliberately unrevealing, even innocuous. The MUP was one of the most powerful ministries in the land, with responsibility for local and national law enforcement. With Radovan's assistance, it became more powerful still, helping to arm civilians and local militias of the self-proclaimed Republic of Serbian Krajina in Croatia, and secretly channeling funds to the RSK's president, Milan Martić.

It was Radovan who had organized the support structures for the Bosnian and Croatian Serb forces during the wars; Radovan who had provided funding for the 'volunteers' recruited to fight in Serb-held territories in Croatia; Radovan who had personally

36

supervised the handover of hundreds of thousands of dollars to the Serbian criminal warlord Arkan, whom he had known of old; and Radovan, ultimately, who had arranged Arkan's assassination in the lobby of Belgrade's InterContinental Hotel in January 2000, when it became clear that it would be better for all, Arkan himself excepted, if he did not live long enough to be questioned about war crimes by the inquisitors of the International Criminal Tribunal for the former Yugoslavia. Without Radovan Vuksan's efforts, the War in Croatia would have been significantly shorter and less genocidal than it was. Yet any blood on his hands was purely metaphorical. He was an organizer – a brilliant one – but with no taste for either committing or witnessing mass murder. Some might even have called him a coward, but they would have been wrong, for Radovan's moral failings were deeper and more complex than the term allowed.

The blood continued to drip from the ceiling. The sound it made as it splashed on the table was unnerving to him. From the position of the spreading stain he thought the old woman, Anouk, was probably the source. She had a lot of blood in her, and the mattress on which they had placed her was thin. It was not a surprise that it had become soaked through so quickly.

Radovan took a handkerchief from his pocket, dampened it at the sink, and used it to clean his pate. The cigarette was calming him slightly, but then the girl, Liesl, began to make a high-pitched mewling noise that he could discern even over the music. Radovan had never heard a human being emit a sound like that. It was beyond any ordinary conception of pain, and he guessed the girl would not last much longer. He turned the music up a notch, and realized he would never again be able to listen to Schumann with quite the same pleasure.

Radovan had tried to talk his brother out of going after De Jaager. Andrej Buha was long dead, the memory of him lost to all but a handful of his contemporaries, and even they would hardly have recalled him with much fondness. Had De Jaager not hired someone to take care of him, the Zemuns would eventually have been forced to kill him themselves. They might even have entrusted the Vuksans with the task in order to avoid a blood feud. Buha had become unstable, which threatened to bring danger to them all. De Jaager, by Radovan's reckoning, had done them a favor of sorts by solving the Buha problem, and the Vuksans had weathered the storms that followed until they, like De Jaager, were on the verge of retiring as wealthy men. They had lived as voluntary exiles for long enough, and home was calling. Concerns had been assuaged, bribes had been paid, and a place had been prepared for them in the new Serbia. In time, they would be laid to rest in its soil. This final act of vengeance for an unloved man was, in Radovan's view, an unnecessary risk to take at such a delicate stage.

Radovan wondered, too, about the assassin De Jaager had employed to kill Buha. The gunman was an American, and his name – as they now knew, thanks to the legat Armitage – was Louis. According to Spiridon, this Louis was no cause for apprehension. He was a professional who had been hired to do a job, and whatever happened in the aftermath would be of no concern to him. Perhaps, if the mood struck, Spiridon might ask one of their friends in the United States to take care of him, but there would be little pleasure in it. Louis was undoubtedly lethal, and would therefore have to be dealt with quickly. He would die largely without suffering, possibly without even knowing the reason for his termination, and what would be the purpose of that? As Spiridon had indicated to De Jaager, only a dolt blamed a weapon for his agonies, cursing the blade that cut him or the gun that wounded him rather than the one who wielded the knife or pulled the trigger. If they did not trouble the assassin, said Spiridon, he would not trouble them. That was how such men worked.

But Radovan was not so sure. Armitage had informed Zivco Ilić – to whom she had first reached out, for reasons still unclear to the Vuksans – that Louis had returned briefly to the Netherlands and was met at the airport by De Jaager's factotum Paulus, who now lay slumped and dead in the kitchen. In addition, the Vuksans' contact in the AIVD, the Dutch General Intelligence and Security Service, claimed that Louis and De Jaager had visited the Rijksmuseum together, and Louis might even have stayed for a time in this very safe house. Armitage had believed Louis and De Jaager to be engaged in some joint endeavor, one involving an American private investigator named Charlie Parker. This, to Radovan, did not look like the standard relationship between a hired killer and his one-time employer, but suggested a deeper connection. One might almost have said a friendship.

He increased the volume of the music still further, and lit another cigarette.

Chapter X

S pecial Agent Edgar Ross did not smoke, drank rarely, and socialized on a level familiar only to the dead. His life, or the productive part of it, revolved to a worrying extent around the private detective Charlie Parker and, to a slightly lesser degree, Angel and Louis. Ross's affection for all three was minimal, although in the context of his largely solitary existence, this served to elevate them almost to the status of boon companions. But his respect for them exceeded his affection by a considerable magnitude, and it was partly this – or so Ross told himself – that led him to make the call to Louis.

Yet Ross, in addition to speaking with Conrad Holt, had also put out discreet feelers beyond Federal Plaza. In every situation, however grave, the question to be asked was: How may this be turned to my advantage? A distinctive duplicity was bred in the bone of those who monitored and investigated others for a living, and Ross was far from immune to it. He was aware that, sooner or later, Conrad Holt would attempt to feed him to the wolves. When this happened, Ross intended to make them fight for their meal.

In the meantime, he would continue to secure his position while sticking to his primary task, which was to identify and destroy a group of men and women known as the Backers. This cabal was powerful, corrupt, and mired in the occult, most particularly the search for an entity called the Buried God, which they believed to be a fallen angel, imprisoned deep below ground. Ross, for his part, didn't much care what they did or did not believe: he knew only that they were a malign influence on the affairs of men, a contaminant, and needed to be rooted out. Ross was prepared to use any and all means toward that end, among them Charlie

Parker and, by extension, Angel and Louis. If that meant protecting those men when required, so be it.

Ross was not entirely surprised when the phone was answered on the first ring. Only a select few were privy to the number, which was changed on a regular basis before the new details were carefully circulated. Until that moment, Louis had not even been aware that SAC Edgar Ross of the Federal Bureau of Investigation was one of those with knowledge of its latest iteration.

'What the fuck do you want,' said Louis, once Ross had identified himself, 'and how did you get this number?'

'To answer the second question first,' said Ross, 'I work for the FBI. It's my business to know these things.'

'Then I need to get rid of you or the number. The number might be easier, but it would give me less satisfaction.'

'You are aware that threatening a government official of the United States is a felony under law?'

'Then I'll go to jail laughing,' said Louis. 'You still haven't told me what you want.'

And Ross said, 'I want to deliver a warning.'

Chapter XI

The Vuksans and their votaries finished their work shortly before 6 a.m. Radovan had fallen asleep in a chair, and was woken by his brother calling his name. He spotted a scarlet smear on Spiridon's neck, and guessed that his sibling must have joined in with the persecution of the women at some point. Behind him, Zivco Ilić was carrying a pair of heavy-duty garbage sacks containing the towels and sponges they had brought with them to clean themselves. Radovan also smelled bleach, but under this was blood.

'Was it worth it?' Radovan asked.

'I believe so,' said Spiridon. 'De Jaager lasted a long time; the young woman, too. The older one had a weak heart, I think.'

Radovan recalled the red rain from the ceiling. He had eventually moved the kitchen table to avoid the spatter, and the pool of blood on the floor was now startlingly large. It was a wonder any of those in the room above had survived as long as they did, but then the Vuksans' torturers were skilled at their work.

Radovan got to his feet. He badly needed to pee, but he would not do it here. He hoped Spiridon and the rest had also resisted the impulse, because the forensic investigators, when they came, would examine the toilet bowls for DNA. Then again, even if they found evidence and used it successfully to identify any of the perpetrators, the Dutch would have to seek their extradition from Serbia. Since that country was not a member of the European Union, this would be a political as well as a legal issue, one that could be postponed almost indefinitely, aided by the Vuksans' allies in the Serbian Ministry of Justice and the brothers' position in the larger Serbian criminal hierarchy. Still, Radovan's preference was that extradition should not even become a subject for debate, because who knew how circumstances might change in the future? Money could not buy loyalty indefinitely, and the word of a politician was written in smoke.

Radovan looked out the kitchen window. An unmarked van was pulling up in front of De Jaager's safe house – and how ironic that nomenclature now seemed. Luca Bilbija was behind the wheel. The younger man had left the killing to the others, preferring to wait in the van. He had no more stomach than Radovan for watching women being killed.

'You have blood on your head,' said Spiridon. 'Did you injure yourself?'

'It dripped through the ceiling. I thought I'd washed it all off.'

'It seems that it's as close as you'll ever come to being blooded,' said Spiridon.

The old argument, even now.

'I've played my part in making us wealthy,' said Radovan.

'As have I. You may think, but I act.'

'Rashly, at times. You, too, have blood on you.'

He pointed at the stain. Spiridon spat on his fingers and used them to wipe away the mark.

'And you're too cautious,' he said, 'always.'

For a moment the two brothers faced off, before Spiridon smiled and kissed Radovan.

'But let's not argue,' said Spiridon. 'It is done, and we are finished here. No more loose ends, and no more killing. We will leave this land and return to our own. We will spend our last days together by Zaovine Lake, drinking *rakija* and speaking of old times.'

And we will do so alone, thought Radovan. *We have no wives, no children: I by choice – in another life, I might have been a monk, for such appetites of the flesh have always been alien to me – and you, Spiridon, because you killed your wife Andjela for cheating on you with Andrej Buha. Monster though he was, his touch was still preferable to yours, or maybe her hatred for you eventually became inseparable from her hatred for herself. Perhaps this is why you were so intent upon avenging yourself on De Jaager, because he deprived you of the possibility of revenge, leaving you with only Andjela to hurt. You took your time with her. When she was dead, your desire for any woman vanished, and you became like me. So yes, we will end our days like the lonely men we are, speaking of old times and old blood, for they are one and the same to us.*

'I need to sleep,' said Radovan.

'It's all the worrying you do.'

'Yes,' said Radovan, 'that must be it.'

Behind his brother, Radovan watched Luca Bilbija and the last member of their group, Aleksej Marković, mount the stairs, and soon after he heard movement from above his head.

'I thought we were leaving,' said Radovan.

Zivco Ilić returned to the kitchen. He held a nail gun in his hand.

'We are,' said Spiridon, 'but there's just one final task to accomplish.'

Chapter XII

The Skadarlija locality of Belgrade was once known as the Šićan Mala, or the Gypsy Quarter. Founded in the middle of the nineteenth century, it gradually became the haunt of writers and artists, giving it a bohemian character that persists to this day. Like many such areas in great European cities, it has now become popular with tourists, attracted by the character of its cobblestoned streets and its traditional inns and restaurants.

One of the less well known of the latter is Tri Lovca, or 'The Three Hunters', which sits at the atrium end of Skadarlija. It is more expensive than its neighbors, yet also less prepossessing from the exterior. Its front door is kept locked and patrons must ring a bell to gain access. All guests require a reservation, which can only be made by calling an unadvertised number. Tourists who try the bell in the hope of securing a speculative table are informed that, regrettably, none is available – assuming they speak Serbian, which, being tourists, they probably don't. The words will therefore be entirely beyond their understanding, although the substance of them will not. The waiters, of course, also speak English. Among them, the staff of Tri Lovca are fluent in ten tongues, although this fact is known only to a select few diners. The waiters, the maître d', and the chefs may communicate only in Serbian, but they listen in a variety of languages.

Tri Lovca is ostensibly owned by a diminutive old man named Ivan Jelić, who greets each diner and will, if requested, entertain them with a selection of folk songs at the end of the evening. For years, patrons have been colluding in this fraud, because Ivan is an amiable soul. In reality, Tri Lovca is owned by Nikola Musulin, head of Belgrade's Musulin crime family, and nephew of Spiridon and Radovan Vuksan through their late sister, Jana. Nikola

Musulin frequently dines in his own restaurant – the food is very good – either alone or as part of a group, because it is useful for entertaining and impressing important visitors. Its exclusivity also makes it a magnet for a certain type of visitor – wealthy, well connected, occasionally criminal – who may not be aware of its owner's base nature, or has chosen to ignore it. Plied with alcohol and fine food, such diners sometimes become careless in their speech, and the waiters and waitresses are always nearby. Even should a quiet conversation escape their ears, it will not elude the microphones located under and around every table, with the exception of a single sheltered booth at the back reserved exclusively for the real owner's use. Thus has Nikola Musulin's investment in Tri Lovca paid for itself many times over in the form of information gleaned from diners, as well as in credit card details skimmed and bank accounts emptied. Musulin is not fussy about how he earns his money, and men of his character are never more than a step removed from the street.

Because the food at Tri Lovca really is rather exceptional, its preparation must begin early in the day. By midmorning, staff will already be at work in the kitchen. Nikola Musulin has even been known to join them, rolling up his sleeves to chop vegetables or debone fish. He has a fine palate, but also wishes to ensure that standards are maintained in his restaurant. It would be easy to allow them to slide, and his presence is a reminder to all concerned that such a deterioration in quality would be not only unwelcome but also inadvisable. After all, accidents have been known to happen, particularly if one's hand is being held down on a chopping board while a blade is applied to the tips of one's fingers.

But often Nikola Musulin will be driven to Tri Lovca early in the morning solely to read a selection of the day's newspapers – the tabloid *Informer*, the leftist *Blic*, the more right-wing *Politika*, as well as the *Sportski Žurnal* for its football coverage – over *burek* and coffee. Radio Nostalgija will be played at a low volume, and the chefs will mind their language because Musulin is a devout member of the Serbian Orthodox Church and disapproves of swearing. He is also, except in very rare circumstances, disinclined to resort to killing in the resolution of difficulties: violence, yes, even mutilation, but he generally eschews murder. It causes problems, draws unwelcome attention, and is frequently counter-productive. As the Serbian proverb has it, 'A dead man pays no debts.'

Nikola Musulin is tall and handsome, but walks slowly due to severe, and worsening, rheumatoid arthritis. The condition curses him with near constant pain and causes him to suffer from constipation. He has also recently noticed a decline in his respiratory capacity, and now avoids stairs whenever possible. His sexual appetite has decreased, a fact on which both his wife and mistress have commented. As a consequence, he has fallen back on Cialis to treat his impotence.

Nikola Musulin is only forty-four, and regards his health problems as deeply unfair, but also perhaps as a punishment from God for his criminal vocation. What man, Musulin reasons, can engage in narcotics, prostitution, people smuggling, larceny, and – if infrequently – murder, and not expect some form of retribution from the Divine?

Nikola Musulin, forty-four, will not live to see forty-five.

The present tense is about to become the past.

The door of Tri Lovca opens before Musulin rings the bell because old Ivan Jelić has been keeping watch for him. Sometimes Musulin arrives unexpectedly, but usually the restaurant receives a call in advance, just so that the *burek* and coffee can be waiting for him, freshly made, when he takes his seat in his booth. The newspapers he will already have, as they are delivered to the gates of his home each morning. A bodyguard in a hut accepts the package, checks it – one can't be too careful – and either sends the papers up to the house or, on those mornings when Tri Lovca is to be the destination, places them on the back seat of a silver Mercedes-AMG G63. Originally designed for military use, Musulin's G63 is, by any stretch of the imagination, an ugly vehicle, but it can go from zero to sixty in under seven seconds. The standard model can do it in fewer than five, but Musulin's vehicle is armored, and therefore heavier.

Nikola Musulin is a careful man – power attracts envy, rivals for the throne – and has inculcated a similar caution in his wife, his two children, and his mistress, but even the most circumspect of individuals will inevitably fall victim to routines. While Musulin varies the days and times of his sojourns at Tri Lovca, his fondness for the restaurant has, nevertheless, been noted.

There is also the matter of the impending return to Serbia of Musulin's uncles. Musulin has made clear the Vuksans' desire to retire to lakeside lodges, there to pass in tranquility whatever years may remain to them. Whatever might be said about Radovan, few of those at the highest levels of Belgrade's political, legal, and criminal communities believe that Spiridon Vuksan is conditioned for peace. What is more likely to occur, they feel, is that his voice will begin to whisper in his nephew's ear. It will speak to Nikola of wealth and ambition. It will warn him of enemies, actual and potential.

It will talk to him of war.

If Nikola Musulin is familiar with these concerns, he has given no indication of it. He is aware of the pretenders, and the strength of his enemies, but he does not see these men – and they are all men – as a significant threat. Musulin has friends in the police, the military, and the government. Some of these allies are loyal to him because of his uncles, and their experiences with them in the wars of the 1990s, although Musulin also ensures that their wallets are kept well filled. Others are indebted to him for their success in life, because Nikola has arranged promotions and transfers, and funded election campaigns. The rest cooperate with him out of fear or greed. In other words, Nikola Musulin has bought all his friends, and therefore has no friends at all.

On this particular morning, Ivan Jelić walks with him to his table and makes jokes about Partizan, Nikola's soccer team of choice, Jelić being a supporter of their bitter rivals Red Star. It is the mark of civilized men that they can disagree without being disagreeable, but Musulin's fondness for Jelić runs deep, and he both tolerates and encourages opinions from him that others would fear to voice. This may be a consequence of the absence of a paternal figure in Musulin's daily life, his father being long dead and his uncles distant – although that, as we have seen, is about to change. Ivan Jelić, long-lived and long-married, has provided good advice to Nikola Musulin about family and relationships. He has listened sympathetically over the years, and has asked for nothing in return beyond the purpose and income afforded him by Tri Lovca – although just because a man does not ask doesn't mean he does not want.

Musulin remarks that Jelić looks fatigued, and Jelić admits that he has not been sleeping well of late. His wife is ill, although the doctors are not sure what is wrong with her. She has lost weight and struggles to keep down solid food. She weeps in the night, and her body odor has changed. He believes his wife may be dying, and it appears there is nothing the doctors can do but watch. Ivan Jelić thinks his wife needs better doctors, but such medical expertise is expensive.

Musulin notes the strong smell of *rakija* in the air. Jelić confesses that he knocked over a bottle the night before and some of it may have soaked into one of the rugs. Musulin tells him not to worry: as the day goes on, and more and more dishes are prepared, the smell will fade. Anyway, says Musulin, a restaurant smelling of good *rakija* is no bad thing.

Jelić has timed the delivery of the owner's coffee and *burek* perfectly, because it arrives just as Nikola Musulin takes his seat. The older man leaves the younger to his breakfast, and puts on his coat in order to step outside and smoke a cigarette, smoking not being permitted in Tri Lovca, another of its owner's quirks in a city that runs on nicotine. Musulin barely looks up as Jelić leaves. He is already absorbed in his newspapers.

Ivan Jelić closes the front door of the restaurant behind him and buttons his coat. He does not light a cigarette, but instead walks away quickly, passing through the early-morning pedestrians on Skadarlija. An acquaintance greets him, but Jelić does not hear, or pays no attention if he does. Jelić is troubled by his conscience. He likes the men and women with whom he works. They are kind and industrious. There are currently six staff members in Tri Lovca, along with two of Nikola Musulin's bodyguards. A third bodyguard sits outside in the Mercedes, staring at the screen of his phone.

After Tri Lovca had closed the previous night, Ivan Jelić had remained behind, ostensibly to go over the books with a glass of quince *rakija*. Shortly before 1 a.m., he answered a knock at the back door and admitted five men, two of whom were expert carpenters. Over the course of the next four hours the carpenters had carefully removed the top of Nikola Musulin's exclusive table, hollowed out the interior, and packed it with C4 explosive. The top of the table was then replaced, the sawdust and woodchips gathered and disposed of, and the *rakija* spilled to disguise any lingering scents of wood and glue.

Ivan Jelić is already some distance from Tri Lovca when the C4 explodes, but the force of the blast still rocks him, and he seeks support from a wall. He looks back to see a cloud of dust and smoke rising from the direction of the restaurant and hears screams and shouts. None of these is likely to be coming from Tri Lovca itself. The blast has not only torn Nikola Musulin apart, and killed everyone on the ground floor of the restaurant, but has also brought the old building down in its entirety, an unanticipated effect which contributes to the minor injuries caused to passersby, although miraculously there are no fatalities beyond the occupants. This is good news. Skadarlija is a tourist street, and it has been made clear that collateral damage must be kept to a minimum.

So, Tri Lovca is no more. Nikola Musulin is no more. They are now of the past.

All is was, all is were.

Chapter XIII

Following the warning from Ross about Armitage's dealings with the Vuksans, Louis deliberated late into the night before making a series of calls to the Netherlands. The difficulty was that De Jaager, the man about whom he was most anxious, was also his principal contact in the country. De Jaager's phone went directly to voice mail, which was not unusual: De Jaager, like Louis, preferred to use his cell phone as a mobile answering service, since he regarded the device as being for his convenience, not that of others. Louis then tried Paulus, De Jaager's nephew, driver, and man-at-arms, and when that number rang out, he resorted to calling Anouk, Paulus's mother and De Jaager's sister-in-law. Her phone also went to voice mail. Anouk was in her seventies, so it was not surprising that she might have chosen to turn off her phone before she slept. As for Paulus, his cell phone rarely left his side and was always on. He was his uncle's right hand and was rarely far from him. Louis tried Paulus three more times over the next hour, until finally the phone stopped ringing, suggesting either that it had been turned off or had run out of power.

Logically, Louis should not yet have been worried. Unlike Charlie Parker, he was not a man to chase after phantoms. But he had learned to trust his instincts, and they told him that something was very wrong.

He had one more person to whom he could turn: the big Dutchman, Hendricksen, who worked as an investigator in the Netherlands, although lately he was devoting most of his time and energy to tracing missing artwork. Hendricksen had no great love for De Jaager, regarding him as a crook, if only on the basis of the company he kept. But Hendricksen was principled and owed Louis a favor, since Louis had helped track down the man responsible for killing one of Hendricksen's colleagues.

Hendricksen, thankfully, did pick up, although he didn't sound happy at being woken early on a Sunday morning.

'*Ja, wat is het verdomme?*' were the first words out of his mouth.

'Is that swearing?' said Louis. 'Because it sure sounds like it.'

'Who is this?'

'We met at a gas station in Belgium.'

'You.'

'Yes, me.'

'The question stands, maybe without the swearing: What is it?'

'I think De Jaager may be in danger,' said Louis, 'and I can't raise him or his people on their phones.'

'How much danger?' Hendricksen already sounded more awake.

'The Serbian kind.'

Louis could hear Hendricksen breathing, marshaling his thoughts.

'Is your phone secure?' he said.

'Is any phone secure?' said Louis. 'It will have to suffice.'

'Perhaps I heard rumors down the years,' said Hendricksen, 'about the death of a Serb nicknamed Timmerman, a killer for the Zemun syndicate.'

'Whatever you heard was probably true.'

'They say he was killed by a black Muslim.'

'Only fifty percent of that is true.'

'But at the instigation of someone in the Netherlands.'

'Certainly true.'

'A mutual acquaintance?'

'Again, true.'

'Jesus.'

'You asked.'

'I did,' admitted Hendricksen. 'What do you know about the current situation here?'

'Not enough.'

'The Netherlands has become a narco state, and is now the logistical center for the world cocaine trade. There are huge amounts of money to be made, but the older generation doesn't have the will or the ruthlessness to fight for its share. The gray-beards are content to leave the shooting and maiming to the young, because otherwise they won't live long enough to spend the loot they've set aside for their golden years. Whatever rules once applied in the Netherlands are relevant no longer. We have teenagers with guns being sent on assassination runs by men not much older than they are. Everyone is a target.'

'Meaning?'

'Meaning I think perhaps you're getting worked up over nothing. The Vuksan brothers, Spiridon and Radovan, who've been the dominant Serb influence in the Netherlands for the last four or five years, are passing on the torch. They're not looking for trouble. I hear they're jaded and want to go home. They've sent out signals to the Korps – the Dutch police – informing them that the Vuksans are not going to be a problem in the future. They may even have thrown a few bottom-feeders to the Korps as a gesture of good-will, a parting gift tied up in a neat bow. It would make no sense for the Vuksans to go settling scores now.'

'Depends on how you look at it,' said Louis. 'To a certain type of mind, now would be the perfect time to settle scores.'

Louis heard Hendricksen yawn.

'I'm not in Amsterdam at the moment,' said Hendricksen. 'I'm in Paris. I'm not due to return to the Netherlands until tomorrow morning, but I can make some calls. I'll let you know as soon as I have news.'

'Likewise.'

Louis hung up. He tried each of the three numbers connected to De Jaager one more time, but to no avail. His own phone was now probably compromised, but he would hold on to it until he heard from Hendricksen.

Angel was right: he needed to sleep. He compartmentalized his worries, locking them away so they would not disturb his rest. Before he closed his eyes, he asked the dead girl from his dreams not to bother him.

And she did not.

Chapter XIV

It was just past 8 a.m. when Louis heard from Hendricksen.

'There's no sign of De Jaager at his home or usual haunts,' said Hendricksen, 'and Anouk and Paulus haven't been seen since yesterday. Obviously, my police contacts are reluctant to go breaking into the residences of private citizens without due cause, particularly ones like De Jaager. They don't always want to know exactly what he's up to, because if they did, they might have to do something about it. He's also a man who lives what could politely be described as a clandestine existence, and so occasional unexplained absences are to be expected. What goes for De Jaager goes for Paulus, too, it seems. Meanwhile, I don't know Anouk well enough to comment either way.'

Everything that Hendricksen said made sense to Louis. De Jaager was a secretive individual, and that desire, even need, for concealment affected all those around him, but especially Paulus and Anouk. While De Jaager rarely went anywhere without the former, Anouk took care of all kinds of incidental details, including catering for De Jaager's more demanding guests, of whom Louis had recently been one. There was no reason for her to be absent as well, not unless all three had gone to ground for their own security, which was, Louis supposed, a possibility. No one could live as long as De Jaager, and move in his unusual circles, without accumulating enemies, Serbian or otherwise.

'What about the Vuksans?'

Hendricksen didn't answer immediately. Louis pressed him.

'I asked you a question.'

'They've gone dark,' said Hendricksen. 'They weren't under constant surveillance by the Korps – that level of manpower just isn't available – but they were being monitored regularly. At the moment, there's no trace of them or their people.'

'I detect an unspoken "but" somewhere,' said Louis.

'But,' Hendricksen conceded, 'it seems a flurry of activity occurred a few hours ago, involving one Zivco Ilić. Ilić is to Spiridon Vuksan what Paulus is to De Jaager. He made a series of pickups, probably cash and easily transportable assets, from a number of businesses and apartments linked to the clan. The Criminal Intelligence Team received a tip-off, but it came too late to target Ilić and find out what he was up to. Then again, as I informed you when last we spoke, the Vuksans are closing up shop, so some element of wealth consolidation is to be expected. The Korps are just glad to see them recede from view.'

'I've heard Ilić's name,' said Louis. He shared with Hendricksen the entirety of the information he'd received from Ross, including the fact that the crooked legat, Armitage, had probably been in contact with the Vuksans through Ilić.

'Maybe Ilić was a rat,' said Hendricksen. 'Armitage could have been using him as a source.'

'If she was, she kept it to herself,' said Louis. 'When did you say you were returning to Amsterdam?'

'You know exactly when, because I told you: tomorrow morning.'

'Can you get back earlier?'

'I could. There's a KLM flight at four forty-five today that would get me into Amsterdam just before six. I have plans, though, the kind that involve a woman.'

'She'll understand.'

'Is it politically incorrect to suggest that only a gay man would speak such nonsense?'

'Probably, but I'll let it pass.'

'If you've made me give up a night of pleasure for nothing,' said Hendricksen, 'you and De Jaager are going to have to compensate me – and the lady in question.'

'I don't tend to worry without cause.'

'That's what I thought. Nevertheless, I don't know what more I can do by being in Amsterdam instead of Paris. De Jaager has friends on the police, and their sources are better than mine.'

'Not entirely,' said Louis. 'They don't have me, or the address of De Jaager's safe house.'

Chapter XV

There was no fool, Radovan Vuksan reflected, like one who believed that fate played favorites. His brother was not a fool, but he was arrogant, and that arrogance – a product, Radovan suspected, of his military background – combined with a certain undeniable good fortune, had convinced Spiridon that the cards would always fall to his benefit. It was this, as much as his blood-lust, that had led him to target De Jaager and the others as his farewell to the Netherlands, but he had overplayed his hand and now events beyond his control had left the Vuksans in peril.

The immolation of Nikola Musulin in Belgrade was a grave and unexpected setback to Radovan and his brother. The Vuksans' original intention had been to return quietly to Serbia via Budapest, where they would be picked up by Musulin's associates at Ferenc Liszt Airport before crossing the border near Kelebija. Radovan, ever cautious, had counseled against flying directly to Belgrade, where they would be under surveillance from the moment they arrived. While the Vuksans were not without allies in law enforcement, neither were they entirely without enemies, and Radovan felt it would be better if they reentered their homeland quietly. Musulin had assured them that everything would be taken care of, but he was, in Radovan's experience, a man who sometimes spoke in the expectation that, by doing so, his words would become truth. But Musulin was dead and his people were biding their time while they awaited the emergence of a new order with which they could cut a deal for their survival.

The Vuksans were unusual in that their operation deviated from the traditional horizontal structures of the Serbian mafia. The Vuksan syndicate was controlled from the top down, which meant Radovan and Spiridon gave the orders, and they were followed without question. The Vuksans were allied by blood to Nikola Musulin, and fed money back to him, but their reputation also endowed his rule with a certain force and legitimacy. An attack on Musulin, therefore, was also an assault on the Vuksans.

Radovan had already been in contact with some of his old colleagues from the Ministry of Defence, who had made it plain to him that Serbia was now hostile territory. In all likelihood, any attempt to return to their homeland would lead to a move against them on the grounds that Spiridon might be in the mood to seek revenge for Musulin's death.

But there was also talk that the Vuksans themselves might have been responsible for what had occurred, since few had believed Spiridon's claims of retirement to begin with. Perhaps the Vuksans had detected signs of weakness in Musulin, or a wavering in his support for his uncles' homecoming, and decided to act conclusively as a prelude to assuming complete control.

Radovan didn't bother to contradict any of the rumors. He understood what was happening. The soil was being sown with salt to prevent them from putting down roots, and the hearsay would multiply their enemies. But they could not stay in the Netherlands because it was only a matter of time before someone connected them to the killings at De Jaager's safe house. Neither could he and Spiridon remain long elsewhere in Western Europe, not given the ease with which international arrest warrants could be served and extraditions arranged. They had to move.

No, they had to flee.

Chapter XVI

Hendricksen made the flight to Amsterdam with thirty minutes to spare, the imprecations of his spurned dinner companion still ringing in his ears. As anticipated, she had *not* understood the reason for his sudden departure. Then again, he did not completely understand it himself. He had no particular obligation to the American named Louis, beyond the fact that Louis had helped put an end to the man who was probably responsible for his colleague Yvette Visser's murder in England. Visser's body had still not been found, and was unlikely ever to be discovered now that her killer was dead. It was not even as though Louis had set out to uncover the truth behind her disappearance, or achieve some measure of justice for her. The culprit's death had merely been incidental to a larger investigation.

But sometimes, Hendricksen thought, we encounter individuals who are beyond the norm, persons who inspire a loyalty and respect that can be neither analyzed nor quantified. If they ask a favor, they do so in the knowledge that another can, and should, be asked in return, and will not be refused. Hendricksen wasn't sure that he would ever require the kind of favor Louis was capable of reciprocating. He certainly hoped he wouldn't, because he suspected it would involve violent death, and Hendricksen was generally reluctant to involve himself in troubles of such magnitude.

He retrieved his car from the external parking facility at the airport Hyatt Hotel, dumped his bags at his apartment, and removed the Glock 17 from the safe in his closet. The Netherlands had some of the strictest gun laws in the world, with civilian ownership restricted to law enforcement, hunters, or those, like Hendricksen, who were members of gun clubs. Even taking one's pistol to a shooting club required that it first be disassembled before being placed in a secure case. Open or concealed carry was forbidden. Hendricksen was a member of a club in Floradorp, but rarely visited the range. He disliked firearms. They held bad memories for him. Unfortunately, in his line of work he occasionally encountered men and women, but mostly men, who demonstrated no small disregard for the Netherlands' gun laws – any laws, come to think of it. The Vuksans undoubtedly fell into this category, and therefore a weapon was advisable. Finally, Hendricksen took a small bag from the base of the closet and placed it in his backpack.

He drove to the Herengracht, parked two blocks from the address of the safe house, and walked the rest of the way, pulling on his gloves as he went. He made two passes of the property, the first from the opposite side of the canal to check for any obvious surveillance or activity in the vicinity, and the second by the house itself in an effort to spot lights or other signs of occupancy. No one appeared to be watching, no lamps burned inside, and the shutters were drawn on the upstairs and downstairs windows.

Hendricksen paused by the front door. He could see no bell. Knocking seemed mildly foolish, but less foolish than breaking in, which he hoped to avoid. He knocked twice, but received no reply. Option Two it was, then.

This stretch of the Herengracht was quiet, even for a Sunday evening in early winter. The sensible approach would have been to inform mutual friends in the Korps that some concerns had arisen for the well-being of *Mijnheer* De Jaager and his family, but this would have necessitated revealing the location of the safe house. Should De Jaager have decided to take a break in the country or in another European city, perhaps with Paulus and Anouk in tow, he would be most unhappy to return and find the location and nature of this redoubt were now familiar to the authorities. In such an eventuality, Hendricksen's already fraught relations with the old fixer would likely suffer a terminal decline.

Hendricksen's eye was caught by a mark on the otherwise pristine paintwork of the doorframe. He used his pocket Maglite to reveal it: a dark oval against the cream, fading to nothing, like a red flare passing over snow. It looked, to Hendricksen, very much like blood. Someone, it seemed, had been careless.

He checked the area one last time for police and found no trace of them. Across the canal, a man and woman were walking arm in arm. From the opposite direction, a small group of young people emerged from a basement bar. Hendricksen waited in the shadows until all had gone their separate ways before reaching into his pack and removing a snap gun and tension wrench. Picking locks was a craft, one that Hendricksen had never had the urge or patience to master. A snap gun did the job faster, although it was much noisier than a lockpick and tended to permanently damage the mechanism, which meant it was useless if one wished to enter someone else's property without leaving proof of intrusion. But then Hendricksen was also carrying a concealed Glock, and so would have larger problems to occupy him if confronted by men and women in uniform.

He took a final look around, inserted the steel needle of the gun into the lock, positioned the tension wrench, and squeezed the trigger. The gun cocked, and Hendricksen increased the trigger pressure, causing the needle to snap into action. It made a sound like nails and concrete being mixed in a blender, but the lock didn't open. Hendricksen adjusted the thumb wheel on the gun, jacking up the impact of the needle, and fired again. A light flicked on in an upstairs window of one of the houses to his right, casting a rhombus of illumination on the cobblestones nearby, but by then the steel rod had driven the lock pins into the cylinder. Hendricksen applied the tension wrench and felt the lock plug turn.

The front door opened, revealing a dark, undecorated hallway. A door to his right was closed, as was another straight ahead, to one side of the stairs. Hendricksen dropped the snap gun and wrench on the hall floor to reach for his Glock, easing the door shut behind him to prevent himself from being silhouetted against it: an easy target. If anyone remained in the house, the noise of the lock being broken would have brought them running, but no one emerged to investigate. Hendricksen smelled blood, and beneath it an odor ranker and more desperate, the involuntary purging of creatures at the end of their suffering.

The house felt empty. Still, he crouched and listened for five seconds, ten, twenty, just to be sure, before he stood tall again. He flipped on the flashlight for a second time. A thick trail of blood stained the stairs, with more blood on the floor of the hallway, where a body – perhaps more than one – had been dragged across the boards. From the pattern of the smearing, Hendricksen guessed that the remains had been brought down rather than up, and deposited behind the closed door to his right.

He stepped around the stain, being careful not to disturb it, and put his back to the wall. He reached across the door with his left hand, found the brass knob, and opened it with a single quick motion before pulling his hand back, his body tensed for the sound of shots. None came, only a stronger stench. Hendricksen tightened his grip on the Glock. He offered up a single short prayer and went in low, the gun in his right hand, the flashlight held beneath it in his left. Gun and light traversed the room together, but found no life.

Only death.

Chapter XVII

The lawyer's name was Anton Frend, and his offices occupied two floors of a beautiful *fin-de-siècle* building in the Neubau area of Vienna. Even by the standards of remuneration available to lawyers of the most expert, mendacious, or downright crooked stripe, the location was enviable, and the rooms concealed behind its walls were worthy of the façade. The building had been in his family's ownership for more than a hundred years, the Frends having provided legal advice to the great and the good – as well as, inevitably, the not-so-good – of Vienna since the early nineteenth century.

The common factor shared by their clients was money, the firm of Frend Rechtsanwälte being disinclined to deal with those whose tribulations extended to cashflow problems. Frend Rechtsanwälte specialized in the protection of the wealthy, and by doing so had enriched itself. The Frends had also proved adept at anticipating the direction of impending political and social winds, enabling them to survive not only the collapse of the Austro-Hungarian Empire and the ravages of World War II but also the various peaks and troughs that had followed over the succeeding three-quarters of a century, all while remaining impressively unremarked, except by those who availed of their expensive services. The Frends had this in common with Austria itself, a country that somehow managed to remain simultaneously part of, yet apart from, the larger European community, and with which most of Europe's citizens would have struggled to make very many associations at all beyond white horses, Danube waltzes, and an unfortunate connection with the progenitor of Nazism.

Anton Frend could have sold the building, invested most of the proceeds, acquired a more modest property with the rest, and still have continued to practice in the most salubrious of surroundings. Alternatively, he could have entered into a comfortable retirement, being unburdened by debt or any familial complications beyond the norm. He was an only child, and an orphan to boot. Now in his sixties, and admirably well-preserved, he was in possession, to varying degrees, of a wife, a daughter, three properties – the others being the family's city residence, and a summer-cum-winter retreat in the Tyrol – and a long-standing mistress whom he occasionally entertained in the apartment above his offices.

Yet retirement would have bored Frend. He enjoyed the law – or more correctly, he delighted in finding ways around it on behalf of his clients, and the money he earned as a consequence was a pleasant bonus. In this he resembled a certain type of gambler, one who takes pleasure in the moments during which the ball is in play on the roulette wheel, or the final card is about to be turned; for whom the anticipation is more pleasurable than the outcome, and who can therefore win or lose with relative equanimity. It helped, of course, that Frend was gambling not with his own money and future but with those of his clients. If he failed these men and women – which, the nature of human existence dictated, he occasionally must – he could only shrug his shoulders and apologize while attempting to limit the damage for all concerned, because there are always gradations of loss.

But Frend's reputation, like that of any good advocate, rested on rarely losing, and for this reason his services were eminently saleable. He was in the enviable position of being able to choose his clients as much as, if not more than, they selected him. Some of those clients, of course, took their occasional reversals better than others; in the case of a very small number, it was best for all involved, Frend included, if they did not lose at all.

Anton Frend, like all gamblers, was in love with risk, and men who become besotted with hazard also grow accustomed to it. In this it resembles other vices: the practice becomes habitual, and what is habitual inevitably becomes dull, thereby requiring greater extremes of behavior in return for rewards that will, at best, plateau. For Frend, this behavior manifested itself as an ongoing immersion in criminal society, and so he resembled a man wading deeper and deeper into colder and colder waters, gradually losing all feeling in his limbs and numbing his senses on the way to an inevitable drowning.

Among the most enduring of Frend's clients in this regard were Radovan and Spiridon Vuksan. Frend had known the Vuksans since the mid-nineties, when Radovan Vuksan had commenced diverting funds from clandestine bank accounts, set up to bankroll Serb-backed militias in Croatia and Bosnia, into safe financial havens where the money could rest and cool. Occasionally, the funds would arrive at Frend's offices in the form of hard cash, delivered in cheap gym bags by associates of the Vuksans – grim-faced men with the eyes of carrion crows – or, if the opportunity arose, by Radovan himself, after which he and Frend would dine together at Griechenbeisl or, after a walk in the hills, Der Pfarrwirt, where they would talk of music and books.

After the end of the Balkan conflict, Radovan and his brother had entered into an association with the Zemuns, who had become aware of some, although not all, of the Vuksans' financial activities. The Zemuns had by then already established footholds in Amsterdam and Paris, and suggested that the Vuksans might wish to enter into an alliance as junior partners, with a considerable upfront investment on the Vuksans' part as a gesture of good faith.

The Vuksans had agreed, the alternative being conflict with the Zemuns that would undoubtedly have resulted in the deaths of Spiridon, Radovan, their families, friends, and anyone who might once have sold them a loaf of bread or given them the time of day, as well as the exhumation of their ancestors' remains, the scattering of said bones on distant, hostile seas, and the destruction of the stones that once bore their names, so that the very memory of them would be erased forever from this world. But the Vuksans were shrewd and ambitious, and eventually outmanoeuvered the Zemuns' representatives in the Netherlands to assume control of the operation, assisted throughout by the best legal and financial advice money could buy in the form of Anton Frend.

In the beginning, when the Balkan wars were still ongoing,

Frend had taken care only of the paperwork, negotiating the potential legalities and illegalities arising from the transfer of funds. He sourced compliant accountants, and bankers who had learned not to ask too many questions about deposits. He had no difficulty in separating Radovan Vuksan from the reports of rape, murder, and attempted genocide appearing nightly on his television screen. Radovan was not stripping victims of their valuables before sending them to the gas chambers, or mining gold from the teeth of the dead. This was not some modern version of Nazi atrocities, no matter what the liberals might have alleged. Radovan was simply claiming a small percentage of war capital as a reward for his efforts, as any good businessman did. In fact, Frend might even have argued that by redirecting money from the Serbian government, money that would otherwise have been used to buy weapons and pay militias, Radovan was actually *saving* lives. Such rationalizations were endemic to Frend's profession, and explained why so many lawyers were destined to burn in hell.

Also, Radovan was an Austrophile who loved the writings of Stefan Zweig and the motets of Anton Bruckner. He had never killed or raped anyone, and appeared to find the savagery that was engulfing the former Yugoslavia deeply unpleasant. Frend, meanwhile, was sufficiently versed in twentieth-century European history to accept that the violence was a consequence of old enmities, held in check by the force of will of the dictator Josip Broz Tito before once again being exposed to the light following his demise in 1980. Frend nodded sympathetically when Radovan opined that it would be best if the struggle played itself out as quickly as possible, resulting in the redrawing of boundaries so that nationalities and religions were separated by clear, internationally recognized borders. This, said Radovan, could most efficiently be achieved by a resounding Serb victory, and Frend saw no reason to demur.

But when the Vuksans joined forces with the Zemuns, Frend was confronted with a clearer moral choice. Previously, he had been complicit in the dispersal and investment of cash illegally acquired from an internationally reviled regime, although the funds themselves were technically clean. Now he would be working with money that came from smuggling, narcotics, prostitution, people trafficking, kidnapping, and contract killings. A closer examination of his conscience might therefore be required.

Except Frend did not have a conscience, which made the whole process significantly easier for him. (In Frend's opinion, a conscience was a poor companion for a lawyer, one that always took but never gave.) But just in case, by some miracle, a conscience began to assert itself, he had made it clear to the Vuksans – or more correctly, to Radovan – that he preferred to dwell in blissful ignorance of the more 'colorful' details of their operations, except on those rare occasions when Spiridon chose to join them for dinner and Frend permitted himself the indulgence of vicarious sadism by listening to the latter's tales.

Frend's distancing also served a practical purpose: the less he knew, the less he would have to hide from the authorities in the event of any unfortunate investigation into his links with the Vuksans; and the less he had to hide, the less reason the Vuksans would have to kill him in order to ensure his silence. By his knowledge and competence, he had made them all wealthier than they might otherwise have been, but no one was indispensable, and the prospect of dying behind bars made pragmatists of even the most cultured of men.

Yet so critical had Anton Frend become to the Vuksans' operation, and they to his prosperity, that the activities of Frend Rechtsanwälte now revolved almost entirely around the brothers' needs, apart from a handful of clients – some honest, a few less so – retained either to keep up appearances or because they would have taken their abandonment ill. As a consequence, the firm's offices, which had once echoed with many voices, now held only two: those of Frend and his secretary of many years, Fraulein Pichler, whose moral sensibilities were at least as nebulous as her employer's.

Anton Frend and Fraulein Pichler existed in a state of mutual dependence, which meant that when one finally elected, or was forced, to retire, the other would have no option but to do likewise. Frend would never be able to find or trust another secretary like Fraulein Pichler, and she, in turn, would never be able to train another employer as she had Anton Frend. Around them, like planets orbiting major and minor suns, revolved an assortment of bankers and accountants of similarly abiding association. It was a delicate construct, built on deceit and moral compromise. Had the light of honesty been shone on its workings, it would have crumbled to dust.

Regrettably, the Vuksans' actions in Amsterdam, and the death of Nikola Musulin in Belgrade, now threatened to undo decades of good work. Frend had, in recent hours, been the recipient of panicked phone calls. He had been forced to rouse financiers from their beds, and conspire in the kind of rapid movement of funds that risked inviting the scrutiny of international law enforcement. He had called in favors, and promised greater favors in return. He was exposed, and his clients were in danger, all because of Spiridon Vuksan's reckless need for revenge.

So Frend sat in his dimly lit office, the banker's lamp on his desk the sole illumination, catching the gold of his antique tie pin as he worked. It was one of a collection of such pins that he maintained, each seemingly more ornate than the last. They were as close to an eccentricity as Frend was ever likely to come, and he had often considered adding some versions of one as a water-mark on the firm's stationery. He had removed his jacket, but not so much as loosened his tie, because certain standards had to be maintained, in private as in public. He had poured himself a glass of Rochelt schnapps, but so far it remained untouched. It would not help, not at this moment. He required a clear head.

Because someone would come, he was sure of this.

Someone would come, and it might be the end of them all.

Chapter XVIII

Hendricksen pulled the door of the safe house mostly closed behind him, returned to his car, and stored the wrench and gun in the well beneath the spare tire. He then called Bram De Jong, his closest contact in the Korps. He informed De Jong of what he had discovered in the safe house, neglecting to mention only that he had been required to disable the lock in order to gain access. Admitting to the crime would serve no purpose. The police might have their suspicions, but proving them would be difficult, even if they were keen to pursue the matter, which seemed unlikely.

Hendricksen walked back to the safe house and waited outside for the police to arrive. He was tempted to call Louis, but decided to postpone any contact until later. It would be better if he were not discovered speaking on his cell phone when the investigators came, although he took the trouble to delete the record of the calls to and from New York when he heard the first of the sirens in the distance.

His mouth tasted sour, and his hands were shaking.

He closed his eyes and saw blood.

Later, after Hendricksen had given the police a sanitized version of events – a worried call from a mutual acquaintance, whom he declined to identify, sharing concerns about De Jaager; Hendricksen's unsuccessful efforts to contact De Jaager and his circle; and finally, the visit to the safe house, about which Hendricksen had heard rumors, and the discovery of the unlocked door and what lay behind it – he phoned Louis in New York.

'They're dead,' he said. 'All of them.'

Chapter XIX

This is what Hendricksen saw when he opened the door to the kitchen of the safe house.

The floor was awash with blood, and a red stain had spread across the white ceiling. At first Hendricksen attributed it to arterial spray until he realized that the pattern was inconsistent with the opening of an artery, and the blood had instead soaked through from above. Two women lay against the far wall, their nakedness barely hidden by the sheets that adhered to their bodies, the cotton now more red than white. The women – one old, one young – had been positioned with the younger holding the older in her arms, the pinnacled weight of their bodies keeping them upright. The younger woman's face was visible to Hendricksen, but he did not recognize her. Even though her facial muscles had relaxed in death, her expression was fixed in her final suffering, and her mouth hung open in a silent howl of agony.

The woman to the right had long gray hair and faced the wall, but Hendricksen did not need to look upon her features to know that this was Anouk. Had he required any further confirmation, he would have found it in the two wedding rings that hung from a chain around her neck, caught between her remains and those of the woman with her.

Beside Anouk lay her son, Paulus. Someone had draped a patterned tablecloth over him in an approximation of a shroud or robe. There was less blood on him, and the gunshot wound to his head suggested he had not suffered as much as the others. His right cheek rested against his mother's bare back and his left hand hung over her shoulder.

The wall behind them was mostly ancient brickwork, broken by a series of vertical wooden pillars that were as much decorative as practical. De Jaager's body had been nailed to two of these posts, his arms outstretched, his feet resting on a stool to take his weight. The nails had been fired through his wrists, the palms of his hands, the elbow joints, and his shoulders, and were buried deep in the flesh. In addition, a rope had been slung around his neck and fixed to one of the ceiling beams: additional security to ensure that the tableau was not ruined by the old man's body yielding to the nails.

Hendricksen held the flashlight on the crucifixion, as though to fix it in his mind, although he knew that he would never forget what he had seen here. On his deathbed, the memory of it would accompany him from this world to the next. De Jaager's eyes were half-open, and for the briefest of moments Hendricksen thought that the old man might somehow yet be alive. Hendricksen advanced a single step before stopping, his left foot inches from the first of the blood, before he realized the foolishness of this.

De Jaager's face was unmarked, his eyelids intact. He had not turned away.

And at his death, he had prayed that others would not turn away either.

Chapter XX

Louis was packing for the Netherlands when his cell phone rang. Angel answered, and the expression on his face showed no warmth as he held up the device.

'You need to change this number,' said Angel, 'unless you're planning on smuggling in the phone when they eventually lock you up.'

Louis tried scowling at him for effect, but Angel had been rendered immune by decades of exposure.

'Who are you,' said Louis, 'my mother?'

'If I was your mother, I wouldn't admit it.'

'Just give me the fucking phone.'

Angel gave him the fucking phone.

'I heard about De Jaager and the others,' said Ross. 'I'm sorry.'

'You tried,' said Louis, 'and for that I'm grateful.'

'I could have made the call earlier.'

'I don't believe it would have changed the outcome. They were marked, and had been for a long time.'

'What will you do?' said Ross.

'Are you asking in your official capacity?'

'What do you think?'

'Then you know what I'm going to do,' said Louis.

'When do you leave?'

'Tomorrow.'

'I'll be at the bar of the St. Regis in an hour. Meet me there.'

'Why?'

'Don't be obtuse. It won't benefit you.'

Ross hung up.

'What did he want?' said Angel, who had returned to filling his own case.

'To talk. In person.'

'Is he going to warn you off?'

Louis carefully folded another white shirt.

'No,' he said, 'I think he wants to help.'

Before departing for the St. Regis, Louis contacted Charlie Parker, who had briefly met De Jaager, Paulus, and Anouk in Amsterdam earlier that year.

'Do you want me to come with you?' said Parker. 'Because I will.'

'No, or not yet. The offer is appreciated, though. I just thought you'd want to know.'

'I'm grateful, and sorry, too.'

'I know, but this isn't on you or me.'

'The Zemuns?' said Parker.

'Someone involved with them from way back. The Zemuns, it seems, are yesterday's news.'

Louis told Parker about the imminent meeting with Ross.

'It won't hurt to hear what he has to say,' said Parker.

'You think he's acting out of the goodness of his heart?'

'Not exactly, unless he's received a transplant. On the one hand, he did try to warn you.'

'Yes.'

Parker heard the doubt in Louis's voice, and couldn't blame him for it. Louis was right to be cautious about Ross, not least because of Louis's own past. It wasn't clear how much Ross knew about it, but he knew enough. Killers and FBI agents made uneasy bedfellows, and Ross probably had the word 'expediency' embroidered and framed above his bed.

'But on the other,' said Parker, 'it's always an exchange with Ross. If he offers assistance, it's because he sees an advantage that can be gained – and not just a favor he can call in down the line, but a direct benefit.'

'Meaning?'

'Meaning it may suit him to have you go after whoever did this.'

'Well that's okay,' said Louis, 'because it suits me too.'

*

The King Cole Bar at the St. Regis was quiet, with only a handful of people scattered amid the wood and brass. Ross was seated at the far end, drinking a dirty martini. Louis joined him and ordered the same. They did not exchange pleasantries, but Ross raised his glass, said 'To De Jaager,' and Louis did likewise.

'I met him once,' said Ross.

'I didn't know that.'

'It was a long time ago, in Berlin, as we were witnessing the end of the Cold War – or the First Cold War, as I think we're now obliged to call it.'

Louis had no idea how old Ross was and had never bothered finding out. He'd just assumed that the FBI man had come out of the womb already looking like a late-middle-aged man with hemorrhoids, at which point his parents had disowned him. But if Ross had already been making Europe appear grimmer by his presence at the start of the 1990s, he was probably at least in his late fifties by now.

'De Jaager fed us some information about a group of hard-core Stasi who didn't like the way the wind was blowing,' Ross continued, 'not that they were unique in that regard, but these particular cold warriors were of a mind to cause trouble. Ordinarily we might just have kept them under surveillance, or let someone else deal with them – maybe their own people, because this was in the days just after the wall had fallen, and we weren't in a position to go chasing down every lead amid the chaos. And some of us were optimists. We thought the end of communism meant a new beginning.'

'Were you an optimist?' said Louis. 'Because I have to say, that would surprise me.'

'I might have contracted optimism once, by association,' said Ross. 'But I got over it.'

'I guessed,' said Louis.

'I was just a young agent back then, attached to the Berlin embassy as a new legat. I wasn't privy to all that went down, because it was an Agency operation and I only learned about most of it later. I became involved in the discussions because we were investigating the death of a young American tourist named Annie

Houseman in Bautzen, and the Stasi knew more about it than they were prepared to admit, even through the back channels which we were using to communicate with them.

'Anyway, the story we were hearing was that one of these rogue Stasi guys might have killed Houseman. He got her drunk in a bar, tried to rape her, she fought back, and it all spun out of control. He ended up crushing her head with his car to hide her injuries, although she was already dead by then. It was put down to a hit-and-run, an unfortunate accident amid the anarchy and celebrations, but De Jaager knew better. He got the story from a functionary looking to relocate to Stockholm via The Hague, who was seeking an honest broker for the documents he had to share. The smarter ones knew that it would be a seller's market at the start, but it wouldn't stay that way for long, so it paid to stay ahead of the competition.

'There was no proof of the killing, of course, but De Jaager's information was never less than cast-iron: this Stasi guy – his name was Buchner – had a lot of blood on his hands, and so did the others in his circle. They'd been around for a long time, and were the go-to crew for advice on torture and execution across the Eastern Bloc, which meant they'd helped to put a lot of our assets in the ground over the years. Letting them fade away to work against us from the shadows started to make less and less sense, particularly when we began to learn more about them.'

Old King Cole stared down at them from his Maxfield Parrish mural above the bar. Everyone in his circle – his courtiers and jesters – seemed to be having a good time, but Louis had never liked the look of him. In his black robe and white collar, he resembled a hanging judge. You could play the buffoon, and make the king laugh, but it wouldn't stop him from killing you when you ceased to amuse.

'The operation was farmed out,' said Ross. 'The Israelis were probably involved, because they had their own reasons for wanting two of these guys, but I can't say for sure. They turned it around in three weeks, which was fast: four men dead, and no wreckage. A week after the last of them was dispatched, De Jaager joined us for dinner. His payment was five US visas, no questions asked.

'I suppose I had scruples in those days, or more of them than I do now. The way it was done bothered me. I wanted Buchner to be arrested and face trial. I still believed in closure, or some semblance of it. De Jaager must have picked up on my unhappiness, because he took me aside as we were leaving. He could have uttered some platitudes about justice being served, but he didn't. He just said "Sometimes, this is how it must be done. It's wrong, and it stains the soul, but it has to be, because the other option is so much worse."'

'And how do you feel about that now?' said Louis.

'Let's just say I've grown more comfortable with the concept as the years have passed.'

'I can't say it ever bothered me,' said Louis.

'I can believe it. I've seen your file.'

'Don't believe everything you read.'

'If even half of what's in that file is true, you earned the "Reaper" epithet. There are plagues that have killed fewer people.'

'Did you bring me here to arrest me?'

Ross actually laughed aloud. For Louis, it was akin to watching a dead man dance.

'If anyone ever arrests you,' said Ross, 'it won't be at my instigation.'

'Because you might end up taking the stand with me, and not as a witness?'

'I'll admit to an aversion to awkward questions where you and your friends are concerned.'

'Then why are we here?'

'I know exactly what was done to De Jaager and his people,' said Ross, 'and I know the reason, otherwise I wouldn't have called to warn you about the contact between Armitage and whatever is left of that Serb syndicate in the Netherlands. De Jaager and his family died because, ten years ago, give or take, he conspired in the killing of a Zemun enforcer called Andrej Buha, also known as Timmerman. At the risk of being excessively blunt, I think you killed Buha, either on contract or as a favor to De Jaager.'

'That must be some file you got,' said Louis. 'I'd like to see it someday. I might even recognize some of what's in it, although it's unlikely.'

'Your denial is noted for the record,' said Ross. 'But De Jaager and the others died because of what was done to Buha, and now you're going to find whoever killed them and put them down. In all likelihood, that means you'll be looking for Spiridon and Radovan Vuksan, unless some of the Zemun old guard have decided to return to Amsterdam and settle scores. But my money is on the Vuksans.

'This is the thing: There are people in law enforcement – here, and elsewhere – who wouldn't shed too many tears if some grave misfortune were to befall the Vuksans. They've been sowing misery since the Balkan wars, but they've always had a particular interest in people trafficking. In the last five years, they've expanded into people smuggling, which is a different beast: container trucks, the holds of ships, fast boats across the Mediterranean from North Africa. There's good money to be made, because the cargo pays upfront. If the cargo drowns, suffocates, or gets caught and put behind wire in a camp in Italy, Greece, or Cyprus, that's their tough luck. It's a high-volume, high-yield business, and casualties don't impact on the bottom line.

'At the other end of the scale, the Vuksans are moving low volumes with a significantly higher individual yield, and they're not big on background checks. That form of cargo travels in more comfort, and has to arrive safe and sound, with not even a bruise. The Vuksans charge Iranian Kurds fifty thousand dollars per head to get to the United Kingdom via Serbia and France, and God bless those who make it. We fucked the Kurds over, so I don't begrudge them a new start.

'But the Vuksans are also taking money from people who don't mean anyone any good, not unless you're in the market for a holy war. Once these men get to Europe – and some of them may be returning after a few years in Iraq, Syria, or Afghanistan – they vanish, and we don't hear about them again until they blow themselves up on a bus or train, drive a truck through a crowded market, or turn a shopping mall into a shooting gallery.

'And they're not even the worst. The ones that really frighten us are those who will never get close to a gun or bomb. They're the organizers, the recruiters, the moneymen. They were Al-Qaeda, then ISIS, and soon they'll mutate and reappear with a new name but the same ideology. Meanwhile, the Vuksans and those like them are banking one hundred thousand dollars for every piece of delicate terrorist cargo landed safely, and that's just the starting price. For a high-value target, and therefore high-risk, the Vuksans will ask for, and receive, a quarter of a million, sometimes more.'

'So why doesn't someone do something about it?' said Louis. 'There's a rule of law, even down in the dirt.'

'I know of some dead Stasi who might express a different opinion, if bones could talk.'

'Suspicions aren't sufficient cause to add a black tag to a file, and last time I checked, our European allies objected to drone strikes on Paris and London.'

'Maybe so,' said Louis, 'but even if you kill the Vuksans, someone else will take their place.'

'Possibly,' said Ross, 'and indeed the word is that the Vuksans are retiring from the game, although I'm not sure retirement is really in Spiridon Vuksan's nature.'

'So why bother with them at all?'

'As punishment for past crimes, and a warning to those who might be of a mind to follow in their footsteps: If you do this, we will find you, and we will make you pay.'

Louis finished his martini and signaled for another.

'Are you asking me to do the US government's dirty work?' said Louis.

'I'm not asking you to do anything. Unless I'm misreading the runes, you're going after the Vuksans one way or another. What I'm saying is that we may be in a position to facilitate your efforts.'

'With "we" being . . . ?'

'Concerned citizens.'

'The worst kind. And how would these concerned citizens facilitate me?'

'Well, my first thought was that a clean phone might help, so I considered offering you one, but then I realized you probably wouldn't be very comfortable carrying around a cell phone provided by law enforcement.'

'You know,' said Louis, 'I wouldn't be very comfortable with that at all.'

'Great minds. I went with an alternative plan instead.'

'Another crooked legat?'

Louis had the pleasure of watching the dart hit home. Armitage's betrayal had left a mess, and everyone in the blast range had suffered damage. Ross wouldn't have escaped unscathed. He offered Louis a thin smile.

'I'd like to believe we learn by our mistakes,' said Ross.

'I'd like to believe that too,' said Louis. 'Obviously I don't, but I'd like to.'

'The Bureau has limited jurisdiction overseas,' Ross continued, 'so given the delicacy of what is being proposed, I've supplied some reading material, and alerted an interested party about your travel plans.'

He stood to leave. A copy of the *New York Times* lay on the bar between them. Ross tapped it, and threw down cash to cover the tab.

'You ought to take a look at today's paper,' he said. 'You might find it informative. Travel safely.'

Louis watched Ross go, but did not immediately reach for the *Times*. Instead, he sat and thought. In the years since he had come to know Parker, Louis's life had changed in ways he could never have imagined. Many of these developments were positive, or at least not actively negative, but coming into contact with SAC Edgar Ross of the FBI was not among the latter. Louis did not doubt that a record of his activities existed somewhere in Federal Plaza, although he suspected that much of it was for Ross's personal amusement only – or that was his hope. Whatever the truth of the matter, Ross's knowledge of Louis was a threat, and hung like a sword over his head. Eventually, something might have to be done about it.

There was also the problem of Armitage and her legacy. If she had been in contact with the Vuksans, and was responsible for setting them on De Jaager, then a trail existed, one the Bureau would prefer to see erased. Ross had just handed Louis a broom and told him to get sweeping.

But if Armitage was the source of the Vuksans' information, what else had she told them? Ross was assuming that Armitage had, in the course of her duties, come across material confirming De Jaager's instigation of the killing of Andrej Buha, but what if this was not all she had discovered? According to Ross, Armitage had made contact with the Vuksans shortly after Louis and Angel left Amsterdam. The possibility existed that it was not only De Jaager she had fed to them but also Louis.

So Louis drank, and mused. When he finally left the St. Regis, he did so with a copy of the *New York Times* under his arm.

Chapter XXI

B y the time Louis returned, Angel had finished packing. They
had discussed the possibility of Angel staying in New York,
but the conversation ended almost as soon as it had begun. Angel
was no longer receiving treatment for his cancer and the latest
tests had shown him to be clear. True, he was not as physically
strong as he once had been, but any diminution was balanced by
a psychological change. Angel had faced physical suffering over
and over, and each time he had come through. He did not consider
himself to be immortal, or even blessed: he simply had little fear
left.

'What did Ross want?' said Angel.

'For us to clean up the Armitage mess. Oh, and to give me his
copy of the *New York Times*.'

'Did you tell him we have a subscription?'

Louis unfolded the newspaper. Concealed in the Arts & Leisure
section was a manila envelope, and inside the envelope was a
dossier on an Austrian lawyer named Anton Frend, along with
an assortment of photographs of Frend with family, professional
colleagues, and, last of all, seated at a dinner table between two
men, one of them thin, bald, and vaguely patrician, the other a
thug. Louis turned over the photograph. Attached to it was a date
– April 9, 2016 – and three names: Radovan Vuksan, Anton Frend,
and Spiridon Vuksan. Louis read the salient parts of the file aloud
to Angel before passing him the picture of the diners.

'Dead men,' said Louis.

'Even the lawyer?'

'We'll see. If he's keeping that kind of company, his conscience
is already reposing. It may be time for the rest of him to follow.'

In addition to the notes on Frend, the envelope contained single pages of data on five other men: Spiridon and Radovan Vuksan themselves; Armitage's contact, Zivco Ilić; Aleksej Marković; and Luca Bilbija. The material included family backgrounds; known aliases and recent addresses; passport details; prison records; sexual preferences; and, in the case of everyone except Radovan Vuksan, a history of military service. This service included allegations of involvement by Spiridon Vuksan, Zivco Ilić, and Aleksej Marković in mass murder during the Balkan wars. Luca Bilbija, meanwhile, had been too young to fight in the conflicts, although he had done six months of mandatory military service in 2006. A photograph of each man was attached to the relevant page. As Louis read a document, he passed it on to Angel.

'These aren't just dangerous people,' said Angel, 'they're dangerous animals.'

'Smart, though,' said Louis. 'Ilić and Marković have spent time behind bars, but not for long, and none of it for any crimes worth mentioning. Bilbija seems clean, and the Vuksans have never seen the inside of any prison, not unless they were visiting someone.'

'Or killing them.' Angel was reading about Ovčara, and the facility at Sremska Mitrovica, where Croat prisoners were tortured, raped, and murdered by Serb reservists. Both Spiridon Vuksan and Zivco Ilić had also been present on specified dates and had, according to witnesses, participated enthusiastically in the carnage.

'It looks like Radovan just took care of the paperwork,' said Louis, 'and made sure that all of his brother's victims were in one place when he and his men got around to butchering them.'

The figures were almost beyond belief: a hundred men here, two hundred there, gradually shading into the thousands; women and children, too. Louis had a vague memory of these wars, of news reports on TV and pictures in the better papers, but he had been a different man back then. Now he found it hard to believe that the civilized world had stood by and allowed this slaughter to continue for so long before finally being goaded into intervening. By that stage, less than half a century had gone by since the fall of Nazi Germany, yet no one appeared to have learned very much from it at all.

But who was he to point the finger? He, too, had blood on his hands.

And soon, he would have more.

Later that evening, Angel explained to Mrs Bondarchuk that he and Louis would be heading abroad for a period of time yet to be determined, and the usual routines would apply, which Mrs Bondarchcuk took to mean that she should maintain her vigil by the window, and sign for deliveries. In the event of a problem, or any matter of even the slightest vexation, she had a list of numbers to call, including those for Charlie Parker; his lawyer, Moxie Castin, to whom Louis and Angel had also begun to entrust some of their affairs; and, in the event that everyone else on Earth ceased answering their phones or vanished into another dimension, the Fulci brothers.

But the number that Angel and Louis always instructed her to call first, should she feel threatened, belonged to a woman named Amy, whom Mrs Bondarchuk had never met. Amy worked for Leroy Frank Properties, Inc., a company that might have been revealed – had anyone been inclined to dig deep enough – as the beneficial owner of the property in which Mrs Bondarchuk currently resided. When Angel and Louis were away, Amy took care of any problems that might arise: plumbing, heating, carpentry, and sometimes more specialized issues, too.

Earlier in the year, while Angel and Louis had been in Europe, Mrs Bondarchuk had become agitated. Three men – two young, one older, all of a disreputable mien – had followed her home from Zabar's, and she became convinced, not without some justi-fication, that they might be about to attempt a break-in, since they had passed the building either alone or in pairs four times in the next two hours, the city gradually growing darker around them.

Under similar circumstances, the Mrs Bondarchuks of this world tended to reach out to the cops, but this particular Mrs Bondarchuk was aware of the ambivalence with which the gentlemen on the upper floors viewed the police. Instead, although not without reservations at potentially being branded a worrywart, she had contacted the mysterious Amy, who – in what could only be described as a dulcet tone – thanked Mrs Bondarchuk for her vigilance, and assured her that her concerns would be addressed. The last Mrs Bondarchuk saw of the three undesirables together, they were being escorted into the back of a van by a group of four men who had embraced them in what, to the casual onlooker, might have been mistaken for friendly bear hugs, assuming bears carried guns. Two weeks later, she passed one of the undesirables while she was feeding bread to the ducks in Central Park. He caught her eye, and took a moment to recall her, before proceeding on his way, the speed of his departure hampered only by the new cast on his right leg and his lack of familiarity with crutches.

'I'll look after everything,' said Mrs Bondarchuk as she fed pieces of sausage to the Pomeranians.

'I know you will,' said Angel. 'Having you here is a weight off our minds.'

He meant it, too, and she knew he did. He patted her hand, and Mrs Bondarchuk grinned fit to burst.

And while Angel spoke with Mrs Bondarchuk, Louis again went over the documents passed to him by Ross, even as he understood that the knowledge they contained was insufficient for his purposes.

Five names.

He had no idea where these men might be. For all he knew, they could already be back in their own country, and Louis's cursory knowledge of Serbian culture suggested that, if this was the case, a black man would have difficulty operating inside its borders without attracting attention. At the minimum he would be an object of curiosity, and that was before he began asking questions about Serbian criminals. A black *American*, meanwhile, might even be a lightning rod for overt hostility, given that US planes had helped NATO bomb some sense into the Serbs in 1999, killing over a thousand soldiers and police, and half as many civilians. If the Vuksans were in Serbia, Louis's hopes of striking at them were minimal.

Only their lawyer, Frend, was immediately locatable, but it

wasn't as though Louis could pull up in front of Frend's Viennese office, Sachertorte in hand, knock on the door, and ask after a bunch of Serbs. For the first time, Louis felt the futility of what he was attempting. He was already out of his depth. With the exception of a Dutch private investigator, everyone he knew in the Netherlands was now dead. He had a vague promise of assistance from Ross, a federal agent whom he did not trust, and an unknown intermediary in the Netherlands, courtesy of that same agent. From what Ross had said at the St. Regis, Louis guessed that the intermediary was, if not a serving spook, then a former one, and nobody could trust a spy.

Louis took the documents and photographs to his office, where he scanned them before emailing them to a secure dropbox. He then placed the paperwork in the fireplace and set it alight. From his armchair, he watched the faces of the five Serbs curl up and burn.

He would try, for the sake of De Jaager and the rest. It was all he could do.

Five criminals. Five Serb killers.

Unfortunately, government agencies are systemically unreliable.

Because unbeknownst to them, there was a sixth.

Chapter XXII

The Vuksans and their people headed first to Germany, avoiding the larger urban centers and keeping electronic communication to a minimum. The Serbs were deeply embedded in the German criminal underworld, mostly through prostitution and narcotics, and many were ex-military. While some might have sympathized with the Vuksans' plight, they would be unwilling to endanger their own lives by offering help, even if – as was likely – Belgrade had not cautioned against it. If the Vuksans turned to them, they risked being betrayed.

But there were some on whom they could still rely, men whose loyalties extended back to the days of Tito, and so the Vuksans traveled to the farm of Gavrilo Dražeta near Kassel in Central Germany.

None of his neighbors knew Dražeta by his old name. Here he was István Adami, a Hungarian of German ancestry, although one with only the most distant of Teutonic relatives remaining alive, and they resided far to the east, or so he told anyone who asked. Thanks to his late mother, Dražeta spoke fluent Hungarian, which helped maintain his cover and hide him from his enemies.

Dražeta was a former security officer with the JNA, the Yugoslav People's Army, who had fought the Croats at Vukovar in 1991, where fewer than two thousand Croatian national guardsmen, supported by civilians, were besieged by more than thirty-five thousand heavily armed Serb paramilitaries and JNA soldiers. The Croats held out for nearly three months before the city finally fell. Dražeta was among those who had supervised the executions and ethnic cleansing that followed, including the massacre of two hundred prisoners at Ovčara farm. It was said that it was he who had come up with the concept of 'running the gauntlet', whereby the prisoners at Ovčara, civilians and wounded among them, were forced to clear two rows of Serbs armed with chains, bats, and blades before being dispatched. Among those who had aided him in this endeavor was the late and largely unlamented Andrej Buha, aka Timmerman.

Dražeta technically remained a person of interest to war crimes investigators, and had long been under indictment by the ICTY, the International Criminal Tribunal for the former Yugoslavia, before it ceased operation in 2017. He had avoided apprehension because his German papers were flawless, thanks to the efforts of Radovan Vuksan. It was the least Radovan could have done for his old partner, for it was Dražeta who had arranged the safe transportation of looted art out of the ruins of Vukovar, and Radovan who had organized its sale. Now Dražeta lived a dull but comfortable pseudonymous existence among dull but comfortable Germans, in a dull but comfortable house with a dull but comfortable wife.

'Are you sure he can be trusted?' Spiridon asked his brother, as their convoy pulled up in Dražeta's yard.

Spiridon had never been convinced of the wisdom of aiding Dražeta's retirement to Germany, not with the indictment hanging over him. It would have been better had he remained in Serbia, where he was less at risk of extradition. Here in Germany Dražeta had undoubtedly grown lazy and soft, and soft, lazy men were vulnerable to pressure when the authorities came calling.

'If he was going to betray us,' said Radovan, 'he could have done so a long time ago.'

'The morals of men can change,' said Spiridon.

'Not those of men like him.'

Dražeta seemed pleased to see his old comrades again. There were hugs and kisses, and the hint of manly tears. He fed them venison washed down with Samtrot wine, and played them the songs of Lepi Mića on an ancient turntable. They kept the conversation neutral, avoiding all references to the Vuksans' current troubles, although Aleksej Marković and Luca Bilbija said nothing at all. They were not sociable men, or not beyond the confines of campfires, bars, and gambling dens.

While the guests relaxed and waited for the strudel to cool, Draẑeta's wife took him to one side. Her name was Wilella, which she had always disliked. Her husband called her Willa, like the American writer Willa Cather. Draẑeta's wife had copies of some of her novels in translation, battered hardbacks of *Frau im Zwielicht* and *Meine Antonia*, but they had never been to her taste. It was enough for her to own the work of a famous namesake.

'What about the other one?' Willa asked.

'What other one?' said Draẑeta.

'I saw someone else in the first car. I think it was a child. Shouldn't we take her something to eat?'

'You're mistaken,' said Draẑeta.

'I'm not,' said Willa, her voice growing louder. 'There's a child with them.'

Gavrilo Draẑeta, a rapist and murderer, had never raised a hand to his wife in all their fifteen years of marriage, and rarely did they exchange harsh words. Even their disappointments, the absence of children being principal among them, had not soured their relationship in any appreciable way. But now, in their kitchen – *her* kitchen – Draẑeta placed his right hand forcefully over his wife's mouth and pushed her hard against the wall.

'Listen to me,' he said. 'You saw nothing. There is no one else out there. Do you understand?'

Willa nodded. She thought her husband looked not only angry but also frightened. She didn't know every detail of his past, but she was aware that he had fought in the Balkan wars, and all wars were dirty. The strangers in her house belonged to this past, and were therefore also dirty. Whatever trouble they had brought with them might well linger after they left, which could be part of the reason why her husband was so scared. Yet it was, she thought, the mention of the child that had really set him off.

Draẑeta took his hand away from his wife's mouth and kissed her.

'I'm sorry,' he said.

'It's nothing,' she lied, but she was disappointed in him – not because of his fear, but because of how he had dealt with it, and her. The fractures in strong men ran deep.

The strudel was served. When they were done, she removed the plates and went to bed, leaving her husband and his friends to talk alone.

The Vuksans' associates had moved to the lounge to smoke and watch TV, leaving the brothers alone with their host and a bottle of brandy. They spoke of what had happened in Amsterdam and Belgrade, including the death of Nikola Musulin.

'If I may speak freely,' said Dražeta, 'Nikola was not as forceful as he might have been. They laughed at him behind his back.'

The brothers had heard these stories, and counseled their nephew to take action. The fact that he had not done so might have contributed to his death, although it was unlikely that any response from Nikola would have prevented it. Spiridon's intended return had damned him.

'He was a figurehead,' said Spiridon, 'a straw man. But he was ours.'

'Such a public killing,' said Dražeta, 'must have been sanctioned at a very high level.'

'Nevertheless,' said Radovan, 'I doubt they expected the entire restaurant to be brought down on him. Someone will have received a rap on the knuckles.'

'With a blade,' said Dražeta, and they smiled.

'Have you been approached by Belgrade?' said Spiridon, and he asked the question so mildly that there could be no mistaking his meaning.

'Not recently,' said Dražeta.

'But in the past?'

'Yes. I have always refused to become involved in contemporary ventures.'

'You're involved now,' said Radovan.

'I would never refuse you – or your brother,' he added, in deference to Spiridon.

'We're grateful,' said Radovan, and they toasted one another again.

'So where will you go?' said Dražeta.

'I don't know,' said Radovan. 'We have to open a dialogue, but without exposing ourselves. We want to be close to home, but not so close that they can strike at us. It's difficult.'

'They'll be watching for you,' Dražeta agreed. 'But Romania is a possibility.'

At points, the Danube narrowed to as little as 150 meters between Romania and Serbia. It was easy to move people between the two countries.

'No,' said Radovan, 'relations between Bucharest and Belgrade are too good right now. If we're found on Romanian soil, we'll be handed over without a second thought.'

'Hungary?'

'Fucking Orbán has Belgrade in his pocket.'

Dražeta did not even bother suggesting Bulgaria. The Serbs had long moved narcotics through Sofia, but conflict with the Bulgarians over the lucrative Balkan route was ongoing. If the Vuksans were not immediately targeted by their own kind, the Bulgarians would be happy to do the job for them.

Dražeta noticed that Spiridon Vuksan was not contributing.

'You're quiet, *ćale*,' he said, using the Serbian term of affection meaning 'papa'. During his time in uniform, Spiridon had liked to believe that his men viewed him as a father figure. No one had ever worked up the courage to disabuse him of this notion.

It was Radovan who answered.

'My brother does not like skulking,' he said. 'It is against his nature. He believes we should return with our flag raised, like Peter the Liberator.'

'The longer we hide,' said Spiridon, 'the weaker we appear.'

'The longer we hide,' said Radovan, 'the longer we live.'

Spiridon drained the brandy.

'My brother is an old woman,' he said to Dražeta, 'and the only battles he fights are with his purse. I'm going to bed.'

Radovan and Dražeta waited until he was gone before resuming. For Radovan, Spiridon's words stung less here than they might have done in other company. Dražeta had only ever killed unarmed men and women, and his greatest physical exertion had involved consigning to the Danube the naked bodies of the dead.

'They may come looking for you,' said Dražeta. 'It would be better if I had an answer to give if they do.'

'Tell them we were speaking of Romania, but were not specific. I'll make some calls to see if bread can be scattered on those waters.'

Dražeta raised the bottle. Radovan shook his head.

'Can this situation be salvaged?' said Dražeta.

'I don't know. Spiridon is an obstinate man.'

'And you are a clever one. You'll find a way.'

'Yes,' said Radovan, and his gaze lay elsewhere. 'I expect I shall.'

Willa pretended to be asleep when her husband at last came to bed. The Vuksans had been given the guest room, while their men were on couches and chairs in the lounge. She waited until her husband started snoring before she got out of bed and removed from beneath it a Tupperware box. It contained a little cold venison with some red onion marmalade, a hunk of bread, and, in a separate compartment, a piece of strudel. She put on her robe and went downstairs. Avoiding the lounge, she used the side door to leave the house and approached the cars in which the men had arrived. All were empty.

Willa paused. Perhaps, she thought, she had been mistaken, until she noticed a small figure moving by a hedgerow, watching. And although she could not have said why, she crossed herself and wished only to be back in the safety of her home.

'Here,' she said, 'I brought you something to eat.'

She placed the box on the hood of the nearest car and went back inside. She locked the door behind her before checking the rest of the exterior doors. One of the men, the one called Marković, emerged from the lounge as she was finishing in the kitchen. He had a gun in his hand.

'What are you doing?' he asked.

'I thought it would be better if we locked the doors,' said Willa. 'Just in case.'

'It's three o'clock in the morning.'

'All the more reason for it.'

Marković looked at her oddly before returning to the lounge. Willa went back to bed and eventually fell asleep. She was woken by the sound of the men leaving. It was still dark. Her husband was no longer beside her, but she had not heard him get up.

Willa went to the window, pulled aside the drape, and watched the three cars drive away. She counted six shapes: the five men who had slept in her home that night, and the other.

Later, outside the kitchen door, she found the Tupperware box. The food was gone, and the box had been washed, but it was not empty. Inside was a single small coin with a hole at one edge, as though it had been removed from an earring or a necklace. The coin was so old that it had been rubbed almost smooth, but she could just discern the outline of a face upon it. Willa placed the coin in a jar by the door and hoped it would bring good fortune to their home. But she washed her hands after touching it, and laid her fingers against the cross on the wall while praying that none of the six would ever return to Kassel.

Chapter XXIII

The next day, while Angel and Louis waited for Alex, their regular driver, to take them to JFK, a call came through from Louis's money guy. His name, rather aptly, was Golden, and he was responsible for ensuring that Louis's bank accounts, whether domestic or offshore, attracted as little federal attention as possible. Golden's store of small talk didn't require more than a single intake of breath to fuel it, but he was very good at his job.

'Do you have a moment?' Golden asked.

'For you, always,' said Louis. 'And I was about to call you about moving some funds. I have travel plans.'

'How lovely for you, but we've had a series of unanticipated deposits. Is there something you forgot to tell me?'

The best way to avoid alerting the authorities to the movement of money was not to move it at all, or certainly not electronically, but the requirements of modern finance made this difficult. The next best way was to move sums of less than $10,000, but not so often as to establish a pattern, while any international transfer over $100,000 was guaranteed to arouse curiosity. American banks in particular were supposed to file SAR – Suspicious Activity Reports – for any cash transfers over $10,000, although the sheer volume of transfers, combined with the natural greed and perfidy of the banking industry, mitigated against total compliance. Golden's clients stayed under the radar by advising him of impending transactions and receiving in turn recommendations on how best to disperse them, expertise for which Golden received a not excessive, but still generous, commission.

'How much?' said Louis.

'One million euros, transferred into seventeen different accounts in transactions of between five and nine thousand euros a time, but not from the same source – or seemingly not from the same source, but in reality, almost certainly so.'

'Not possible.'

'With money,' said Golden, 'anything is possible.'

'And have you established the source?'

'No, I haven't begun running back the cat. I thought I'd contact you first, just in case a million euros had somehow slipped your mind. One of the deposits did come with a message, though. It reads: "From one Hunter to another, with thanks", and a capital "H" for "Hunter". Does that mean anything to you?'

Louis knew that De Jaager had been planning to dispose of most of his physical assets. The old man had spoken of his intention to keep only what he needed and distribute the rest of the proceeds. Louis could not have imagined that some of the money would find its way to him, yet now it seemed apt. It was almost as though De Jaager had somehow anticipated what was to come and prepared the ground for retaliation.

'Yes, it does,' said Louis.

'Should I be worried about the source?'

'The source is dead.'

'That wasn't what I meant.'

'No, he would have been careful. That money is clean.'

'I'm glad to hear it. Carelessness costs extra. Now, how much did you want to move, and where?'

From memory, Louis named figures and accounts, and requested the transfer of the euro equivalent of $500,000 to prepaid credit cards, the cards to be made available for collection from a courier in Amsterdam. Golden said that he'd take care of it and hung up.

'A problem?' said Angel.

'De Jaager sent me a million euros before he died.'

'I always liked him. What's a million euros in real money?'

'Maybe a million-ten, a million-fifteen.'

'If I'd known how wealthy he was, I'd have been nicer to him.'

'I don't think he ever placed much value on money,' said Louis. 'But that's a rich man's luxury, I suppose.'

Alex's limo pulled up outside. Angel touched Louis gently on the arm.

'At least we're putting it to good use,' he said.

Louis thought about De Jaager. He thought about Paulus, and Anouk, and the girl named Liesl. He recalled the latter from the library at the Rijksmuseum, glancing up at Louis and De Jaager as she and another girl, Eva, trailed a book dealer named Cornelie Gruner from the library's reading room. Dead now, every one. For just a moment, Louis looked back on the path of his life and saw it littered with bodies.

'Fuck it,' he said. 'Let's go.'

Chapter XXIV

They flew not into Amsterdam but into Brussels. Louis and Angel had been with Parker at Amsterdam's Schiphol Airport when Armitage came to meet them, which meant that their images were on record and might well remain connected to the investigation into the legat's death. Louis didn't know how much cleaning up the FBI and its confederates had managed in the Netherlands, but he wasn't about to bet his liberty on the assumption that it included erasing video images obtained from airport security footage, or advising Dutch law enforcement that the men photographed with Armitage in Amsterdam should no longer be regarded as persons of interest.

They passed through Belgian immigration without incident, helped by the fact that they were traveling on clean US passports under names only marginally different from their own. The passports had cost Louis a lot of money, and had deliberately been kept unused, and therefore untainted, in case of the necessity of sudden flight from the authorities. Now he and Angel were burning these identities not on their own behalf but that of friends. They had no regrets about this.

They collected their luggage and passed through the terminal building to the sidewalk. A light drizzle was falling on a world that bore only a superficial resemblance to their own, for even the air smelled different here. They caught an airport shuttle bus to the Van Der Valk Hotel on Culliganlaan, but did not check in. Instead they walked to the parking lot, where an eight-year-old midnight-blue BMW stood waiting. As they approached, the trunk popped open. They placed their bags inside, closed the trunk, and got in the car, Louis in the front passenger seat, Angel behind him. The driver greeted them.

'I would say welcome back,' said Hendricksen, 'but it seems inappropriate under the circumstances.'

The three men drove to Amsterdam without stopping, Angel napping on and off in the back seat. His recent brush with cancer (no, more than a brush: a head-on collision) had left him with less bowel, more gray hairs, and pain lines on his forehead and beside his eyes. Louis watched him in the rearview mirror as he slept, and thought he looked as though he was suffering, even in repose.

This man, this beloved, infuriating man.

At Louis's insistence, Hendricksen once again went through the circumstances of his discovery of the bodies, step-by-step. He'd had the foresight to use his cell phone to document the scene before the police arrived, and these pictures he'd printed out and placed in a plastic folder for Louis's use.

'I don't suppose there's any point in warning you about the contents?' said Hendricksen.

'None,' said Louis, yet still he was shocked by what he saw. The flash on Hendricksen's phone had created a chiaroscuro effect, accentuating the pallor of skin while deepening the surrounding shadows. The result was a vision of brutality that resembled the most anguished imaginings of medieval and Renaissance art. He felt the final agonies of these four people and allowed the rage to build inside him. But as the wave broke and the tide subsided, he raised barriers that he would not permit to be breached again. Emotion would only hamper his efforts, and he had long ago learned to compartmentalize his hatreds.

Yet his features displayed none of this, remaining impassive throughout.

'They made De Jaager watch what was done to the women,' said Louis. He had moved on to the photographs of the upstairs bedroom, with its two bloodstained beds, its reddened boards, and a single chair lying on its side, a pair of cable ties nearby. 'These are foul men.'

'Go to the last of the photos,' said Hendricksen.

Louis did, and discovered a series of images of a van, obtained from what must have been a building's external security camera. The date and time on the pictures indicated that they were taken on the morning after De Jaager's final, long night. In the third image, the driver's face was almost visible. The pictures that followed were enlarged and enhanced versions of the same face. Louis wouldn't have been able to swear to it in court, but he was reasonably certain that the driver was Luca Bilbija. A second man sat beside him, but his face was turned to the right, and was therefore not visible.

'Where were these taken?' asked Louis.

'About half a kilometer from the safe house,' said Hendricksen.

'Did you get them from the police?'

'No, these emerged from my own inquiries.'

Louis was impressed. He could only imagine the kind of dedication this had required.

'I have police contacts,' Hendricksen continued, 'good ones, but I decided it might be wiser not to use them unless absolutely necessary.'

'And why would that be?' said Louis, although he already guessed the answer.

'Because I doubt you're here to perform a citizen's arrest on these men.'

'No, I'm here to kill them.'

Better it was said aloud so that Hendricksen would not have to lie to himself, now or later.

'As I thought.'

'And how do you feel about that?' said Louis.

'I would have preferred it to be otherwise,' said Hendricksen. 'Perhaps I yet retain some hope that a legal solution might present itself. Incidentally, do you see where we are?'

They were passing a sign for the truck stop at Meer, close to the Belgian-Dutch border. It was here that Louis and Angel had first met Hendricksen, in the company of De Jaager and his only nephew, Paulus.

'Yes,' said Louis, 'I remember this place.'

'It's as though the old man ordered it this way, that we should be speaking of him now. He had a talent for manipulating the direction of human affairs.'

Louis considered this a peculiar way of describing it, although he couldn't entirely disagree. Minutes later, they crossed the invisible border with the Netherlands.

'To return to your original question,' said Hendricksen, 'if there is a way that they can be taken alive and handed over for trial, will you allow it?'

'I'll consider it,' he said, which he felt was a suitably gnomic reply, 'but not if this is the only evidence of their guilt.' He held up the picture of Bilbija at the wheel of the van.

'The women were raped,' said Hendricksen. 'There was semen present, so the men who did it weren't using protection. If they were negligent in that way, they may also have been negligent in others. There will be DNA evidence. With that will come leverage.'

Louis wasn't so sure. These were hardened men, with military as well as criminal backgrounds. It would take a great deal of pressure to make them turn on one another.

'You already sound like you're trying to talk me out of what I came to do,' he said.

'I don't believe I'm capable of doing that. I'm just suggesting that there may be alternatives.'

'Not if they return to Serbia.'

Hendricksen conceded with a shrug. The Serbian justice ministry adjudicated extradition requests on a case by case basis, generally linked to political relations between Serbia and the country in question. Relations between the Netherlands and Serbia were good, the Dutch being supporters of Serbian efforts to join the European Union. But extradition proceedings could drag on for years, even with the political will to facilitate them, and that was before one took into account the possibility of corruption. The Vuksans had money, and a degree of influence. If they managed to embed themselves in Serbia, the brothers would be long dead before anyone got around to signing their extradition papers. There was little purpose in putting a corpse on trial, and cadaver synods were only for popes.

'Still,' said Louis, 'the first step is to find them.'

'Finding them will be time-consuming,' said Hendricksen, 'and expensive.'

'We have money.'

'Very expensive.'

'Lots of money.'

'Well, then,' said Hendricksen, 'perhaps it won't be so time-consuming after all. Money, I find, hastens progress.'

Behind them, Angel woke, stretched, and stared out at the flat landscape.

'If I was rich and lived here,' he said, 'I'd build a mountain and declare myself king.'

'If you lived here, everyone else would leave,' said Louis. 'Anyway, you think that's how royalty works?'

'Pretty much,' said Angel. 'I've read books.'

'You know, he has a point,' said Hendricksen.

'Don't tell him that,' said Louis. 'He'll start believing he has more of them.'

'When I'm king,' said Angel, 'I'll outlaw golf.'

'Is that all?' said Louis.

'Golf, cell phone conversations taking place anywhere near me while I'm trying to read, and using "action" as a verb.'

'Jesus Christ,' said Louis.

'No,' said Angel, 'he'll be okay.'

'You gonna be lonely in this kingdom of yours?' said Louis. 'Because I can't see you being inundated with subjects.'

'No,' said Angel. 'You'll be there.'

'You think so?'

'I know it,' said Angel, and went back to sleep.

Chapter XXV

The Vuksan convoy, now reduced to two cars, had paused at the Raststätte Donautal in Passau, just northeast of the Austrian border. There the men sat outside eating German sausage and fried potatoes, and drinking pilsner beer, all except Radovan, who kept himself apart while he made a call to the lawyer Anton Frend. The two men spoke for fifteen minutes, but although a lot of information was communicated, neither took notes. When they were done, Radovan made a second call, and this time wrote down an address. He then removed the SIM card from his phone, destroyed it, and replaced it with another.

Spiridon wiped the grease from his fingers as his brother returned to the table.

'What does the lawyer say?' said Spiridon.

'Through intermediaries, he has found us a place to stay,' said Radovan. 'I felt it would be better if he did not know the exact address.'

'Did he object?'

'He suggested I send him a signed declaration to that effect, just in case anyone came asking, but I think he was joking.'

Radovan did not really believe that Frend would turn a blind eye to their location, because it was not in the lawyer's nature to deny himself knowledge. Still, the pretense would serve its purpose.

'You and he are too close,' said Spiridon.

'So you never tire of telling me. Had I listened to you, we would have hired a Serbian lawyer, and he'd probably be dead by now.'

Zivco Ilić and Luca Bilbija turned their heads away, finding new sources of interest in the passing traffic and dull buildings. They were by now so used to the brothers' bickering that they were able to tune it out or reduce it to white noise, but it was wise to make their lack of curiosity obvious.

'Frend is your lawyer,' said Spiridon, 'not ours.'

'I didn't realize there was a distinction.'

'I did,' said Spiridon, 'a long time ago.'

Radovan let the argument go. When his brother was in this mood, persistence only encouraged him. Radovan glanced at the nearer of the two cars, where a small figure sat unmoving in the back seat.

'Has she eaten?' he said.

'She said she wasn't hungry. She may have scavenged food from Dražeta's kitchen while we slept. She has her ways.'

'Aleksej told me that Dražeta's wife got up during the night,' said Radovan. 'Perhaps she fed her.'

'What of it?'

Spiridon's tone was sharp, for him. He was always defensive about the girl. It was tiring. No one had ever suggested that there was anything improper about the relationship, or not within earshot of Spiridon. Unnatural, yes, but that was another matter.

'Nothing,' said Radovan. 'It was just an observation. We should be going. Vienna is still three hours away, and I'll feel safer once we're there.'

He had been against stopping, but the men had wanted to use the restrooms, and then hunger had gotten the better of them. There were too many people here, too many strangers, and Belgrade was watching for them. They had been reduced to the status of prey, hiding from the light.

Spiridon signaled to the others, and they began to walk to the cars. It was left to Radovan to clear the debris from the table. Spiridon stared back at him.

'What are you doing?' he said.

'Look around you,' said Radovan. 'See all the law-abiding Germans and Austrians disposing of their waste? If we wish to remain unnoticed, we must behave as they do.'

He divided the litter and food waste between the appropriate containers, and arranged the the glasses and trays.

'We are not like them,' said Spiridon, as his brother fell into step beside him. 'And we never will be.'

'Small details will betray us,' said Radovan.

'No,' said Spiridon, 'only small men.'

Chapter XXVI

On their previous visit to Amsterdam, Angel and Louis, with Parker, had done their best to avoid letting Ross know their location and movements. They had stayed in De Jaager's safe house, an option that obviously no longer presented itself. But making it difficult for Ross to contact him now seemed counter-productive to Louis, so he and Angel were booked into the Conservatorium in Oud-Zuid, and a secure email had advised Ross accordingly. Once they had freshened up and changed their clothes, they joined Hendricksen in the hotel lounge, where they ordered food.

'You really must have money if you're staying in this place,' said Hendricksen. 'I feel as though I'm bringing the tone down just by being here.'

'Me, too,' said Angel.

'You'd bring down the tone of a Super Eight,' said Louis to Angel. 'Anyway, it's not our money, it's De Jaager's.'

'I don't understand,' said Hendricksen.

'He wired me a million euros before he died.'

'To what end?'

'Possibly because it amused him.'

'And now you'll use it to avenge him.'

'That's right.'

A waiter arrived with coffee, a pot of tea, and the neatest sandwiches Louis had ever encountered. The coffee smelled strong and bitter, and the bread tasted freshly baked.

'And you?' said Louis to Hendricksen. 'Where do you stand? I brought you into this, but you have no obligations to me or De Jaager, not unless you've been hiding something from us.'

Hendricksen finished a bite of sandwich before responding.

'You know what my background is?'

'Military.'

'That's right. Did De Jaager tell you?'

'No, because I never asked,' said Louis. 'I picked up on it the first time we met.'

'I served eight years in the Dutch army,' said Hendricksen. 'I joined when I was eighteen: Airmobile Brigade. I was twenty-two when we were told we were to form part of an *infanteriebataljon* – in our case, Dutchbat Three – to be sent to the Balkans as part of the UN peacekeeping mission, except nobody had figured out how to keep peace in a place where everyone around you was committed to war.

'Our mission was to enforce UN Security Council Resolution 819, which was supposed to make the town of Srebrenica and its surrounding areas a safe haven for civilians under attack from Bosnian Serb paramilitary units. But the mission was flawed: keep the peace, but don't shoot anyone; guard the civilian population, but don't get too involved, just in case someone takes offense. The UN didn't want to be drawn into another bloody war in Europe, but we were already there. We *were* involved; it was just that the UN wasn't prepared to acknowledge the implications. Eventually, we were going to have to pick a side, and it wasn't going to be the Serbs, but no one wanted to make that admission, not then.

'By July 1995 we were marooned in the town, surrounded by Ratko Mladić and his cutthroats. There was a constant flow of refugees – men, women, children, mostly Muslim – all looking to us for protection, but we couldn't even protect ourselves. We numbered fewer than five hundred men with each rotation, armed with a few heavy machine guns and a pair of RPGs. They had tanks and artillery, we had armored personnel carriers. They cut our supply lines, and when we made incursions into their territory, we took fire. We called in air support, but the Serbs were holding fifty of our men hostage and threatened to kill them if the planes attacked, so the bombing run was called off. And all the time, the number of civilians inside the town kept growing and growing: fifteen thousand, twenty thousand, twenty-five thousand. They were terrified, and we were terrified, too.'

Hendricksen was no longer looking at Angel and Louis. He was staring at the floor, as though in its devices he might be able to discern some version of the patterns in his own life, the paths that had led him at last to this place, and this admission of guilt.

'The Serbs entered Srebrenica on July eleventh and we handed the town over to Mladić. We watched the Muslim women and children being taken away in buses. I don't know what happened to the children, but most of the women were probably being raped within hours. The men and boys stayed. Mladić told us they'd be transferred to camps later, but we knew better, even before the executions started. The Serbs killed eight thousand at Srebrenica: old men, young men, teenagers. We stood by and let them do it, and when it all became too much we drove away. I've heard it said that we had no choice, but we did, because there is always a choice.'

'And what should you have done?' said Louis.

'We should have stood our ground,' said Hendricksen. 'We were soldiers. We should have fought.'

'You'd have died.'

'Perhaps,' said Hendricksen, 'but sometimes that's not only a soldier's duty but also his destiny. Had we died in the service of those people then the UN, and the Americans in particular, might have been forced to act sooner. And even if we had been killed, we would have died heroes. Instead, we were blamed for what happened. We returned home in disgrace. It's a stain upon our personal honor, and our nation's, that can never be erased, not unless some opportunity to make reparation comes around.'

'So you see the Vuksans as a chance to do the right thing?' said Angel. 'If you'll forgive me for saying so, I'm not sure that equates.'

Hendricksen tore his gaze from the floor.

'Spiridon Vuksan was there, at Srebrenica,' he said. 'He was one of Mladić's advisors, sent by Belgrade to judge the length of his leash. I saw Spiridon with my own eyes. I heard a lieutenant ask him if the male prisoners should be separated according to age, which might make them easier to handle, and Spiridon told him that the Turks – that was what he called the Muslims, "Turks" – wouldn't be a problem for long.

'And then he noticed me listening, and he looked at me and smiled. I wanted to shoot him then. I wanted to shoot them all. He saw it in my face. He spread his arms wide, and spoke to me in English. "Do it," he said. "Be a man." But I did nothing.'

Hendricksen still held a half-eaten sandwich, but whatever appetite he once had was gone. He placed the sandwich on a plate and wiped the crumbs from his hands.

'We're not on a crusade,' said Louis.

'Aren't you?' said Hendricksen. 'I think the circumstances of your previous visit to this country might suggest otherwise. But regardless, you need my help. You don't have any friends in the Netherlands, present company excepted, and you don't have any contacts. I have both, and that extends to almost every country in Europe. I've been in this business a long time. I'm owed some goodwill.'

'Even in Serbia?' said Angel.

'Even in Serbia.'

'You have a job,' said Louis. 'You work as an investigator for Dutch lawyers. You can't just drop everything to help us.'

'I operate on a contract basis, so I work as I choose. At the moment, I have no obligations so urgent that they cannot be set aside.'

'What we're here to do could take a while,' said Louis.

'I repeat, I have no obligations.'

Louis poured himself a fresh cup of tea. Back in the United States, he stuck to coffee, and couldn't understand why anyone drank tea, even in those fancy Manhattan tearooms. But he'd developed a taste for tea in England. Europeans did this kind of stuff well, he thought.

'If you work with us, we pay you,' said Louis.

'I don't want payment.'

'I don't care what you want. This isn't about acts of kindness, or making up for past failings. I don't know you well enough to work on trust alone, and that kind of help is too subject to second thoughts. It's not our money, it's De Jaager's. Accept it, or walk away.'

'Then I accept,' said Hendricksen. 'But I'll take payment when we're done. You can decide then how much my assistance was worth.'

'Agreed.'

'Now that's settled,' said Hendricksen, 'I have good news for you, and bad.'

'I'm a bad-news-first kind of guy,' said Louis.

'I guessed. I made some more calls while you were checking in. The Vuksans have vanished. That van was found burned out on waste ground about an hour after the picture was taken. I've commenced trawling for witnesses, but so far no one saw anything.'

'Do you believe them?' said Louis.

'I don't think these people have any reason to lie. For them, it was just a van fire.'

'What about your other contacts, the ones who might have a reason to lie?' said Angel.

'I'm working on them, but I've come up with nothing yet. I can go back with an offer of money, but I suspect the answer will remain the same in most cases. De Jaager was well-liked, and even those with reason to feel aggrieved at him still retained a degree of tolerance for his activities. If they knew anything, they would have shared it, for the sake of the murdered women as much as De Jaager. But I haven't exhausted every avenue, so who knows what may emerge?'

'And the good news?' said Angel, who was, by contrast, a good-news kind of guy, having heard enough bad news to last a lifetime.

Hendricksen smiled.

'The Vuksans can't go back to Serbia,' he said, 'not yet.'

'Why?' said Louis.

'Because someone has started blowing up their relatives.'

Chapter XXVII

By common consent, the area around the Stalingrad Métro stop, at the border between the 10th and 19th arrondissements in northeastern Paris, was regarded as being among the less salubrious spots in the city in which to linger – and that was even before the building of a migrant camp near the avenue de Flandre. The camp had since been forcibly dismantled by French police, leading to running battles with residents, but its removal had not done much to raise the tone of the locale. By day it was mostly fine, but night brought out the predators.

Aleksej Marković was not unduly worried by the possibility of predation, mostly because he was more dangerous than any other predator on the streets. Marković had murdered his way across whole swathes of Bosnia in the company of Ratko Mladić, Spiridon Vuksan, and the VRS, the Bosnian Serb Army, during the wars in the former Yugoslavia. If there was a man in the vicinity of Stalingrad who had killed more men or raped more women than he, Marković might have enjoyed shaking his hand, although only after making sure that he was dead, because Aleksej Marković had grown circumspect in middle age.

He had never expected to survive his twenties, but as the years went by, and his collection of scars increased without putting an end to him, Marković had decided that the concept of living to old age was not without its appeal. He had watched other men fall by the wayside, rendered harmless by bullets, disease, prison, poverty, and even domesticity, while he flourished. Much of his felicity he ascribed to the proximity of the Vuksans. If ever Marković needed confirmation that God had been on their side in the war against the Turks, the Ustashe, and their Western allies, it lay in the potency of Spiridon and Radovan Vuksan. God would not have blessed them with wealth and long life otherwise. Their success was a tribute to the righteousness of the Serbian cause, and Aleksej Marković had benefited as a consequence, so he did not question their orders or doubt the wisdom of their decisions. This included the recent action against De Jaager and the others who had found themselves in the Amsterdam safe house – or, more accurately, the unsafe house – at the wrong time.

Marković recognized that some conflict had arisen between the brothers on the subject, with Radovan urging caution, or a less public display of vengeance: a quiet abduction for De Jaager, followed by the disposal of his remains in an anonymous grave. But Spiridon had wanted to make a statement, to offer a final farewell to the Dutch. In addition, Spiridon required De Jaager to understand that his very existence had poisoned the lives of all those around him, and their suffering was a consequence of his behavior. Although he was not asked for his opinion, Marković had sided with Spiridon, because he always did.

Also, truth be told, Marković liked killing, and had not lost his taste for rape.

All had not gone according to plan, but Marković had no regrets. Spiridon could not have anticipated a move against Nikola Musulin, a violent usurpation of the established order. Perhaps it was better that Musulin's death should have occurred now, while they were out of the blast range, rather than later, when they were already back in Serbia. Musulin's killers had made an error. Had they waited, they might have succeeded also in taking out the Vuksans. Now the Vuksans' enemies were obliged either to come after them, which would be difficult and dangerous, or negotiate an agreed return – or so Spiridon had informed Marković and the others when the news of Musulin's death came through, although Marković noticed that Radovan remained silent throughout and did not voice his support for Spiridon's opinion of their circumstances.

But Marković didn't much care one way or the other. He wasn't sure that he wanted to return to Serbia. Even had he gone back with the Vuksans, he doubted he would have stayed. Western Europe offered more possibilities, more ways for a ruthless man to earn money. Marković was a follower, not a leader, and his recognition of this reality had probably contributed more to his survival than he might have realized. At home, he would have been obliged to ally himself with one of the local groupings and swear allegiance to small men. Eventually, he would have become caught up in the kind of internecine feuding that had cost Nikola Musulin his life, resulting in a transfer of loyalties to another small man under threat of injury or death. The problem was that every such move caused a diminution in one's value and an increase in the amount of suspicion one attracted, until finally it was safer for someone to put a bullet in one's head rather than have one roaming free, accumulating grievances. No, regardless of whatever deal the Vuksans finally managed to strike – assuming they could strike any deal at all, because that expression of doubt and worry on Radovan's face had made an impression – Marković would find gainful employment in Europe, Asia, or even North America. A man with his skill set would never want for work.

For now, though, Marković was in Paris, staying in a hotel that reeked of standing water and bad food. He had taken an early-morning train from Cologne, dumping the car at the Tiefgarage Hauptbahnhof with the keys in the ignition and €500 in the glove compartment. On the way to the station, he had made a call to ensure that the car would be disposed of within the hour.

Despite the precariousness of their position, the Vuksans still had certain obligations that needed to be fulfilled, and it was to Marković that they had entrusted this responsibility. The cargo soon to arrive at the Gare de Lyon had landed at Port-Vendres some days previously, following a circuitous journey from Syria via Egypt and Algeria. It would have been simpler to have routed them through Serbia using established channels, but these men had business to be concluded in Cairo and Algiers before they could depart for Europe, and had indicated their preference for the Port-Vendres back door. Given recent events in Belgrade, it was now fortunate that they had elected to bypass Serbia. The Vuksans would have been unable to guarantee them safe transit, and might even have been forced to return the portion of their fee already delivered. Port-Vendres, although riskier, had proven to be a blessing.

Back in the glory days of France's imperial odyssey, Port-Vendres had benefited from being the southernmost French port to the colonies in Africa. While it was too far from the industrial cities to be a useful shipping center for goods, it had flourished as a terminal for passenger traffic to and from Algeria, because the crossing was smoother than over the Gulf of Lyon. Now the little commune was a tourist destination best known for its seafood restaurants, where fishing boats landed their catches at the quai du Fanal. Some security checks on incoming vessels were inevitable, but they were far fewer than might be anticipated at Toulon or Marseille. For this reason, and in order to preserve the integrity of the route, the Vuksans used their Port-Vendres contacts for only the most high-value cargo.

Marković found a table outside a Turkish café and lit a cigarette. He might have loathed Muslims, but he could not fault their coffee. Also, one never knew what one might learn by sitting in their presence and pretending not to speak French. Marković also had a smattering of Turkish, some Arabic, and adequate Spanish, as well as fluent English. He cultivated the aspect of an ignorant man, and his English deliberately remained heavily accented, but he was no dullard. The Vuksans did not employ dolts, or not for long.

And as Marković smoked his cigarette, and flicked idly through his cell phone, his image was captured and dispatched three hundred miles north, where a phone in Amsterdam pinged in the lounge of the Conservatorium, notifying the recipient of the message's arrival.

Chapter XXVIII

At the Conservatorium, Louis was discussing with Hendricksen the information contained in Ross's dossier on the Vuksans, and particularly that which concerned the Viennese lawyer named Anton Frend.

'The name isn't familiar to me,' said Hendricksen, 'but I can ask around. I've had some dealings with Austrian lawyers.'

'How were they?' said Angel.

'They were lawyers,' said Hendricksen.

'That bad, huh?'

Hendricksen nodded glumly.

'Is the intel solid?' he said.

'I trust the intel,' said Louis, 'but not the source.' He had shared with Hendricksen the generalities of his conversation with Ross, omitting his deeper concerns about Ross's motives.

'And you say Ross is putting you in touch with a contact in Amsterdam?' said Hendricksen.

'So he claimed. If you're right about the repercussions of Musulin's death, we now have a window of opportunity, but it may not remain open for long. Ross's spook buddies will understand that just as well as we do.'

But even as he spoke, Louis had to quell his unease. In his old life he had prided himself on preparation, including intimate study of a target through multiple forms of surveillance, sometimes lasting weeks, or even months. Whenever possible he took on much of that responsibility himself, because he placed the appropriate value on his own skin. Only on rare occasions had he killed without taking precautions, and the premium charged had not been worth the peril: twice he had come close to being apprehended, and once he had almost died. Now he was hunting on unfamiliar territory, and dependent on the goodwill of strangers.

Which was when a waiter appeared with a note for him, and said, 'Your guest is waiting for you at the bar.'

Chapter XXIX

R adovan and Spiridon Vuksan had rarely been apart during
the past twenty years. They were, in their way, symbiotic
beings, or two aspects of the same brain. Radovan was the cere-
brum – thinking, learning, planning – while Spiridon was the
cerebellum, governing the movement of the muscles. Radovan
adjudged, and Spiridon acted accordingly. Separate, they were
individually weaker. Together, they were greater than the sum of
their parts.

On the other hand, for such a relationship to work, these two
aspects of the brain had to be in perfect accord, and in recent
years Radovan's caution had increased in seemingly direct proportion to Spiridon's recklessness. Spiridon no longer considered his
brother's counsel, and even when he did, it was dismissed as often
as it was accepted. Had he not known better, Radovan might have
said that Spiridon was intent upon their ruination.

For the first time, Radovan Vuksan was contemplating the
excision of his brother from his life.

But for now they remained united, because Spiridon was giving
the impression, if not of heeding his brother's advice, then at least
of weighing it. Initially, after the death of Nikola Musulin, Spiridon
had spoken only of revenge: of returning to Serbia, gathering their
forces, and punishing those responsible. But a night's sleep at the
farmhouse of Gavrilo Dražeta appeared to have mellowed him
somewhat, if only temporarily, and on the long drive southeast,
Spiridon had listened more than he had spoken.

If they went back to Serbia, Radovan explained, they'd be killed.
No one in Belgrade – not in government, not in the police, not
even among the gangs and syndicates – wished to see a descent
into open criminal warfare. It would be bad for the country's

image, especially as it attempted to present its best face to the European Union. Shortly after their return, the Vuksans and anyone who stood alongside them would be quietly vanished, and nothing would ever be heard of them again.

There were also established cultural reasons for maintaining the status quo. Back in the good old days of the Socialist Federal Republic of Yugoslavia, under the firm hand of Marshal Josip Broz Tito, criminals were generally allowed to go about their business as long as they conducted it beyond the country's borders and repatriated some of their profits to benefit Yugoslav society. Following Tito's death in 1980, the country had become economically and politically unstable, leading to fractures along ethnic and nationalist lines, and, ultimately, war.

Now, more than two decades after the first eruption of the conflict, something resembling stability reigned, admittedly with certain qualifications. The Chinese were investing heavily in Serbia in preparation for the country's eventual integration into the EU, and the Russians, as usual, were doing their best to sow discontent in the region, including working to prevent the former Yugoslav federal state of Macedonia – or North Macedonia as it was now known – from joining NATO. Meanwhile, a version of Tito's law once again applied to the more ambitious forms of Serb criminality: it was strictly export-only. In Serbia, as in Russia, the real criminals now wore suits and roamed unchallenged through the National Assembly.

All of which meant that Nikola Musulin's death must have been sanctioned at a high level – in theory, if not in actual practice, since even the most pragmatic of Serbian politicians would have balked at a bomb attack at the heart of one of the country's tourist hot spots. It was Radovan's opinion that the main reason for Musulin's assassination had been to prevent Spiridon's return to Serbia because he represented a potentially destabilizing influence – although, as with all such maneuverings, there were undoubtedly other forces at work, since Musulin's death opened the way for a redistribution of wealth and influence. If their foes were prepared to sanction Musulin's public immolation, they would not hesitate to do the same for the Vuksans.

But the brothers were also vulnerable if they remained in Europe, because the Serbian gangs had insinuated themselves throughout the continent. It was, therefore, unwise for the Vuksans to linger where they might be spotted by unfriendly faces. Unfortunately, Spiridon had so far proved resistant to the idea of relocation to another continent. Spiridon *wanted* to be acknowledged as a threat, and the closer his proximity to Belgrade, the more his enemies had reason to fear him and thus – according to his rationale – the more cause they would have to seek an accommodation with him.

Nikola Musulin's death had not affected Spiridon on any personal level, beyond the inconvenience it was causing him. Blood ties aside, the two men had never been close, and if the bomb had not blown Musulin to pieces, someone else would have usurped him down the line because, as Gavrilo Dražeta had noted, he lacked foresight and ambition. When, or if, Serbia was finally accepted into the European Union, it would be open season for the criminal syndicates and their political allies, and a lot of people stood to become very wealthy. This was why the government was making superficial efforts to appear to be tackling corruption and economic crime, even if it stopped short of large-scale arrests and prosecutions, or the seizure of notable criminal assets.

Serbia was what is known as a captured political system: It was corrupt from the top down, and picking off the bottom-feeders did little to affect the big fish. Those big fish had decided that Musulin was surplus to requirements. It would be interesting, thought Radovan, to see who would take his place. It would not be Spiridon, though, whatever unspoken hopes he might entertain; his time had passed. The question of succession mattered only in terms of the ease or difficulty of brokering a deal with the new occupant of Musulin's throne, and the extent to which the political forces that had facilitated Musulin's murder were prepared to bend on the issue and form of the Vuksans' survival.

It was dark as the Vuksans drove into Vienna, a city Radovan had always loved. Here, he believed, they would be safe for a while. He trusted Anton Frend, even if the two men would be unable to meet while the Vuksans bided their time. Too many individuals were aware of Radovan's professional relationship with Frend, even if they did not – or so Radovan hoped – realize the depth of the personal connection. It was too risky for Radovan and Frend to be seen together in public, so most of their communication would have to be conducted via dropboxes, temporary email addresses, and burner phones. If necessary, Zivco Ilić would act as a personal intermediary, because he was very good at seeing without being seen. Ilić would have some help in this, as he and the Other were close.

And the Other had gifts beyond all understanding.

Chapter XXX

The man sitting at the bar of the Conservatorium was staring at an iPad showing coverage of a news conference by a floundering senior US politician railing against his enemies, both real and imaginary. The man had a single earbud in his left ear, and a hearing aid behind his right. Louis guessed that he was in his sixties, with the patrician air of one who didn't like any money that wasn't old. Generations of good breeding had left him with all his hair, a body that was refusing to succumb to senescence, and – judging by his eyes as he glanced at Louis – a mind that was likewise raging against the dying of the light. He was wearing a gray suit and a black knit-silk tie, with a polka dot pocket square to offer a hint of levity.

'As soon as paranoia sets in every politician begins sounding like Nixon on the final White House tapes,' said the man, gesturing at the screen as Louis appeared beside him, 'and that's never a good image. Take a seat. Would you like a drink?'

Louis sat. 'What are you having?' he said.

'A Dutch Negroni, made with *oude genever*. You know *genever*?'

'I know it.'

'Of course. You've been here before – and left your mark, by all accounts. So: a Negroni?'

'Sure.'

The man raised a finger, and a bartender was pulled toward them.

'A Negroni for my friend, and a fresh one for me.'

'Are we friends?' said Louis.

'The alternative is less pleasant to contemplate, and harder to explain to bartenders.'

'You could start with a name.'

'You can call me Hermes.'

'Get the fuck out of here,' said Louis. 'I'm not calling you Hermes.'

'The patron of travelers and thieves. You could do worse.'

'Not a whole lot worse.'

'A pity,' said the man. 'Those cloak-and-dagger aliases always remind me of more innocent times. Then Harris will do, I suppose.'

The feed across the bottom of the iPad showed the politician inveighing against plotters and turncoats, and the anti-democratic maneuvers of the Deep State.

'Look,' said Louis, 'he's talking about you.'

'People love conspiracies,' said Harris. 'They find them reassuring. It's the consolation that someone, somewhere, might actually have a design in mind. The fearful embrace conspiracies for the same reason they believe in God.'

The Negronis arrived. Harris raised his glass.

'To great designs,' he said.

Louis made the slightest of gestures in return, and drank. The Negroni tasted smokier than he was used to, but he thought it might grow on him.

'As it happens,' said Harris, removing the earbud and putting the iPad to sleep, 'my father served under Nixon. Well, he served under people who served under Nixon, which is pretty much the same thing. He told me that he'd never encountered a stranger bunch of men than those in the Nixon White House. He spent one evening watching *Triumph of the Will* in the basement with the rest of the staff at the insistence of Gordon Liddy, although there was popcorn. Liddy then announced that the Special Investigations Unit, the dirty tricks brigade, was to be code-named ODESSA, after the former SS veterans' organization, and showed my father the nine-millimeter parabellum pistol he'd acquired from the CIA, just in case Bud Krogh asked him to assassinate anyone.'

Harris tasted his second Negroni, and seemed to find it just as satisfactory as the first.

'You know,' he concluded, 'Nixon's White House had its share of nuts and crooks, but back then Gordon Liddy wasn't a nut or a crook. Gordon Liddy was completely batshit crazy.'

'Is there a point to this story?' said Louis.

'The point is that we survived Nixon and his cadre, just as we survived all those who came before them and we'll survive all those who come after, God willing. Politicians are like hemorrhoids: they're a torment to be endured. Meanwhile, the greater game goes on.'

'Not for De Jaager,' said Louis, who was growing tired of listening to a stranger philosophize at a bar, 'or those who died with him.'

'No,' said Harris, 'not for them. I liked De Jaager. Ross and I met him together, back in the day.'

'The Stasi business?'

'Did Ross tell you about it?'

'He did.'

'So much for secrets. We farmed the wet work out to the Israelis, just like we're farming the Vuksans out to you.'

'So Ross indicated. Why did the Israelis take on the job, if you don't mind me asking? That wasn't entirely clear to me.'

'Because they have long memories,' said Harris. 'The Stasi funded terror groups in West Germany – the Red Army Faction, the Baaders – when it suited them to have bombs going off and executives being kidnapped. The Reds, with Stasi money, helped Black September plan the attack on the Olympic Village in Munich in 1972 that left eleven Israelis dead. Buchner, the Stasi who murdered Annie Houseman, was believed to be one of the the bagmen for the RAF. Seventeen years or so later, when the opportunity for payback arose, the Israelis took it. If I remember right, they sent us a couple of cases of Judean wine as a token of appreciation. But then, those were more civilized times.'

'And who do you work for,' said Louis, 'or is it impolite to ask?'

'Officially, I'm retired.'

'Unofficially?'

'I help out, on occasion.'

'So, start helping.'

Harris smiled.

'The Vuksans and their people haven't used any of their known passports – we're on top of those, so I'm certain on that front

– which means they're either still in Europe or they've acquired new identities. If it's the latter, they did so through Anton Frend. He's not a passport broker, but he has access to individuals who specialize in that area. You know about Nikola Musulin?'

'I heard he got blown up by a table,' said Louis.

'Apparently they're still searching for his head,' said Harris. 'The family is reluctant to bury him without it.'

'Funny how sentimental people can be.'

'Isn't it? Thanks to the elimination of Musulin, the Vuksans have been forced into hiding. But if they can stay alive for long enough, they may be able to cut a deal and return to Serbia.'

'Cut a deal with whom, Musulin's successor?'

'Nominally with his successor, but actually with whichever branch of the Serbian political and judicial establishment signed off on Musulin's assassination. In the meantime, the Vuksans will soon be hemorrhaging money, if they aren't already, because you can be sure that someone in Belgrade is going after their assets in order to push them further into a corner. Frend almost certainly has access to a slush fund, but it's unlikely to contain enough to support the Vuksans in a lifetime of exile.'

'So Frend is the key,' said Louis.

'A very crooked key, and one that won't easily be turned. If you try by force, you'll alert the Vuksans. They'll have set up a series of tripwires: calls at strictly scheduled times, code words, warning signs. The moment Frend fails to follow whatever routines they've established, they'll know he's been compromised.'

'Which doesn't help me.'

'No, but some other information might,' said Harris. 'I know Ross gave you a dossier on Frend. Did you notice that he has a daughter?'

'Pia. She's in London, and also a lawyer. Must be a fault in the genes.'

'Pia is estranged from her father, to the extent that she has reverted to her mother's maiden name: Lackner. Our understanding is that she hates Anton while he, like most men who find themselves rejected by a woman, pines for her approval and remains hopeful of a reconciliation.'

'Huh,' said Louis.

'Second – and I hope this will brighten your day – one of the Vuksans' men, Aleksej Marković, has come up for air. He's in Paris, staying at a hotel in the tenth arrondissement. Do you have email on your phone?'

Louis reached into a pocket and removed a primitive Nokia.

'What the fuck is that?' said Harris.

'It's a Nokia.'

Louis also possessed an iPad mini, but he was scrupulously careful about its use.

'So I see,' said Harris. 'Does it have a winder?'

'No, but it has something more useful: anonymity.'

Harris conceded the point. He checked to make sure they were not being watched before rousing the iPad from its sleep. A tap of his fingers produced an image of a man drinking coffee outside a café. Louis recognized Marković from the material supplied by Ross.

'When was this picture taken?' said Louis.

'About twenty minutes ago.'

'That's fast work.'

'He was careless – not very, but it doesn't take a lot.'

'Why isn't he in hiding like the rest of them?'

'Necessity,' said Harris. 'What do the Vuksans require?'

'Money.'

'Exactly. We think that Paris may be the last stage in one of their people-smuggling ratlines. From there, the cargo either vanishes into the banlieues or, for an additional charge, is moved to the United Kingdom or elsewhere. The only reason for Marković being in Paris is to ensure that a delivery will be concluded safely.'

'Ross said that the Vuksans might be helping terrorists gain access to Europe.'

'They are,' said Harris. 'Terrorists pay well, and the Vuksans don't ask security questions.'

'So why don't you just lift Marković from the street and see how long he can breathe underwater?'

'For the same reason that you can't approach Frend directly. If we apprehend Marković now, whoever he's waiting for will be alerted and the cargo will be lost. Also – and I'm not privy to every detail, so you'll have to take this on trust – Marković operates through cutouts. He never meets the cargo directly, but monitors proceedings from a distance. And finally, the French don't take well to foreign agencies operating on their territory without permission, but if we bring them in, you'll never get to Marković. We could let the French interrogate him, and listen in as guests, but he won't give up the Vuksans or the others, even if he knows exactly where they are – and my guess is that he doesn't, just in case he's picked up.'

Louis had not missed the flash of the blade: *if we bring them in, you'll never get to Marković.*

'You want me to take care of Marković?' he said.

'Isn't that why you're here?'

The hearing aid was in Harris's right ear, away from Louis, but he appeared to be having no trouble with his left. Louis guessed that Harris could probably hear perfectly well with his right, too. Transmitters and receivers came in all shapes and sizes.

'You must have me mistaken for someone else. I'm a tourist.'

'I'm not recording this conversation,' said Harris.

'You say.'

'If I was recording, I'd be more circumspect. If it makes you any happier, yes, we would like you to take care of Marković. We want him wiped from the map. Consider it payment for our help.'

That was all Louis wanted to hear. Harris might not have been recording their conversation, but Louis was.

'And his cargo?'

'We'll look after that. As for the Vuksans themselves, the lawyer is the wedge you need.'

'And his weakness is his daughter,' said Louis.

'That's right. You ever consider going into the kidnapping business?'

'No,' said Louis, 'but there's a first time for everything.'

Chapter XXXI

Louis and Harris spoke for a while longer, but Louis understood that Harris had provided all the intelligence that was likely to be forthcoming, at least for the present.

'Should I ask about weapons?' said Harris, as he reached for his hat and coat.

'I wouldn't,' said Louis.

'I figured you'd have your own sources, but I thought it was only polite to offer.'

Harris recited a telephone number, which Louis didn't write down, but memorized. It was a US number, with a 571 area code.

'It's message-only,' said Harris, 'but if you call, I'll get back to you immediately.'

Louis thought that 571 might be Virginia, in which case he would have bet a crisp dollar bill that the number would ring somewhere in Langley, home of the CIA. He decided that he'd have to be in a whole lot of trouble before he called it.

Angel arrived to check on Louis.

'Did I miss something,' said Angel, 'other than a round of drinks?'

'This is Harris,' said Louis, 'or maybe Hermes, if you want to view him as a luxury lifestyle choice. Personally, I prefer Harris. Harris, this is Angel.'

The two men shook hands.

'Ross warned me about you,' said Harris to Angel. 'Is it true that you're tormenting Connie Holt about restroom keys?'

Ross's superior was being driven slowly crazy by a series of anonymous missives claiming knowledge of a secret network of FBI restrooms situated in strategic locations around the United States. The latest communication received by Holt had included

125

a packet of Dr Singha's Mustard Bath (single size) from the National Mustard Museum in Middleton, Wisconsin; a desk calendar from the Museum of Bad Art in Somerville, Massachusetts; and a framed wreath made from human hair, stolen from Leila's Hair Museum in Independence, Missouri, and repurposed by replacing the photo of a deceased nineteenth-century woman at its heart with a picture of Conrad Holt himself. This final artifact had particularly enraged the FBI man, who was sensitive about his hairline. Each item came with a key attached, and a typed note complaining that the key in question did not fit the lock to the restroom. As with a number of the most recent letters to Holt, the envelope used was stamped *Greetings from the Great Lost Bear, Portland, Maine. Remember: Good Bears Eat Their Honey!* Holt was now of the opinion that the bar in question should be raided and its owners taken into custody. If they were not actively involved in his persecution, they were facilitating it by permitting the use of one of their rubber stamps.

'Holt,' said Angel, his face assuming an expression of wounded innocence that would not have shamed the Archangel Gabriel himself. 'I gotta say, the name doesn't ring a bell.'

'You boys sail close to the wind, I'll give you that,' said Harris. 'It was good talking to you. I wish you good luck in your endeavors.'

They watched him leave.

'Another legat?' said Angel.

'No, a spook,' said Louis. 'He says he's retired, but that's like claiming to be an ex-alcoholic.'

'Did he help?'

'Some,' said Louis. 'He gave us a lead, and a bead on our first target.'

'Here?'

'Paris.'

'When do we leave?'

'I leave for Paris in the morning. You don't.'

'So what am I doing?'

'You're going to London,' said Louis. 'You're about to arrange a kidnapping.'

Louis, Angel, and Hendricksen ate that evening at Mama Makan, an Indonesian restaurant on the Spinozastraat recommended by Hendricksen. When they were done, Hendricksen took them to the house in which De Jaager and the others had died. There was no indication that anything untoward had occurred there, beyond a strip of red-and-white tape and a police notice in Dutch that Louis did not require a translation to comprehend.

'You're sure you want to do this?' said Hendricksen. 'There's nothing to see, except blood.'

'Then I'll look at blood,' said Louis. 'What about an alarm?'

'Deactivated since the killings.'

Angel took care of the new lock with his own pick set. Hendricksen stayed outside by the canal to keep watch, although little danger remained of the police or anyone else coming to investigate further. He simply had no desire to enter that building again. He watched Angel and Louis go inside, the door closing softly behind them, and felt a chill enter his bones.

The shutters were drawn, but both Angel and Louis carried small flashlights, the bezels wrapped with Scotch tape to narrow the beams, thereby reducing the risk of attracting attention. The bloodstains had turned to ocher, but Louis thought that he could still taste copper on his tongue and pick up the smell of a charnel house. The two men moved from room to room, first downstairs, then upstairs, concluding in the bedroom where the women had died. They exchanged no words, but instead bore silent witness. Theirs was an act of empathy, an attempt to grasp the depth of the suffering that had occurred here. The photographs might have been enough for some, but not for them. Sometimes you had to walk the ground. This they had learned from the private detective named Charlie Parker.

Finally they returned to the front door. Angel opened it slightly and waited for Hendricksen to confirm that it was safe to leave. He nodded once, and they joined him by the water.

'So?' said Hendricksen.

'As you warned us: blood,' said Louis.

'I'd like to say that I'd never seen so much before,' said Hendricksen, 'but it would be a lie.'

'I don't understand it.'

'Is there something to understand?'

'All that pain,' said Louis, 'just to avenge a life as worthless as Timmerman's.'

Hendricksen stared into the dark water of the canal. 'Spiridon Vuksan may be insane. I hope so. It would be more frightening were he not.'

'What about the men with him, and his brother?'

'His men are rapists and butchers, and if Radovan ever had a conscience, it was extirpated a long time ago. So what now?'

'I have some calls to make,' said Louis, 'and you need to book a flight.'

'To where?'

'Vienna.'

'The lawyer?'

'Yes,' said Louis, 'the lawyer.'

Chapter XXXII

The Vuksans had been advised to keep their heads down, and avoid leaving the suburban safe haven sourced for them through the efforts of the lawyer Frend. The kitchen was well stocked with food and alcohol, and the rear garden, although small, was secluded. There was a TV with a Netflix subscription, and a selection of fiction and nonfiction books – none in Serbian, but that was probably for the best. Had Frend instructed the intermediary to source some titles, it would rather have given the game away. In any case, of the three men destined to be sequestered in the house, only Radovan was a reader, and his English and German were both adequate to enable him to read in translation. Should he have been obliged to conceal himself alone, he would have been quite content with these quarters.

Unfortunately, Spiridon Vuksan had no patience, and disliked being contained for long. He did not value books, could watch television only in short bursts, and slept just four or five hours a night. Had he not been permitted to leave the apartment at least once a day, he would have torn it apart in the process of going crazier and crazier, driving his brother mad along with him.

So, barely fifteen hours after their arrival in Vienna, Spiridon was already out walking the streets, disguised as best he could and accompanied by a similarly camouflaged Zivco Ilić.

And shadowed by the Other.

Nahid Hasanović had been traveling to and from Heitzing, Vienna's 13th District, for more than fifteen years, ever since deciding that Bosnia-Herzegovina was no longer a country in which he wished to live. He had tried to make a life there, but the memories of the conflict were too painful and the price he

129

had paid was too high: he had lost two brothers, five cousins, three nephews and a niece, who had variously been shot by snipers, bludgeoned to death in ditches or, in the case of his niece, left to bleed out after multiple sexual assaults. This would have been ample cause for any man to leave his homeland – that, or take up arms until a bullet found a way to put him out of his misery – but Nahid had chosen to remain, if only for a while. He stayed, worked, prayed, and waited until the bodies of each of his relatives had been dug up and identified before taking advantage of ties in Austria to move his immediate family – a wife, two sons, and a daughter – to Vienna before someone decided to shoot, bludgeon, or rape them to death, too.

And, yes, a lot of Serbs had also made their way to the capital, because the Serbs had been migrating there since the nineteenth century, and the Habsburg Empire had once encompassed both Bosnians and Serbs. But the city also had a large Muslim population that had been in place for longer than the Serbs, dating back to the fifteenth century, when Vienna first became an object of imperial desire to the Ottomans. The Ottoman Empire failed to take the city, but a more gradual, gentler Muslim influx had followed, and Muslims now formed about one-eighth of Vienna's population, even if the memory of the Turkish assault on Vienna had never quite been permitted to fade from the Austrian collective memory, or from Austrian history books and school texts.

In Vienna, Nahid had rented a small apartment in the Rudolfsheim-Fünfhaus area, where more than half of residents had a foreign background. With money borrowed and money saved, he set up a small laundry and dry cleaning business in the 13th District. The 13th was among the most desirable residential areas in the city, although not as expensive as some, with easy access to parks and gardens on one hand and the city center on the other. Those who lived in the grand Biedermeier and Jugendstil villas had no great desire to do their own laundry, and Nahid's collection service meant they didn't even have to leave their homes to drop it off. He soon expanded into repair work and tailoring, and now owned three satellite laundries along with a large central facility, but when possible he still preferred to operate out of

Hietzing, where he kept an office and a couch on which to nap. He enjoyed the beauty of the area, and the fresh air. He liked the zoo in the grounds of the Schönbrunn Palace, to the extent that he retained an annual membership. He loved the smell of roses and freshly cut grass.

In all that he did, he was trying to forget, yet Nahid could never truly forget. He had watched two of his cousins being taken away while he hid in an outhouse. He had held one of his brothers, Adin, in his arms after he was shot by a Serb sniper while trying to flee Bostahovina, their village in the Srebrenica municipality, and could remember attempting to push a fragment of Adin's skull back into place because his brains were leaking from the cavity. He had stood with his wife as a United Nations digging team showed them the remains of their niece, her schoolbooks preserved in the pink satchel that lay beside her in the hole, her name stitched clearly above the buckle.

Nahid did not hate all Serbs. Nahid tried not to hate anyone at all.

But sometimes, it was very hard.

Nahid himself had only barely evaded capture and murder. He had been traveling to Srebrenica with his wife, and what was then their only child, because they, like the other Muslims, believed that the UN-protected town offered safe haven from the Serbs. But as they drew nearer, it became apparent that the Serbs had blockaded Srebrenica. Refugees were still getting through, but to Nahid it smacked of entering a mosque before the doors were locked and the whole edifice was set alight. So he had turned his wife and daughter away from the town, despite the risk of having their throats slit by the Serbs, and had found sanctuary in the basement of a farmhouse owned by one of the few Quakers in the country. His brother and his family, along with two male cousins and their families, had continued into Srebrenica.

The men, and their older sons, were never seen alive again. Only in the years after did Nahid discover documentary evidence of their fate. A piece of news footage showed a group of Muslim prisoners descending from a truck and being led to a grove of trees. There, Nahid subsequently learned, they were tortured by their captors, members of the Serb paramilitary unit known as the Scorpions. Finally, they were dragged to a hole that had been dug by an earthmover, and there they were shot. From the film, Nahid had identified his brother, his nephews, and one cousin among the prisoners in the truck. Later, he had helped war crimes investigators locate the scene of the massacre, and worked with them to exhume the bodies for identification and reburial, because it was important that they should all have a name and a formal resting place.

No, he did not hate all Serbs.

But some he *really* hated.

Nahid watched a mother walking her toddler on the grass of the Schönbrunn, the woman crouching to hold the child's arms as his chubby legs carried him, half-stumbling, along. What people often forgot when it came to violent death were the connections, the links not only to those left behind but also to lives and worlds that might have been. Nahid found some consolation in the theory of multiple universes, and the idea that in a parallel existence those he had lost continued to live and breathe. Children were born, then grandchildren, on and on for generation after generation. These were potential states of being that did not conclude in sexual torment, in torture and murder.

Sometimes he heard them, the local Viennese Serbs, as they spoke dismissively of Muslims and Croats, just as others uttered calumnies about Jews or Blacks, creating a hierarchy of misery and pain, a tacitly accepted list of those whose destiny it was to suffer and die. What the ignorant did not understand was that the executioners were always the same, and only the uniforms changed. In that sense, the identities of the victims – their race, their color, their religion – were irrelevant: reduced to bone, we are all identical. When it came to mass murder, any prey would do, and those who would kill one would kill all. They who remembered this, they who had helped to excavate from pits the bones of men, women, and children, could only keep watch in the hope of warning the world when the next batch of executioners made themselves known.

Two men, one older, one younger, passed across his field of

vision, breaking his train of thought. They took a shortcut over the grass, and in doing so crushed the edge of a flowerbed beneath their shoes.

'Hey!' said Nahid, in German. 'Watch where you're treading.'

'Fuck you,' said the older man, not even bothering to look back.

'Fuck me?' said Nahid. 'Fuck *me*? No, fuck you. Fuck you!' He took out his cell phone to film the two men trampling the blooms. You could say what you wanted about the Austrians, but they placed a premium on law and order, and they really liked their flowers. Nahid planned to show the footage to the park authorities, and perhaps post it on the Internet as an example to others.

Nahid found himself lapsing into Arabic, as he often did when fury got the better of him, the Arab tongue being even more creative than German or Serbo-Croat when it came to insults. '*Kess ikhtak!*' he shouted, and then, just in case the object of his ire didn't have a sister, he added '*Kess ommak!*', on the basis that he certainly did have a mother, and so could go fuck her instead. If she was living, all the better. If she was dead, he could dig up her corpse and fuck that.

The older man stopped, and now he did turn back, even as the younger one with him tried to steer him away.

'*Ya kalb!*' he screamed at Nahid. 'You immigrant dog! You fucking Turk!'

The expression on Nahid's face changed, and he lowered his phone.

'I know you,' he said, so softly that he might almost have thought that it had gone unheard were it not for the way the younger man's head tilted slightly in response. 'I *know* you. From the film . . .'

The man was older now, his face softer, his body thicker, but the more Nahid stared, the more certain he became. Here before him was one of those who had walked with General Ratko Mladić through the streets of Srebrenica after the surrender, preening for the cameras as they sat down over coffee to nego-tiate the terms of departure for the Dutch battalion, even as they were setting in motion the mechanics of the genocide to come.

133

Fucking Mladić: a butcher who did not even have the guts to stay and supervise the slaughter he had ordered, but instead traveled back to Belgrade so he would have an alibi should the war turn against the Serbs.

In Mladić's absence – physical only – the abandoned UN base at Potočari was used as a staging point for the thousands of Muslim men and boys bound for execution, and later still Potočari became a cemetery for those same dead as their remains were exhumed from forests and glades to be taken there for reburial, as though to haunt the Dutch forever. Now, in Vienna, the past had assumed human form in order to torment Nahid Hasanović too. This man, on camera, had forced Nahid's male relatives from a truck in woodland and lined them up before a pit. He had watched as fathers were made at gunpoint to sodomize their sons, and old men were bludgeoned to death, before organizing the militias into firing squads. It was all that Nahid could do not to throw himself on this animal and sink his teeth into his flesh, to punch and kick him as he and his soldiers had punched and kicked defenseless civilians. But the other, younger man had already tensed, torn between wanting to silence Nahid but also to protect his charge, and Nahid knew that the moment he took a step forward, they would hurt him, and hurt him badly. Yet if Nahid could find a policeman, perhaps he could explain. Here was a war criminal. There was evidence on film. The United Nations was still looking for these people. They'd found Mladić and put him in the dock, and his puppetmaster Karadžić, too. One could still hope for justice.

Swiftly, Nahid began to walk away. He heard the younger man calling after him, and speeded up his footsteps until he was running, his right hand holding tightly to the phone in his pocket. He risked a glance over his shoulder, expecting to see at least one of the men pursuing him, but they were now continuing their journey through the gardens, although with perhaps a little more haste than before.

But Nahid had the footage on his phone. He could send it to the police, and if they did not provide satisfaction he would find a way to pass it to the United Nations, because he had aided them in digging up the bodies. He still had the names of some of the men and women he had met in the course of that work. They would listen to him, because they knew he was not one to tell lies.

So lost was Nahid in his thoughts, and so intent on the sight of the two men growing smaller, that he bumped into someone on the path. He instinctively apologized, and saw that he had almost sent a young girl tumbling to the ground. She was small, perhaps still in school, although she was not wearing a uniform.

'I'm sorry,' said Nahid. 'Are you all right?'

The girl nodded, and checked the front of her tan coat, as though worried that she might discover a stain upon it following the collision.

'Yes, I'm fine,' she said. 'And you? You seem distressed.'

She spoke in heavily accented German, and her voice was deeper than he might have expected from someone of her age.

'I had a bad experience,' said Nahid, 'but I will be okay. I think I winded myself, though.'

He saw that the girl was not as young as he had first thought – not a girl at all, in fact, but a woman, although one that had not grown to adult height. Her eyes were brown, the same color as her hair, and her skin was of an almost luminescent pallor, as of a creature bred in darkness.

Nahid's stomach hurt. He must have taken her elbow in his gut, he thought. He ought to sit, but he needed to be on his way. He looked down at his belly and saw a stain spreading across the front of his white shirt. It was very red, like beet juice. The stain would be difficult to remove, but there were ways . . .

'I think you should rest for a moment,' said the woman, as she helped Nahid to a bench. He sat heavily and the pain caused him to cry out. The woman's hand punched at him once, twice, and this time he felt the blade slice through his insides. Then she was searching his pockets and taking his cell phone from him. Finally, she wiped the blood from her right hand on his coat, and fastened the buttons.

'What is your name?' she said.

'Nahid.'

'Good. I like to know names.' She tested the word in her mouth: 'Nahid. Na-*hid*.' When she had memorized it to her satisfaction, she said, 'You can sleep now, Nahid.'

But Nahid Hasanović was already dead.

Chapter XXXIII

It was Radovan Vuksan's opinion that one could account neither for the vagaries of fate nor, if one were a believer, for the possibility that God appeared to have a sense of humor, although one that, like so many of His ways, passed all human understanding. Yes, Radovan had advised his brother not to leave the apartment, and to maintain instead a low profile while overtures were made to Belgrade and Frend went about his work. Yet short of narcotizing him, there was little Radovan could do to prevent Spiridon from seeking exercise and fresh air. But that he should have been spotted by a Turk capable of identifying him represented misfortune on a grand scale, a calamity that had been heightened by the killing of said Turk, and further underscored by leaving the body on a park bench.

'What were we supposed to do,' said Ilić, 'carry it back with us?'

'Not killing him might have been a start,' said Radovan.

His ambivalence about Ilić – no, call it what it was: his dislike – was hardening with every hour. That Ilić had certain talents was undeniable, but like all sadists, he lacked self-control, and his loyalty to Spiridon meant that he was unable or unwilling to rein in his worst impulses. Radovan was convinced that Zivco Ilić was the wrong man to be acting as his brother's right hand under these circumstances. Unfortunately, he was the only man currently available.

'The Turk was shouting,' said Ilić. 'The police would have come.'

'And by the time they came, you would have been gone.'

'You can't say that for sure,' said Ilić. He was unhappy at being upbraided by Radovan, but if he reacted with anger both brothers would turn on him, because only Spiridon could censure his brother, and vice versa. 'Anyway, I didn't kill him. The *vedma* did.'

Radovan winced at the use of the word, but did not contest it. He tried to have as little as possible to do with Spiridon's shadow, but he knew what his brother and the rest of them thought of her. While not a superstitious man himself, Radovan understood the advantages of cultivating the superstitions of others. If Ilić was convinced she was a witch, he would not contest it. It bothered him more that Spiridon was similarly credulous, because it was one thing to indulge – even exploit – the gullibility of others, but quite another to fall prey to it oneself.

But Radovan could not deny the oddness of Zorya, to use her given name – or the name by which she identified herself, which was not necessarily the same thing – since little about her could be confirmed, and all of Radovan's meticulous yet discreet inquiries had yielded hardly any useful knowledge about her. He knew only that she came from the country of the Vlachs, an ethnic minority of Romanian descent that inhabited small communities in the harsh, isolated landscape of eastern Serbia. The Vlachs had long been associated with both black and white magic, even after adopting Orthodox Christianity, or some version of it that permitted them to invoke Jesus and the Virgin Mary alongside whatever other non-Christian deities they also worshiped. The more sensationalist Serbian newspapers and media outlets occasionally ran stories ascribing blame for murders and ritual killings on Vlach witches, all of them nonsense. Like most allegations of witchcraft since the dawn of time, they were largely aimed at elderly women living in communities that sometimes lacked even the most basic of support structures for the more vulnerable, whether medical, psychological, or emotional.

The Vlachs, often marooned in countryside dotted by abandoned or barely functioning mines, frequently mired in poverty and, like many in Serbia, watching their young folk leave to seek better lives elsewhere, were forced to rely on one another, and so a people with their own dialect and traditions became more anomalous still. Their name was derived from the Old High German word meaning 'walh', or 'foreigner'. They were perennial outsiders in a nation that was suspicious of strangers, yet still they survived. During the conflicts that had followed the disintegration of Yugoslavia, their close familial bonds kept money flowing into the country from abroad, and they had shared some of that modest income with their non-Vlach neighbors. Radovan would never have considered describing his Serbian brothers and sisters as tolerant of those unlike themselves, but it was as good a word as any to describe the texture of their relationship with the Vlachs.

Spiridon had discovered Zorya living rough in the Braničevo District of eastern Serbia. How long she had been living there she would not say, or why she had been ostracized, because it was clear that the locals wanted nothing to do with her, given that she was enduring a solitary existence. Within sight of the home she had made for herself in a rocky hollow lay a village, accessed by a stone bridge over a stream. In Vlach culture, Radovan knew, a boundary existed between the realms of the living and the dead, and the dividing line was often running water. Caves, too, were associated with the next world, but while the Vlachs would visit those places to leave gifts of supplies for the souls of the dead during their seven-year period of wandering the earth, they did not live in them. Zorya, whether coerced or by choice, had made her dwelling in an umbrous region. It was the opinion of one of Radovan's sources that perhaps Zorya was not Vlach at all, but something stranger, something older . . .

None of which was sufficient to explain Spiridon's decision to bring her back to Belgrade with him, and then on to Amsterdam after the Vuksans had allied themselves with that particular faction of the Zemun clan. No, Spiridon had finally embraced Zorya following two warnings given by her, exhortations that turned out to be true. The first, that Spiridon was the target of a Bosniak hit squad seeking to avenge the massacre at Srebrenica, had resulted in the killing of three Sunni Muslims from the Croatian town of Bakar and an end to that threat. The second, that a UN war crimes investigation team was closing in on Spiridon, based on testimony from five witnesses, led to the demise of the witnesses in question, crippling the inquiry. Spiridon took care of the Bosniaks personally, but it was Zorya who had dealt with the witnesses – three women, two men – all of whom died from poisoning.

After that, Zorya became Spiridon's own guardian goddess, just like the Auroras from whom she took her name. Without her, Spiridon would have been dead long ago, although even Zorya had tried to dissuade him from targeting De Jaager. When that failed, she had attempted to have him limit his rage to the old Dutchman, leaving the others unharmed, but lately it seemed that Spiridon's taste for blood exceeded even her own.

Now here was Ilić, with a sly look on his face, acknowledging his belief in Zorya's eldritch nature, and inviting Radovan to deny it, thus angering his brother. Radovan elected to end the conversation. All they could do was hope that no eyewitnesses emerged. Ilić was convinced that he and Spiridon had not been followed from the park, and Radovan was inclined to believe him.

As for Zorya, wherever she now was, woe betide anyone who dared to follow her.

Zorya paused at the Zollamtsbrücke, the green metal bridge over the Wien that connected Vienna's Innere Stadt from Landstrasse, and watched a train traverse the U-Bahn crossing beneath. The Wien trickled below, but all rivers were as one to her, and the name of this one barely registered in her consciousness. She wore the hood of her jacket raised, which concealed her unsettling appearance, and the steady rain encouraged the passing Wieners and tourists to keep their heads down.

Not surprisingly, the discovery of Nahid Hasanović's body had made the news, and although his death had not been observed, police were eager to talk to a girl dressed in tan or brown who was glimpsed in the vicinity of the park at the time. Zorya had since changed her clothing, and it was not as though the police were suggesting that a child might have been responsible for the killing, not yet, but caution would be required for a while. She always dressed in layers, whatever the weather, because it disguised the curvature of her spine. Scoliosis: that was the medical name for her condition. There was no cure for it, but its severity could be reduced by surgery in more serious cases in order to prevent further deterioration and alleviate pain. But Zorya was not about to submit herself to a surgeon's knife, and her condition was relatively mild. Also, since she no longer grew, her deformity did not worsen; the pain, she could live with.

If Radovan Vuksan attributed Spiridon's encounter with Hasanović's path to bad luck or some strange act of God, Zorya, by contrast, believed it to be part of a deeper pattern of tribulation that included the assassination of Nikola Musulin, with an inception that could be traced back to the murders of De Jaager and his kin. She felt a profound sense of enclosure, of darkness encroaching, but had not yet spoken of it to Spiridon. He was already acting incautiously, and she had begun to suspect that his natural belligerence and his tendency toward cruelty were degenerating still further into a form of dementia. Reasoning with him had always been difficult, but he had followed her counsel more often than not. Now, though, he heard her out but did not follow her guidance, even as his faith in her abilities to protect him appeared to grow. Yet this trust was likely to be shaken by recent setbacks. If they continued, it would surely be only a matter of time before he began to question her usefulness to him. When that happened, she would be faced with a difficult choice: to stay or to run; to remain or to begin again with another whom she could mold.

Zorya looked over the river to Landstrasse, the ornate decorative tops on the pillars of the bridge like skulls against the sky. Crossing was always hard because an ancient, atavistic part of her fought against the impulse. She had to will her feet to move. Even then, they advanced only reluctantly, as though her body were resisting this flirtation with dissolution. The air became colder as she advanced, and Landstrasse grew fainter instead of more distinct. By the time she had reached the far bank, its buildings had vanished entirely, and Zorya stood alone in a featureless gray landscape across which shadows moved like the drifting contours of unseen clouds.

Except clouds did not move in such patterns or with such agency, and they were not drawn to the living.

The lands of the quick and the dead were distinct territories, but overlapped at the margins. If one knew the paths, and could see what others did not – because most people remained barely conscious of their immediate surroundings, never mind those that lay beyond simple perception – then it was possible to move between them. But the journey came at a price, because the living did not belong among the dead, and they left behind a little of themselves each time they crossed.

And if one lingered too long, and fell prey to the lassitude that was a prelude to the final sleep, well, then one would remain among the dead. In the ordinary world, the world of bridges and trains, of rain-filled gutters and baroque architecture, a body would be discovered, perhaps still warm and without a mark on it. Its heart would simply have stopped beating because sometimes hearts just gave out. No questions would be asked and no mystery would attach itself to the death – or none beyond the mystery that follows every death, which is the matter of what comes after, and to that a body cannot testify.

But Zorya could have answered, had she wished. She could have spoken of wandering souls, and the whispering of angels – or worse. She might have talked of a lake, barely glimpsed through mists, and the endless host of the dead in a state of constant subsumption by its depths and the sea beyond. Sometimes she thought she perceived the distant figure of a girl by the lakeshore, facing the water, but Zorya had never approached her to investigate further. It was better to pass through this terrain unnoticed, to find out what one came to discover and depart without being seen.

But this girl both intrigued and frightened Zorya because she, like Zorya, did not belong here. She was dead, yet she chose not to follow the rest. Instead she waited, and Zorya sensed that whatever knowledge she herself might have possessed of this land paled beside the intensity of the other's cognizance. But if the girl was aware of Zorya's presence, she gave no indication of it.

Or had not done so, until now.

As the lineaments of the realm of the dead grew more apparent to Zorya, she saw the girl's head turn in her direction. The girl was interested in her, and Zorya sensed that the girl knew who she was, *what* she was.

Then the girl spoke.

'Jennifer,' she said.

The girl was dangerous.

'My name is Jennifer Parker.'

Very, very dangerous.

'Come closer. Let me see you.'

But Zorya remained within sight of the bridge, and the crossing back to her own world. This was far enough. From here she could see all that she needed to see, because the shadows in this place were not only those of the dead but also of those who brought death with them. Zorya glimpsed them now: two men, radiating purpose.

And approaching fast.

II

Is it justice to make evil, and then punish for it?
James Fenimore Cooper, *The Last of the Mohicans*

Chapter XXXIV

Louis's flight arrived at Paris-Charles-de-Gaulle Airport shortly after 9 a.m. He took a taxi to a small hotel in the 16th arrondissement, regarded as the most boring area in the city. Nothing exciting had happened in the 16th arrondissement since 1794, when an explosion at the Grenelle gunpowder factory in the almost equally boring 15th arrondissement caused body parts to soar across the Seine and land in the streets and yards of its marginally more nondescript neighbor. He supposed that, after a rain of limbs, centuries of tedium might seem like a blessed relief.

Louis checked into a room decorated by someone who had never encountered a shade of gray he didn't like, and waited for the arrival of a courier carrying four Rohrbaugh R9 Stealth Elite pistols, each weighing less than a pound and built without a slide lock, magazine release, safety catch, or sights, all to ensure that the weapon didn't catch on clothing. The Rohrbaughs retailed for in excess of a thousand dollars each, and the four Osprey suppressors that accompanied them cost only slightly less, but Louis's delivery had still totaled €12,000, the premium reflecting the various gradations of illegality involved in the transfer of the goods, and the absence of any questions afterward.

Louis trusted Harris about as much as he trusted Ross, which meant that he did not trust him at all, but he had fulfilled government contracts in the past, even if they had never been formally identified as such. Many administrations preferred to farm out their wet work, in part because this made it easier to avoid telling the truth at inquiries, but also because men and women willing to kill at close quarters without the imprimatur offered by a uniform, or even a plausible reason for the sanction, were comparatively few, and often ill-suited to the strictures of intelligence agencies. Even the Russians, who were as close to conscienceless as one could get in this modern age, liked to maintain the illusion of distance and the comfort of deniability.

If, by some misfortune, Louis were to be apprehended by the French, he could anticipate no help from Harris or anyone else with US government credentials. He would be expected to keep his mouth shut and suck up his punishment like a big boy. Then, in a year or two, he would be quietly repatriated from a French jail, in theory to serve out the remainder of his sentence on home ground, but in reality to walk free with his anonymity compromised and his ability to perform any task riskier than taking out the trash permanently limited.

Louis did not intend to be caught by the French.

He checked the pistols. All four were new, but his premium had also ensured that a hundred rounds of Speer Gold Dots had been run through them before delivery. Two boxes of Gold Dots, fifty rounds each, came with the Rohrbaughs, but Louis hoped that would be significantly more than required. The ammunition was on the house because Louis was a returning customer and loyalty deserved its rewards.

Louis turned on the TV in the room, keeping the volume slightly louder than might have been preferable for his fellow guests. In the bathroom, he test-fired each of the pistols with an Osprey to muffle the sound; to absorb the bullets, he used a stack of old Bibles couriered from Amsterdam for just that purpose. Once he was satisfied that the guns were fit for use, he put the ruined Bibles in an anonymous white cotton bag and dumped them in a trash can on the way to buy an espresso and a croissant. He carried his purchases to the Passy Cemetery, watching always for recurring faces. He was curious to see if Harris had tagged him, but no one showed signs of taking an undue interest in him, and the cemetery was quiet as he sat by a grave and ate his pastry. He wandered the tree-lined avenues of Passy for a time before taking the Métro to Jaurès and walking the rest of the way to Stalingrad. While he could have traveled direct to the station, he knew better than to leave that kind of trail.

Aleksej Marković's hotel overlooked the Quai de l'Oise, and

was about as unprepossessing as a pension could get without hanging dead rats from its sign. According to the information provided by Harris, Marković was staying in room 42. He might even be in there now, Louis thought. A call to the hotel would confirm this, but might also spook the target. Either way, it had been made clear to Louis that he was not to move against Marković until the Vuksans' cargo had been safely apprehended or neutralized. Harris and his people didn't want any more jihadis roaming free. The French had more than enough of them to contend with already.

Louis wondered how many people the Americans had on Marković. Two teams would be standard practice, and three would be better. But if they were keeping tabs on the Serb – audio and visual – then any action against him by Louis would also be recorded, and Louis was averse to shooting a man while agents of his own government recorded the event.

He had also briefly considered the possibility of taking Marković alive, if the opportunity presented itself, in the hope of obtaining from him the whereabouts of the Vuksans, but had dismissed it on a number of grounds: the risks involved, the likelihood or otherwise of Marković having anything more than an email address or burner number for the brothers, and his willingness to share that information with Louis, even under duress. Louis wasn't in the torture business, but he knew enough about it to be aware that any intelligence obtained through abuse was often unreliable and could be difficult or time-consuming to verify. He was also certain that the Vuksans would have procedures in place should Marković fail to make contact, which meant that whatever Louis might learn from him would ultimately prove useless. No, the Viennese lawyer Frend still seemed the best path to the Vuksans, which made Marković dispensable. In addition, his death would alarm the Vuksans, and any reaction from them would create ripples that might be traced back to their source.

He found a bench, removed a book from his pocket, and commenced not reading it. He spent an hour watching the comings and goings at the hotel, but saw no trace of Marković. It didn't matter. By the time Louis was done, he had a better sense of the environment, to which he added by taking a stroll through the neighborhood. He checked his watch: the overnight Delta flight from JFK to Paris-Charles-de-Gaulle had landed by now, so it was time to return to his hotel and wait for his guests to arrive. While he hoped to take care of Marković himself, circumstances dictated that this might not be possible. Whatever happened over the next twenty-four hours, one thing was certain: Aleksej Marković would not be leaving Paris alive.

At Paris-Charles-de-Gaulle, two slight figures passed through immigration with hand baggage only, attracting barely a second glance from the staff. Both men wore glasses, had neatly trimmed black hair, and spoke heavily accented English. They carried US and Japanese passports, but were traveling on the former to avoid any questions about their arrival from a US airport. They smiled a lot, because they had learned that Western people held preconceptions about Asians, both positive and negative, which could be used to gain an advantage. Over the years, they had carefully cultivated an image that traded on harmlessness, politeness, and conviviality, even though they had once killed a man by adding sodium cyanide to the chlorine-dosing system of his indoor swimming pool. This had been carried out at the instigation of Louis. The two men always enjoyed assisting Louis. He paid up front, and had been known to present them with intellectually stimulating challenges. Through him, they got to encounter new and interesting people, and find new and interesting ways to kill them.

Chapter XXXV

Zorya sat in a deep armchair before Spiridon Vuksan, her feet not quite touching the floor. Behind her, Radovan leaned against the window frame and thought that, in her stillness and the oddness of her mien, Zorya resembled a malformed mannequin. She glanced at him, as though picking up on his thoughts, but he did not look away. Zorya didn't need to be a mind reader to know how he felt about her. She held too many secrets for Radovan's comfort.

'You say you saw a girl?' said Spiridon.

'A dead girl,' Zorya corrected him.

'What is she to us?'

'I don't know, but she is connected somehow. She would not have sensed my presence otherwise.'

'Connected?'

'To the hunters.'

Spiridon switched his attention to his brother, who shrugged.

'We've heard nothing from Belgrade,' said Radovan.

An uneasy and temporary limboid state of being existed between the Vuksans and the new emerging criminal order in their home country. The delineations of that order remained unclear, but from his contacts in Serbia – or those still willing to accept his calls – Radovan had learned that the voice of Matija Kiš was currently speaking loudest and most persuasively. This did not entirely surprise Radovan: Kiš was a figure of respect in the nebulous structures of the Serbian mafia, not only because of his cleverness and careful use of violence but also thanks to his extensive political connections. These included senior members and associates of the ruling Serbian Progressive Party, among them a cadre involved in consolidating influence and investment in the country's infrastructure in advance of Serbia's anticipated entry into the

European Union. They, in turn, were backed by Russian money, which meant Putin.

Meanwhile, on the more blatantly criminal side, Kiš had close ties to Simo Stajić, the dominant figure in the Kosovan underworld. Stajić had graduated from car theft to extortion, loan sharking, money laundering, and the smuggling of fuel, cigarettes, and drugs. He enjoyed free rein in Kosovo, untroubled by police interference, thanks to his reputation as a protector of minority Serbian rights in the disputed region. He was ruthless where Kiš was restrained, and crazy where Kiš was practical. Effectively, Stajić was a dog on a chain, which Kiš could unclip at any time. Now, it seemed, Kiš was seeking to expand and consolidate his influence, aided by Stajić. It was Radovan's view that Stajić had in all likelihood designed and planted the bomb responsible for reducing Nikola Musulin to fragments of meat and bone, in collaboration with Matija Kiš and with the blessing, tacit or otherwise, of a cabal within the SPP.

Radovan had shared none of this with his brother. He did not want Spiridon to call in whatever favors he had left in an effort to punish Kiš or, God forbid, Stajić by targeting some of their people. Instead, overtures would have to be made to these two men, which was why Anton Frend would soon be traveling – albeit reluctantly – to Belgrade in order to find a solution satisfactory to all parties involved.

But Zorya's talk of hunters was troubling. Perhaps Kiš and Stajić had decided that negotiations with the Vuksans were likely to be more trouble than they were worth, and it would be better to cut the head off the snake than allow it to slide into the dark, from where it might strike at some future date.

'The hunters are not Serbian,' said Zorya.

'What, then?' said Spiridon.

'The dead girl had an American accent.'

Spiridon looked to his brother, who shrugged.

'De Jaager dealt with the Americans,' said Radovan, 'but then he dealt with everyone. The Americans would have no more reason than others to take his death personally.'

'One of the men I saw was black,' said Zorya.

'Ah,' said Spiridon. 'Could this be Louis, the one the legat identified as Andrej's killer?'

He looked to his brother for confirmation.

'Perhaps,' said Radovan. He was reluctant to accept Zorya's warning unconditionally, but he was not so foolish as to dismiss it entirely. After all, she had been correct in the past. Her instincts, supernaturally gifted or not, were good.

'If he wants to make a personal matter of it, so be it,' said Spiridon. 'Let him come.'

'It's a further complication we could do without,' said Radovan, 'especially when we are vulnerable.'

'Don't use that word,' said Spiridon. 'To speak it is to make it so.'

'To ignore reality is worse. Whatever action we choose to take, we first need to confirm this man's identity. If we do not know who he is, how can we cope with the threat he poses?'

Radovan looked to Zorya, but it was clear from the blankness of her expression that they had reached the limits of her knowledge, or however much of it she wished to share with them for the present.

'This girl in your visions,' said Spiridon, 'could you talk with her?'

'No,' said Zorya.

'You've communed with the dead before.'

'But I will not commune with her.'

Spiridon smiled. 'Why? Are you frightened of her?'

'Yes,' said Zorya. 'Very much so.'

And Spiridon's smile faded.

Chapter XXXVI

Angel arrived at London Heathrow on a late-afternoon flight. He retrieved his bag without incident, although the airport remained baffling to him. It seemed to have been designed as a means of actively discouraging people from traveling. Had he been forced to change terminals for a connecting flight, he might have wept.

As he exited the baggage hall, a man appeared by his side: Paul Canton, one of the FBI legats attached to the US embassy in London.

'Welcome back,' said Canton.

'I don't remember booking a driver,' said Angel. 'And if I had, it wouldn't have been you.'

Angel kept walking, following the signs for the Heathrow Express. Canton fell easily into step beside him, given that he had at least six inches on Angel and was a couple of decades younger. Canton had crossed paths with Angel, Louis, and Parker during their previous visit to London, one that had ended – perhaps inevitably, given those involved – in bloodshed. Canton had proven helpful, and probably saved them some time behind bars, but that didn't mean Angel ever wanted to see him again. Like Louis, Angel was of the opinion that far too many US government employees had developed an interest in their affairs. Pretty soon, someone would be offering to strike a souvenir silver dollar with their faces on it.

'I've been instructed to facilitate you,' said Canton. 'You have no idea how hard it was to say those words, by the way.'

'If it's any consolation, they were just as difficult to hear. Can you find me a gun?'

'No.'

'How about getting me my health back?'

'Can't do that either.'

'Then what good are you to me?'

'None at all, I hope.' He handed Angel a card. 'Just in case. The number has changed, by the way. I'm moving up in the world.'

'It's nice to see virtue rewarded,' said Angel. 'Your mother must be very proud.'

He didn't look at the card before dropping it in his pocket. A crowd of people waited impatiently before the elevators for the Heathrow Express. Angel resented standing in line for anything. He associated it with prison. He glanced at his watch. Given the time, and the hordes in the terminal building, the Express was likely to be busy, and he'd be arriving in central London just in time for rush hour.

'You have a car, right?' he said.

'A black one,' said Canton. 'It's very clean.'

'What's that supposed to mean?'

'Just that I don't want to get it dirty.'

Canton looked pointedly at Angel's suitcase, which had certainly seen better days but was too old to remember them. Angel followed the direction of Canton's gaze, and reluctantly conceded the point.

'Maybe we ought to just tie it to the roof,' he said.

'No, we can put it in the trunk. I have some plastic sheeting.'

'What about me, do I have to go in the trunk, too?'

'I guess you can ride up front.'

'Will I have to talk to you?'

'Only if you're bored.'

'Then lead the way. I figure my taxes are probably funding the car anyway.'

'Not your taxes,' said Canton. 'You don't pay any.'

'Even better,' said Angel. 'And I hope you have candy.'

In the event, there was candy – boxes of Swedish Fish and Milk Duds – and some polite conversation passed between Angel and Canton on the journey, the former's animosity toward the latter being general rather than specific, and arising from the aforementioned distrust of federal law enforcement. Canton's radio was tuned to one of those classical music channels aimed at those anxious to improve themselves but hampered by short attention spans.

'I don't suppose you'd care to tell me why you're here?' said Canton at last, as they turned off Euston Road and entered London's congestion zone.

'I want to catch up with a friend,' said Angel. 'I may even take one of those bus tours. I didn't have a chance last time I was here.'

'Well, you were otherwise occupied, what with you and your buddies leaving a trail of bodies and all.'

'A "trail" might be an exaggeration. And a couple of them were down to you, or so the newspapers said, unless you plan on demanding a retraction.'

'Thankfully, I wasn't actually named.'

'You shouldn't hide your light under a bushel,' said Angel.

'It wasn't my light I was hiding.'

Which was true. Canton had taken the heat for killings that would otherwise have left Parker, Angel, and Louis with awkward questions to answer. It didn't seem to have hurt his career, Angel thought, unless he was being forced to moonlight as a limo driver to make ends meet.

'So this isn't a business trip?' said Canton.

'It's personal all the way.'

'Huh,' said Canton. 'I wasn't aware that SAC Ross had expanded into leisure tourism.'

'I think he's planning for his retirement,' said Angel. 'You know how much he hates idle hands.'

They crossed Oxford Street and edged into Soho.

'Nevertheless,' said Canton, 'if you anticipate problems arising out of your activities here, I expect to be informed *before* they happen, not after. For old times' sake.'

'Is that a warning?' said Angel.

'Call it a government advisory,' said Canton. 'Unofficial, of course.'

'Sure,' said Angel, as they pulled up in front of Hazlitt's on Frith Street. 'By the way, you got any "Get Out of Jail Free" cards, just in case?'

Canton stared at him, stony-faced.

'No,' he said, 'I don't.'

'I'll just take the candy, then,' said Angel. He liberated two boxes of Milk Duds, dropping them into his pocket. 'And thanks for the ride. Five stars, no question.'

Hazlitt's had been recommended to Angel by Bob Johnston, a retired Maine bookseller who was now living happily in London with a woman named Rosanna Bellingham. Johnston and Rosanna had a number of shared interests, among them books, gin, and each other. Johnston had opted to stay in London after traveling over from Maine to help Charlie Parker with some research on a case. This had resulted in Johnston being rendered permanently deaf in one ear and having a number of his fingers broken, which was what sometimes happened to people who entered Parker's orbit.

Angel unpacked, freshened up, and met Johnston and his inamorata at the Phoenix Arts Club on the Charing Cross Road, where they ate decent comfort food while resting actors sang show tunes around a piano. During the lulls between songs, Angel explained to Johnston and Rosanna his reason for being in London, and requested their assistance with what was to come.

'A kidnapping?' said Johnston.

'The appearance of one,' said Angel.

'I've never kidnapped anyone before,' said Rosanna.

'And you're not about to start now,' said Angel. Rosanna Bellingham, he thought, looked to be worryingly enthused by the idea of an abduction. He believed she might have missed her vocation.

'What if she doesn't want to be kidnapped?' said Johnston.

'Nobody wants to be kidnapped,' said Angel. 'And for the last time, an actual kidnapping is not what it is.'

'Bob's right,' said Rosanna. 'What if she says no? Because you'll have played your hand, and if you let her walk away . . .'

'Then,' said Angel, 'we'll have a problem.'

'No,' said Rosanna, 'you'll have a kidnapping.'

Later, Johnston and Rosanna walked Angel back to his hotel and said good night, but when he got to his room, he found he could not sleep. He was struck by a wave of depression, the latest in a succession both unpredictable and unrelenting in their ferocity. Angel had always been prone to bouts of melancholy – given the abuse he had suffered earlier in life, it would have been surprising had he not experienced periods of profound emotional distress – but the nature of them had altered following his recent illness, growing deeper and more emphatic. He wondered if it was a form of survivor's guilt. He thought about speaking with Louis, but instead used his cell phone to call another number, because he knew one man who might understand how he was feeling. The call was picked up on the second ring.

'So how is Europe?' said Parker.

'Full of Europeans.'

'I detect a certain absence of joy.'

'I hurt,' said Angel simply. 'In my heart and in my head.'

'Then let's talk.'

And they did.

Chapter XXXVII

A cell phone, unsolicited, was delivered to Louis at his hotel shortly after seven the following morning. It was fully powered, came with a Bluetooth earpiece, and rang five minutes after it arrived. Louis picked up, and Harris spoke.

'Marković is on the move,' he said. 'We have eyes and ears in his room, but he's using a clean burner phone. He received a text message about twenty minutes ago, armed himself, and left. We're trying to get a trace on the sender and the message, but that will take time.'

'Any idea where he's going?'

'We think it's Gare de Lyon. Our information is that it's the Vuksans' preferred final destination for important deliveries.'

'Okay. By the way, I thought you were retired.'

'Semiretired,' said Harris. 'Plus, I've always liked France. We're going to patch you into the coms group, so keep the earpiece in place and you'll hear what we hear. The phone has a fifteen-hour battery life, so don't worry about charging it.'

'I'm on my way,' said Louis. He inserted the earpiece and dropped the phone in his coat pocket, but not before muting the microphone on the device. It was one thing permitting himself to be tracked by Harris and his people, another to have them listening in on his conversations. He placed one of the Rohrbaugh pistols in a hip holster under his jacket. The other already had its Osprey suppressor in place because he didn't want to waste time trying to fit it if he needed to use the Rohrbaugh in a hurry. That gun now hung vertically from a custom Velcro strap beneath his coat, and could be released with a single hard yank. The setup wasn't ideal, but neither was the world. The remaining two pistols had gone to his guests.

159

When he was ready, he made a call on his own cell phone. 'Game on,' he said.

Aleksej Marković took a seat in the Costa Coffee at Gare de Lyon, which gave him a good view of the station concourse and the exit onto rue de Châlon. At no point would he make direct contact with the two men arriving from Port-Vendres. Their shadows, acolytes of the Vuksans, would stay with them until they left the station, at which point the Syrians' own people would take over; and that would be the last Marković or anyone else at the Vuksans' end would see of them, at least until their photographs appeared on BFM, the BBC, or Sky, alongside images of rising smoke and fleeing bystanders, of blood and broken glass.

He watched the Syrians, Saad and Mahdi, emerge separately. Both were in their forties, which made them old by jihadi standards, and dressed in business suits that looked more expensive than they were. Marković knew this because he had supervised their purchase himself, just as he had chosen the clear-lens glasses and overnight bags. The men had trimmed their beards and now resembled middle managers for some modestly successful business, or academics at one of the lower-ranked colleges.

A few meters behind them walked Baba and Fouad, the shadows. Both came from the northern suburbs of Paris, the banlieues where immigrant unemployment was high and opportunities for advancement were few. Fouad, the Algerian, was Muslim, although far from observant, while Baba, the Senegalese, was a Christian from that country's Casamance region. The two men were not close, but managed to work well together. Marković preferred dealing with Fouad because he didn't feel compelled to talk about God quite as much as Baba did. Every two years, Baba made a pilgrimage to Popenguine, on Senegal's Atlantic coast, where he prayed before the Black Madonna and asked her to intercede on his behalf and that of his extended family. How Baba balanced his deep Christian beliefs with a capacity, even a propensity, for extreme violence was one of the mysteries of his particular brand of worship. But then Marković, a devout member of the Serbian Orthodox Church, was hardly in a position to criticize the contradictions of others, not with all the blood on his own hands.

Marković had not informed Baba and Fouad that he would be present for the handover, if only as an observer. His appearance had altered since last he'd met the two operatives. He was now bearded, and his hair was a few shades darker. Up close, they might have recognized him, but not from any kind of distance. He wasn't sure what they knew of the Vuksans' current situation, but he had seen no reason to enlighten them if they were ignorant of it. Both Baba and Fouad were shrewd, which was why they'd been entrusted with the care of the Syrians; but if they became aware of the Vuksans' problems, the smart move would be to walk away, and Marković couldn't afford to let that happen. Their eyes scanned the crowd, always returning to the Syrians. Fouad struck Marković as the more uneasy of the two, but he was by nature a nervous animal. Baba was always calmer. Even when he was hurting another human being, he remained implacable.

The four men entered the concourse. Fouad glanced to his right, and his gaze froze before moving on. It was only the minutest of pauses, but Marković caught it, and it seemed to him that Fouad slowed down, falling farther behind Baba and the Syrians. Marković saw a couple, a man and a woman, cease their examination of a ticket machine and begin closing fast on Baba and the Syrians. Meanwhile, by the exit, a young black man in a clean tracksuit and an older male in a dark suit, a *misbaha* wrapped around his fingers, brightened as they took in the Syrians' approach.

Suddenly there was shouting, and the couple from the ticket machine reached for guns, the butts visible to Marković beneath their jackets. At the same moment, heavily armed officers from RAID, the National Police's tactical unit, emerged from a pair of unmarked doorways and moved in on the Syrians. Marković instinctively looked around, expecting to see more armed personnel closing on him. He was carrying a pistol but wasn't so foolish as to believe he would stand a chance against a cadre of antiterrorist operatives. The best he could hope for was to be taken alive. So far, though, it seemed that he remained unnoticed, and so he began planning his escape.

Curiously, at that point the couple quickly separated, vanishing into the crowd, and Marković thought he saw at least three other men, all in civilian clothing, head for the exits. They didn't run, unlike some of the passengers at the station who had immediately panicked at the sight of assault weapons, nor did they remain frozen in place like so many others. In common with Marković, who was already on his feet, their instinct was to remove themselves from the scene before they were spotted.

Marković immediately identified it for what it was: a fuckup, two operations being conducted independently of each other on the same target. One unit was clearly French, given the presence of RAID, but the likelihood of two French teams working in ignorance of each other was slim. The French had learned a lot of hard lessons from the terrorist attacks of 2015, one of which was the importance of integration and coordination. UCLAT, the Unité de coordination de la lutte antiterroriste, representing all branches of the National Police, was responsible for the centralization of operational information and decisions. It existed to ensure that, theoretically at least, the *main gauche* always knew what the *main droite* was doing. Regardless of divisional rivalries, no French agency would risk a takedown at a site such as the Gare de Lyon without first clearing the operation at the highest levels. That left a foreign power or independent operators as the second team, and Marković was leaning toward the former.

Fouad, he noticed, was nowhere to be seen. Baba, on the other hand, had peeled away as soon as the police appeared, but only managed to walk a few feet before he was surrounded. He was now lying on the floor with three assault weapons pointing at his head. The Syrians were still standing, their hands raised, although the two men who had been waiting for them were gone. The Syrians had their backs to Marković, but one of them – Marković thought it might be Saad – was shouting at the police in Arabic. Around them, passengers huddled low or lay flat on the ground, giving the officers clear fields of fire if required. Saad's right hand dropped, and he reached inside his jacket. At least three RAID officers opened fire simultaneously, two with pistols and one with a Heckler & Koch G36. They drew no distinction between Saad and Mahdi. Within seconds, both men were dead.

Louis was at the main station entrance when he heard swearing in his Bluetooth earpiece, before Harris's voice gave the order to abort the operation. Louis listened for a while longer, until a woman's voice announced that they'd lost Marković. Almost immediately, his own cell phone buzzed, and he answered.

'We have him,' said the voice on the other end. 'He's on Place Henri-Frenay, heading north.'

Louis took out the Bluetooth earpiece and replaced it with a wired earpiece and microphone connected to his own phone. He removed the SIM card and battery from the Android device that had been delivered earlier that morning, and debated breaking the SIM card in two. Instead he put it in his pocket, but dumped the phone and battery in a trash can. He wouldn't have put it past Harris to embed a tracker in the phone, one that operated independently of the battery.

Louis walked away as more police vehicles pulled up outside the station, along with a pair of ambulances. His taxi was waiting on the street; the driver had come highly recommended, as selectively blind and deaf as the evolution of his breed would allow. As Louis got in, the voice in his ear told him that Marković had been making for the Reuilly-Diderot Métro station, but now looked as though he might be reconsidering. Moments later, Marković had hailed a cab, and his trackers were now following, all the time keeping up a constant flow of information from their cell phones to Louis's earpiece.

'North at present,' Louis heard. 'Do you think he's going back to his hotel?'

'Only if he's dumb,' said Louis, 'and Marković doesn't strike me as that.'

Louis was frustrated. Harris's operation had gone south fast, but at least Marković wasn't in the wind, not yet.

Marković's cab held the straightest route north, only veering east as it approached Gare de l'Est. For a moment it seemed possible that Marković might just be foolish enough to return to his Stalingrad base, but the cab passed Stalingrad and continued over the Bassin de la Villette and on to Pantin, where it stopped outside a budget hotel near the quai de l'Aisne that was only marginally more appealing than Marković's original lodgings. There was no other hotel in the vicinity. Marković did not enter immediately but instead took a seat in a nearby coffee shop, from which he could watch the hotel while making a series of calls.

He was still there when Louis's taxi arrived. By then one of the men tracking Marković had already paid cash for a room at the hotel, and he slipped the card keys to Louis as they passed each other on the street: one for the door that separated the lobby from the interior of the hotel, including the elevator, and another for the room itself. If, as seemed likely, Marković was keeping a second base at the hotel, Louis now had the means to follow him inside. Louis bought a newspaper, found a bakery, and took a space by the window that gave him a clear view of Marković.

Marković was patient, but only up to a point. He waited forty-five minutes before leaving the coffee shop and walking toward, then entering, the hotel. Louis was behind him, tapping the copy of *Le Monde* against his right leg as he went, although he hoped that no one tried to test him on his knowledge of its contents, his command of the French language not extending to the intricacies of the newspaper's political commentary. From his pocket he removed a baseball cap and placed it on his head. Louis hated baseball caps, but sometimes indignity was the better part of valor.

Marković glanced back as he reached the security door in the lobby, aware of the presence at his back, but relaxed a little when he saw Louis flipping a card key between his fingers. They waited for the elevator together, each man giving the impression of studiously ignoring the other. When the elevator arrived, Marković went in first and took up a position in the corner farthest from the panel of buttons. Louis noted the camera above Marković's head, protected from vandalism by a wire cage.

'*Votre étage, monsieur?*' said Louis.

'*Trois,*' said Marković, then he added, '*S'il vous plaît.*'

Louis pressed the buttons for the third and fifth floors. No one else entered and the doors slid closed. The elevator rattled upward and did not stop until it reached the third floor. The doors opened again, and Marković exited. Louis nodded at him as he passed, but Marković did not respond. Just as the doors were about to close for the second time, Louis halted their progress with a foot, stepped out, and called to Marković.

'*Monsieur, vous avez oublié quelque chose!*'

Louis was holding up a key card. Marković turned back, saw the key card, and displayed his own, which was when Louis shot him twice with the Rohrbaugh concealed in the folded newspaper. The first bullet took Marković in the belly, the second in the chest. Marković stumbled backward, landing hard against the wall, and slid to the floor, leaving a smear of blood on the paintwork. Louis advanced and fired one more time as Marković raised his right hand as though to shield himself. The third bullet passed through the palm of Marković's hand and entered his brain through his right eye. The hand dropped, and Marković was still.

The shots had sounded loud in the low hallway, even with the suppressor, but no one emerged from a doorway to investigate the source of the disturbance. Maybe, Louis reflected, the hotel was under-occupied; that, or its residents were endowed with enough sense not to display obvious interest in what might have been gunfire. Either way, Louis wasn't going to wait around long enough to find out. He took the stairs to the lobby and left through the front entrance. There was no point trying to hide his face as his presence had already been recorded by the cameras in the lobby and the elevator, but the baseball cap would help, along with the inability of ignorant men to distinguish one Black face from another. What mattered now was getting out of Paris. Harris and his people could sort out the mess, which would be easier for them if the police hadn't yet laid hands on a suspect.

Louis turned right at the corner and climbed in the back of the rental Peugeot idling by the curb. It pulled away quickly but not recklessly, and attracted no attention. The two Japanese men in the front did not look back at him, although the driver raised an inquisitive eyebrow in the rearview mirror.

'One down,' said Louis. 'Four to go. You have my stuff?'

'It's in the trunk,' said the driver.

'Then take me to the airport.'

The two Japanese did not return immediately to New York after dropping Louis at Charles de Gaulle. They took a room at Le Bristol, and dined that evening at Dersou on rue Saint-Nicolas, because Paris was always pleasant for a few days. Admittedly, they had not been required to dispose of anyone in a new and interesting way, but into every life a little rain must fall, and they remained hopeful that Louis might need them again before his work was done.

They were, in their way, optimists.

Chapter XXXVIII

Pia Lackner, the estranged daughter of the lawyer Anton Frend, operated from an old brownstone near Blackfriars Bridge, within easy reach of the Inns of Court. Her firm shared the premises with three others, although Lackner's was the only one specializing in environmental law and human rights. Angel felt more virtuous just by standing in its general vicinity.

He had decided against tackling Lackner on her home ground, opting instead for more neutral territory. He had selected the Black Friar, a nineteenth-century pub that occupied a wedge-shaped building on Queen Victoria Street. A phone call to Lackner's office informing her that he might have information of interest was enough to draw her out, any concerns that she might have had about meeting a stranger being allayed by the choice of venue and an envelope that Angel had placed in the company mailbox earlier that morning.

The envelope contained a series of documents – provided by the enigmatic Harris – relating to the mining practices of multinational conglomerates in four African countries. A recent judgment by the Supreme Court in London had ruled that a mining company based in the United Kingdom could be held to account for the actions of one of its subsidiaries in Zambia, enabling the case to be held in England, where the claimants believed they had a better chance of achieving a measure of justice. The ruling opened the way for similar suits to proceed against a series of corporations. Lackner's firm was representing litigants in West Africa who were taking an action against a big oil company for the pollution of their farmland. The firm's resources were more limited than those of its larger rivals, so any help was likely to be gratefully received.

Angel was already seated at a corner table when Lackner arrived, a cup of coffee and a copy of the *Guardian* in front of him. Lackner was a small, heavyset woman with very bright blue eyes, and an expression set somewhere between bemused and skeptical, although Angel accepted that he might be the cause of both in this instance, with bemusement appearing to be winning out. Lackner had probably been anticipating an encounter with someone wearing a suit, or at the very least an individual who didn't look as though he was more familiar with being the client of lawyers rather than their abetter.

'Mr Angel?' said Lackner.

He stood to shake her hand.

'Just Angel.'

'Is that your real name?'

'It's the one I've settled on, so I guess it is. Can I get you a coffee, or a tea?'

'Coffee will be fine, thank you.'

He ordered a coffee from the bar and returned to his seat. Lackner was examining the main story on the front page of the newspaper, something to do with the Middle East. Angel had barely glanced at it.

'Are you a regular *Guardian* reader?' said Lackner.

'I just bought it to impress you. It doesn't have enough funny pages for me.'

She regarded him thoughtfully.

'I can't tell if you're being serious or not.'

'I suppose it has *Doonesbury*,' continued Angel, 'which kind of counts. I once owned an Uncle Duke T-shirt with "Death Before Unconsciousness" written on the front, but it was only amusing when I was younger. As I grow older, and death assumes an objective reality, unconsciousness doesn't seem like such a bad option.'

Lackner's coffee arrived. She added sugar and milk, heavy on both.

'So,' she said, 'those documents.'

'Yes.'

'Where did you get them?'

'From a third party.'

'I thought as much. You don't strike me as someone with a direct line to an oil company. Do you or your source have more papers like them?'

'Possibly.'

'And what do you want in return for them, money? If so, that's not how our firm operates.'

Angel delved into the messenger bag at his feet and displayed a thick manila folder held together with rubber bands before putting it away again.

'Whatever I have is in that folder,' he said. 'I can't claim to understand all of it. As you've already surmised, it's not my area of expertise. Still, the fact that you're sitting here based on the first taste means it's probably gourmet stuff. You can have it, in return for a few minutes of your time. Oh, and you'll be required to look at some photographs. You may find them disturbing. It depends on how strong your stomach is.'

'What exactly is this about?' said Lackner.

Angel produced a thin envelope, marked *Do Not Bend*.

'Photos first, then we can progress to details.'

'What if I don't want to look at any photographs?'

Angel considered the question before retrieving the folder from his bag and placing it on the table.

'Then you can walk away with this, and do with it as you please. You'll never see me again.'

He waited. Lackner didn't reach for the folder.

'Show me the pictures,' she said.

She was seated against a wall, which meant she was in no danger of sharing the contents of the prints, but Angel suggested it might still be preferable for her not to set them on the table. He watched as she progressed through the images. The first four were enlarged passport photos of De Jaager, Anouk, Paulus, and Liesl, the dead of Amsterdam. The remaining photographs came from the crime scene at the safe house. Angel had excluded none. If Lackner was to be convinced, she had to see everything. He did not speak as she went through them. He did not even watch her, but took in the bar and its occupants, and wondered if the

Doonesbury slogan could be repurposed as 'Death Before Obliviousness'. Most people, he thought, would choose obliviousness.

Pia Lackner was putting the photographs back in the envelope, but not before first returning to the images of De Jaager and the others as they had been in life.

'Who were they?' she said.

Angel gave her their names.

'Why were they killed?'

'Because they crossed a Serbian crime lord, or De Jaager did, and the others paid for it alongside him. A while back, a Serbian enforcer named Andrej Buha, sometimes known as Timmerman, was assassinated in Amsterdam. He enjoyed crucifying men and women, so he was no great loss. The deaths of these four people were revenge for the killing of Buha.'

'What has this got to do with me?' said Lackner.

But something in her tone told Angel that she already suspected the truth.

'The man who ordered and supervised their torture and murder is Spiridon Vuksan. He's one of your father's clients.'

'I don't have anything to do with my father,' said Lackner. 'I have even divested myself of his name.'

'I'm aware of that, just as I know that he sends you flowers on your birthday and a case of champagne at Christmas.'

'You're very well informed.'

'I also know that you give away the flowers and champagne.'

Lackner gestured at the envelope and its photographs. 'Wouldn't you, under the circumstances?'

'I don't like champagne,' said Angel, 'and flowers make me sneeze. The point is that your father still cares about you.'

For the first time, Lackner looked worried.

'Are you threatening me?'

'No, not at all. We would like to use you, though – with your consent, obviously.'

'Oh, obviously,' she said, with enough sarcasm to turn honey sour. 'I wouldn't be used any other way. But I still don't understand what you want from me. And who is "we", by the way?'

'My friends and me.'

Lackner glanced around the bar.

'Are they nearby?'

'No, they're on the Continent.'

'Doing what?'

'Hunting down the men who did this, or trying to. We believe there are five of them, including Spiridon's brother, Radovan. They're in hiding. They thought they could kill these people before retreating to Serbia, where they'd be safe from retribution, legal or otherwise. They were wrong, but the situation remains fluid. We'd like to find them before the balance tilts in their favor.'

'You specified retribution both legal *or* otherwise,' said Lackner.

'Yes,' said Angel. 'We would be the "otherwise".'

'Does otherwise include murder?'

'I thought lawyers never asked a question to which they didn't already know the answer.'

'Perhaps I do know it.'

'Then why ask?'

'It would have been remiss not to,' said Lackner. 'And you want me to collude in this?'

'Spiridon Vuksan has been slaughtering innocents since the last century, aided by his brother. He was at Vukovar, at Srebrenica, and a whole lot of other places I can't spell or even find on a map, but I know what happened in them, and I know the part Spiridon and his men played in it. The law has largely failed their victims so far because it has its limits. We, on the other hand, do not.'

'Jesus.' There was neither bemusement nor skepticism on Lackner's face now. She was a picture of misery. 'And my father knows where these people are?'

'We think so. Your father has been helping the Vuksans since the Balkan wars. Without him, they might never have survived. Who else would they turn to in their time of trouble?'

'Do you want me to ask him where the Vuksans might be?' said Lackner.

171

'Would he tell you if you did?'

'I doubt it. I may be his daughter, but he's still a lawyer.'

'Well, then,' said Angel, 'I think we may have to find another way.'

Chapter XXXIX

A nton Frend, the subject of this discussion, was currently at Vienna International Airport, sitting in the Austrian Airlines business lounge while he waited to board his delayed flight to Belgrade. He had left home without saying goodbye to Mina, his wife, who had already departed for her regular yoga class, to be followed by an abominably healthy late breakfast with some of her abominably healthy friends. She was now absent from the house so often that Frend might almost have suspected her of conducting an affair had she not lacked the appetite or imagination for infidelity.

Frend knew that his wife was aware of his mistress even if, in typical Viennese fashion, she chose to ignore the fact of her existence. Mina, though, was probably grateful to be spared his advances. She had always found sex distasteful – the mess, the noise, the smells, the fluids. It was why they only had one child: after she had successfully given birth to Pia, Mina had seen no further reason to engage unnecessarily in the mechanics of intercourse. Pia was enough for her, or perhaps regular sexual activity with her husband was too high a price to pay for expanding the family.

They could have divorced, of course, but the process and aftermath would have been socially awkward for both of them. In addition, Mina did not trust Frend to behave generously in any settlement, or not to use his contacts in the legal community to make life as difficult as possible for her, which suggested a degree of acuity on her part. But Mina was also Frend's only remaining point of contact with their daughter, and fed him tidbits of information about her life, as much to taunt him as anything else.

Were they to separate, even this modest line of communication would be severed, and Pia would be rendered a complete stranger to him.

As for Radka, his Bulgarian mistress, Frend was under no illusions about her reasons for being with him. He had bankrolled her boutique in Neubau, and he paid for their expensive weekly dinners in restaurants where the minimalism of the décor reflected the paucity of food on the plates. In return, he received from her the sexual favors denied him by his wife, and, equally importantly, enjoyed conversations with an element of human warmth to them. A private investigator hired by Frend had assured him that Radka appeared to be faithful to him, although whether out of genuine affection or a reluctance to endanger her financial position was unclear.

The display screens indicated that the Belgrade flight was now boarding. With what might have seemed like a degree of resignation, Frend unfolded himself from the chair and placed his newspaper in his overnight bag. In the past he had enjoyed his intermittent visits to the Serbian capital, the food being some of the best in Eastern Europe thanks to the enduring culinary influence of the Turks. This trip, though, was more problematic, and carried with it certain risks. He was representing the Vuksans, and the Vuksans were currently personae non gratae in Serbia. Despite this, a formal channel of communication had to be opened following the death of Nikola Musulin. The Vuksans wanted – needed – to return home. It was Frend's task to discover the price of this repatriation.

Hendricksen watched Frend leave the lounge, but took his time before following. Thanks to Hendricksen's efforts, and the expenditure of an eye-watering amount of Louis's money, all transactions on Frend's personal and business credit cards were now being monitored. Minutes after Frend's secretary had booked the return trip to Belgrade for her employer, Hendricksen had obtained seats on the same flights. It might have been better to have reserved a seat in economy, if only to lessen any possibility of Frend becoming familiar with Hendricksen's face. On the other hand, the investigator wanted to be within earshot if Frend used his cell phone on the plane.

They boarded, and Hendricksen took the aisle seat that had been reserved for him directly behind Frend, who stood aside to allow a young woman to occupy the window seat beside him. Hendricksen saw Frend take in the woman's figure and wondered if the lawyer might be considering trading in his Bulgarian girlfriend for a newer model. Details about Radka had been included in the dossier on Frend. The possibility of using her to get to her lover had been raised by Louis, only to be dismissed after Hendricksen had succeeded in chasing up a series of payments to one of her bank accounts. They originated from a holding company in Amsterdam, the same company responsible for running two nightclubs in the city operated by associates of the Vuksans. Evidently the brothers were not the trusting kind, not even when it came to their own legal advisor, which explained why they'd survived for so long. Either the Vuksans had deliberately introduced Radka to Frend, or they had recruited her after the relationship began in order to have another set of eyes on the lawyer. Whatever the sequence of events, she was a tripwire: had Louis and Hendricksen tried to exert pressure on Frend through her, the Vuksans would have been alerted immediately.

Frend used his phone only to send texts and emails while boarding continued. It would have been useful to be able to monitor his cell phone and email communications, but that kind of surveillance was beyond the capabilities of the hunters, and when Louis had suggested it to Harris, the spook just laughed. It seemed that Harris's interest in the Vuksans – and, by extension, that of the American authorities – began and ended with nailing Aleksej Marković and intercepting the delivery of his cargo. Now that Marković and the two Syrian undesirables were dead, Louis and the others could expect little help from that quarter.

Frend stuck to coffee when refreshments were served. Hendricksen did likewise. He spent the duration of the flight refamiliarizing himself with the geography of Belgrade even though he had a driver, Dušan, waiting for him at the airport. Dušan was a former interpreter for the UN, and now ran his own limousine company. He, like Hendricksen, had been at Srebrenica.

Hendricksen had not expected to return to the Balkans; the region held only bad memories for him. Perhaps the outcome of the Frend pursuit would alter that situation, but he doubted it. The best he could hope for would be to make up for past deficiencies – his own, and those of others.

Chapter XL

Spiridon and Radovan Vuksan watched the ongoing coverage of the Paris shootings on the television in the living room while Zivco Ilić worked the phone and monitored online chatter.

Two things were clear. The first was that the Vuksans would not be receiving the final portion of their fee for the safe delivery of the Syrian cargo, which was unfortunate. The second was that those who had entrusted the Syrians to their safekeeping would want to know why two of their most senior people had been martyred at a Paris railway station. They would already be trying to establish if they had an informant in their ranks, but only as a formality.

If the traitor were at their end, he would have passed on details of the operation long before Saad and Mahdi ever boarded the boat to France, a drone strike in the North African desert being easier and less dangerous than a confrontation at a crowded Parisian transportation hub. Similarly, the two men could have been intercepted shortly after they landed at Port-Vendres, or while they were in the safe house outside the town. Instead, the French had waited until they arrived at Gare de Lyon before moving on them, with the associated risk of civilian casualties should the men have been in possession of explosive devices, or had they elected to fight it out.

To Radovan, this suggested necessity rather than choice on the part of the French. While they might have had some foreknowledge that valuable ISIS operatives were headed for their territory, they didn't know how, or when, until the Syrians were actually on the train to Paris. Radovan knew that Marković would have stuck to established procedure and isolated all stages of the operation, meaning that only he and the Vuksans were aware of all the arrangements, including false trails involving misinformation, unused cars and apartments, and associates placed on alert who would never be called upon to act. Marković had also decided to split the long journey to Paris between road and rail in order to minimize the risk of interception, so that even Baba and Fouad were not aware of the final destination until they boarded the TGV to Gare de Lyon at Perpignan. No, the leak had occurred only once the final phase of the trip was confirmed, which meant that either Fouad or Baba had betrayed them.

The latter was currently in police custody: there was footage all over the internet of his apprehension by armed police. Of Fouad, there was as yet no trace. The fact that the French had seized Baba did not mean anything. If he was the informant, it would have been natural for the police to spirit him away as quickly as possible; if he was not, the same principle applied. But if Fouad was innocent, why had he not made contact? Yes, Marković was dead, and Fouad had no direct line of communication to the Vuksans, but he had not even been in touch with some of his own people. Fouad, it seemed, had vanished. Perhaps the French had also picked him up and were keeping silent about it, but that was unlikely. Thus Radovan was leaning toward Fouad as the traitor.

But this suspicion, even if it were to be confirmed, would not avail them if, or when, it came time to explain to a bunch of aggrieved Arabs why Saad and Mahdi – accomplished ISIS strategists and moneymen, and therefore beloved of the Prophet – had come to a violent end while ostensibly under the Vuksans' protection. Spiridon and Radovan would be held accountable. Financial compensation would be demanded, which the Vuksans were not in a position to pay. And if money was not forthcoming, the men in black would seek a more painful and permanent form of restitution.

Meanwhile, Marković was dead, killed in what was being described as an undercover police operation linked to the events at Gare de Lyon. If Fouad had betrayed the operation to the French, it was probable that he had sold out Marković as well. Yet according to the Vuksans' source on the hotel staff, the police had arrived only after Marković was shot – and, the source opined, they had appeared as puzzled as anyone else by his murder.

All of which made it more urgent than ever that Frend reach an accommodation with Belgrade, one that would permit the Vuksans to retreat to the safety of their rural fastnesses in Serbia. Radovan was working on other options, just in case, but he did not wish to spend the rest of his life running from his enemies, waiting for the inevitable moment when they found him. Like Spiridon, he wanted to be buried in Serbian soil, but unlike Spiridon, he was intent on postponing that interment for as long as possible.

Chapter XLI

Zorya stood amid a grove of trees on Danube Island, observing the young mothers pushing strollers or walking hand in hand with their toddlers on the gravel beach. She had no memory of her own parents. There was only darkness, then light; she had been birthed from the cave as though from a stone womb. She knew only that she was both very young and very, very old, and was filled with hate for those who were not like herself, which meant all of humanity.

She was still shaken from her trip across the Danube to the island. Zorya had not crossed water since her vision of the dead girl by the lake, although there was no logic to her reluctance. After all, not every journey over a river or stream involved a movement between worlds: that choice was one for Zorya to make, and previously she had always been the observer, never the observed. But the girl's awareness of her presence had deeply unsettled her, as well as complicating her relationship with Spiridon Vuksan. Zorya could be of benefit to him only if she could see what he could not, and to do that she needed to be able to explore without impediment.

She had decided to visit the island in order to clear her head, because the city, in all its grandeur, was oppressing her. Back in the Netherlands, she had regularly ventured outside Amsterdam to find relief from concrete and crowds – sometimes alone, at other times with Spiridon or one of his men, if only to avoid attention from those who might be curious as to why one who appeared, at first glance, to be a child was traveling without adult supervision. In Vienna, she had found her movements more restricted because the Vuksans were supposed to be in hiding. After the incident with the Turk Hasanović, the necessity for concealment was greater still, even for Zorya. Yet she could not remain indoors for long. It was too much like another death, too much like the cave.

So she had taken the U-Bahn from Leopoldstadt to Danube Island almost without thinking, keeping her head down while the train left the station, the hood on her sweatshirt raised and a magazine open but unread on her lap. As the train approached the Reichsbrücke for the short journey across the river to the island, she had experienced a tightening in her belly and a pressure on her skull. The lights in the carriage flickered as the train reached the bridge, and the commuters and tourists around her grew faint before melting away entirely. In their place was the dead girl from the lakeside. She was staring at the floor, her hair hanging loosely over her face. Dark fluid dripped from beneath the blond strands and pooled at her feet. It took Zorya a moment to realize it was blood. The dead girl raised her head, and Zorya glimpsed the empty sockets of her eyes, and the flesh and tendons of a face scoured of skin.

The dead girl spoke, her voice transformed by the journey from her world to this one.

found you, she said. *found you at last*

And then they reached the island, and she was gone. There were only commuters and tourists, and soon the train was slowing for its entry into the Donauinsel station. Zorya had exited in a daze, and now here she was, watching the women and children on the beach, terrified of returning to Leopoldstadt because to do so would require crossing the river again, where the dead girl might be waiting.

But the contact between them was not all one way, because Zorya knew the girl's name.

Jennifer. Jennifer Parker.

And that could be used against her.

Chapter XLII

Frend arrived at Belgrade's Nikola Tesla Airport feeling vulnerable and exposed. He was here representing men whom many might have preferred to see dead. It was possible that Frend was walking into a trap instead of a negotiation, and might soon find himself in a basement in Palilula with a blowtorch being applied to his genitals before vinegar was poured onto the wounds.

Frend knew all about the Serbs' interrogation methods. Radovan Vuksan had sometimes spoken of them over postprandial drinks, although he had differentiated between torture for the purposes of eliciting information and torture for its own sake. Burning and vinegar were best for persuading someone to talk, but pure sadism offered more scope for experimentation – theoretically, at least. It had been a source of some regret to Radovan that his countrymen displayed a marked lack of imagination when it came to inflicting suffering on others. Bats, chains, axes, and blades were the preferred instruments of the Serbs, Radovan explained, the sessions fueled by tequila, vodka, narcotics, and violent pornography. Oh, and rape: the Serbs enjoyed using sexual assault as torment for both men and women. Now, in Belgrade, such abstractions were assuming disturbingly concrete forms for Anton Frend.

There was also the small matter of Nikola Musulin's head. Despite a careful search of the ruins of Tri Lovca and the immediate vicinity, the head had still not been recovered, and Musulin had finally been laid to rest without it. The Vuksans believed that the head might have been taken away by those responsible for the explosion, an act designed to further antagonize and humiliate Musulin's family and allies. Musulin's widow very much wanted the head restored to her in order that it might be placed in the

182

coffin with the remains of her husband – 'remains', in this case, being the operative word, since the C4 had contrived to separate Musulin into a great many pieces, and he weighed much less in death than in life. One of Frend's tasks would be to establish if, in fact, the head was in the possession of Matija Kiš or Simo Stajić, both of whom would be at the meeting, and potentially secure its safe return.

All of these thoughts passed through Frend's mind as his passport was examined for what felt like a very long time before the stamp was applied and he was admitted to the country. He went straight to the exit, carrying only his overnight bag, and was relieved to see the familiar face of Miloje, who had regularly driven him around Belgrade in better times. Miloje, Frend knew, was distantly related to the Vuksans. They trusted him, even after all that had occurred, which was why he had been given the task of picking up Frend from the airport. Miloje was a mute: Bosniak soldiers in Konjic had removed his tongue with hot pincers during the war. In his pocket he kept a notebook in which he wrote questions or comments. In addition to his native Serbian, Miloje also understood English, German, and a little French. In his notebook he now scribbled the question *Hotel?* and showed it to Frend.

'No,' said Frend, 'let's go straight to the restaurant.'

He had reserved a room at a boutique hotel in Vračar, but the delayed flight had cost him two precious hours, and he did not think it would be politic to arrive late for the meeting. Miloje showed Frend to a gray Audi, sheltering him from the rain with a black umbrella. They then crawled toward the city, Belgrade's notorious traffic rendered even more chaotic by the bad weather. Serbian flags hung from every second lamppost along the motorway, a reminder, if any were needed, that Serb nationalism remained a potent force. The journey was soundtracked by a cacophony of blaring horns, and accompanied by a cortege of taxi drivers measuring out their lives in missed fares.

Frend's cell phone rang. Only Radovan had the new number.

'Where are you?'

'Passing the Sava Centar,' said Frend, naming the huge Tito-era conference facility close to the river. 'The flight was late, but I'll soon be at the meeting place.'

'Good, because I just received a call.'

'From?'

'A North African client inquiring about a lost delivery.'

Frend knew the substance, if not the details, of the botched operation in Paris.

'What did you say?'

'That we were looking into the reasons for the failure.'

'And?'

'It did not diminish the client's unhappiness,' said Radovan. 'He has requested a meeting. Naturally, I demurred.'

'Naturally,' said Frend. As if their situation wasn't bad enough, the Vuksans now had homicidal religious lunatics trying to track them down. 'Did you offer to return the portion of the fee already paid?'

'Are you trying to be funny?'

Frend wasn't, and told Radovan so. He watched a pair of police cars speed by, followed by an ambulance: an accident farther up the road, which might have explained some, but not all, of the delay. This was Belgrade, so there was always an accident somewhere.

'I now believe,' said Radovan wearily, 'that the reputational damage suffered would not be undone by a refund, even were we willing or able to offer it. We need that money. I'm informing you of the complaint only because it makes reaching a settlement with Belgrade even more urgent than before.'

'I understand. Do you think Belgrade knows about your involvement with the cargo?'

'I hope not, but you'll find out soon enough.'

Frend noticed that his left hand was shaking. He used the armrest to steady it as the Audi reached the Gazela Bridge and crossed the Sava. The traffic began to ease. Miloje was texting as he drove. Frend tried to read the message, but it was in Serbian. Miloje glanced at him in the rearview mirror before returning his attention to the road. An earlier conversation with Radovan came back to Frend:

I would trust Miloje with my life.

You're not trusting him with your life, but with mine.

'I remain concerned for my safety,' Frend now said to Radovan, as the connection briefly lapsed.

'You should have told me that before you left Vienna,' said Radovan.

'I did.'

'I mustn't have been paying attention.'

'Would it have made any difference if you had?'

'None at all,' said Radovan, before killing the call.

The Cathedral Church of St. Michael the Archangel was now coming into sight, which meant that they were near the location for the meeting. After some back-and-forth, it had been agreed that it should take place at a neutral venue, and one some distance from Skadarlija, where the unfortunate Nikola Musulin had met his end. This was not a question of sensitivity, since those willing to blow a man apart before stealing his severed head were unlikely to be troubled by the feelings of his bereaved intimates. Yet even allowing for a degree of collusion between the authorities and the killers, it would still have been unwise for those suspected of involvement in Musulin's assassination to be seen wining and dining within shouting distance of the crime scene. The Serbian media might be largely cowed or corrupted, with the few remaining quality publications struggling to survive, but one could not underestimate the tenacity of a handful of principled journalists and newspaper proprietors, or the anonymity of the internet. It would be embarrassing, at the minimum, were pictures of a gathering of the alleged conspirators to have appeared in *Danas* or online, particularly if Frend were also to be identified.

No, better to steer clear of Skadarlija entirely, which was why an appropriately removed site had been rented for private use. The tavern was among the oldest in the city, with dark wood floors, low chairs and stools, and waitstaff in white shirts and black waistcoats. The separate dining area had blue check tablecloths, and served a traditional menu that changed according to the mood of the chef, while the walls were decorated with paintings of brooding Serbian landscapes and the ruins of ancient fortresses.

Miloje found a place to park before escorting Frend into the bar. Two men were seated at one of the tables to the left of the door, wearing the ubiquitous cheap leather jackets of the professionally thuggish. They were drinking coffee, and nodded at Miloje, who nodded back. Miloje held his hands out from his sides, inviting a search. One of the men rose and scanned Miloje with a handheld metal detector before patting him down, just in case he'd accessorized with a ceramic blade or rigged himself to explode as an act of revenge. They didn't even bother checking Frend. Perhaps, Frend thought, he didn't look like a threat, or they were betting that a lawyer wouldn't be self-sacrificing enough to lay down his life for a client, in which case they would have been absolutely correct.

Miloje took a seat at the table to the right of the door, leaving Frend to proceed into the restaurant. Three more bodyguards were arranged inside, two by the window and the other by the far wall, and only one of the tables was set for dinner. Two men were already waiting at it, drinking Vinjak XO brandy as an aperitif.

Frend had met Matija Kiš on a number of occasions, finding him to be uninteresting company, although Radovan had advised against underestimating him and, it seemed, had been right. Kiš was tall and dark-haired, but most of the color came from a bottle. He was wearing a slim-cut black suit that looked a size too small, even though Kiš was not a particularly heavy man. Frend blamed the Daniel Craig incarnation of James Bond, whose Tom Ford suits were too tight and narrow-shouldered for someone of his build. A whole generation of would-be sophisticates had now grown up believing that a man's suit jacket should be cut an inch too short and ripple outward from the center button.

Seated to Kiš's left was Simo Stajić, whom Frend knew only from photographs. Frend did not believe Stajić had ever owned a suit. Even at funerals, Stajić dressed as though he operated a market stall selling stolen cell phones: jeans, a leather jacket, a shirt that could have been mistaken for designer wear only in poor light, and anonymous sneakers for a speedy getaway. Whatever Stajić spent his money on, it wasn't fashion. He kept his head shaved and had the build of a long-distance runner. He blinked a lot, so that his eyes resembled the shutters of a camera perpetually recording everything they saw, and he smoked obsessively, even by Serbian standards. Already the ashtray before him held four butts, and Frend was only a few minutes late.

Both men stood to shake his hand – Kiš firmly, with a double grip, in the manner of a politician seeking reelection, and Stajić more desultorily, possibly because he had to switch the cigarette to his left hand to do so, thus depriving himself of valuable smoking time. Frend was relieved not to be subjected to the ritual of kisses, at least.

'You had a good flight?' said Kiš in English. Frend wondered if it was for Stajić's benefit. Radovan was of the opinion that Stajić did not know German, but had learned English because it was the international language of criminality.

'We were delayed,' said Frend.

'So I understand. May I offer you an aperitif? It's very good.'

'It's very strong.'

'That, too. But strong is good, right?'

'I'll stick with wine,' said Frend. 'Prokupac, please.'

Kiš passed the order to a waiter, and a bottle was produced. Almost as soon as the wine was poured, food began to appear: salads and flatbreads, followed by a variety of meats, including kidneys and pig trotters. Frend avoided the latter and ate only lightly of the meats. He preferred the new Serbian cooking to this more traditional fare. There was, he had long ago decided, only so much that even the best of chefs could accomplish with grilled flesh. He and Kiš kept up a polite conversation, touching on sport, culture, the weather – anything but the real reason for Frend's presence in the city. Stajić didn't contribute much beyond the occasional grunt, and kept a cigarette burning throughout the meal, but Frend saw that he was listening intently, his eyes moving back and forth between the interlocutors. It made Frend wonder which of the two, Kiš or Stajić, was the real power here.

Finally, when they had all eaten their fill, having barely made inroads into most of the food, the table was cleared, coffee was poured, and they got down to business.

187

'So how is Spiridon?' said Kiš. 'And please don't tell me he's the same as ever or I shall be disappointed at his continued inability to evolve.'

'He is concerned,' said Frend, 'as is Radovan.'

'Oh, Radovan I can believe is concerned. Radovan is always concerned. Spiridon, I imagine, is more than that.'

'Enraged, then. Is that more acceptable?'

'Accurate, perhaps. Acceptable is another matter.'

'May I speak frankly?' said Frend.

'There is little point in your being here if you do not.'

'Spiridon thinks you may have some knowledge of who killed Nikola Musulin.'

Which was a diplomatic way of putting it. Frend did not even glance at Stajić, the man who was probably responsible for planting the explosives that ended Musulin's life, because the lawyer remained hopeful of making it back to Vienna alive.

Kiš's expression of benevolent interest did not alter.

'And if I did?' he said. 'Would Spiridon want revenge?'

'Spiridon wants only to come home. He wishes to spend his remaining years by a lake in the mountains.'

'In peace, with no thoughts of vengeance?'

'In peace. As for his thoughts, they cannot be policed, but his intentions are clear.'

'Really?' said Kiš. 'If so, it would be the first time.'

Now Stajić spoke. His voice was raspy, and his breath smelled of a thousand ashtrays.

'Where are they?' he said. 'Where are the Vuksans?'

'I can't tell you that.'

'But you know?'

'Actually, I don't. I felt it was wiser to dwell in ignorance.'

'Safer, too,' Kiš suggested.

'Indeed.'

'I don't believe you,' said Stajić.

'That's unfortunate,' said Frend.

'Yes,' said Stajić, 'it is.'

Kiš made a calming gesture to his colleague. Stajić lit another cigarette, puffed on it until the tip glowed red, then held it upright just outside Frend's field of vision. Frend could almost feel the heat of it close to his ear.

'If they are in hiding,' said Kiš, 'which they are, of course, from whom are they hiding? Us?'

'Among others,' said Frend.

'They have no need to hide from us,' said Kiš. 'No one wants more deaths. It would draw too much attention.'

'But one can always disappear, which is less awkward,' said Frend. 'And a death can be postponed.'

'Your clients have bigger problems elsewhere. Soon an Interpol Red Notice will be issued in their names, or so we have been informed. That's what you get for crucifying an old man these days, unless you're an ISIS Turk.'

A Red Notice was a request to locate and arrest a suspect, pending extradition. It was the modern equivalent of the Wanted posters that had once been put up outside sheriffs' offices in the American West. Frend had been aware that a Red Notice for the Vuksans might be on the horizon, but so far his sources had suggested it was not imminent. Kiš might have access to more recent intelligence but Frend doubted it. Still, the man's confidence worried him.

'There are places they can go,' said Frend, 'countries in which Red Notices are difficult to enforce.'

'Yes, North Korea,' said Kiš. 'Or perhaps the Vatican. They can convert to communism or Catholicism!'

He laughed, noticed he was the only one doing so, and stopped.

'If Interpol doesn't get the Vuksans, ISIS will,' he said.

Which meant, Frend realized, that Kiš knew about the events in Paris. That was regrettable, and weakened the Vuksans' bargaining position.

'And if ISIS doesn't,' Kiš continued, 'someone else might. Maybe that someone has already started.'

'What do you mean?'

'Do you think Aleksej Marković was really killed by the French? I hear that Marković was already dead when the police found him.'

Frend might have been a lawyer, and therefore gifted – or cursed

– with a lawyer's countenance, but he could not entirely hide the fact that this was news to him.

'The Vuksans didn't tell you?' said Kiš. 'Of course, why would they? You'd only have begun to worry. You might even have considered abandoning them to their fate. The Dutchman, De Jaager, had friends, the kind it doesn't pay to antagonize. Your clients have made those friends very angry.'

'How do you know this?' said Frend.

Kiš tapped a forefinger to the side of his head. 'Common sense. Also, questions are being asked, inquiries that come with the promise of rewards attached. Money is being put on the streets in an effort to trace the Vuksans. Soon, they'll make a mistake. They'll turn the wrong corner, board the wrong train, look out the wrong window. Then a call will be made, and – poof!'

Kiš made a gesture with his hands, as of something vanishing – or exploding.

'So where does that leave us?' said Frend.

'It leaves you as buyers in a seller's market,' said Kiš. 'The Vuksans wish to purchase a comfortable old age in their homeland, where any attempt at extradition will move at the pace of a dead man. Here they can live out their lives, perhaps under new names, safe in the knowledge that Serbia will not join the EU until 2025 at the earliest, by which time their sins will have been forgotten, if not forgiven. They'll have their own people around them, which will make them harder to target, either by the Turks or the friends of the Dutchman. It seems to me that the guarantee of such an untroubled existence must come at a price, not to mention a secondary sum to be set aside as a guarantee of good behavior, just in case Spiridon begins to confuse thought with action.'

'How much?' said Frend.

'Four million euros,' said Kiš, 'with a further two million to be placed in escrow, half to be returned to the Vuksans' beneficiaries following the death of each man, minus a twenty percent holding fee. Should the Vuksans breach the terms of the agreement, which broadly means displaying any signs of aggression, the money becomes forfeit and they will be killed.'

This time, Frend managed not to give away his thoughts.

'I'll have to discuss it with my clients,' he said.

'Take all the time you want,' said Kiš. 'We're in no hurry.'

Stajić placed a hand on Frend's right arm.

'Or you could just tell us where they are,' he said, his eyelids fluttering.

'Yes,' Kiš concurred, 'you could just tell us that.'

'I repeat,' said Frend, 'I don't know where they are. They were relocated through a third party so I could work without being vulnerable to coercion.'

Stajić's grip grew tighter. He kept his nails very sharp, and Frend could feel them pricking at his skin.

'Yet you are still vulnerable here and in Vienna,' said Stajić, 'regardless of what you do or do not know.'

Frend waited them out. He had no choice. Eventually, Stajić's grip eased. Kiš, meanwhile, was smiling again.

'Go back to Vienna, Herr Frend,' he said. 'Talk to your clients. We look forward to hearing their response to our proposal.'

Frend did not move from his chair.

'There is one more thing,' he said. 'It relates to Nikola Musulin.'

'You know,' said Kiš, 'I was just about to talk to you about Nikola. I think we may have found something that belonged to him.'

Kiš waved his right hand and one of the bodyguards came forward with a velvet bag. Its contents were roughly circular, and rolled slightly as the bag was placed on the table before Frend.

'Feel free to open it,' said Kiš. 'But if I were you, I'd just accept our word that it's his.'

Frend picked up the bag. He had never held a severed head before, so he could not say that it was lighter or heavier than anticipated. It was just a head.

'We'll be in touch,' he said.

'Of course you will,' said Kiš. Stajić only blinked.

Frend walked through to the bar area, where he was relieved to find Miloje still waiting. Miloje led the way to the Audi, neither man looking back, yet both fearing to hear the sound of footsteps approaching from behind.

*

Hendricksen took fresh pictures of Frend and the driver, concealed by the smoked glass of a Mercedes. As the Audi pulled away, Dušan asked if Hendricksen wanted to follow the car, but he demurred. He was waiting to see who else might emerge from the tavern. Barely two minutes later, the door opened and the first of the bodyguards appeared, checking the street, to be followed by Matija Kiš and Simo Stajić.

'Fuck,' said Dušan. 'Put the camera away.'

'They can't see us,' said Hendricksen.

'I don't care. Put it away.'

Hendricksen did. He had the shots he needed.

'Who are they?' he said, as Kiš, Stajić, and the others climbed into a pair of BMW people carriers.

'Devils,' said Dušan.

'There are no devils,' said Hendricksen, 'only men who act like them.'

'You're wrong,' said Dušan, as he started the engine, 'but then, you don't have to live here.'

In the back of the Audi, the severed head beside him, Frend was writing down the license number of the Mercedes. Miloje had spotted it shortly before they entered the city. Frend thought it might have been sent by Kiš or Stajić to keep an eye on them, but he had reconsidered when he saw it parked near the bar as they emerged, the driver still in place.

Miloje was writing in his notebook with his right hand while driving with his left. He showed the page to Frend. The message read *Do Not Go To Hotel.*

'Where, then?' said Frend, and Miloje raised a hand to let him know that the matter was being taken care of.

They drove for half an hour, making cutbacks and illegal turns until Miloje was sure they were not being followed, before stopping at a surburban hotel frequented by Eastern European tourists on strict budgets. Miloje went inside and came out a short time later with a key. He returned to the notebook and wrote *Stay In Your Room.*

'What about tomorrow?' said Frend. 'I have to fly back to Vienna.'

Not From Belgrade. Timisoara.

Timisoara Airport was in Romania, about 160 kilometers away, by Frend's reckoning.

'How?'

We Drive.

'When?'

5 a.m.

Frend thanked him. There was no one at reception as he passed, and he entered his room unnoticed. It contained a single bed, a television that did not work, and a bathroom that reeked of human waste.

Six million euros. The Vuksans did not have access to such funds. Even had they been able to lay their hands on that kind of money, it was a deliberately absurd price. Kiš and Stajić wanted the Vuksans dead. Had Frend gone to his original hotel, Stajić's people would have been waiting in his room. He would have been drugged and removed without fuss. Then, in some quiet basement that smelled of vinegar and burning, Stajić would have gone to work on him.

Frend stayed awake until Miloje came to collect him the following morning. Only when they crossed the Romanian border did he begin to feel safe, and he did not truly relax until he was on the Tarom-Romanian Air flight to Bucharest with an onward connection to Vienna.

As for the velvet bag, Miloje delivered it to Nikola Musulin's widow.

He did not stay to watch her open it.

But he did hear her screams.

Chapter XLIII

At thirty-one, Luca Bilbija was the youngest of the men who had assisted the Vuksans on the night De Jaager and the others were murdered. He had known only that a final job was to be done, one that would necessitate violence, after which he would receive a bonus and be free to seek employment elsewhere, if he chose; alternatively, he could return with the Vuksans to Serbia, where Radovan had promised him a position as his personal driver and bodyguard.

In common with Radovan, Bilbija was an avid reader, and they shared an affection for early twentieth-century Serbian poetry. Bilbija had a degree in Serbian Literature and Language from the University of Belgrade, and had intended continuing his studies at the postgraduate level until the family's money ran out, forcing him to consider working for a living instead. Unfortunately, jobs were not in plentiful supply in Belgrade, and even less so in his home village in the east, close to the Danubian border with Romania. The village boasted three hundred houses but only two hundred inhabitants. Those with ambition, or of sufficient desperation, had departed to work in other countries – Austria, in the main – leaving the rest to survive as best they could. It was, like so many other Serbian communities, fit only for old men and women, and then barely. Bilbija had not wanted to go back there, but neither was he convinced that he wished to wait tables in Viennese restaurants or deliver parcels from a van in Berlin.

And then, through Zivco Ilić, who was a friend of Bilbija's uncle, he was offered a door position at one of the Vuksans' clubs in Amsterdam. After a couple of weeks of bouncing drunks, he was assigned the task of driving prostitutes to their clients; Bilbija might have possessed the heart of a poet, but it was housed in the body of a wrestler. He liked his new role, and took a proprietorial interest in the young women under his care, although this did not stop him from inflicting pain on them when they tried to hold money back,

Six months into his time in Amsterdam, he helped Zivco Ilić dispose of a body. The victim was a dealer who had begun to dip into his own supply and ended up owing the Vuksans more money than he could ever hope to pay. He was given one chance to make up for his lack of self-control by transporting a consignment of heroin from Amsterdam to Brussels. Unfortunately, his drug-induced paranoia led him to believe that he was being followed by the police – or possibly demons dressed as police, the precise details were unclear – which caused him to dump all five kilos in a pond near Brecht.

Ilić and Bilbija tracked him to an unfurnished room in Matonge, which Ilić proceeded to redecorate with the dealer's blood while Bilbija waited outside in the car. When Ilić had finished, he summoned Bilbija to help cut up the victim and place the remains in black bags, which would then be dumped at various locations around Brussels. Unfortunately, just as they began cutting off his arms, it became apparent that the dealer was not as dead as Ilić had believed, but Bilbija finished him off before he could make too much of a racket. Bilbija had never killed anyone before. He found the experience messy but interesting, and later wrote a poem about it in the modernist style of Vasko Popa.

After that incident, Bilbija became an integral part of the Vuksan hierarchy, especially once the Vuksans assumed complete control of operations in Amsterdam. He took his orders from both brothers, but always ran Spiridon's commands past Radovan before proceeding. In this way, a certain amount of unnecessary violence was avoided, if at the cost of complete trust between Spiridon and Bilbija. This trust had been further eroded by Bilbija's refusal actively to engage in rape and femicide at the house in Amsterdam. He might have been prepared to hurt females, but he drew the line at killing them himself, and he was not a rapist. Among his tribe, Luca Bilbija was what passed for a man of principle.

Bilbija did not like what he had witnessed at De Jaager's safe house. It had caused him to reconsider his future relationship with Radovan Vuksan. He was aware that the Dutch police would soon connect the Vuksans to the killings, and it was entirely possible that he would be connected to them in turn. This seemed terribly unfair. He had not harmed anyone at the safe house. He had tied the women to the beds, and later helped nail De Jaager to a wall, but by then the old man was already dead. Bilbija's role in what had occurred was, therefore, largely limited to driving and cleaning up after, and in his view hardly merited a custodial sentence.

When the Vuksans' situation grew more complicated following the death of Nikola Musulin, Bilbija decided that his period of employment with them had come to its natural end. He had privately informed Radovan Vuksan of his decision to leave the fold while they were hiding out at the farmhouse of Gavrilo Dražeta. Radovan had placed a hand on his shoulder and whispered:

'Say nothing of this to Spiridon or the others. For now, you remain one of us.'

'Why?' said Bilbija.

'Because circumstances have changed,' said Radovan. 'We are wanted men, and any desire to depart will be viewed by Spiridon as a prelude to treachery. He will have you killed the moment you turn your back on him. Zivco will do it in a heartbeat.'

'But Zivco is my friend.' Bilbija was surprised to hear his voice catch with emotion.

'You have no friends, not even me.'

'Then why are you telling me this?'

'Because I've read your poetry,' said Radovan. 'You are a terrible poet, but better to be a terrible poet than no poet at all.'

So Bilbija had kept his mouth shut, and within hours events had swung in his favor. Radovan had prevailed upon Spiridon to split his forces to avoid attracting attention. Aleksej Marković was on his way to Paris anyway, and Bilbija was told to lie low but remain in contact. Radovan had given him the number of the lawyer Frend in Vienna, and an email address that would be checked four times daily. On Radovan's instructions, Bilbija had headed east, to Prague, which was no great imposition. Bilbija had always loved the city, and thought that if he had to hide out somewhere, at least it might as well be in a place for which he had some affection.

Luca Bilbija's particular vice was gambling, but he did not enjoy wagering in solitude and took no pleasure from staring at a screen. He relished the ambience of casinos, the excited anticipation of men and women waiting on the spin of a wheel or the turn of a card. He liked gaming tables, and the smell of a new deck. He did not consider gambling to be a character flaw because he was both lucky and careful, and so won more often than he lost. But as any gambler will tell you, luck always runs out eventually, and that is when a man becomes most reckless.

Prague had no shortage of casinos.

And people were watching and listening for Luca Bilbija.

Chapter XLIV

F rend heard the ping of an incoming email as he was showering
at home. His trip from Belgrade to Romania, and on to Vienna,
had been tense and unpleasant, but he had almost succeeded in
washing Serbia from his skin. He remained troubled, though, by
how close he had come to becoming a prisoner of Simo Stajić.
He'd have told them where the Vuksans were, of course, abandoning dissimulation and confessing all at the first sight of the
blowtorch, but he knew that talking wouldn't have saved him.
His long death would have been recorded on a cell phone, but
only for private distribution. The killing of an Austrian lawyer on
Serbian territory would have caused untold problems for Belgrade;
his disappearance, less so. Eventually, to throw the Austrians off
the scent, Frend's papers would have been discovered in a Bosnian
or Croatian whorehouse, perhaps with a little of his blood dotted
around for appearances' sake.

Toweling himself dry, Frend checked his in-box. Miloje, his
bodyguard in Belgrade, had located the Mercedes that had followed
them from the airport, the city's community of limousine drivers
being relatively small. Miloje had convinced the owner of the
Mercedes to divulge the identity of the person who had hired him:
a Dutchman named Hendricksen, who had spent the night at the
Radisson before being driven back to the airport for an early-
morning flight to Vienna.

Frend put on a robe and set to work finding out all he could
about this Hendricksen. Like any good lawyer, especially one who
operated in more legal and moral gray areas than the norm, Frend
had contacts in credit card companies, banks, and the government,
including the Austrian foreign ministry. Somewhere, there would
be a record of Hendricksen's movements. It took Frend thirty

minutes, and the transfer of some of the Vuksans' remaining funds, to secure a scan of Hendricksen's passport. Within an hour he had also obtained Hendricksen's residential address in the Netherlands, bank and credit card records, and home and cell phone numbers, as well as a partial client list, because Frend learned that Hendricksen was a former Dutch soldier now working as a private investigator. The majority of his income in recent years had come from three law firms, one of which specialized in cases relating to the art world. The credit card information, meanwhile, showed that Hendricksen was currently staying at a chain hotel in Vienna's Innere Stadt, and had been for a number of days, apart from his brief sojourn in Belgrade.

Frend heard his wife moving about downstairs, and music playing on the radio. Mina was probably making herself a gin and tonic, because it was about that time. She called up, asking if he'd like a drink, and he told her he'd be right with her. They needed to talk. Frend might no longer have loved his wife, but he retained some residual affection for her and did not wish any harm to befall her, as much for the sake of their daughter as for her own. Frend might have managed to escape Belgrade unharmed, but that did not mean he was safe. He did not doubt that the reach of Kiš and Stajić extended beyond the Serbian border, and there was no shortage of Serbs in Austria. If Kiš and Stajić decided to move against the Vuksans, their lawyer still remained the most obvious means of applying pressure.

With this in mind, Frend had decided that, until the Vuksans' difficulties were resolved, it might be best if he took steps to safeguard his family and himself. His daughter, he felt, was reasonably secure in London, where she had been living under her mother's name since moving to England to study law. Even had he attempted to contact Pia in order to share his concerns, he was certain she would have laughed at him, assuming she agreed to accept his call to begin with. In any case, he doubted she would be willing to alter her routine on her father's say so, even at risk to herself. He suspected she would prefer to die just to spite him.

His wife was another matter; his mistress, too, come to think of it. He would deal with Radka later, although there wasn't much he could do other than advise her to be careful. She was as willful as his daughter – which was hardly surprising, given how close in age they were – and would be unlikely to entrust the running of her boutique to an assistant for more than a day or two.

Anyway, Frend thought it more likely that his immediate family would be the preferred targets: mistresses, however lovely, were temporary, but family was for life. Yet in the reptile part of his brain, Frend debated how he might act should Radka or Mina be used against him. Objectively, he would be prepared to renounce either or both of them for his own safety, which was intimately connected to the continued safety of the Vuksans, whom he could not betray. The brothers might have been isolated and grievously weakened, but they were not without friends. Were he to hand them over to their enemies, word would get out, and Frend's days would be numbered. Only for Pia would Frend be willing to sacrifice himself, and even then with a degree of understandable vacillation . . .

He went downstairs and accepted the glass from Mina. He then led her to the kitchen, where he spoke with her quietly and seriously for ten minutes. He did not share with her every detail of the problem, but told her enough to make her understand the necessity of absenting herself from their home. He was surprised that she did not complain, or even blame him for this enforced exile. She merely accepted with a shrug, and he saw in her face that their relationship, such as it was, had finally reached its belated end.

'I always knew you were crooked,' she said. 'I knew it from the day we met.' Curiously, she did not use the word *unehrlich*, meaning dishonest, instead opting for *verkrümmt*, as in bent or warped, as though his perfidy was so ingrained as to have manifested itself physically. 'But,' she continued, 'perhaps I, too, was guilty. I enjoyed our lifestyle. I just chose not to ask how we could afford it.'

She looked around the kitchen.

'I don't think I'll ever sleep under this roof again,' she said. 'I hope you realize why.'

'I do,' said Frend, and recognized the irony of using these two words upon the dissolution of a marriage. Now that she was leaving him at last, he desired only for her to stay. He was not so unhappy with Mina as to prefer a life without her, and he knew that Radka would ultimately forsake him. 'I don't wish I was a better man, but I do wish I had been a better husband.'

'You cannot be one without the other. We should both have come to terms with that a long time ago.' She sipped her gin. 'Does she make you happy?'

'Who?'

'The woman you fuck when you're not with me.'

He thought about the question.

'Sometimes, but there is always guilt.'

'Even for you? I'm surprised.'

'Even for me.' He felt empty and weary. 'If I survive this, I believe I will conclude the relationship. All things considered, I'd rather embrace solitude.'

'That might be best for everyone.' She stood. 'I suppose I'd better start packing.'

'Where will you go?'

'I was thinking of London. I could see Pia.'

He shook his head – 'I wouldn't' – and the look he gave her made the reason clear.

'Jesus,' she said.

'There is only a small chance.'

She stared at him for a moment before throwing the contents of her glass in his face.

'Listen to yourself!' she said. 'A "small chance". This is your child you're talking about!'

He used a clean dish towel to wipe away the gin.

'I know that, which is why we have to stay away from her.'

Mina placed the empty glass on the table and leaned toward him.

'If anything happens to her,' she said, 'I'll kill you myself.'

Mina had an old friend, a widow, who lived in Kufstein in the Tyrol. It was a pretty town, and her friend would welcome the company. Frend provided Mina with €20,000 in cash from the safe and advised her to avoid using her credit card or making withdrawals from ATMs.

'How long?' she asked, as she waited for a taxi to arrive.

'A week, I should think, or just a little longer.'

In truth, he did not know. Perhaps it would never end, or not as long as the Vuksans remained alive.

'What about you?'

'I cannot leave the city,' said Frend. 'I have obligations. I'll move to the apartment above the office.'

The first two floors of the building were rented to a security firm, which had also paid to have a vault installed in the basement. In addition, the firm had assumed the lion's share of the cost of double security doors at the front and back entrances, and at least one of its staff was on monitoring duty 24/7. The firm did not specialize in personal protection, but Frend was sure that it might be in a position to recommend someone should he choose to engage a short-term bodyguard. He would advise Fräulein Pichler to take a trip to visit her sister in Helsinki, with all expenses covered. She would require no explanation, and would know better than to ask for one.

Frend thought that if Kiš and Stajić decided to come after him in Vienna, it would be as a last resort. Vienna was not Belgrade, no matter how many Serbs might be employed in the city. By escaping from Serbia intact, Frend had bought himself some time. Now, he hoped, Kiš would restrain Stajić while they waited for the Vuksans to make their next move. If Kiš could not, Frend had a card he might yet play.

The taxi appeared. Frend placed his wife's bags in the trunk.

'I'll arrange to collect the rest of my things once this is resolved,' said Mina. 'I have a lawyer in mind for the divorce. She's young, and doesn't move in your circles.'

'You don't have to worry,' he said. 'I won't make things difficult for you. You have my word.'

'It's a little late for that kind of promise, isn't it?'

He couldn't help but smile, and she responded in kind.

'I suppose so.' He placed his hands in his pockets. 'Were they all so terrible, these years we spent together?'

'Not terrible, but such a waste.'
'Except for Pia,' he said.
'Yes, except for her.'
'You know that by losing you, I also lose her?'
Mina's smile faded.
'You lost us both a long time ago,' she said.

Chapter XLV

As arranged, Angel waited for Pia Lackner at a parking lot on Queen Victoria Street, a short walk from her office. Lackner arrived carrying only her purse, as briefed. For the purposes of the narrative being constructed, she was not permitted to bring with her any clothing or possessions from her apartment, not even a cosmetics bag. She had provided Angel with a list of her requirements, including her measurements, and Rosanna Bellingham had taken care of the purchases, assembling sufficient clothing and toiletries for two weeks. Angel had assured Lackner that two weeks represented a worst-case scenario, and she, in turn, had informed him that he had a week, and no more.

Rosanna was sitting behind the wheel of a Ford Galaxy, Bob Johnson beside her. Lackner quickly climbed into the back as Rosanna started the engine. A comfortable cottage had been rented for them on Cornwall's Lizard Peninsula, equipped with provisions and diversions. Lackner would have to remain hidden for the duration of the stay, but the cottage had its own secluded beach, and the nearest neighbors were some way off. She wouldn't be going into Helston for dinner and drinks at The Greenhouse, but neither would she be entirely a prisoner, if one of her own choosing. As for her job, it was already Friday, which meant they had three days before she would be required to begin justifying her absence. A call complaining of being ill would suffice. Even if Frend decided to check with the firm, it would make sense for his daughter's kidnappers to ensure that her employers were not made anxious about her.

With Angel's assistance, Lackner had recorded three video messages for her father. She was, he thought, a pretty good actress, communicating fear at her situation and anger at him for placing

204

her in jeopardy. The first video would be sent to Frend after Angel arrived in Vienna.

Lackner pressed a button to lower the window of the MPV.

'Will I see you again?' she asked Angel.

'Only if things go wrong.'

'My father won't call the police, if that's what you mean. He won't put me in further danger.'

'Well, that's only one of the ways the plan could go south, but it's reassuring to hear.'

'I'm placing a lot of trust in you,' said Lackner.

'As I am in you,' said Angel.

She bit her lip.

'I don't want him to get hurt,' she said. 'I may hate him, but he is still my father.'

Angel patted the side of the vehicle, and it began to pull slowly away.

'We won't hurt him,' said Angel. 'I promise.'

We probably won't have to, he thought. *If he betrays the Vuksans, someone else will do it for us.*

Chapter XLVI

Frend stood in the bedroom he had shared with his wife for so long. He tried to remember the last time he and Mina had made love here – made love anywhere – and failed. They could, of course, have elected to occupy separate bedrooms, but the issue had never arisen. Perhaps, even in their reduced state, they still had not wished to be alone in the dark.

Although Mina had packed hurriedly, there was no mess in the bedroom, and only his own possessions now remained conspicuous. It was very like her to be able to excise so efficiently any obvious evidence of her existence. When eventually the divorce was finalized, and their severance complete, it would be as though she had never played a part in his history. They might meet at Pia's wedding, he supposed, assuming Pia ever found time to marry, and he was invited to the ceremony. Otherwise, Frend believed that he and Mina might never be found in each other's presence again until one of them died and the other stood dry-eyed in the church as some version of a life was recalled for the benefit of the congregation.

His cell phone rang. For a moment he hoped it might be Mina calling, but the number was withheld. He answered it anyway to distract him from his thoughts.

'Lawyer Frend,' said the voice in his ear. 'This is Matija Kiš.'

Frend moved to the window, keeping to one side of it, and used a finger to lift the drape, half expecting to see Kiš or Simo Stajić standing by the gate, but the street was empty.

'Yes?' said Frend.

'You left Belgrade very suddenly.'

'I was concerned for my well-being.'

'I don't blame you. In fact, I admire your courage for being willing to come to Belgrade in the first place. Few lawyers would choose to jeopardize their lives for their clients. In that sense, I concede, you are a credit to your profession. May I be honest with you?'

'I would welcome it,' said Frend.

'With regard to your clients, my colleague and I have encountered a difference of opinion on how to proceed. In part, it comes down to our contrasting natures. Simo is impulsive, and prone to seeking terminal solutions. He acts first and thinks after. Sometimes, I fear he does not think at all. Do you understand?'

Kiš's problem, Frend reflected, was that he had been born a decade too late. There was a time when someone so obviously mired in criminality would still have been electable in Serbia – in fact, in any number of territories that were once part of the Soviet bloc – but such was no longer the case and now he had to work through others. Nevertheless, he had a politician's tongue and was careful to avoid saying anything over the phone that might impact negatively upon him in a court of law.

'I have experienced no difficulty in following you so far,' said Frend.

'I, on the other hand, am of a more cautious disposition. So, too, are many of my acquaintances.' Kiš's political allies, no doubt, eager to contain an outbreak of implicitly state-sanctioned murders. 'It is our belief that your clients cannot return home. They are a contaminant, carriers of profound instability. Their word cannot be considered their bond, and even pecuniary evidence of their goodwill might not be sufficient to make up the shortfall in trust.'

'Then why was that option proffered?'

'To see if you – or they – would bite,' said Kiš. 'The end result would have been the same. I think you know what I mean.'

'Except that you and your friends would have been significantly wealthier.'

'Not compared with the wealth that accession to the European Union will bring. In our opinion, the benefits of removing your clients from contention would not have compensated for the hazards involved. We need no more ruined restaurants in Belgrade.'

'But your dinner companion does not hold a similar view.'

'No,' said Kiš. 'He wants the money *and* his fun. He struggles with the concept of delayed gratification.'

'Does he realize that his time is coming to an end? If, as you say, EU accession promises affluence and opportunity, blatant thuggery will be an inevitable casualty. Even the Russians have to maintain the pretense of legality.'

Ever wary, Kiš said, 'That confrontation with Simo must be saved for another day.'

'I look forward to reading details of the outcome. I hope the photographs are in color, and that he suffers no more than he deserves to.'

'I'll pass that on to the individual in question, if you like.'

'Do as you wish,' said Frend. 'He has no great love for me anyway.' He tried to sound offhand, but the tremor in his voice betrayed him. He had only narrowly avoided an inquisition at the hands of Kiš's ally. 'So where does that leave us?'

'Your clients have a week to get out of Europe. If they do not, their prospects will diminish rapidly.'

Which was an interesting way to describe a death sentence, thought Frend.

'I'll have to discuss it with them,' he said. 'Their hearts were set on a base closer to home.'

'I would have thought they'd be happy to leave. As discussed over dinner, we are not alone in finding them an aggravation.'

'I can only repeat that I will talk to them.'

'I have faith in your persuasiveness, Herr Frend, particularly since your destiny is so intimately tied up with theirs. I look forward to hearing from you.'

Kiš hung up, and Frend put down the phone. It was moist from the sweat of his palm. One week: it might be enough, if Spiridon could be talked around, but his agreement would resolve only one of their difficulties. There remained the fallout from the botched handover of the Syrians, but that issue might yet be settled with blood money. Frend was sure that the Vuksans had access to funds unknown to him, because Radovan was too clever not to have squirreled money away. A payment in cash would surely assuage the anger of the Islamists.

But if Kiš was right about friends of De Jaager seeking revenge for his death, then the killing of Aleksej Marković in Paris took on an even more troubling aspect. Whoever was responsible for Marković's assassination would not stop there, which meant that the Vuksans and all those around them remained in danger. This was a problem that could not be solved by departing Europe, or paying compensation to anonymous men in tieless shirts. It would require more direct action.

Frend looked again at the photograph of Hendricksen. It was time, he thought, to establish who exactly was hunting the Vuksans.

Chapter XLVII

Louis had taken the train from Paris to Prague, the long journey made more tolerable by the comforts of first class and the knowledge that he could hold on to one of the Rohrbaugh pistols without fear of awkward security questions. Another Rohrbaugh, the one used to kill Aleksej Marković, was already at the bottom of the Seine, and his Japanese guests had presumably disposed of the remaining pair.

Louis made no calls from the train, and slept between Paris and Frankfurt. For the remainder of the journey, he alternated between newspapers and a copy of James Fenimore Cooper's *The Last of the Mohicans*, which Angel had given to him. Louis had a vague memory of encountering the comic book adaptation when he was younger, which probably hadn't been the best response to give when Angel had asked if he'd ever read the novel. Now here he was, on a train to Prague, trying to make amends for his ignorance.

Ever since Angel's illness, Louis had been working his way through a list of the one hundred greatest works of world literature. He was doing well, he felt, just as long as he didn't go looking at too many rival lists. Surely, he thought, the finest critical minds could have reached a consensus by this stage, permitting a man reasonably to set himself the target of filling the gaps in his literary knowledge without fear that a whole new set of gaps was lurking in the bushes, waiting to be revealed. At this rate, he might never be done with reading.

It was nightfall when the train finally arrived in Prague. Louis had booked himself a room in a small hotel in Malá Strana, on one of the back streets near Kampa Island. There he showered, changed, and touched base with Angel and Hendricksen. He ate alone at U Modré Kachničky on Nebovidksá, where years earlier he had dined with Parker and Angel. Back then, he wouldn't have bet heavily on their prospects for survival, yet somehow all three of them had endured.

The world, he reflected, was full of surprises.

The following morning, Louis met the man named Most in the basement bar of the Hotel U Prince in Prague's Old Town Square. Technically, the bar didn't open until after 5 p.m., but exceptions tended to be made for Most. His nickname translated as 'bridge', since Most prided himself on making connections, often between individuals seeking something illegal and the illegal item in question. It also served to describe Most himself. As Angel had once observed, Most could have linked both banks of the Vltava by draping himself across the river. He was a massive figure: grayer now, and walking with the aid of a cane, but still imposing.

'You appreciate the venue?' he said to Louis, as he eased himself onto a leather banquette.

The bar was called Black Angel's. Louis had last come to Prague during the search for a statue – or an entity, depending on one's beliefs – called the Black Angel. Given the number of people who had ended up dead as a consequence, the choice of bar appealed more to Most's sense of humor than Louis's.

'It's certainly got atmosphere,' said Louis.

'Like a cave,' said Most. 'And it's quiet. Later, there will be many tourists. Now, only us.'

'Your English seems to have improved since last we met.'

'I took lessons. We must change with the times, and the times require good English. You want a drink?'

'It's too early for me. Just coffee.'

Most looked disappointed. To make up for Louis's abstemiousness, he ordered two cocktails for himself. They arrived quickly, along with Louis's coffee, before the bartender left them in peace.

'What happened to your leg?' said Louis.

'Arthritis. It runs in the family.' Most tasted both of his cocktails, reducing them to one cocktail between two glasses. 'I also got shot, a long time ago. That did not help.'

'It wouldn't.'

Louis added milk to his coffee, but set the sugar aside.

'I hear you got shot, too,' said Most, 'but not so long ago.'

'That's right.'

'Painful?'

'Then, or now?'

'Now, obviously. It's always painful at the time.'

'A little.'

'When men like us say "a little", we mean a lot. You ought to drink more alcohol.'

'Is it working for you?'

'Not yet, but that may mean I'm not drinking enough. I'm happy to keep trying until I find the perfect dosage. How is Angel?'

'He hurts, too.'

'A bullet?'

'Cancer.'

Most winced. 'I am very sorry.'

'They cut most of it out, poisoned the rest. Angel, I'm happy to say, is very hard to kill.'

Most raised both glasses. 'Then *dobré zdraví*,' he said, 'for what it's worth.'

Louis lifted his cup.

'Good health,' he said. 'Have you found Bilbija?'

'He was not so hard to find,' said Most, producing a photograph of Luca Bilbija from his jacket pocket and placing it on the table. 'He's been spending money, which makes a man conspicuous, although this one has been spending it in the right way and in the right places, which makes him less conspicuous.'

Louis moved the photo closer. It was definitely Bilbija.

'Where was it taken?'

'At a casino in Zbraslav, south of the city. Very private. He has rented a house nearby, courtesy of the casino owners.'

'Alone?'

'Entirely. But there is a difficulty.'

'Isn't there always?'

Most added five more pictures to the first. They showed, from various angles, what looked like a fortified blockhouse: a single-story dwelling with narrow windows, surrounded by a high wall. The wall had a vehicle door built into its southern side, leading to a smaller entrance into the main house.

'This is where he's living?' said Louis. He sounded incredulous.

'It is not, I admit, the home of a man at ease with the world,' said Most.

He tapped the topmost photo with a straw from one of his drinks.

'See here? Cameras, on the outer and inner walls. It also has lights triggered by motion sensors, and an alarm connected directly to the casino's private security system. The door into the house is reinforced steel, and the windows have security shutters of the same material. Even if the power is cut off, the house has a backup generator, and any failure automatically triggers an alert. The casino can also choose to involve the police, if required. There is, I'm informed, an understanding between them.'

Most handed Louis another photo, a trio of men in their fifties, one of whom was pointing a gun directly at the lens of the camera.

'The Novákovi,' said Most. 'They own the casino, and Bilbija's is one of five properties in the area that they keep for high rollers, the kind who prefer not to stay in hotels. They also rent them to those who may have certain security problems, including temporary difficulties with enemies or the law.'

'What about that understanding with the police you mentioned?'

'The police don't ask questions of the Novákovi, as long as there's no trouble,' said Most. 'Some of them even do security work on the side, officially and unofficially. You see here?' He indicated the northern corner of Bilbija's house. 'That's the guards' residence. Two are present at all times. They're relieved every forty-eight hours. The gate in the outer wall is opened, a car drives in, the occupants are checked by this camera on the inner wall, and only when the guards inside are satisfied that all is well do they open the door to the main house. The guards also take care of deliveries, so they bring in food, wine, women, whatever the guest requires.'

'Weapons?'

'Heckler and Koch UMPs, and Phantom pistols. But even if the guards were armed only with small stones, taking Bilbija at the house would not be an option. You might get to him, if you were lucky, but by the time you did, you would be surrounded. Fighting your way out, assuming you could, would involve killing police, and no one would be happy about that, including me.'

'But Bilbija must leave on occasion,' said Louis.

'Only to go to the casino. He eats, he gambles, maybe he takes a woman upstairs to one of the private rooms, then he returns to the house.'

'Let me guess,' said Louis. 'He doesn't travel alone.'

'He likes to drive himself – the Audi TT in the second picture is his rental – but an escort car from the casino arrives to bring him in, joined by a police vehicle. One car in front, one behind, and Bilbija in the middle.'

'And the casino?'

'No guns are permitted on the premises, or not for guests. There are metal detectors and hand scanners. The cars are parked securely underground, so it would be hard to get at Bilbija's Audi. As with the house, killing him at the casino would be difficult, but not impossible. Getting away with it is the challenging part. I suppose it is a question of how badly you want him dead.'

'Very badly.'

'Ultimately, he will make a mistake. It's just a matter of time and patience.'

'I don't have much of either.'

'You could contract it out.'

Louis stared at Most.

'Or maybe not,' said Most.

'Show me the route from the house to the casino,' said Louis, and was pleased to see Most unfold a map of the area instead of using Google Earth on his phone. Most, like Louis, did not like leaving an electronic trail.

'Here is the property,' said Most, once again using the straw as a pointer, 'and this is the casino. The distance between them is three point two kilometers, all of it on private roads through Novákovi land.'

'So that's where he's most vulnerable.'

'No,' Most corrected Louis, 'he is *not* vulnerable there. We would have to get onto the land unnoticed, which means evading cameras and sensors, then find an ambush point and an escape route after. We are also talking about four armed men, including at least two police, as well as Bilbija himself. Once again, I remind you that we are not in the business of engaging the police in gun battles.'

'I wasn't thinking of a firefight.'

'Maybe an RPG? I can get you a grenade launcher, no problem. It will open the Audi like a tin can and blow Bilbija to pieces. But we'll still be on foot, pursued by armed men, with more rushing to join them. We won't get out alive.'

'I wasn't considering RPGs either,' said Louis.

'What, then?' said Most. 'You will ask God to help you obliterate Bilbija from above?'

Louis returned the photographs to Most for disposal.

'Yes,' he said. 'That's exactly what I'm going to do.'

Chapter XLVIII

Frend contacted the Vuksans using a fresh SIM card. He kept a stock of them in his safe for emergencies, and it had already been decided with Radovan Vuksan that neither of them would use the same number to remain in contact for more than a couple of days. Frend had made sure to send, by encrypted email, a list of the numbers at his disposal so that his calls would be identifiable, and Radovan had done the same.

Frend had packed a bag in preparation for the move to the apartment above his office. He kept some changes of clothing there – shirts and underwear, for the most part, along with a spare suit and basic toiletries – but not sufficient for his current needs. He would not be happy to return home until the problem of the Vuksans was resolved, but it seemed increasingly unlikely that the solution on offer would satisfy either of the brothers.

'Well?' said Radovan, when he answered Frend's call.

'You can't go home,' said Frend. 'And they have given us an ultimatum: You have one week to leave Europe, or face the consequences.'

Radovan was silent for a time.

'Spiridon will not go,' he replied at last.

'Then, with respect,' said Frend, 'Spiridon will die.'

One hour later, Zivco Ilić was waiting for Frend at Café-Restaurant Corbaci in the Museumplatz. Corbaci's modest exterior belied what lay within, including a beautiful vaulted ceiling of oriental tiles. Ilić looked out of place among the mix of tourists and Viennese, but it was hard to think of anywhere Ilić would not have looked out of place, apart from under a rock. Frend had never warmed to the man, but thankfully his exposure to him had always been limited.

Curiously, Ilić did not appear to be alone. A teenage girl was sitting opposite him drinking a hot chocolate, her face mostly hidden by a black hooded sweatshirt bearing the name of some band of which Frend had never heard but that he knew he would have hated from the first note. No young girl had any business being around a man like Zivco Ilić, thought Frend, not unless her business *was* being around men like him. She did not look up as Frend approached the table and took the chair to Ilić's right.

'I wasn't expecting us to have company,' said Frend. 'Who is the young lady?'

Only now did the girl peer out at him from under her hood, and Frend felt a great urge to get up and walk away, to abandon the Vuksans and his own existence in order to hide away from creatures such as this. Here was no teenager, only a mockery of one. Her eyes were rheumy and old, the teeth discolored, and her skin was covered in very fine lines, like a piece of fruit in the process of decay. Her fingernails were unpainted and tapered to points, reminding him uncomfortably of Simo Stajić's. Frend experienced a profound sense of absence: a dearth of feeling, of morality, even of good or evil, as though her antiquity and her otherness made a mockery of those concepts. One might as well have expected to encounter such higher functions in a spider or a scorpion, entities barely altered since prehistory.

'This is Zorya,' said Ilić.

Here, then, was Spiridon Vuksan's witch. Frend had paid little attention to Radovan's references to her, dismissing her as one of Spiridon's indulgences, another indication of his innate primitiveness. Now, exposed to her presence at last, Frend accepted that he had been wrong. Spiridon Vuksan might have been a superstitious peasant by birth, but for this credulity he deserved to be excused. Zorya was *unheimlich*. A century earlier, Freud himself would have come running from his rooms on Berggasse just to set eyes on her.

'Were you careful?' said Ilić.

'I believe so,' said Frend. 'But then, I advised against this meeting to begin with. A drop could have been arranged.'

'Spiridon wanted it this way. I just follow orders.'

Spiridon, not Radovan. Frend thought this was interesting, but also worrying.

'Did he say why?' asked Frend.

'I didn't ask. That's why they call it an order.'

A waiter arrived, and Zorya hid her face once again. Frend asked for a tea that he didn't want and placed a folded copy of *Der Standard* on the table. Inside was a picture of Hendricksen and an envelope of €100, €200, and €500 notes: €10,000 in total. By prior arrangement, Ilić would take the newspaper and photograph with him when he left.

Frend was conscious of Zorya appraising him, but he tried not to look at her. She smelled of a combination of dryness and dampness, like an ancient cavern through which water had once flowed.

The waiter returned with the tea. Ilić watched the sightseers go by in the courtyard, following the prettiest of the girls, molesting them with his eyes. Frend reflected that the hour of Ilić's death could not come soon enough.

'You say this Hendricksen is ex-military?' said Ilić, his gaze still fixed on young flesh.

'He served in the Balkans,' said Frend. 'His battalion was at Srebrenica.'

'Is he trying to atone?'

'Who knows?'

'We'll have to find out. Zorya will ask him.'

'What about Spiridon?' says Frend. 'Has there been any change in his position regarding Belgrade?'

Ilić shrugged. 'Radovan is trying to reason with him, but Spiridon does not believe in running away.'

Frend pinched the bridge of his nose and closed his eyes. He was largely immune to headaches, except in extreme circumstances, but he could feel the pain of one coming on now.

'And you,' said Frend, for want of a better question, 'what do you believe in?'

'Money. Pussy. What else is there?'

'God?' Frend suggested. He was half-joking. Even after all this time, he struggled to balance these men's devotion to Serbian Orthodoxy with their relish for sadism and murder. But Ilić appeared to be giving the question his serious consideration.

'Zorya says there is an existence beyond this one,' conceded Ilić, 'and she does not lie. But even if she's right, I won't see God when I die, or not for long. You won't either, so you shouldn't concern yourself with the mechanics of His existence.'

Frend felt a pressure on his right hand: the nail of Zorya's index finger was tracing a pattern over the veins, writing a word. Three letters: P-I-A.

Pia.

'That's your daughter's name, isn't it?' said Zorya. Her voice was too deep, too cracked.

'Yes,' said Frend. 'Did you learn that from Spiridon?'

'Spiridon has never mentioned her, and neither has Radovan. Would you like me to share more with you about her?'

'No.'

She ignored him.

'I can tell you that you're never going to see her again.'

'I don't think I want to have this conversation,' said Frend.

One of Zorya's fingernails scratched the back of his hand. He quickly withdrew it from her reach. Ilić sniggered.

'She has all kinds of parlor tricks,' said Ilić. 'I wouldn't let her bother you, though.'

Zorya hissed at Ilić. It was a peculiarly adolescent action, although it struck Frend as being almost entirely without malice. Zorya gave the impression of liking Ilić, or not actively disliking him. In Frend's opinion, it didn't say much for either of them.

'They tracked down Fouad,' said Ilić.

It took Frend a moment to recall the name: Fouad, the missing man from Paris, the one Radovan suspected of betraying the two Syrians to the French. Frend had long known of the Vuksans' activities in the area of people smuggling, particularly the movement of high-value individuals, but as with most of their affairs, he had managed to keep his distance from the particulars.

Unfortunately, he no longer had that luxury. Had the Vuksans consulted him on the matter, he would have advised against consorting with suspected terrorists. It was depressing, he thought, that he might even have been required to offer such counsel.

'Who found him?' said Frend.

'The Turks, we believe,' said Ilić. 'They tortured him to death in a basement in Marseille.'

'And how did Radovan react to this?'

'He has made contact with the Turks through an intermediary. It seems Fouad claimed to be working alone with an American handler, and exonerated Spiridon and Radovan of any involvement in the failure of the operation.'

An American intelligence handler: that was curious, thought Frend. Had the Americans then fed the Syrians to French intelligence? It was unlike them to give up a prize so easily, but a new order prevailed in Washington. Islamist plots were of less interest than the maneuverings of the Chinese and the mischief of the Russians.

'That vindication is good news,' said Frend.

'Not good enough to absolve us of responsibility for trusting Fouad to begin with,' said Ilić. 'The Turks still want their blood money.'

'Then you may have to pay it.'

Ilić looked at Frend as though he were a fool.

'Paying won't make any difference,' he said. 'By now, the Turks must be aware that we're running out of friends. They wouldn't have dared target Fouad otherwise. If we pay them the money, they'll still kill us as an example. If we don't pay them, they'll kill us for not paying *and* as an example. Therefore, we don't pay.'

'But they won't stop looking for you,' said Frend.

And what about me? he thought. *What do I tell them if, or when, they come for me?*

'We're working on it.' Ilić patted Zorya on the shoulder. She stood, pulling the hood closer to her face with its drawstrings.

'Tell Radovan I'll be in touch again tomorrow evening,' said Frend.

Ilić nodded, and guided Zorya toward the door.
'Let's go talk to a Dutchman,' he said to her.
But Zorya did not move.
'Wait,' she said.

III

My yesterdays walk with me. They keep step, they are gray faces that peer over my shoulder.

William Golding, *Free Fall*

Chapter XLIX

Gavrilo Dražeta arrived back at his farmhouse with bread, fruit, fresh sausage, and a bottle of Sekt for him and his wife to share, as their wedding anniversary would fall over the coming days. Some of their neighbors might even join them in a toast – *István und Willa, Zum Wohl!* – although István technically did not exist, and his marriage, however happy, was therefore a lie. But the fiction had now become the reality, for he thought of himself more as István Adami than Gavrilo Dražeta, and the latter's crimes – if crimes they ever really were, which he disputed – now sometimes seemed like the actions of another man, or the dreams of an alternative reality. Had István Adami been rigged up to a lie detector and confronted with a litany of his alter ego's offenses, he might well have evinced a confusion that was compelling even to himself, and passed the test without difficulty.

Anyway, few in Kassel wished to speak of conflicts, whether recent or more distant. Allied bombers had destroyed most of the city by 1943; whatever was spared was renovated in the aftermath, while the rest was later reconstructed from the rubble. As a consequence, the people of Kassel had an ambivalent attitude toward the trials of war. And who deserved to be judged for their failings only in the eyes of others? If that were the entire measure of the law, no one would be declared innocent. A man was more than the sum of his imperfections. This is what Gavrilo Dražeta might have told the UN investigators had they succeeded in dragging him before one of their tribunals, but Gavrilo Dražeta was no more. Now there was only István Adami, a man who loved his wife, cared for his cattle, extended a helping hand to his neighbors, and volunteered with local groups that supported the elderly and the poor. István Adami lived a blameless life, even if he cast the shadow of another man.

But since the visit of the Vuksans, this specter of Gavrilo Dražeta had assumed renewed substance. He could not have turned his back on his old comrades in their time of need, but he dearly wished they had not darkened his door. Every contact left a trail, and a trail could be followed. Following the Vuksans' departure, he had begun carrying his little Walther pistol in his pocket, because one never knew who might come calling.

Now he entered the house through the kitchen, his arms heavy with shopping, and called his wife's name. He placed the bags on the table and stretched his shoulders. He had already been up for many hours, and his day was only half-done, but he had a mind to take a nap before he tended to the cows again.

The first blow to the back of his head sent him to his knees.

The second sent him to oblivion.

Chapter L

Hendricksen had received an email from Angel notifying him of his imminent arrival in Vienna and confirming that Pia Lackner's removal from London had gone as planned. In return, Hendricksen had shared with Angel and Louis the pictures taken in Belgrade, along with the identification of the principals made by Hendricksen's driver. Even without access to what had been said in the restaurant, they surmised that Frend had been attempting to negotiate the terms of the Vuksans' return to Serbia. From their access to his credit card transactions, they were also aware that Frend had elected to re-enter Austria from Romania, despite having a return ticket on the Belgrade-Vienna route. Either Frend had encountered sudden pressing business in Timisoara, which seemed unlikely, or the negotiations with Kiš and Stajić had not gone well, which meant the Vuksans still had no safe haven in Serbia, and so remained exposed.

Now Hendricksen watched from the Architekturzentrum as Frend emerged from the Corbaci café and began walking toward the U-Bahn station. Frend had taken two taxis to Corbaci, ditching one halfway to walk for a time, probably in a vague effort to shake off any surveillance, but Hendricksen was too experienced to lose a quarry to such a simple ruse.

Frend had brought with him a briefcase and an overnight bag. Hendricksen was concerned that the lawyer might be about to take another flight, but his credit cards showed no reservation. Despite Corbaci's large windows, Hendricksen had not been able to get a good look at Frend's dining companions because of where they were sitting, and had not wanted to risk being seen inside by the lawyer. He knew only that Frend had been at a table with two people, one of whom appeared to be a young girl. As far as

227

Hendricksen was aware, the Vuksans were not in the habit of keeping company with teenagers – or if they were, it was not for any moral purpose. Hendricksen had managed to take a couple of pictures with his phone, but the distance was too great and the faces remained unclear.

Had Angel or Louis been present, they could have split surveillance duties with Hendricksen. As things stood, he could either stay with Frend or follow the man and the girl. So far, only Frend had come out, and Hendricksen was at risk of losing him if he waited much longer. He chanced a quick glance into Corbaci, but could see no sign of Frend's companions. He decided to stay with the lawyer.

Later, as he was dying, he would conclude that this had been an error of judgment.

Zorya and Ilić emerged together from the restroom. They attracted one or two curious looks, but no one said anything, this being Vienna.

'It's safe now,' said Zorya. 'The feeling is gone.'

'Do you have any idea what caused it?'

'Danger, but perhaps we should leave Hendricksen for a little while.'

Which had been enough to make Zivco Ilić concur. Unlike Radovan, he was no skeptic when it came to Zorya. His people were from Negotin in eastern Serbia, and he'd grown up with the Vlachs. His family had turned to them in times of need: when a job had to be secured, a proposal of marriage accepted, a run of bad luck ended. He remembered his mother's funeral, and the old women forming a watchful phalanx around the open coffin, because it was not unknown for the unscrupulous to place beneath the corpse a small possession belonging to an enemy – a key, a button – in order to hex them. The item would be buried with the dead, and shortly afterwards the target of the curse would die in turn.

Many would have laughed at these superstitions, but Ilić knew better. Zorya might have discouraged any investigation of her origins, but her nature had something in common with that of the Vlach witches, which was enough for Zivco Ilić. He looked after the girl, and hoped the girl might look after him in turn. So far, the arrangement appeared to be working.

'Well?' said Ilić.

'The lawyer is hiding something.'

'Treachery?'

'No,' said Zorya, 'it wasn't that strong, and it's not recent. It goes back years. But he's frightened, and his commitment is wavering.'

'Is that what you'll tell Spiridon?'

'I'll tell Spiridon what he needs to hear.'

'And if he asks me?' said Ilić.

'You'll inform him that I shared nothing with you.'

They walked on.

'What you said to Frend, about his daughter—' Ilić began.

'Yes?'

'Was it true?'

'Have you ever known me to lie?'

'No, I have not.'

They walked through the Museumplatz, but drew no attention. Zorya would have sensed it.

'What about me?' said Ilić.

'What about you?'

'I, too, have a daughter. Will I ever see her again?'

Katarina was eight. Ilić and her mother had not stayed together for very long, but he still sent money regularly, and spent time with the child when he could. He thought he perceived a little of himself in her dark looks, but no one else had ever agreed. Perhaps that was best, for the girl's sake. Zivco Ilić had never contemplated modeling as a career option.

Zorya stopped.

'Do you really want me to tell you?' she said.

'I think so.'

She reached out and took his right hand in her left. She closed her eyes and squeezed. Her grip was very firm and very cold. After a time, he felt it ease, and her eyes opened again.

'No,' she said, 'you will not.'

229

Ilić nodded once. 'I guessed,' he said. 'You're not the only one who experiences intimations of bad luck.'

'I'm sorry, Zivco. I wish it were otherwise.'

She released his hand. He glanced down at the imprint of her fingers and thumb upon his skin. He waited for the marks to fade, but they stayed, like burns.

'I've never asked you this before,' he said, 'but can you see, you know, the moment?'

'Of a man's death?'

'Yes.'

'No, I cannot.'

'Then how can you be sure?'

'I see shadows, clouds. They draw nearer and nearer, until finally the person is swallowed by them.'

'And these shadows, can they be dispelled?'

'Sometimes,' said Zorya. 'I've watched sick people get better, and then the shadows retreat, but they're always present. They never go away, not entirely. The shadows are with us when we come into the world and they are with us when we leave.'

'And mine?'

'Yours are very close now, and very black.'

'What about Spiridon and Radovan?'

'I can't tell you that, but you were never going to live to be old, Zivco.'

'Not like you.'

'No, not like me.'

'May I ask one more question?' said Zivco.

'Of course.'

'Do you ever see your own shadows?'

'Lately I have begun to glimpse their approach,' said Zorya, 'but they are not just shadows. A figure walks among them.'

'What is it?'

Zorya shivered.

'It's a girl.'

Chapter LI

G avrilo Dražeta's head hurt, and he had vomited on himself. He was slumped in his favorite armchair, his hands secured behind his back. He had a vague memory of being dragged across the floor of his home and into the living room, but it was more a recollection of movement than actual images. His wife was sitting on the couch opposite, her hands also tied. Behind her stood a huge man with a heavily scarred forehead. In his right hand, he held a long knife. His left rested almost possessively on the head of Dražeta's wife.

A second man entered from the kitchen. He was carrying a glass of water, which he now placed to Dražeta's lips.

'Here,' he said, 'drink. It will make you feel better.'

Dražeta drank, because he really did feel very bad. He thought he might be sick again, but he managed to keep the water down. He'd taken blows to the head in the past and hadn't enjoyed the experience. He knew it would take him days to recover from this latest concussion, assuming he was allowed to live.

The glass was placed on a side table and the second man returned to view. He was smaller than his companion, with sallow skin and a neatly trimmed beard. He wore a dark suit and a crisp white shirt without a tie. He moved an upright chair so that it faced Dražeta without obscuring his view of his wife, and sat down.

'Gavrilo Dražeta,' he said, 'killer of Muslims, Croats, and Kosovar Albanians, among others. You're a wanted man.'

Dražeta did not answer. There was no point in either confirming or denying it.

'Does your wife know about the blood on your hands? Should I share with her the details? But then, who has that kind of time?

There is, after all, so much blood, and we don't have very long. She will, I think, have to take it on trust.'

'Who are you?' said Dražeta.

'My name is Mr Rafi. I'm here to ask you some questions. I expect you to answer them honestly, because I'll know if you're lying. The first time you lie, my colleague will cut off one of your wife's ears. The second time, he'll cut off her other ear, then her nose, and finally, he'll progress to her eyes. But frankly, I don't imagine we'll be forced to resort to that level of savagery, not unless you really hate your wife. Do you hate your wife, Gavrilo?'

'No.'

'Not even a little? Because most men do.'

'No.'

'Good,' said Mr Rafi. 'So, tell me: Where are the Vuksans?'

The scarred man washed the blade clean in the sink, overseen by Mr Rafi. Gavrilo Dražeta was dead, but his wife remained alive. She had watched her husband's throat being cut before she passed out, and was now lying bound and gagged in the basement of the house. Someone would find her, eventually. Perhaps, Mr Rafi thought, it might have been wiser to kill her, but he was a devout man. Did the Holy Quran not state that 'he who slays a soul, unless it be in punishment for murder or for spreading mischief on earth, shall be as if he had slain all mankind'? The killing of Gavrilo Dražeta was justified on both counts, but his wife was blameless – or her fault was not so grave as to merit death. Mr Rafi knew that others might have questioned his reasoning, but they were not present. He was scrupulous in his sadism, which he found enhanced the pleasure, and the Prophet's true enemies were virtually numberless.

He checked his watch. It was time to leave. Two seats had already been booked on the evening flight from Frankfurt to Vienna, and he hoped to have the current unfortunate state of affairs resolved within days. It was he who had been entrusted with the responsibility of getting the two Syrians safely to Europe, and his failure to do so had left him in disfavor. The Vuksans would have to pay so that he would not.

He listened for a moment before departing the house. Dražeta's wife was quiet, and the scarred man had locked the basement door. In time someone would free her to mourn her husband. For now, she could contemplate the nature of the defects and iniquities that had cost him his life.

The scarred man dried the knife and followed Mr Rafi across the yard to the car.

In the basement of the farmhouse, Willa lay still and silent. Her eyes were closed but her throat was open, and her blood soaked the dirt floor.

In her final moments, the scarred man had been almost gentle with her.

Chapter LII

That night, Luca Bilbija gambled as usual at the casino in Zbraslav. His Audi TT arrived as the middle vehicle in a convoy of three, with a black Land Cruiser leading the way and a police car bringing up the rear. The casino, housed in a small nineteenth-century villa, was surrounded by a low wall with two entrances: the main one, with a security barrier and a guardhouse, and a second access point at the rear, which was gated and used only by staff and delivery drivers.

Bilbija had not come alone. A younger man rode alongside him in the front of the car, and joined him at the blackjack table and the roulette wheel. According to Most's source – a waitress and occasional escort who worked at the casino – the second man had arrived at the rented house sometime the previous evening, and he and Bilbija had later eaten at the casino's restaurant. Bilbija had introduced his companion to acquaintances as his younger brother, Mirko. The two men subsequently spent four hours moving between blackjack and the wheel, losing about €4,000 in total, the euro being the casino's currency of choice. Although women were available, the Bilbijas instead withdrew to one of the lounges, where they kept their own company. Most's waitress said that Luca Bilbija, who had a naturally melancholic disposition, seemed even more subdued than usual. After a couple of brandies, the men were escorted back to the safe house.

The night of travel to and from the casino had been observed by Louis and Most with the aid of a heavily adapted DJI Phantom 3 Pro drone fitted with a lightweight thermal imaging camera. The Phantom wasn't entirely silent – no commercial drone was – but the fact that its battery, motor, and wires were concealed in the body made it quieter than similar models, and the propellers were securely wound, reducing their noise level. The Phantom was software-limited to a height of five hundred meters, but Most had bypassed the restriction, meaning that there was little chance of the drone being heard from the ground. Also, the casino did not monitor its airspace, although Most had heard that the introduction of an advanced drone detection system was imminent. Privacy mattered to the Novákovi and their clients.

'There they go,' said Most, as his iPad screen showed the greenish image of the Audi disappearing behind the walls of the safe house. 'You think Luca's brother is in the same line of work?'

Most's car was parked behind a ruined factory four kilometers from the casino, but still within the range of the drone. Louis had resigned himself to metric measurements for Most's sake. Confusion over distance was, he thought, best avoided, given what they planned to do.

'Luca Bilbija doesn't have a brother,' said Louis.

'Huh,' said Most. 'Boyfriend, maybe? I know he sleeps with girls, but I am not one to judge.'

'More likely someone he trusts from home,' said Louis. 'He's cooped up in that house, killing time until the Vuksans give him the all clear. He's bored, but he's also scared. He wants companionship, and an extra gun for reassurance.'

Louis began guiding the drone back to the car. He and Most had spent the afternoon practicing with the equipment until Louis was happy that he could handle it without difficulty.

'You think he cleared Mirko's arrival with the Vuksans?' said Most.

'I doubt it. They probably don't even know he's frequenting the same casino every night, and renting accommodations on-site. If the Vuksans find out, they'll make him stop. Sloppiness may cost them their lives.'

'He believes himself to be safe,' said Most. 'The Novákovi have a reputation to protect, and it would be lamentable if a guest were to die violently on their most upscale property.'

'Has that ever happened?' said Louis.

'Not to my knowledge.'

'Well, there's a first time for everything.'

Most grunted.

'Are you worried?' said Louis.

'I'll only start worrying if we get caught,' said Most, 'and I would strongly advise against that. The Novákovi use the woodland as their personal cemetery. If we're lucky, we'll be dead before they put us in the ground, but lucky men wouldn't get caught to begin with.'

The drone came into sight, and Louis brought it down to earth. It landed heavily, and Most flinched.

'Please tell me you'll be gentler tomorrow,' he said.

'If it's any consolation,' said Louis, 'neither of us will know a great deal about it if I'm not.'

'That,' said Most, 'is no consolation at all.'

Chapter LIII

Zorya and Zivco Ilić sat with the Vuksans, the drapes closed against the dark. On the table before them was a picture of the Dutchman, Hendricksen.

'Could he be one of those who killed Aleksej in Paris?' said Spiridon.

'No,' said Ilić. 'I checked his hotel reservation. He was in Vienna when Aleksej died, but he may be working for the same people.'

'Then why is he still breathing?'

'The timing wasn't right,' said Zorya.

'We didn't know enough about him to act without caution,' Ilić added, exchanging a look with Zorya. Under the present circumstances, it didn't seem wise to tell the Vuksans that they had decided not to target Hendricksen because Zorya had experienced a premonition of danger.

Ilić noticed that Radovan appeared distracted.

'Is there something we should know?' said Ilić.

'Gavrilo Dražeta and his wife are dead,' said Radovan.

'How?'

'Their throats were cut.'

'By whom?'

'Does it matter?' said Radovan. 'It probably didn't even matter to them. A cut throat is a cut throat. But if I had to guess, I'd say it was the Turks.'

'What could Gavrilo have told them about us?' said Ilić. 'He didn't know where we were going, did he?'

Radovan was quiet for a time. When he finally opened his mouth, he did so only to lie.

'No,' said Radovan, 'Gavrilo didn't know anything.'

*

Zorya and Ilić departed, leaving the brothers alone.

'Why didn't you tell him the truth about Gavrilo?' said Spiridon.

'Because the odds are already against us, and Zivco has an instinct for self-preservation that may outweigh even his loyalty to you. If he feels we're without hope, he could decide to cut his losses and run, and we need him. Also, if he's located by our enemies, what he knows could endanger us. We have to keep him close.'

'You shouldn't have shared anything with Gavrilo,' said Spiridon. 'It was a mistake.'

'How could I have anticipated what would happen in Paris?' said Radovan. 'As far as we were concerned, our only worry was Belgrade, and it wouldn't have dared permit action against Gavrilo, not even if it meant laying hands on us. Gavrilo had too many old friends back home, all of them with long memories.'

Spiridon's eyes went vacant for a moment. Radovan thought he might be remembering a time when he had more friends, at home and elsewhere.

'How do you want to proceed?' said Spiridon.

'Zorya and Zivco will speak with the Dutchman, and then we'll know more.'

'And Frend?' said Spiridon. Zorya had told him that she believed the lawyer to be wavering.

'He's looking for a way out,' said Radovan, 'for all of us.'

In the apartment above his office, Frend listened for a moment more before hanging up the phone. He poured himself a drink. His hands were shaking. Eight of the Vuksans' accounts had been emptied entirely, and the funds transferred to accounts in Belgrade. Five more had been frozen on the orders of Interpol's Financial Crimes Unit. Four minor accounts remained undiscovered, and Frend had taken steps to close them and move the money, but the action was too little, too late.

The Vuksans had just been pauperized.

Chapter LIV

Angel was less comfortable than Louis in foreign climes. Before the two men formed their personal and professional partnership, Angel had regarded even certain parts of New Jersey as dangerously exotic, and anywhere without sidewalks as essentially barbarous. Now here he was, traversing the continent of Europe, arranging an approximation of a kidnapping in one country and aiding the planning of multiple assassinations in others, all without the benefit of any communication skills beyond American English, a little Spanish, and a few words of Greek learned from a restaurant owner on West Seventy-fourth Street, most of them grievously insulting.

While he still remained uneasy far from home, and had yet to encounter anywhere preferable to the Upper West Side, he had to admit that Vienna looked exactly the way one might have expected Old Europe to look, and therefore was not a disappointment. Also, as with the Netherlands, everyone appeared to speak better English than he, which didn't seem fair. Frankly, Angel blamed the American education system, even allowing for his own limited participation in it.

Hendricksen was not in his room when Angel arrived at the hotel, and neither was he answering his phone. Angel was not unduly worried; although he trusted Hendricksen, he was not yet familiar with the man's routines, and was aware that tracking Frend had already necessitated one unanticipated side trip to Belgrade. He had to trust that, wherever he was, Hendricksen knew what he was doing.

Angel freshened up before eating dinner alone at Ilona Stüberl on Bräunerstrasse, which had been recommended to him by the hotel concierge. It was a small Hungarian restaurant with a white, wood-beamed ceiling, and china plates on the walls, resembling less a big city establishment than a village inn. The waitress fussed over him, delivering a helping of goulash and pasta that could have fed a small family, and chided him gently for not finishing it. He wanted to tell her that it was the largest portion of food he'd tackled since his diagnosis, but decided this was more information than she required. He wondered how Louis was faring, but did not contact him. Where Louis was concerned, no news tended to be good news. If there was an issue, Angel would find out about it in due course.

The waitress brought coffee, which he drank while reading Graham Greene's novelization of *The Third Man*, because he'd seen it in the window of a bookstore near the hotel and decided that if he was going to read one book set in Vienna, *The Third Man* might as well be it. Since it was really a novella, it was also short. As Angel grew older, long books became less appealing to him. He was increasingly conscious of his own mortality, an inevitable consequence of surviving cancer, and was therefore aware that, sooner rather than later, he would start a book he would not live to finish. There was, he had decided, little point in trying to get to grips with Proust's *In Search of Lost Time* at this late stage of his life, but if he were suddenly to be taken ill with *The Third Man* in his hand, he could probably manage to finish it in the ambulance.

His cell phone beeped. He checked the message, expecting to see something from Hendricksen, but the text had come from Louis. It read simply: *LB located and marked.*

So, Luca Bilbija had not only been found but was also in Louis's sights. All things going well, Bilbija would soon be dead. The effect on the Vuksans, Angel knew, would be similar to throwing a flaming torch into an ants' nest. The Vuksans would now be aware beyond any doubt that they and their people were being targeted. Their choice would be to remain wherever they were hiding or seek new ground. Angel figured they'd stay where they were; to break cover would mean revealing themselves.

Louis was convinced that the Vuksans were, if not in Vienna, then in the vicinity of the city, because they would want to be close to Frend. If the Vuksans trusted the lawyer as much as Harris and his fellow spooks seemed to believe, then he had access to funds, documents, even passports. Now that the Vuksans were the subject of an Interpol Red Notice – a communication from Ross had informed Louis of this latest development – it meant that receiving electronic transfers of large sums of cash would become difficult for them, especially since their known accounts were being monitored. Whatever they required would have to be sourced and delivered the old-fashioned way, which meant that, at some point, Frend would have to meet the Vuksans face-to-face, or work through someone who was only one step removed from them. Hendricksen might already have made progress on that front.

Angel threw back the last of his coffee and paid the check in cash. He took a detour past the tiny Loos American Bar on the Kärntner Passage but the music was too loud for him and the patrons had spilled out onto the street. Instead he returned to the hotel and tried Hendricksen's room and cell phone. Once again, he received no reply.

Only then did he begin to worry.

Chapter LV

Louis and Most were sitting in an old BMW X3 amid the ruins of the roofless factory, waiting patiently to take a man's life.

It was a cold, clear night. Most was keeping the car warm in order to prevent condensation from limiting their visibility. The factory stood almost within sight of the eastern boundary of the Novákovi territory, which was as close as Most was willing to get, and closer than he would have preferred. He had parked so that the road behind them could be seen in both directions through the glassless windows of the building. A low wall cut off the property from the road, with a gap on either side wide enough to admit a truck. Most had laid a spike strip at each entrance, which would puncture the tires of any vehicle that tried to approach. Ahead of them, a dirt track cut through waste ground, ending in a small patch of woodland. If everything went awry, and their location was discovered, the spike strips would buy them enough time to make for the woods, ditch the car, and continue south on the powerful motorcycle that Most had concealed under a tarpaulin among the trees. Louis hoped it wouldn't come to that. He disliked being a passenger at the best of times, but he particularly wished to avoid riding pillion on a motorcycle. Not many things made Louis nervous, but motorcycles were one of them, especially when they were under the control of a man who walked with a cane and admitted to not always being able to feel his right foot.

Louis checked his watch. According to Most's source, Luca Bilbija typically spent between two and four hours at the casino each night. Given that Bilbija now had a visitor from home, Louis guessed that tonight it was likely to be closer to four – more, should Bilbija and his companion decide to seek some female entertainment. If they did, it was doubtful that they would bring the women back to the house. A man who was spending money on a police escort, and living in a secure compound, would be reluctant to imperil himself by admitting strangers to his accommodations, even girls screened by the Novákovi.

Or so Louis hoped. If Bilbija did decide to take girls home, the hit would have to be postponed. Louis and Most were not prepared to kill innocents. Mirko, the man who claimed to be Bilbija's brother, was less of a concern; he should have chosen his acquaintances more judiciously. Whatever happened, Most's contact would let them know just as soon as Bilbija was ready to leave the casino. He would then have to wait for his car to be brought to the main door, and for the two escort cars to arrive. Even so, the window of opportunity would be very small.

To pass the time, Most and Louis listened to some Czech jazz – solo piano music by a young pianist named Beata Hlavenková – followed by the BBC World Service. After two hours, the two men got out, opened the trunk, and removed the primary drone, a DJI S1000, bigger and heavier than the Phantom. The Phantom had a spec weight of about two and a half pounds, or just over a kilo, which meant that it couldn't easily fly with a camera, a load of high explosive, and a detonator. The DJI could, but it was noisier than the Phantom, so they had chosen the Phantom for the initial surveillance and the DJI for the drop. With its eight arms, the DJI resembled a black-and-red spider. Most carried it to the edge of the lot, as far from the factory as possible. Then, while he watched nervously, Louis packed two pounds of C4 behind the drone's camera before adding the detonator.

'Have you done something like this before?' asked Most.

'You mean blow stuff up? What do you think?'

'I meant with a drone.'

'No. I'm a novice in that way.'

Most didn't look any happier to hear this, and he already looked very unhappy indeed.

'You should let me do it.'

'I'm not going to put Luca Bilbija's death on your conscience,' said Louis.

'Who said anything about a conscience? I just don't want you to drop that thing on my car.'

Louis wasn't worried about blowing them up so much as hitting an overhead wire or an unanticipated tree. Well, perhaps he was slightly worried about blowing them up, but he decided not to share this with Most. The DJI had a flight time of fifteen minutes, but they couldn't risk bringing it close to the casino until Bilbija was on his way back to the house. That way, the engine noise from the convoy would cover the sound of the drone.

They returned to the vehicle and resumed their vigil, this time in silence. When Most's phone pinged, it surprised them both.

'They're on the move,' said Most, as he read the message. 'They've asked for the Audi to be brought up, and there's a police chaperone on the way. Five minutes, but no more than that.'

Louis started the propellers and they watched the drone rise. Both men held their breaths. Two pounds of C4 was a significant quantity of explosive, and the detonator was primed to go off as soon as it hit a hard surface. If the drone cut out, the explosion would leave a hell of a crater.

'Shit,' said Most, as the phone pinged again.

'What is it?'

'A problem. Some kind of disagreement at the door.'

'Bilbija?'

'Unclear.'

Most kept his eyes on the phone. Louis held the drone hovering five feet in the air. Now that it was started and airborne, he was reluctant to bring it down again. It was one thing getting the machine off the ground, but another to land it softly, especially with a mass of C4 attached.

'A fight,' said Most. 'Bilbija and Mirko have both drunk a lot. One of the bouncers has taken a punch.' He paused, as another text message came in. 'She can't see everything that's happening, but she thinks – wait, the escort cars have arrived, and the Audi is leaving.'

Louis sent the drone higher, taking it well above the trees

scattered around the perimeter of the lot before turning it toward the casino. The screen on the controller displayed the view from the DJI's high-definition infrared camera, the terrain clearly visible below.

'They're heading for the gate,' said Most. 'Thirty seconds.'

Louis had the drone flying fast now. His eyes didn't deviate from the screen. The road appeared and he directed the drone to follow it. Ahead lay the entrance to the smaller track leading to the house. The track was lined with evergreens, which would make it almost impossible for Louis to target Bilbija's car. If he was going to make the strike, it would have to be on the main road. He also wanted to come at the Audi from the front, in the hope of hitting the windshield or the hood, or even allowing the drone to be dragged under the vehicle. Wherever the drone struck, the Audi's forward momentum would work in their favor.

'They've left,' said Most, before he swore for a second time.

'Tell me,' said Louis.

'There's only one person in the car.'

'Who is it?'

'She doesn't know. She's trying to find out.'

'Tell her to try harder.'

The drone reached the intersection between the main road and the secondary trail. Louis turned it to face south along the road, and held it in place as the drone's available flight time ticked down. Ten minutes. Nine-fifty-nine, nine-fifty-eight, nine-fifty-seven . . .

'One of them has a broken nose,' said Most, reading from the screen. 'The other was told to go home because he was making the situation worse.'

'I don't care about injuries,' said Louis. 'I only want to know which of them is in the car.'

Most's thumbs tapped out a reply. He was still typing when the drone's camera registered the headlights of the lead car.

'I have them,' said Louis.

'She's still working on it!'

The drone continued in the direction of the small convoy, descending as it went. Using the drone's precision altimeter Louis would have to fly only a meter or so above the first car in order to hit the second. The more distance there was between the two vehicles, the easier it would be. At the moment, he judged them to be about twenty meters apart. He didn't want them to get any closer.

'Most,' he said calmly, 'I need to know now.'

They would only have one chance with the drone. If they hit the Audi and Luca Bilbija wasn't in it, they would lose him. Bilbija would bury himself deep and all their efforts would have been for nothing.

The drone was closing in rapidly on the convoy. Five hundred meters, four-fifty, four, three-fifty, three, two-fifty. Soon the lead car would fill the lens of the camera. Its headlights, thought Louis, might even pick out the incoming threat.

Two hundred meters.

'Abort,' said Most. 'It's not Bilbija.'

Louis lifted the drone fast. The screen showed the three cars passing just beneath it. The drone continued to rise until it was well above the road.

'Wait!' said Most. 'Bilbija's outside the casino. He's making a call. She thinks he's asking Mirko to come back for him. He doesn't want the guards to drive him, and they don't want to take him unless they have to. He's made himself unpopular.'

'Is he alone?'

Most tapped the question. The phone pinged.

'Yes, he's alone.'

Louis brought the drone down again, following the road south.

'Confirm his position,' he said.

Most realized his intention.

'Seriously?' said Most.

'Seriously,' said Louis.

Most tapped again. The reply came instantly.

'He's smoking a cigarette on the lawn and talking on his phone. She says there's no one else nearby.'

The casino was in sight. Louis tilted the drone west. Seconds later, it was passing over the gatehouse, and the camera picked out a guard looking up, trying to determine the source of the noise. The lawn appeared, the figure of a man visible upon it. By now the drone was below tree level. The man turned toward the drone. In the final seconds, Louis saw Luca Bilbija's face.

There was a flash, and the camera went dead. A moment later, they heard the explosion.

Chapter LVI

Frend broke the news about the accounts to Radovan Vuksan over the phone. Frend was very glad that circumstances necessitated his remaining isolated from the Vuksans, because this was not information that he would have cared to deliver in person.

'What about the bankers?' said Radovan. 'Why didn't they protect us?'

Frend thought it was unlike Radovan to be so naïve, but then, he was distressed. One of the problems with using crooked bankers – or rather, bankers who were more crooked than the norm – was the obvious: their essential dishonesty. They would always buckle under the right kind of pressure. But faced with Interpol on one side, and what might well have looked like a perfectly legal series of transfers to accounts in Serbia on the other, perhaps even the bankers were not entirely to blame in this instance. Frend endeavored to explain as much to Radovan, but he was not in the mood to listen. Frend permitted him to vent for a time before pointing out that he had managed to move some funds to secure accounts: not as much as he would have liked, but sufficient for their needs over the coming months.

'What needs?' said Radovan. 'Bread and water?'

'The position is not quite so grave as that.'

'Is that really what you think, Anton? If so, I fear you may not have been paying attention. In fact, my brother may be of a similar opinion when I tell him that his war chest is now empty. He will be looking for someone to blame, and you're nearer to hand than any banker.'

Frend waited. He was good at waiting. All lawyers were, if only because they charged by the hour.

'Are you done, Radovan?' he said, once blessed silence had reigned for a while.

Radovan sighed. 'Yes, Anton, I am done. I apologize.'

'There's no need,' said Frend. 'I understand the pressure you're under.'

For a moment, Radovan was tempted to share with him the fact of Gavrilo Dražeta's murder. In the past, Frend had acted as a sounding board and source of good counsel, but also as a release valve for Radovan. They were close, he and the lawyer: Frend by name, friend by nature. Yet Radovan was also a good judge of people, and knew that Frend was already scared enough. Informing him that another hunter was closing on the Vuksans might well break him.

'Work on getting us out of Europe,' said Radovan. 'Quickly.'

'What about Spiridon?'

'I'll deal with Spiridon.'

'What you require will cost money, more than you have to hand.' Frend did not offer Radovan a loan from his own funds. Even had he that kind of cash, which he did not, its disappearance from his accounts might draw attention later, especially if everything ended badly for the Vuksans. But it was also poor practice: lawyers did not lend money to clients.

'Don't worry about the money,' said Radovan. 'There are ways.'

Chapter LVII

M ost and Louis disposed of the Phantom surveillance drone by dousing it in gasoline and setting it alight in a dumpster. Most then drove Louis to a guesthouse on the outskirts of Lidice, just a short distance northwest of Václav Havel Airport. In June 1942, in reprisal for the assassination of the Reich Protector Reinhard Heydrich in Prague, the Germans had razed Lidice and sown the ground with salt. They had also executed every male over the age of fifteen and sent the women and children to Chelmno to be gassed, apart from a handful adjudged physically acceptable enough to be Aryanized. The current village overlooked the site of the original settlement. A line of trees concealed it from the view of those staying at the guesthouse.

No one at the desk asked Louis for identification or payment. An elderly woman showed him to a tiny, spotlessly clean room, and left without offering a word. The earliest direct flight from Prague to Vienna left at 8:15 a.m., and Most had decided that Louis should not spend the intervening hours waiting in an airport lounge. Most thought it unlikely that any connection would be made between the explosion at the casino and the departing American, but in the event of such a misfortune befalling them, it would be best if Louis were somewhere other than a terminal building filled with cameras and armed police.

Louis did not sleep, or even remove his shoes, although in deference to his hosts he placed a towel at the foot of the bed so as not to mark the comforter. The TV in the room did not have a cable or satellite connection and was limited to terrestrial Czech channels. He turned on his iPad and tried using the guesthouse's internet to check local news reports, but most were in Czech and none mentioned anything about an explosion at a casino. After an hour he heard a knock at his door, and Most's voice called his name. Louis admitted the big man, who just about managed to fit into the room's single chair. Most had arranged for the motorcycle to be collected by one of his nephews, and all traces of their presence at the factory to be erased, right down to the tire tracks of the BMW.

'Well, they have no leads yet, so we weren't seen,' said Most. 'Bilbija's definitely dead, but it'll take them a while to gather all the bits of him. Two members of the casino's staff were injured in the blast, one seriously, but he'll pull through. The police know it was a drone attack because the guard at the gate caught a glimpse as it passed over. They'll be looking for fragments in the hope of finding a serial number, but that's long gone. The explosive was tagged, but it was the only C4 I held from that particular batch, and they won't be able to trace it back to me. I was saving it for a special occasion.'

C4 usually contained a chemical marker to give it an odor and enable its source to be established. By a strange coincidence, the C4 used to kill Luca Bilbija would subsequently be identified as part of the same batch used to assassinate Nikola Musulin in Belgrade. Such were the vagaries of fortune.

'What about your contact at the casino?' said Louis.

'She's a smart girl. She destroyed the SIM card and the phone I supplied. She still has her own phone, and she used it to send a couple of emojis to her boyfriend while she was texting me, just in case the police or the Novákovi start asking why she was seen using it. The kids in there all have phones stuck to their hands anyway, so she won't have been the only one. She'll be okay.'

'And you?'

Most grinned.

'I'm good,' he said. 'But you won't be when you see my bill.'

After some reflection, Louis decided not to fly to Vienna but take another train instead. The high-speed Railjet would get him and his baggage, both legal and illegal, from Prague to Vienna in just over four hours, enabling him to continue holding on to the unused Rohrbaugh pistol along with a Glock sourced for him by Most.

While he could have picked up replacement weapons in Vienna, it would have involved reaching out to second-tier contacts, ones with whom he was not personally acquainted. Every such transaction involved a degree of unmasking, and it was unwise to expose himself more than was necessary. Louis booked a first-class ticket for the 8:44 a.m. departure, and Most escorted him into the station at 8:30, but not before first checking the concourse for any signs of unusual security activity, the Czech having an eye for such matters. They parted with a handshake and Louis took his seat on the train, his bags now heavier by the weight of the Glock and fifty additional rounds of ammunition.

Three to go, he thought.

Chapter LVIII

Zorya sat in an armchair in the Vuksans' safe house, eating Spanish strawberries from a china bowl. The berries were staining the tips of her fingers red, but Radovan could still see a deeper scarlet lodged beneath her fingernails. A sluggish dawn was forcing its way through the gaps in the shutters on the windows only to expire amid the shadows of the room. The house smelled of coffee and greasy food. Radovan was growing sick of it. He wanted to be done with all this skulking. On the other hand, he did not wish to die.

Beside Zorya, Zivco Ilić was drinking a glass of milk. He had declined anything stronger. Radovan thought that Ilić looked unsettled, as though he had recently received some bad news, although it might have been a consequence of what had been done to the Dutchman. Ilić and Zorya had not been confident of abducting him and so had been forced to interrogate him in his hotel room. Once Frend had informed them of Hendricksen's presence in the city, Ilić had gone to the streets to obtain a master key card for the hotel, a variation on the type given to maids and concierge staff. Such key cards were in wide circulation, cloned from stolen or expired versions, if one knew the right people to ask – and Zivco Ilić did.

Unavoidably, he and Zorya would have been caught on camera while entering and leaving the hotel – they had circumvented the elevators, at least – but Zorya had changed her clothes for the visit, and Ilić's buzzcut had been disguised by the simple addition of a hat, a cheap wig, and thick-framed glasses, as well as a stone in his left shoe to alter his gait. It was very possible that the Austrian police might connect the girl at the hotel with the one spotted at the Schönbrunn Palace on the day the Turk Nahid

Hasanović was killed, but Vienna was not lacking in teenage girls. Anyway, Zorya was not one of them, not really. Wrap her in the right clothing and she might even have resembled some *baba* from the old country, smelling of cheap cigarettes and empty churches.

Now Radovan and his brother waited while Zorya ate and Ilić brooded. Inflicting pain, Radovan had decided, gave Zorya an appetite. She finished the final strawberry and licked her fingers before her tongue progressed to the human matter beneath her nails. It probably tasted salty after the fruit.

'The man hunting us is definitely Louis,' said Zorya, when she was done, 'the same one who killed Andrej Buha in Amsterdam. It's what he does, or used to do: killing for a living. He is a faggot – ' she used the Serbian slur *peškir* – 'and has a *furundžija*, Angel, who travels with him.'

Spiridon shook his head sadly.

'This is what we are reduced to,' he said, 'being hunted by a *gejša*.'

He waited for a laugh from Ilić, but none came.

'A *gejša*,' noted Radovan, 'who has so far killed three of our men.'

'Two,' corrected Spiridon.

'Three. Luca Bilbija has just joined Andrej and Alexsej in the next world.'

Even Zivco Ilić now gave Radovan his full attention.

'When?' said Spiridon.

'Last night, outside a casino in Zbraslav. He was blown apart by a drone packed with explosives.'

'And you're only telling me this now?' said Spiridon.

'I've just learned of it myself, from the Novákovi.'

'Why the delay in informing us?'

'I suspect,' said Radovan, 'that the Novákovi were deciding how best to deal with the fallout. They have not taken sides between Belgrade and ourselves, and prefer to operate their casinos as neutral territory. Having clients obliterated on their grounds is bad for business.'

'And we are sure this man Louis is responsible?' said Ilić. He looked even more ill than before, for which Radovan could not blame him. Apart from the Vuksans, Ilić was now the last of those who had been present for the killing of De Jaager and the women in Amsterdam. Unless the threat to them was dealt with quickly, Ilić would soon be keeping his deceased comrades company in whatever corner of hell they currently occupied.

'No,' said Radovan, 'we don't know for certain that this is his handiwork, but logic suggests it. Belgrade would not risk offending the Novákovi by carrying out a hit on one of their properties, and killing with a drone is not the Turks' style. They prefer to cut throats.'

Spiridon might have been listening to his brother, but his attention was fixed on Zorya.

'Aleksej and Luca were careless,' said Spiridon. 'We have been cautious.'

He seemed to be waiting for Zorya to confirm his thesis, but she did not. Instead she reached out her left hand to Ilić, and he responded by taking it in his right. Radovan saw his brother frown. Spiridon regarded Zorya as his personal property, even if Radovan doubted that Zorya saw their relationship in quite the same light. Radovan wondered if she and Ilić might not be sleeping with each other. The thought disturbed him, although whether because of how she looked at that moment – very young – or what she was – very old – he could not have said.

'Not so cautious,' said Radovan, 'as to have kept Gavrilo and his wife from harm.'

'That's a different issue,' said Spiridon.

'Perhaps, but whoever killed Gavrilo and his woman is now on the way to Vienna, or may already be in the city. Now Louis is closing in on us. We can't just sit here waiting for him or the Turks to track us down.'

'Which of them concerns you more?' said Spiridon.

'Louis. We might still be able to reason with the Turks, even at this late stage, but we cannot reason with him.'

'Perhaps we could find him before he finds us?' said Ilić.

'We no longer have those resources,' said Radovan.

'What, then?' said Spiridon.

But it was Zorya who answered. She had learned information

from Hendricksen to which even Zivco Ilić was not privy, knowledge whispered to her as she explored the concavities of the Dutchman's body with her sharp nails. She knew of Parker, the private detective in Maine, friend and confidant of Louis – and, more to the point, father to a dead girl named Jennifer. There might be a way to strike at Jennifer through Parker, hurting one by hurting the other, just as long as Zorya could keep her distance from the specter of the girl.

'You could divert the hunter's attention,' she said.

'How?' said Radovan.

'By killing one of his friends.'

Chapter LIX

When there was still no word from Hendricksen after 9 a.m., Angel decided to check his room. A DO NOT DISTURB sign hung from the doorknob, but Angel placed no store by it. Whenever he stayed in a hotel. Angel left a similar sign on his door for the duration of his stay. If he needed extra towels, he asked for them, and he was capable of making his own bed. Only a sucker gave strangers more access to his life than was necessary.

He knocked on the door, but received no reply. He took a look at the key card lock, but it was a new model. This particular company's old locks had been vulnerable to hacking through the insertion of a microcontroller into the DC socket at the lock's base, which enabled the 32-bit key to be read and played back, opening the door. The company had been forced to tackle the flaw, at considerable expense. So far the fix was working, but Angel knew from experience that the ingenuity of lockmakers was exceeded only by that of lockbreakers.

He found a maid, told her his name was Hendricksen, and said that his key card wasn't working. He demonstrated this for her with the key card to his own room. She seemed reluctant to oblige him by opening the door, but the sight of a twenty-euro note assuaged her concerns.

The room was dark and the bed unmade. Angel called Hendricksen's name once the door had closed behind him, but again was met only with silence. A suitcase stood on a metal stand, but most of its contents were strewn across the floor. The bathroom door was closed, and as Angel drew nearer to it he heard a tap dripping. He sniffed the air. It smelled bad, like an unflushed toilet, but with a meatiness underpinning it. Angel was familiar with that odor from personal experience: it was the smell of suffering.

A room service tray lay on the table by the window. It held a coffeepot and the remains of a sandwich. Angel took the cloth napkin from the tray and used it to grip the knob on the bathroom door. As he did so, he thought he picked up the softest of sounds from within, the slightest swish of skin against ceramic.

Angel suddenly wished he had a gun.

He paused, took a breath, and turned the knob, using the wall to provide some protection for his body. The door opened, and the smell grew stronger, but no one rushed him. He risked a glance.

Hendricksen lay naked in the bathtub, his lower body mired in a shallow pool of his own congealed blood. His eyes were closed and tape was wound around his head, covering his mouth. His hands and feet had been bound so tightly with cable ties that the plastic had dug deep into the flesh, turning the extremities purple. The interior of the tub was almost entirely red, with spots of blood extending up the wall to pattern the ceiling with dark stars. Angel saw wounds in Hendricksen's chest, belly, legs, and arms. They appeared to have been made by a boxcutter or a very slim, sharp knife, but they were all wider at the center, where the incisions had been explored. He could not have said why, exactly, but he thought a finger might have been used, perhaps even two or three fingers.

Angel touched a hand to Hendricksen's neck. The body was cold, and he could find no pulse at first. But then, incredibly, he felt the faintest of beats. Hendricksen's eyelids fluttered.

'Jesus,' said Angel. 'Hold on, you hear me? You hold on.'

Hendricksen was trying to speak. Angel noticed a pair of scissors in a toiletry bag, and used them to cut the tape over Hendricksen's mouth. Angel needed to summon help, but removing the tape would help Hendricksen breathe, and it was clear that the wounded man had something to say.

The adhesive was strong and the blood around Hendricksen's mouth had dried. Angel gradually worked the tape free, his left arm supporting Hendricksen's head. His tormentors had probably been forced to keep Hendricksen gagged while they worked on him, only loosening the tape for long enough to get answers to their questions. If he couldn't talk, he was of no use to them. But judging by the extent of his wounds, Angel thought that whoever was responsible for this had kept hurting Hendricksen even after he had told them all he knew. They had continued because they liked it.

'Dead . . . girl,' said Hendricksen. 'Dead girl did . . . this.'

Angel thought he'd misheard.

'We'll find her, but you need to stay alive to describe her.'

Hendricksen shook his head.

'No,' he said. 'Dead.'

'Not yet,' said Angel.

He found the phone by the toilet, and hit the button for reception. The call was answered instantly.

'I need an ambulance,' said Angel. 'Now.'

Hendricksen was dying in the hotel room.

He was still dying in the ambulance.

But he died at the hospital.

Chapter LX

L ouis received the message on his cell phone as he alighted from the train at Vienna's Central Station.

Find another hotel, it read. *Hndksn 187*.

It was the police code for homicide. Louis did not call Angel, but responded with a simple *OK*. Behind the two letters lay a weight of sudden grief and anger. He had liked Hendricksen a great deal, and Louis did not like very many people at all. He took a few moments to find alternative accommodation to Angel's, as advised, selecting an upmarket boutique place on Führichgasse. The room was expensive, but six bottles of wine were included in the price, and Louis felt as though he could drink most of them before lunch. He caught a taxi to his lodgings, checked into his room, and waited for Angel to get in touch.

From his window he could see the Albertina. In another life, another time, he might have gone there to view the Dürers in its collection, but not now, not with the weight of the dead pressing upon him. Reflecting on Dürer brought to mind De Jaager, who had enjoyed haunting the Rijksmuseum, and generally adored Dürer, but suffered a curious blind spot when it came to the art of engraving – and the Rijksmuseum, if Louis remembered right, held, with the exception of a single drawing, only Dürer's engravings. Perhaps, Louis thought, he might visit the Albertina after all, circumstances permitting, because De Jaager would have wanted it.

Two hours went by, then three. He did not move from the bed, and was not in the mood to resume his immersion in Fenimore Cooper. There were books on the shelf in his room, but most of them were in German. The only English work he could find was a volume of essays on morals and ethics. He started reading it before deciding that the best of its contents he already knew, and the rest he didn't need to know. He opened one of the complimentary bottles of red wine and drank a single glass. From the wall opposite his bed, a life-size photograph of a girl stared back at him. The girl looked poor: an immigrant, or a lost soul. Louis considered it an odd choice of décor, unless it was intended to evoke feelings of guilt in the observer for being able to afford one of the better rooms in Vienna.

His phone rang. He answered.

'What happened?' he said.

'They must have come for him sometime after eight in the evening,' Angel replied, 'because Hendricksen signed for a room service tray at seven forty-five. He was tortured and left to die in the tub, but somehow, he held on. He lived long enough to tell me that a young girl hurt him. He seemed to be saying that she was dead, but he was in a lot of pain, so who knows what he meant. He passed away shortly after they got him to Vienna General. The police are looking at the security footage from the hotel right now. There are cameras in the elevators and the lobby areas, and one on every external door, although not on every corridor. Unless whoever killed Hendricksen magicked a way in and out, they'll be caught on camera somewhere.'

'What did you tell the police?'

'That Hendricksen and I were friends who happened to have crossed paths in Vienna. We'd agreed to meet for dinner, but Hendricksen didn't appear. When he didn't make it for breakfast either, I grew worried. I asked a maid to let me check on him – I didn't mention the bribe – and found him dying in the tub.'

'And they believed you?' said Louis.

'Not completely, but they accept that I didn't kill him, although I get the feeling at least one of the detectives thinks I know who did. She can think whatever she wants. It won't get her anywhere.'

'Will you be able to get a look at that security footage?'

'I'm sure I'll be asked to view it, just in case I recognize anyone. But Louis, what was done to Hendricksen was strange.'

'What do you mean, "strange"?'

'He was very weak when I found him, but while we were waiting for the ambulance, he said the girl used her fingers on him. She cut him with a blade and then dug deep, working on him with her nails. What kind of child does that to another human being?'

Louis didn't have an answer to the question, although he felt certain that if anyone could find such an individual, it was the Vuksans.

'It means there'll probably be prints,' he said.

'I saw smudges, but no obvious fingerprints. I guess you're right, though. Where are you, by the way?'

Louis gave him the address.

'The police have told me not to leave the city, and to inform them if I change hotels,' said Angel. 'It makes sense not to move, and I wouldn't want to draw attention to you.'

'If this is the Vuksans' work, then they know about us by now,' said Louis. 'Did Hendricksen say what he'd told them?'

'No, but judging from what they did to him, I'd say he gave them everything he knew.'

'Then we need to move on Frend.'

'I have his number,' said Angel, 'and the first of the videos of his daughter. I'll send the footage this afternoon, and a text warning him to resist the temptation to go running to the police – not that I think he will, not with his client list, but you never know.'

'No,' said Louis, 'you never do. On second thoughts, hold off on sending the first video until tomorrow. Let's give the police twenty-four hours to lose some of their interest in you, because I can't handle Frend alone. Once Frend has the video, we'll leave him to stew for a few hours.'

He stared at the girl on the wall, and she stared back. Louis thought he might have to ask for a change of room.

'I wonder how the Vuksans found Hendricksen,' he said.

'Bad luck.'

'Maybe we brought it with us.'

'We always seem to have some to spare,' said Angel. He paused. 'I liked Hendricksen.'

'I liked him too.'

'We'll make them pay, won't we?'

'Yes,' said Louis. 'Every one of them.'

Chapter LXI

The French prison system was, by general consent, a mess: a collection of overcrowded, underfunded institutions, with a significant Muslim population that was ripe for radicalization. Baba Diop had spent time behind bars in his native Senegal, most notably at the notorious Rebeuss Prison in Dakar, but even by those standards Fleury-Mérogis, Europe's largest penal institution, was a grim environment in which to be incarcerated. If Diop was seeking straws at which to clutch, he had at least avoided La Santé. A cousin of his had spent three years there before emerging convinced that the place was both cursed and haunted, a consequence, he believed, of having provided a home for the guillotine until the 1970s.

Diop had passed the days since his capture at Gare de Lyon in a series of French police interview rooms. This had not been a happy experience, not least because he had proven unable to provide his interrogators with the intelligence they required, namely any deep insight into the channels through which Islamic terrorists were making their way into Europe from the Middle East and North Africa. All Baba Diop could tell the French was that he had been hired by Aleksej Marković to escort two Syrians – whose names he had never learned – from Port-Vendres to Paris. He had done similar work for Marković in the past, although on those occasions he had been shepherding human cargo from the Serbian border to Paris.

As Diop understood it, most of these individuals were respectable middle-class citizens – doctors, businessmen, accountants – seeking to escape the turmoil of war and persecution in Iraq, Syria, Somalia, even Pakistan, by buying themselves a new life in Europe. Sometimes they brought their families with them, although only the wealthiest could afford to do so since the Serbians charged $50,000 per head to move illegal immigrants through Serbia and on to France, and did not offer discounts for bulk. Another arm of the operation worked with poorer cargo, the kind that was transported like cattle in the backs of trucks, there to live or die according to the vagaries of heat and cold, and the relative availability of essentials such as food, water, and oxygen. Baba Diop preferred not to involve himself in that kind of haulage. He found it depressing, and incompatible with his Christianity.

As for the two men killed at Gare de Lyon, Diop informed the police that he had been ignorant of their terrorist backgrounds. His policy had always been to ask as few questions as possible. He trusted Marković to share with him all the necessary facets of an operation; anything more, Baba Diop was better off not knowing. Yes, he was aware of the Vuksans, but only peripherally through Marković, because he had never met the brothers himself. He thought that Fouad Belkacem, his colleague who had also been present at Gare de Lyon on that fateful afternoon, might have had some dealings with the Vuksans directly, but he could not be sure. He and Fouad did not talk very much, Diop told the police solemnly. They had little in common, Fouad being a Muslim, a drinker, a smoker, and a fornicator, while Baba Diop was none of these things.

Oh, and Fouad was also apparently a traitor. He had betrayed Baba Diop, Aleksej Marković, and the two Syrians, which meant that Baba, the police stressed, should feel under no obligation to withhold information in order to protect him. Fouad was one of their assets, and had already told them a great deal. Baba Diop's testimony was required only to corroborate certain details, they said, but he should be careful not to lie because, thanks to Fouad, they would know if he was dissembling, and would punish him accordingly.

But Baba Diop did not believe all of this. He had served for a number of years with the Senegalese National Gendarmerie before his arrest for gross corruption – the reason for that involuntary three-year stay at Rebeuss – and had participated in his share of interrogations. He suspected that whatever information the French might have got out of Fouad Belkacem, it had not been enough to satisfy their curiosity.

And so the questioning had continued until, having deprived Diop of sleep, restricted his access to food and water, and beaten him a little, his interrogators decided that he had told them all he could, and it was time for him to languish in a cell until the courts got around to trying him as an accessory to terrorism. Only as he was being taken to Fleury-Mérogis did Diop learn of Fouad Belkacem's murder. He already knew that Marković had been shot and killed. The police had appeared curious to learn who might have been responsible, which surprised Diop since he had assumed that the police had themselves killed Marković. Now, it seemed, Fouad was also dead. Baba Diop found this troubling because he recognized that, depending on the culprits, he might be next in line.

All of which explained how Baba had come to be confined in Fleury-Mérogis. After being brought before an investigating judge, he was remanded to a supposedly secure unit of the prison's *maison d'arrêt des hommes*, where he was likely to remain for the foreseeable future. Following his eventual trial, the end result of which Diop could gloomily predict, he would most likely end up back at Fleury-Mérogis, or even be given the opportunity to find out for himself whether La Santé was, in fact, cursed, or if its refurbishment had succeeded in banishing the hex. This was how Diop saw the next decade or so of his life unfolding. It made him sad. He was not a wicked man. He had tried not to hurt people unless absolutely necessary, but it had been his misfortune to fall into bad company on many occasions, and in at least four different countries.

Diop was not unalarmed at the prospect of incarceration in Fleury-Mérogis. He was aware of its large Muslim contingent and its reputation as a font of radicalism. Amedy Coulibaly, the Malian who murdered a policewoman and four Jews in Paris in 2015, and Chérif Kouachi, one of the two brothers who shot twelve dead at the Paris offices of *Charlie Hebdo* magazine, had both been radicalized by their time at the prison. Diop, one of his fellow detainees warned him as they were placed in the van, would be entering an environment that was unsympathetic at best to non-Muslims, and policed by unarmed guards who preferred not to risk their lives by stepping into the exercise yard when the prisoners were at liberty there.

Baba Diop spent the final thirty-six hours of his life at Fleury-Mérogis. At 11 a.m. on the second day, he was stabbed in the throat with a sharpened comb while being led under escort to the governor's office. His murderer was a young French-Algerian named Ahmed Beghal, who declared that he had taken Diop's life as revenge for his part in the deaths of the 'martyrs' at Gare de Lyon. Beghal, with no previous history of violence, and not yet on the watch list of firebrand inmates, declined to say whether he might have been ordered by another party to kill Diop. He also refused to share with police or prison staff the source of his information about Diop, whose identity had been kept secret in order to protect him against just such an act of retaliation.

And in Vienna, the Vuksans felt the noose tighten another inch.

Chapter LXII

The official term is 'identity management'; the unofficial one is 'passports for sale'. It's a lucrative trade, worth about $3 billion annually, and shows no signs of abating in this age of isolationism, Brexit, tax evasion, and terrorism. Basically, if you're wealthy enough, any number of countries may be willing to provide you with a passport. The most valuable of these documents offer visa-free access to most of the world, including those European territories in the Schengen Area. For this reason, poorer Caribbean island nations are particularly popular, aided by their status as offshore tax havens and their desire to attract outside investment. The price, generally speaking, is quite reasonable: $100–$200,000 for an Antiguan passport; $100,000 for a Dominican; $150,000 for St. Kitts and Nevis, or Grenada. European passports are more expensive: an Austrian passport will cost the buyer upwards of $3 million, a Cypriot passport $2 million, a Maltese $1 million. In addition, fees may have to be paid to a broker, which can add as little as $20,000 or as much as $500,000 to the final cost.

The attraction of such passports is plain for respectable businesspeople from countries with restrictions on access to leading economic markets, but even more obvious for disreputable individuals seeking to avoid the attention of the authorities. On paper, the nations involved in these sales are committed to due diligence, investigating – or claiming to investigate – all applicants thoroughly, and refusing to sell to anyone suspected of altering their identity or those who might be the subject of a criminal investigation.

But the reality?

Well, that's more nebulous.

*

In Simmering, just beyond Vienna's southern limits, lies a small, rarely visited cemetery. This is the Friedhof der Namenlosen, or the Cemetery of the Nameless, and it is the final resting place of more than one hundred people, the majority of them unidentified. For centuries, the Danube's currents caused the corpses of those who had drowned in the river, or whose remains had been thrown into it for disposal, to wash up on a nearby stretch of the bank. In 1939, the construction of the Albern grain dock altered the currents, and the Danube's dead were forced to make landfall farther down the river.

The old cemetery, which accepted corpses until 1900, is now hidden by forest and marked only by a sign among the trees. The new cemetery contains 104 bodies, their plots marked, for the most part, by identical crucifixes, some with candles or wreaths placed there by well-wishers or the fishermen of Albern, who gather to remember these unfortunates each All Saints' Day. The named – Gutman, Molner, Kochinger, Behnken ('*aus Hamburg 11.12.1860 – 15.3.1923*') – repose largely on the left side of the cemetery, as though to distance themselves from those who remain anonymous – *Unbekannt, Namenlos*. A little church, the Chapel of the Resurrection, sits above the graves. To its right rise silos and industrial buildings, and to the left is a patch of wilderness, a place of weeds and dead or dying trees. Behind, but now some distance away, flows the Danube.

Anton Frend had never before set foot in the Friedhof der Namenlosen. He made a point of avoiding graveyards, and had last stood at a graveside seven years previously when his father had been interred in the family plot at Vienna's Central Cemetery. He had not visited the grave since. If there was a next life, which he doubted, then the best of his parents was at peace there; if there was not, they were nowhere. Either way, he saw no point in making obeisance to moldering bones.

He had not slept in the apartment above his office the night before, but had elected to stay at a small hotel in Hackengasse. Frend tended to dismiss talk of sixth senses or bad feelings, but as he approached his office building after leaving Zivco Ilić and the girl, he had spotted a car parked within sight of the entrance, and observed, from behind, two men in the front seats. The driver was entirely concealed by shadow, and Frend could see only the side of the passenger's face: dark hair, a beard, and a sallow complexion accentuated by a white dress shirt buttoned to the neck. Spiridon Vuksan, Frend thought, would have described him as a Turk. The passenger was smoking a cigarette, which he finished while Frend watched. The butt was dropped from the open window to the street below, where it came to rest near three others. Almost immediately, Frend had experienced the strongest urge to run, but controlled himself sufficiently to retreat round the corner and walk to the nearest U-Bahn station, all the time glancing over his shoulder, anticipating the sight of the bearded man in pursuit; but he was not followed and made it onto the train without incident.

Once he had arrived at the hotel, he called his wife and stressed to her again the importance of not returning home or using her credit and debit cards until the current crisis was dealt with. Then, because he wanted to hear her voice, he tried his daughter's cell phone. It went straight to messaging. She usually simply rejected the incoming call if she recognized his number. Once every year or two, she might connect to speak a few monosyllables to him in person.

But not that evening.

Finally, he had contacted Radka, his mistress. She wanted to know where he was. He told her he was staying at a hotel, although he did not share the name with her. She offered to join him. He was tempted to say yes, if only for the company – his sexual appetite had diminished in inverse proportion to the escalation of the Vuksan problem – but decided it would be better if they were to remain apart for the time being. He asked about any suspicious activity, or any odd inquiries made concerning him, but she could recall none. He advised her to lock up the shop for a few days, or leave it in the care of her assistant, Sophia, but Radka only laughed and informed him that Sophia would have the business run into the ground within twenty-four hours, and what was he so worried about anyway?

Frend tried telling her, but without mentioning the Vuksans by name. He advised her of delicate negotiations, of men who might or might not have been watching his office, and others who were probably doing the same thing at his home. He spoke of sending his wife away to safety. He told Radka that he did not want anything to happen to her, but there were those who might attempt to use her to get to him. By the end of the conversation he was no closer to convincing her of the need to absent herself from the store, but she had at least agreed to exercise some caution, whatever that might mean.

Unbeknownst to Frend, Radka had then made a call of her own, this one to Zivco Ilić, informing him that forces unknown might be closing in on Anton Frend.

Now Frend was in Simmering in the cold, gray light of morning. A taxi had dropped him at the entrance to the complex of factories and silos. He had elected to walk the rest of the way to the cemetery, following the direction indicated by a sign on the road, because the fewer witnesses there were to his ultimate destination, the better. He asked the driver to wait for him, but the man refused because Frend could not confirm how long he would be. He could always call another taxi, the driver pointed out. If not, there was a bus stop by the entrance to the industrial area, so he had a couple of options. Frend wasn't so sure about that – two buses an hour would be a generous estimate, and who knew how long a taxi might take to arrive? – but he had little choice in the matter. In better circumstances, he would have driven himself, but his car was parked in a private garage by his office; if he was right, and his business premises were under surveillance, then his vehicle also might be.

He passed no one as he walked. The buildings were deserted, this being Sunday. Flocks of small birds rose above the silos before settling again, the pattern repeating itself three times. He could see no cause for the birds to be alarmed, but perhaps they sensed the presence of predators; that, or the fear of predation was now so ingrained that they were reluctant to stay in one place for too long. In either case, the metaphor was not lost on Frend.

He descended a short flight of steps that brought him under a railway line and within sight of the cemetery. A woman was standing among the graves, smoking a cigarette. She was entirely alone, apart from the dead. She looked up as Frend approached the little chapel, but did not acknowledge him, even as Frend descended to join her and the *namenlos*.

The woman was taller than Frend and ascetically thin, as befitted one who subsisted on coffee and cigarettes. Her silver hair was cut too short for his liking, although his liking, Frend knew, was of no concern to her. The frames of her large spectacles were clear, lending them a protective aspect, so that Frend felt her regard as a laboratory specimen might, the sharpness of her attention like a scalpel ready to cut. She was wearing a beige coat that flared slightly from the waist and ended just below her knees, her legs concealed by high leather boots of a reddish brown, like blood and mud mixed. She was, she claimed, a distant descendant of the painter Angelica Kauffmann, although this might have been a lie, for Hannah Kauffmann was adept at creating falsehoods.

'Hannah,' said Frend. 'You look well, as always.'

Kauffmann flicked at the flattery with a fingertip, the movement causing a pillar of ash to tumble from her cigarette to the plot by her feet.

'If you came out here to exchange compliments,' she said, 'your journey will have been wasted, because you, Anton, do not look well. Are you sure you're getting enough rest?'

'Not lately, but you may be able to assist with a solution.'

'I can offer you pills. I have no shortage of them.'

'I was hoping for something more long-term.'

She waved at the graves with her right hand.

'Then you're in the right place,' she said.

Frend smiled without humor. He had not chosen this venue for their meeting. He would have preferred somewhere closer to the city, and less depressing, but Hannah Kauffmann had always indulged a taste for the dramatic. It might have been a consequence of her love of opera. She was a benefactor of the Vienna State Opera, which meant that she donated at least €10,000 per season. Frend could think of many better ways Kauffmann could have spent €10,000, among them getting her teeth fixed. She was an otherwise attractive woman, but her mouth was a ruin, the enamel stained from decades of caffeine and nicotine, with gaps in the upper row where she had lost molars to decay. Her grin reminded him of the skulls in the crypt of the Stephansdom.

'I was going to ask why we were here,' said Frend, 'and not in more convivial surroundings.'

'You don't like cemeteries?'

'Not particularly, but this one seems more cheerless than most.'

'Really?' Kauffmann frowned. She appeared genuinely surprised. 'I don't think that at all. Most of these people may be nameless, but they have not been forgotten. Every year, for one day, they are remembered. The fishermen leave flowers for them, and set a boat of wreaths adrift on the Danube. That is more than is done for many who have families to recall them, or who lie beneath memorials more lavish than a simple cross. And someday, we will be as they are. When there is no one left alive to recall us, no one for whom our mention causes even a flicker of recognition, then we, too, will have become nameless, whatever the stone above our head may say to the contrary.'

She finished her cigarette and stamped it out on the ground, which detracted somewhat, in Frend's view, from the impact of her testimony.

'Or,' she resumed, 'one could look upon it as a lesson in the transitory nature of identity.'

Ah, thought Frend, *that's more like it. Now we break through the bone to get to the marrow.*

Kauffmann was a lawyer, specializing in banking and capital markets law, but she also maintained a lucrative sideline as a broker of passports, because some of her clients occasionally had need of such a service. From Austrian Bar gossip, Frend was aware that Kauffmann's contacts in the Caribbean were second to none, although she had been forced to sever her ties with Cyprus and Malta following their inclusion on an OECD blacklist of countries believed to be facilitating tax evasion through their passports-for-sale schemes. There was also the case of the Maltese journalist Daphne Caruana Galizia, who had been killed by a car bomb outside Mosta in 2017 while investigating Maltese government corruption, including the trade in passports. Her death had brought unwelcome international attention on the Maltese and the conduct of their affairs.

'One should always be open to change,' said Frend. 'I currently have clients who share this view. One might even say they're quite passionate about it.'

Kauffmann lit another cigarette. The tips of the fingers on her right hand were as yellow as her teeth. Frend imagined her body as a veritable petri dish of cancers.

'I know the circles in which you move,' said Kauffmann. 'That's why we're meeting out here and not at Café Landtmann. There are rumors, Anton.'

'There are always rumors. It would not be Vienna otherwise.'

'These rumors come from farther afield,' said Kauffmann. 'Podgorica, for example.'

Podgorica, capital of Montenegro. Four hundred thousand dollars for a passport, give or take. Independent from Serbia since 2006, but still with deep ties to the old union. During the wars in the 1990s, the Montenegrins had bombed Dubrovnik for the Serbs and handed over Bosnian refugees to be tortured and executed. The Vuksans might once have had friends there, but not any longer.

'And what do you hear from Podgorica?' said Frend.

'That your clients have overstepped, and a price has been put on their heads, not to mention the Interpol Red Notice currently in their names.'

'Which is why they are seeking new names and new passports. An agreement has been brokered with Belgrade, but my clients have to leave Europe soon. A delay might be misconstrued as a prelude to hostilities.'

'Some in Belgrade would contest the existence of any such agreement.'

'Would Simo Stajić be among them?'

'Perhaps,' said Kauffmann.

'Stajić is a thug. It is Matija Kiš who speaks for Belgrade.'

'A city from which you recently barely escaped with your life, if the tales are true. Do you really think that Kiš would have stepped in to save you had you not made it to Romania?'

'Kiš is a gangster trying on a politician's clothes for size – or perhaps it's the other way round: one can never be sure with men of no principle. Whatever his true nature, any further bloodshed might damage his standing beyond repair.'

'Kiš is a pragmatist,' said Kauffmann. 'If he gets blood on one set of clothing, he can exchange it for another. But my guess is that he would be clever enough to keep his distance from any carnage, and let Stajić do the butchering.'

Frend did not like the turn the discussion had taken.

'Have you been warned against becoming involved?' he asked.

'If I had, do you think I'd be talking to you now? I'd like my skin to remain uncharred. For the moment, Kiš is probably prepared to forget about your clients as long as they leave the Continent. Later, though, who can say?'

'Later is for providence, not for us,' said Frend.

'Because you want the Vuksans gone just as badly as Kiš does.'

She had consented to name them at last, Frend noticed.

'More so. I'm at risk as long as they're here.'

'And not only from Belgrade,' said Kauffmann.

'More rumors?'

'Facts this time, as indicated by a growing trail of bodies. Someone seems even more intent than Simo Stajić on wiping out the Vuksans. Even Belgrade is intrigued to know who that might be. Stajić thinks it's Muslims, but then Stajić believes everything is a Muslim plot. Kiš isn't so sure. You wouldn't have any ideas, would you?'

'No,' said Frend.

'I don't believe you, but perhaps it's better that I don't know.'

'From my proclaimed position of ignorance, I can only assume so. Can you help me, Hannah?'

'It will be expensive. Traveling with baggage always costs extra, and the necessity for new identities may complicate matters. It would be cheaper and easier for you to bribe someone in Greece or Italy in return for documentation.'

'I don't have those contacts,' said Frend. 'Also, the passports have to be cast-iron, and come with guarantee of safe haven. My clients may be forced to reside in the territory in question until the Red Notice has faded to a soft pink.'

Kauffmann tired of the second cigarette and sent its butt to join the first.

'I should have an initial response in twenty-four hours,' she said.

'And the cost?'

'That depends. Jordan is probably out, given what happened in Paris. The Jordanians' ties with France are too close, and they prefer to avoid inviting the attentions of extremists. Don't look so shocked, Anton. I know about Gare de Lyon, too. Anyway, the Jordanians charge a million per document, and that's before fees and overheads. With that in mind, I have a feeling your clients may be destined for the Caribbean. Given the complicating factors, I'd anticipate somewhere close to two hundred thousand per passport – and that's at the lower end of the scale – plus my twenty percent.'

'Dollars?'

'I think we'll make it euros. In cash. It's just two passports, correct?'

'Most likely three.'

Frend was not sure that Zivco Ilić had the necessary funds required to purchase a new passport for himself, but the Vuksans might be willing to fund him. They would not want to be trapped in unknown territory without someone they could trust to watch their backs. As for Zorya, he did not believe she would travel with them. According to Radovan, she wished to return to Serbia. He did not know why.

'I need a definite answer,' said Kauffmann.

'I'll check, but assume three for now.'

'What about photographs?'

'I have them ready to send. I just require an email address.'

Kauffmann consulted her phone and supplied a secure address consisting of random numbers and letters, which Frend knew would cease to exist after the image files had been downloaded. He sent the encrypted files from his own phone, and waited for Kauffmann to confirm that they'd been received safely.

'Done,' she said. 'Now, I have somewhere to be. Is there anything else?'

'No, I think that's all.'

Kauffmann tightened the belt on her coat and took in the cemetery one last time.

'Have you considered adding your name to that passport list?' she said.

Frend shook his head. 'I have a business here, and friends.'

'I notice that you fail to mention a family. How is your wife?'

'Elsewhere.'

'Permanently?'

'Probably.'

'And your mistress?'

'You are very well-informed.'

'Just because you don't parade her doesn't make her a secret. Are you attached to her?'

'I am fond of her, but no more than that.'

'And your daughter remains in England?'

'Yes, but we are estranged.'

Kauffmann laid a hand on Frend's right arm.

'Even should you succeed in getting the Vuksans out of Europe,' she said, 'they are leaving wreckage behind, and you will be swimming in it. Too many people know of your ties to these men, and they may refuse to believe that you have severed them completely. You have money, and property that can be sold. By all accounts your wife is a civilized woman who will behave honorably in the event of a divorce. You have fewer obligations here than you think, and a business is not worth a life.'

'And what would I do in some Caribbean backwater?' said Frend. 'Drink too much, and seduce the occasional lonely tourist?'

'There are men who dream of such a life.'

'I am not one of them.'

She patted his sleeve.

'I advise you to reflect upon it. Where did you park?'

'I didn't drive. I took a taxi.'

'Why would you do that?'

'I was being careful.'

'I'd offer you a ride,' she said, 'but—'

'But you're being careful, too,' he finished for her.

'Exactly.'

Frend watched her walk away. Her silver coupe was parked by one of the silos. He did not recognize the make, but then he had never been very interested in cars. He took one last look at the cemetery as Kauffmann drove off. He hoped never to return there, and God forbid that he should ever be laid to rest in such a desolate place. He used the steps to knock the dirt from his shoes before heading back the way he had come, leaving the dead to sleep on in peace.

Chapter LXIII

Louis sipped a coffee at Kaffee Alt Wien on Bäckerstrasse while he waited for Angel to join him. The café was less grand than some of the city's more famous nineteenth-century coffeehouses such as the Café Central or the Café Schwarzenberg, but Louis liked that about it. The walls were decorated with posters for bands of which Louis had never heard and recitals that he had no intention of attending, but the coffee was very good and the ambience was better still. Using his iPad, he accessed the *Vienna Times*, the online English-language newspaper, and read the report on the discovery of Hendricksen's body. A police spokesman claimed that a number of definite lines of inquiry were being followed, which was probably true, and some progress had already been made, which was almost certainly untrue.

Angel had endured another awkward conversation with detectives that morning, but so far, his story appeared to be holding up. He'd also been asked to look at security footage of two people from the hotel's cameras, but it was apparent to Angel from first glance that the male party was wearing a cheap but effective disguise. As for the girl with him, she kept her sweatshirt hood raised throughout, like a recalcitrant teenager. For the purposes of identifying culprits, the footage was worth exactly nothing.

Still, Louis did not like the idea of the Bundespolizei nosing around his partner's affairs, because what affected Angel also affected him. If the Austrians persisted, Louis might have to call in a favor from Ross. The FBI man wouldn't be happy about it, but since Ross never seemed happy about anything, the request wouldn't significantly impact his quality of life.

Louis was in a state of combined anticipation and frustration, the two being intimately connected. Unless the Vuksans made an error that revealed their whereabouts, he was now reliant on Frend succumbing to pressure via his daughter. It was only Harris's opinion that Frend cared enough about Pia Lackner possibly to betray the Vuksans, but the Judas kiss was just one of the options available to the lawyer. He could always turn to the police or private operatives, or even to the Vuksans themselves should he decide his fortunes were irrevocably tied up with theirs. Those actions would be unhelpful to Louis.

He also blamed himself for Hendricksen's death. The Dutchman shouldn't have been left to work alone in Vienna and Belgrade, but Louis's contacts in those cities were nil. Still, they should have had better eyes and ears on Frend, both electronic and human. Harris and his fellow Langley spooks could have stepped up to the plate, but Harris had gone dark since the events at Gare de Lyon. Louis wasn't too surprised, given that Harris had now obtained most, if not all, of what he wanted. The operation might not have gone entirely according to plan, the French, thanks to their mole, having intercepted and killed the two Syrians before Harris and his people could lay hands on them, but a clear message had been sent out nonetheless. In the aftermath, carefully placed and anonymously sourced reports had appeared in a number of the better newspapers in Europe detailing the involvement of Serbian criminals in people smuggling, including the kind of individuals who masterminded attacks on Western civilians. Belgrade had been embarrassed into acting, closing down the access routes through Serbia from the Middle East, however temporarily.

But by involving Louis in their affairs, both Harris and Ross had offered hostages to fortune. They might not have cared to admit it, but Louis had a hold over them, just as they had over him. Ignoring his calls wouldn't negate it.

'A terrible business,' said the man who was seating himself at the next table. He wore a dark suit with a white shirt. A black overcoat was folded neatly on the red banquette opposite. His skin was sallow, and his beard neatly trimmed. He had the kind of face that smiled easily, which caused Louis to form an instant dislike for him. Sometimes Louis worried that he had more in common with SAC Edgar Ross than he was prepared to admit.

'I'm sorry?' said Louis.

'I couldn't help noticing the story on your device. Very unfortunate for the gentleman involved, not to mention the hotel.'

The stranger positioned with his back against the wall, so that Louis had to pivot slightly to watch him. A second man, burlier and less well dressed than the first, but also bearded and Middle Eastern, had taken a table near the door, and was scrupulously failing to pay them any attention.

A waiter arrived. The stranger ordered an espresso.

'What about your friend,' said Louis, 'doesn't he want something, too?'

That too-easy smile spread wider in response.

'He also will have an espresso,' he told the waiter, before folding his hands in his lap and regarding Louis with a semblance of amicability. Louis's jacket remained buttoned, and he could feel the presence of the gun concealed beneath it – not that he anticipated having to use it in Kaffee Alt Wien, or not because of this man and his associate. Only a dialogue would be conducted here. Whatever might follow would unfold elsewhere.

Louis continued to watch without speaking. Louis was very good at remaining silent. The concept of awkwardness was alien to him. From the corner of his left eye he saw the second man take delivery of his espresso, his attention all the while fixed on the entrance to the café and the street beyond. Here, thought Louis, were individuals with enemies.

'My name is Mr Rafi,' said the stranger finally, after his own coffee had been brought to the table. He pronounced every syllable slowly and with care, like a man reading unfamiliar words from a card.

'If you say so.'

Had the smile widened any further, Mr Rafi's lips would have split at the corners.

'You don't believe me?'

'It's not that,' said Louis. 'I just don't care.'

The smile didn't falter, but any residual warmth left Rafi's eyes. He was someone, Louis recognized, who valued the trappings of politeness, if only for their usefulness in disguising whatever reality they, like his smile, were trying to conceal. Mr Rafi, whoever he might be, would be polite even as he was cutting out your tongue or puncturing your eyeballs. He would beam benignly as gasoline was sprayed over a purpose-built steel cage before you were set alight. He might even apologize before slitting your throat while a camera filmed your passing for the internet. Mr Rafi was a sociopath, and one who had found a black flag of convenience under which to operate. This, of course, was not to say that Louis considered every Arab to be a potential killer, only that he knew a killer when he saw one.

'You should care,' said Mr Rafi.

'And why is that?'

'Because I found you so easily. A man in your line of work ought to be more prudent.'

Louis was forced to admit that Mr Rafi had a point. Perhaps he was growing negligent in his old age. On the other hand, he was in the process of killing his way across Europe, so it was not so much a question of not drawing attention as the level of attention one might inevitably draw.

'Maybe you're just good at finding people,' said Louis. 'Like certain dogs.'

Mr Rafi added a great deal of sugar to his espresso and knocked it back in a single gulp before it had a chance to grow even slightly cool.

'You appear intent on causing offense, Mr Louis,' he said.

'Well, I wouldn't like to think the effort was being wasted. And it's just Louis. Adding "Mister" makes me sound like a gentleman tailor.'

'Just Louis, then,' said Mr Rafi. 'Well, Just Louis, it seems we have interests in common.'

'I sure hope not,' said Louis.

'The Vuksans.'

'Oh,' said Louis, with relief. 'I thought it might have been something important, or really anything at all. Unfortunately, I don't know who, or what, the Vuksans are. You may have mistaken me for someone else.'

'Are you worried about a wire? You shouldn't be. You can search me if you wish, but it might prove awkward in such a public place.'

'I'll pass on touching you, but thanks for the offer.'

'I'm hurt,' said Mr Rafi. 'I understood that you enjoyed touching men.'

'I do, but I'm very particular, and I don't like getting my hands oily.'

But Louis was unhappy at what he was hearing. Mr Rafi was disturbingly familiar with his background, and there were only two ways he could have become so: by paying people a lot of money or by hurting them.

'We know you're looking for the Vuksans,' Mr Rafi resumed. 'We know that the Vuksans killed your friends in Amsterdam, and you've killed two of their people in turn. We also have reason to be interested in the Vuksans.'

'And why is that?'

'We entrusted them with cargo. That cargo was lost. Someone has to pay.'

'This cargo wouldn't have been lost somewhere around the Gare de Lyon, would it?' said Louis.

'Somewhere around there, yes.'

'That's a shame. You know, we *really* don't have anything in common. This conversation is coming to a welcome end.'

Louis signaled for the check.

'The lawyer, Frend, has gone to ground,' said Mr Rafi. 'And please don't tell me you have no idea who he is. That would be wearisome.'

Louis gave it three seconds, because comedy was all about timing.

'I have no idea who he is,' he said, and was pleased to see that Mr Rafi's smile was by now under severe strain, like a rope bridge about to collapse.

'We're anxious to speak with the Vuksans,' said Mr Rafi.

'And I still don't know who they are,' said Louis. 'But even if some misfortune were to befall these Vuksans – because who can say? – why should it matter if you have a hand in it or not? It's all the will of God, and the end result is the same.'

The waiter brought the check. Louis reached for his wallet, but Mr Rafi beat him to it by placing ten euros and change on the plate.

'For all of us,' he told the waiter, before returning his attention to Louis. 'And this is why it matters.' In his hand, Mr Rafi held a small roll of bills.

'Compensation,' said Louis.

'If you kill them, we get nothing.'

'And if these Vuksans, whoever they are, pay you, then all will be forgiven?'

'What do you think?' said Mr Rafi. His pupils had grown larger, turning his brown eyes almost black, as though in anticipation of the suffering they might soon witness.

'I think,' said Louis, 'that I may have to find somewhere else to drink my morning coffee in future, at least until something happens to you.'

Mr Rafi produced a card. It was blank, apart from a telephone number written by hand in blue ink. He slid the card toward Louis, who ignored it.

'I'd advise you to take it,' said Mr Rafi. 'What harm can it do to leave open a channel of communication?'

Louis hesitated before, with studied indifference, taking the card and vanishing it into a pocket.

'You have a good day,' he said.

'*Ma salama*,' said Mr Rafi.

The smile was back with a vengeance. Louis decided that it would be an act of public service to wipe it permanently from Mr Rafi's face, and erase Mr Rafi from the face of the earth immediately after.

Louis headed for the door, passing Mr Rafi's companion. He bore a jagged scar that ran from above his right eye, and across his forehead, to behind his left ear. It looked as though someone had tried to unfasten his skull with a can opener.

Louis paused in front of him.

'Yo,' said Louis, 'Harry Potter.'

The man glanced up.

'Made you look,' said Louis, and continued out the door. He patted the pocket containing Mr Rafi's card. He now had a bargaining chip.

Perhaps Harris and Ross might be disposed to do him a favor after all.

Chapter LXIV

Frend summoned a taxi to pick him up from the shadow of the silos. The app suggested it would be a twenty-minute wait, and he suddenly felt very exposed. Damn Kauffmann and her cemetery theatrics, and damn her, too, for making him doubt the wisdom of staying in Vienna once the Vuksans were gone. A bus was idling at the stop, and the driver was putting his phone away in preparation for departure. Frend decided to cancel the taxi. He did not wish to be out here with only birds and the dead for company. He took a seat behind the driver and was the sole passenger for the journey back to the tram terminus at Kaiser-Ebersdorfer Strasse, the trip offering him only a glum vista of warehouses, fields, and farm equipment. This was not Frend's Austria. It was the preserve of those who ate lunch standing up.

He distracted himself from the landscape with his phone, where he learned of Hendricksen's murder. So absorbed had he been by the presumed surveillance of the previous evening, and the impending meeting with Kauffmann, that he had failed to keep up with the news, which was unlike him. He could have lied to himself and pretended that he had not known how the Vuksans would react to Hendricksen's involvement, but such dissembling was beneath him. He would have preferred them to have gone about their business in a less gruesome and more private manner, though. The Vuksans appeared intent on making an already precarious position more unstable still.

The burner phone he used to remain in contact with the Vuksans beeped as he stepped from the bus and waved down a passing taxi. The message was a short, simple text: *We need to talk*. It was, Frend considered, a little late for that. The time to talk would have been before Ilić and the girl – because it was surely their handiwork – had set about torturing Hendricksen in the bathroom of a city hotel before leaving the dying man to be discovered by some unfortunate chambermaid or duty manager.

It was as Frend climbed into the taxi that he realized the implication of one element of the story: the *dying* man. Did Hendricksen remain conscious for long enough to supply information to whomever had found him? More to the point, how much had he shared about Frend with whomever had engaged him to make the trip to Belgrade to begin with?

Which was when Frend noticed a new email in his in-box, containing a video attachment. When he opened the message, three lines of text greeted him.

We have your daughter.

Wait for a call.

Breathe a word, and she dies.

Angel was waiting for Louis in the doorway of the Oswald & Kalb restaurant when the latter emerged from Kaffee Alt Wein.

'Are we making friends?' he asked, when Louis joined him. Angel had been watching the interaction between Louis and Mr Rafi from the street, but had seen no reason to make his presence known. He had faith in his partner's ability to handle most problems, as long as they did not require excessive diplomacy.

'Not unless you're planning to convert,' said Louis as they walked down Bäckerstrasse, 'and I don't think they're looking for our business anyway. I take it you got pictures of them?'

'From a distance, but the images will clean up nicely. What do they want?'

'The Vuksans. Alive.'

'Why?'

'So they can shake them down for blood money before killing them.'

'Did they tell you that?'

'Not in so many words.'

'And obviously they'd prefer if we didn't kill the Vuksans before they have a chance to do it themselves?'

'That would definitely be their preference, yes.'
'So what are we going to do?'
'We,' said Louis, 'are going to fuck them up.'
'That,' said Angel, 'sounds like a very good plan.'

Chapter LXV

In the privacy of his hotel room, Anton Frend replayed the video over and over. His daughter looked frightened and desperate. How could she be otherwise if it was to him she was appealing, the father she had disowned, the man whose very name she had sloughed?

'Papa, they say they'll hurt me if you don't help them.'

Papa: How long had it been since she called him that? Not since childhood.

'They say they'll kill me.'

His wife had cautioned against continuing to work with the Vuksans once they joined forces with the Zemuns to carve out a grubby empire in the Netherlands. She might have turned a blind eye to her husband's activities, but that required an awareness of them to begin with, and even she occasionally felt compelled to raise her concerns. Yet somehow she had managed to hold her nose while spending dirty money on trips to Venice and Milan, on expensive bags and fine clothes, on the nips and tucks that kept her looking youthful even as their marriage bed grew cold. He did not know why she bothered with the surgery, apart from indulging her own vanity. He might have respected her more had she taken a lover. It would at least have justified the expense.

'You have to reply to the email to confirm that you've received this message. Once you do, they'll be in touch.'

Were his wife here now, she would have told him to go to the police. Had he refused, she would have contacted them herself, and probably condemned their daughter to death in the process. It was as well that she was elsewhere. Decades of working with the Vuksans had given Frend an insight into how men of their stripe operated. They did not make idle threats. The questions, of course, were: a) Who had his daughter? and b) What did they want from him in return for her? The first step was to find out the answers, which would determine his next move. Already he had some inkling, but best to be sure.

'Papa, they showed me films. They've done this before. They showed me what would happen if you contacted the police. Papa, don't let them do that to me.'

The video ended. He replied to the email. A single word: *Received.* Two minutes later, his cell phone rang. The caller's number was withheld. He answered immediately.

'Yes?'

'Anton Frend?' The voice was disguised by software. It sounded almost female, but he could tell it was a man speaking.

'That's correct.'

'You saw the film?'

'Yes,' said Frend. 'What do you want?'

And it was as he had feared.

'We want the Vuksans.'

Bob Johnston took the call at the cottage in Cornwall. In the kitchen, Pia Lackner was playing cards with Rosanna Bellingham. The two women were getting along well enough, but the peculiar combination of boredom and tension had already begun to get to Pia. She was growing more short-tempered, which was hardly surprising. There were only so many games to be played, books to be read, and shows to be watched. Eventually, Johnston knew, her patience would run out. If she wanted to leave, he and Rosanna couldn't stop her. Well, they could, but it would be counterproductive, and would turn the operation from a simulacrum of a kidnapping into the thing itself.

The game stopped as soon as the phone rang. Pia and Rosanna watched Johnston answer it. He listened, said 'I'll let her know,' and hung up.

'Your father has made contact,' he told Pia. 'It'll move fast now.'

And Pia Lackner burst into tears.

Chapter LXVI

The Great Lost Bear had been in business since 1979, when Dave Evans, along with his wife and a cousin, had arrived in the city of Portland from North Conway, New Hampshire, and decided to open a bar of his own after years of working for other people who did a lot of stuff right and, sometimes, even more stuff wrong.

During those decades in Maine, Dave had seen just about everything, or thought he had until the Fulci brothers came into his life. Since that fateful event, Dave had been forced to reconsider his attitude to existence, and now steeled himself each morning to face the possibility of some degree of social interaction with Tony and Paulie Fulci. Such a day would potentially be open to chaos and destruction, and cause Dave to go to bed that night wondering if there really was a God and, if so, what had He been thinking when He created the Fulcis.

The Fulci brothers had once tried to agree on how many jails and prisons they'd been inside, but had lost count once the total reached double figures. Dave was surprised they could even count that high, but decided this was why God had opted to go with ten fingers, just so the Fulcis could divide aspects of their world into Things That Numbered Up To Ten, which were easily reckonable, and Things That Were More Than Ten, which were not. They'd run into similar difficulties coming up with an estimate of the number of psychiatrists who'd treated them, and the number of heads they'd busted over the years. As for the quantity of different pharmaceuticals they'd been prescribed, mostly unsuccessfully, during their long and fraught relationship with the medical profession, it easily ran into three figures, although Dave thought that might be erring on the low side, even if he chose to keep this opinion to himself.

The Fulcis were by now in middle-age, and no longer busted quite so many heads as they once had. Neither had they seen the interior of a cell for a number of years, a development due in no small part to their involvement with the private detective named Charlie Parker and his colleagues, Angel and Louis. The Fulcis looked up to all three of them: Parker with a deep respect, Angel with much affection, and Louis with an awe approaching that of the centurion Longinus upon having his blindness cured by the blood of the crucified Christ.

Dave Evans was far from an ingénue, and had no illusions about the natures of Parker, Angel, and Louis. He liked all three of them, and was close to Parker in particular, but he recognized that these were violent men, and not, therefore, ideal role models for the Fulcis, who were easily led. On the other hand, it could not be denied that Parker and the others lived by a moral code and – if even a fraction of the stories, both reported and unreported, were true – had brought a great deal of wickedness to an end. If they were not strictly good, they were whatever was required to face down evil. This, Dave accepted, sometimes necessitated methods that were not entirely legal or, in the case of Parker's occasional utilization of the Fulcis, even strictly wise.

The Fulcis were not without some admirable personal and professional qualities. They loved their mother. They were unswervingly loyal to their small circle of friends. They only busted the heads of those who were asking to have their heads busted. They were kind to animals. After this, the list of positives petered out, but as Dave's wife Weslie liked to remind him – a lot of people in the world couldn't boast even that many decencies. This, Dave had to admit, was certainly true, but as far as he was aware, the majority of those dubious individuals did not drink in his beloved Great Lost Bear, whereas the Fulcis practically lived in it.

Views differed on which of the brothers was the least unbalanced, an argument so esoteric, the differences involved being minute, that even St Thomas Aquinas himself might have elected to take a pass on it. Those familiar with the Fulcis felt that Tony, the older of the two, was now marginally less crazy than Paulie, and kept his brother somewhat in check. Since they looked almost identical (each being roughly as wide as he was tall), dressed in the same clothes, spoke in similar tones, and held interchangeable views on the world, the point was probably moot – especially if one of them was hitting you, since they also punched with indistinguishable force, like being hit by a cement block carved into the shape of a fist.

Currently Paulie Fulci was curled up on a bench beneath the bear head that was the bar's mascot, working on a crossword puzzle. Dave, who was checking accounts at the bar, had almost fallen from his stool in shock upon being told this, only to discover that it was a crossword puzzle in a comic book with a pony on the front cover. Still, it represented progress, of a sort.

The bar was quiet, even for early on a damp Sunday afternoon. Dave enjoyed this time. He found it conducive to the kind of concentration the accounts required, which was why, once a month, he liked to come to the Bear to do them. But once evening arrived, Dave would be gone. The Bear didn't need him around at night, and the line chefs would only stress him out.

In a corner booth, Charlie Parker was speaking softly with a young woman, most likely a client, who was obviously in difficulty if Parker was meeting with her on a Sunday. Parker often received clients, prospective or otherwise, at the Bear. He didn't have an office of his own and his home was out of bounds. Dave knew that Parker occasionally used the premises of his lawyer, Moxie Castin, if circumstances required it, but preferred more informal settings. Moxie ate at the Bear a couple of times a month, usually with Parker. He seemed to be the unhealthiest man Dave had ever met, because his diet would have frightened Ronald McDonald, but he continued somehow to walk the earth. Dave had even started to use his services because Moxie's legal connections were second to none, and being a bar owner in this town meant dealing with the cops and the courts on a regular basis, whether one liked it or not.

The young woman with Parker had begun to cry. Parker caught Dave's eye, and Dave told one of the staff to take her a glass of water and see if she wanted a coffee or a soda, too. Parker's face was alive with feeling for the woman opposite him: not pity, or not solely that, but more a profound empathy. It was why Parker did what he did, why he was good at it, why Dave would never wish for Parker's absence from his life, and why Dave would never judge him harshly for any of his actions. As long as the Bear existed and was under Dave's control, Parker would always be welcome; Angel and Louis, too. And okay, fine, even the Fulcis, although Dave expected time off in purgatory for what he'd endured on earth as a consequence of their presence.

Speaking of which, Dave wondered what Tony was up to. Tony and his brother were usually inseparable, but Tony had headed out two hours earlier and not been seen since. This was potentially bad news for civilization, depending on what he was doing. Dave glanced over again at Parker and the young woman. Cupcake Cathy had arrived with a glass of water, as well as two empty mugs and the coffeepot. Dave trusted that the young woman would be okay. She was with Parker now. He would do his best for her.

Dave returned to his accounts, but Tony Fulci's absence continued to nag at him. He hoped Tony wasn't in any trouble, because if Tony was in trouble, it would certainly be as a result of causing trouble for someone else. Dave wasn't sure how he had ended up feeling some responsibility for the Fulcis' actions, but that had come to be the case. In his weaker moments, he even worried about them. He hoped he wasn't becoming fond of them.

Dear God, he thought, not that.

Chapter LXVII

Tony Fulci was not stupid.

Of course, there were persons in Portland and farther afield who liked to joke that Tony was dumb as a rock, while his brother was dumb as two rocks, or half a rock, depending on where one stood on the whole dumbness/rock comparison index. They did not offer these opinions to Tony's face, or not a second time, but Tony was aware that they circulated, and had taken note of the identities of those responsible. It wasn't so much the aspersions being cast on his intelligence that bothered him as the mockery of his brother. Tony was very protective of Paulie and had promised their mother that he would always look out for him. The world was more confusing to Paulie than it was to Tony. It was frequently too loud, too fast. The unkindness of strangers toward those more vulnerable than themselves, whether human or animal, conspired to rouse Paulie to an excess of righteous indignation that tipped easily into outright violence; yet in all his life, Paulie, like Tony, had never hit anyone smaller than himself, not unless they really, really deserved it. Paulie lived by the principle that a man should punch up, not down. He might have struggled to express the range and complexity of his better feelings, and consequently the unobservant and judgmental concluded that he had no such feelings available to express, but Tony knew better.

When the opportunity presented itself, Tony would have a quiet word with individuals known to have belittled his brother. These conversations typically took place in alleyways or restrooms, and had a tendency to be very one-sided. They also generally resulted in a permanent alteration in behavior, because once Tony Fulci told you something, you stayed told.

To repeat, then: Tony Fulci was not stupid. But he was slow. He did not absorb information quickly, but absorb it he did, in the end. He had learned to listen carefully because he missed crucial details otherwise. Later, in solitude, he would contemplate all that he had heard and try to come to some conclusions about it. He would sit up late into the night when his mother and brother were asleep, his elbows on the kitchen table, his chin in his hands, and stare at the wall, lost in what appeared to be a trance. But the kitchen wall was made of bricks, and on each brick Tony had learned to visualize a word or concept. In his mind, he could then move the bricks around, although it was often sufficient just to leave them in place, having broken a subject down into manageable pieces. For particularly intractable problems, he would resort to writing on the bricks with a piece of chalk, making sure to wipe them clean before he went to bed. Mrs Fulci did not approve of people writing on her walls, not even in chalk.

Tony worried about appearing ignorant and was therefore reluctant to reveal his thought processes, or his doubts, to more than a handful of people. If he did not understand something, he tried to find somebody to explain it to him, someone who would not laugh at his lack of cognizance. This was why Tony and his brother liked the Great Lost Bear: Dave Evans, when he was not busy, or not looking perturbed by the Fulcis' continued presence in his bar, was always willing to listen and offer advice. So, too, was his wife, who reminded the Fulcis a little of their mother, but without the accompanying terror.

For very serious matters, Tony would cautiously approach Mr Parker. Tony felt uncomfortable calling him by his first name – it just didn't sit right – and referring to him by his last name alone seemed rude. Tony respected Mr Parker more than any man he had ever met, even Louis, and he secretly and not-so-secretly worshipped Louis. Tony had never before encountered one so willing to risk his own life to end another's pain as Mr Parker. As far as Tony was concerned, the private investigator had a moral authority that even God lacked. If you asked God for help, there was no guarantee it would arrive, or that God had even listened.

But with Mr Parker, if you were a good person in distress, and you asked for his help, you got it.

That was why Tony and Paulie stood by him any chance they got. The brothers had messed up a lot in their lives, and Mr Parker represented an opportunity to put some of that right by redressing any existing imbalance in favor of the good. Tony thought Angel and Louis had allied themselves with Mr Parker for a similar reason: because they had messed up, too – Louis especially, although Tony wasn't about to judge him for it, even if Louis frightened him at times – and siding with the detective was a way to make up for it. Tony also secretly suspected that it gave Louis an excuse to shoot people and not feel too bad about it.

All of which was a roundabout way of explaining that Tony Fulci was neither as intellectually or as emotionally limited as some believed him to be. And like a lot of men and women who think slowly, he had a habit of coming to the right decision at the end of his deliberations. He had now spent ninety minutes sitting in the cab of the monster truck he shared with his brother, eating a box of Crown Fried Chicken and watching the two men parked over by Coastal Trading & Pawn. Earlier, by coincidence, he and Paulie had been five vehicles behind Parker as he drove along Forest Avenue to the Bear, where his car currently sat in the parking lot. Four cars behind Parker, and therefore immediately in front of the Fulcis, had been a blue Chevy Avalanche with New York plates and what looked like two male occupants. When Tony had stepped out of the Bear to call his mother – he didn't like forcing others to listen to his cell phone conversations, especially not with his mom – the Chevy had been parked outside Skillful Home Recreation, still with two guys sitting in the front. It had since relocated twice while always keeping the parking lot of the Bear in view.

It hadn't taken Tony long to figure out that the two men were watching and waiting for someone in the Bear and the available evidence, given the vehicles that had already entered and exited during the time that Tony had spent observing it, suggested it could well be Mr Parker. On the other hand, Tony knew, he might just be jumping at shadows where none existed. He could call

Mr Parker and tell him what he was seeing, but then what? The investigator might confront the two men – because a certain rashness was part of his nature – but he was currently alone, Angel and Louis being elsewhere, and if the men in the car meant him some ill will, he would be walking straight into their sights. If the cops were called, they could only question them before moving them along, unless something offered probable cause for further action. Again, if the watchers meant Mr Parker harm, they'd either vanish only to materialize again later, or pass the job on to someone else.

Tony really wished Angel and Louis were around.

Just then the Chevy pulled away from the curb and headed east along Forest Avenue toward the entrance to I-295. Rain had been falling steadily since morning, and the streets were nearly empty of people. Tony waited, and a minute or two later the Chevy reappeared in his rearview mirror, passed him, and pulled up at the intersection with Ashmont Street. The driver kept the engine running as the passenger got out. He was shorter and less well built than Tony – there were parking garages less structurally impressive than Tony Fulci – and was, in theory, not the kind of individual Tony should have been inclined to hit. But Tony, who was essentially a good person, had an unerring sense of badness in others. God did not always mark the worst of men, but He did brand some of them, and He had certainly taken the time to differentiate this one from the rest of the herd, if only – because say what you wanted about the Divine, He had a sense of humor – by giving him virtually no distinguishing features at all. From the top of his smooth head to the soles of his no-brand shoes, here was an unfinished man, a moral absence given human form.

Tony knew this because he had encountered similarly incomplete versions of such an entity before, often in prison and even, on occasion, in positions of authority. The best of them were willfully cruel, either to distract themselves from the prospect of their own inevitable damnation or to indulge their basest impulses, seeing no merit in depriving themselves of entertainment if their perdition was already assured. But in others nature and nurture had conspired in a grave error, giving the resulting creations no other option but to behave as they did, just as a bullet fired from a gun can only go in one direction until stopped by an impact or rendered harmless by the laws of energy and decay. They did not recognize concepts such as viciousness and sadism, just as any attempt to explain their opposites would be met with stares of absolute incomprehension. They were as content to inflict hurt as not to inflict it, and if they dreamed, they did not recall their visions. In repose, they gazed out on a featureless vista and heard only white noise. They were humanity's detritus and the devil's foot soldiers.

And now one of them was entering the parking lot of the Bear, carrying a brown paper bag in his right hand and supporting its base with his left. All this time, he and his companion had been waiting for the perfect moment: rain, temporarily empty streets, an almost deserted lot. Tony alighted from the cab of his truck and moved toward the Bear, ignoring the Chevy and its driver for the present because he could deal only with one man at a time. He arrived at the lot to see the human doll kneeling by Parker's car, one hand under the front-left wheel well. The doll looked up to see Tony Fulci standing above him and reacted swiftly, his left hand leaving the wheel well while his right moved simultaneously toward the inside of his coat. Tony let the tire iron slip from his sleeve to the palm of his right hand before swinging it in a single sharp motion toward the doll's head. It caught him just behind the right ear, and Tony heard the bone crack. The doll's eyes rolled upward as he toppled, and blood began to flow from his ear canal.

Now Tony heard footsteps behind him and turned to face the new threat. The driver had emerged from his vehicle. In his right hand he held a short-barreled revolver. Tony threw the tire iron, missing the driver's head by inches.

'You fucking asshole,' said the driver in an accent Tony did not recognize, but Tony was by then already charging at him like a rhino in polyester. If Tony was going to die, he intended to make his killer work for the pleasure, except that the ground was slick with rain, and Tony might have had bulk but he did not have speed, not until he'd built up momentum. He needed more distance than he had, but he realized this just too late.

Which was when the head of a bear hit the driver full in the side of the skull, followed shortly after by Tony's considerable weight impacting on his chest from the front, and seconds later by Paulie Fulci's own bulk connecting with him from the right. The revolver went off, but it was pointed at the sky, and by then the driver had hit the ground with the best part of a six hundred pounds of prime Italian-American beef on top of him. His ribs snapped like dry sticks, and his left arm and left leg immediately shattered. A number of his vital organs either burst or collapsed, and that was before the blows began to land, rendering him mercifully unconscious.

Figures appeared, but Tony saw them only through a red mist. Paulie, by contrast, didn't see them at all, so absorbed was he in pummeling what was left of the life from the man with the temerity to have pointed a gun at his brother.

'Motherfucker!' yelled Paulie, as another bone broke beneath his punches. 'Mother*fucker*!'

When a combination of Dave Evans, Charlie Parker, and a handful of off-duty Portland PD officers finally managed to drag the brothers away, it came as a surprise to them to find that the driver was not dead, although it was not for want of trying. Neither was his companion, who remained unconscious where he had fallen. Attached by a magnet to the wheel well of Parker's car was a device composed of five pounds of plastic explosive, two pounds of nails and shotgun pellets, and a mercury tilt switch so delicate that it would have been activated as soon as the car began to pull out of its parking space.

The two seriously injured men were carrying New York State driver's licenses in the names of Borko Zorić and Miroslav Tomić. Both were naturalized US citizens, originally from Serbia but now living in Queens. They'd been in and out of prison, if only for misdemeanors and minor felonies, but the gun used by the driver, Tomić, would later be linked to fifteen murders, including those of three women and two children. It was, Tomić would subsequently tell prosecutors through wired jaws, his lucky gun, and he hadn't wanted to throw it away. As for Borko Zorić, he would not utter a word during his interrogation or subsequent trial, not even to confirm his own name, and appeared totally indifferent to his fate.

But all that was to come. For now, there was a bar to be evacuated while the police dealt with the car bomb, and later a bear head to be reattached to a wall. Local and national news media would interview the Fulcis. The front page of the following day's *Portland Press Herald*, featuring Tony and Paulie flanking their proud mother, would be added to the memorabilia collection of the Great Lost Bear. The Fulci brothers had saved the Bear, but in doing so had become part of its structure and history, forever inseparable from both.

It was, Dave Evans would later reflect, one of the worst days of his life.

IV

'I incline to Cain's heresy . . . I let my brother go to the devil in his own way.'

Robert Louis Stevenson,
Strange Case of Dr Jekyll and Mr Hyde

Chapter LXVIII

S piridon Vuksan had not survived for as long as he had through good fortune alone. He accepted that luck played a part in every man's life, but so also did preparation, decisiveness, and ultimately, ruthlessness. Neither was Spiridon blind to his own flaws, not least of which was pride, although he balked at categorizing it as a sin, particularly when it came to his relationship with the country of his birth. It pained him that men like Matija Kiš and Simo Stajić were preventing him from returning to his homeland, a country that he and his brother had fought to build from the wreckage of Tito's former dictatorship. Spiridon was a patriot. He had the scars to prove it. Kiš and Stajić were scavengers, filling their bellies from the battlefield sacrifices of braver men.

Now others were striking at Spiridon from the shadows: a *peškir* killer, a negro, a *crnac*, seeking revenge for De Jaager's death when he bore some of the responsibility for having fulfilled the original contract on Andrej Buha; an American, too, which meant it was his people who had bombed Serbian troops from the sky in 1999 because they were afraid to fight them face-to-face.

As well as this Louis there were the *muslimani*, the Turks, no better than the *balijas* Spiridon had euthanized in the woods of Srebrenica and Žepa, descendants of the Ottomans who had beheaded and impaled patriots for rebelling against their rule. If Spiridon ran from men such as these, how could he ever hold his head high again? Better to let his beard and hair grow long like a monk's than look upon his reflection in a mirror and see only a *kukavica*, a coward.

But his brother was counseling caution: a 'strategic retreat', Radovan termed it, while they consolidated their forces and waited to see what might emerge from the Kiš-Stajić axis, because

Radovan, like Spiridon, was convinced that the union would not hold. Kiš was too politically ambitious and Stajić too unpredictable. Soon one of them would turn on the other, and Radovan's opinion was that Stajić would end up with a bullet in the back of his head. Every killing left a vacuum, Radovan told his brother, and the Vuksans, with planning, could be in a position to fill it. They just had to bide their time.

But Spiridon knew that Radovan was lying. Once Radovan was in possession of a new passport and a new identity, with a house in the Caribbean and a small boat from which to fish, he would not want to return to Europe. Radovan was not a fighter, not like Spiridon, and had no concept of ignominy. He would live out his days in the sun, feeling no shame. Spiridon, by contrast, was a guerrilla at heart. He would do what his ancestors had done. He would gather his people and head into the mountains. He would make ghost villages and abandoned houses his own. Others would join him, because men like Matija Kiš and Simo Stajić did not inspire loyalty. They looked like the future only to those with no comprehension of the past, but Spiridon Vuksan knew different. Serbia's past *was* its future. It had been an empire once, and could be an imperial force again. The wars in Croatia and Bosnia had been fought on the basis of that conviction.

Spiridon wondered where Zorya was. He had not seen her since the day before. She would have to be told of his plan, because he would need her by his side. He knew that she, too, wanted to return home, not spend years hiding on an alien island, waiting for enemies to die at the hands of other men. She was a creature of the cold and dark. Zorya had winter blood.

The door opened behind Spiridon. He looked back, expecting to see her, but it was Radovan who entered. Spiridon did not mind. A conversation with Radovan was required, but not about the choice they faced. There was another, more pressing matter to be discussed.

He rose to hug his brother, and they exchanged three kisses.

'Sit,' said Spiridon. 'I have a question for you.'

Radovan took the nearest chair. It left him seated slightly lower than his brother. Spiridon would have avoided placing himself in a similar position of inferiority, even among family, but Radovan had never concerned himself with such details. He was content to let others believe he was weaker than he was because he felt it gave him room to maneuver. Sometimes, though, the perceptions of others concretized into fact. Let people believe you were weak and they might well decide to move against you. No one feared a weak man, or not beyond the potential damage his weakness might cause. Unbeknownst to his brother, recent events were causing Radovan to examine the implications of this.

'What is it?' said Radovan.

Spiridon took his brother's hands in his own.

'How close are you and Anton Frend?' he said.

'You know the answer,' said Radovan. 'We have been colleagues, and more, for a long time. He has never given us cause to mistrust him. Why do you ask?'

'Because they will come for him, after we are gone: the Turks, the American killer. It is a wonder they have not done so already.'

'What about Hendricksen?'

'Hendricksen was just the advance guard,' said Spiridon. 'The ones that will follow are the real threat. They can't get to us, not yet, but they can get to Frend.'

'We need him. He is organizing the passports, and our route out of here.'

'No, we need only the lawyer, Kauffmann. We know she is his contact. He told us so.'

'She will not work with us directly,' said Radovan. 'We are too toxic.'

'Or so Frend would have us believe.'

'He is not lying about Kauffmann. This is Anton's world, and he understands how it works. Clean hands: it is the Austrian way.'

'It may be their way, but it is not ours,' said Spiridon. 'Even if Frend's days are not numbered, do you really believe that Interpol and the Dutch police will fail to connect him to us? If Hendricksen could do it, so can they. And then Frend will talk, because he will not risk prison for our sakes.'

'Brother, Frend and I have been very vigilant.'

'Not vigilant enough to stop our money from being seized.'

'Money can be replaced. The kind of relationship we have built with Frend cannot. His contacts are our contacts. Without him, we are entirely alone.'

'And I tell you they will come for him,' said Spiridon. 'Even if the hunters miss the spoor at first, what is to prevent Matija Kiš from allying himself with them in order to harm us? He will feed Frend to them, and Frend will sacrifice us to save himself. As long as he is alive, we are at risk.'

Radovan did not know what pained him more: to hear his brother speak like this about a man for whom Radovan had much affection, or to know that he might well be correct. Frend was the weak link, but Radovan was not prepared to sacrifice him, not yet. And all this because Spiridon had insisted on marking his departure from the Netherlands with rape and murder.

'Let me think on it,' said Radovan. 'Now I have news for you, and once more, it is not good.'

Radovan had advised against targeting the private detective in Maine. It was a chance they did not need to take, but Spiridon again had ignored his guidance, with Zorya whispering in his ear. Why she had urged Spiridon to strike at Parker, Radovan did not know. He was beginning to wonder if he was the only sane one left in their circle.

'Well?' said Spiridon.

'The attempt on Parker's life failed, and the men sent to take care of it are in police custody. Our friends in Ridgewood are very upset.'

'Will they talk, these men?'

'My information is that they were both seriously injured in the course of events. For now, they are incapable of saying anything at all.'

Spiridon stared at his hands and flexed his fingers. Radovan knew the uses to which Spiridon was putting those hands in his mind.

'Perhaps they'll die,' said Spiridon.

Radovan stood to leave.

'Death does not solve every problem,' he said.

'Actually,' said his brother, 'it does.'

Chapter LXIX

Detective Sharon Macy lounged at a table in the Great Lost Bear, sipping a diet soda. Seated around it with her were two detectives from the Portland PD's Criminal Investigation Division, Tony and Paulie Fulci, Charlie Parker, and Dave Evans. The bomb technicians from the Hazardous Devices Unit had successfully dealt with the IED, the two injured men had been taken under escort to Maine Medical, and the Bear had reopened for business. A brief debate had taken place about whether the bear head used against one of the men should be seized as evidence before it was decided that it was probably just as easy to leave it at the bar. It was now back in its place on the wall, its fur damaged from the impact with either the ground or a Serbian skull. Macy had to concede that Paulie Fulci had quite the pair of throwing arms, because that bear head wasn't light.

A couple of months had passed since last she'd visited the Great Lost Bear. Macy was trying to drink less as part of a new fitness regimen, which meant she was avoiding bars, most restaurants, and pretty much anywhere else she might have a little fun. It was playing hell with her socializing, not to mention her love life. She'd started going to bed earlier, too, because there wasn't much else to do when one didn't drink or go out. This, she decided, was how women ended up in nunneries.

While still a working detective for the Portland PD, Macy also functioned as the liaison between the department, the state police, federal agencies, and the governor's office, particularly in matters relating to serious crimes. Trying to plant a bomb outside the Great Lost Bear counted as serious in anyone's book, but it took on an added gravity when Charlie Parker was the target. Any number of people wouldn't have minded seeing the private detective blown sky high, but even they would probably have preferred it not to happen in the parking lot of one of Portland's best-loved drinking establishments. That Parker wasn't already dead was a miracle, if not necessarily the kind that encouraged faith in divine judgment.

The investigation was complicated by the fact that Macy and Parker had dated briefly. They hadn't managed to get it together – circumstances and timing as much as anything – but there were no hard feelings, so now, as well as being the official point of contact between various branches of law enforcement and state government, Macy was also the unofficial mediator between some of those same agencies and one of the most problematical private investigators in the state, if not the entire country.

Macy and the detectives asked the Fulcis and Dave Evans a few more questions about what they'd witnessed, and clarified the series of events that had led from Dave spotting the first of the Serbians entering the lot on the CCTV to Paulie lobbing a bear head, before telling them they could go. Parker, she asked to stay.

'So you're telling me you have no idea why a pair of Serbian hitmen would decide to place a bomb in the wheel well of your car?' she said.

'I haven't annoyed any Serbians,' said Parker, 'not that I know of.'

He was a man of slightly above average height and build, with graying hair and eyes that veered between blue and green, depending on the light. He was easy to dismiss at first glance, Macy thought. If you looked harder, though, the lines of grief on his face became more pronounced, and his sense of coiled energy, even violence, grew more perceptible. He had killed; some were deaths of which the police were aware, but others, she felt sure, remained unknown to them. Macy had also taken lives, and the memory of it still troubled her. She did not know if Parker was tormented by a great deal of what he had done. She suspected that, as in the words of the Confiteor, he was haunted more by all he had failed to do.

There were those who felt Parker should be behind bars, including half-a-dozen district attorneys and at least three state attorneys general. That he was not was a matter of frustration, but Parker had luck on his side and some influential protectors both inside and outside the law. Yet he also had a strangeness to him, an element of the preternatural. Even his aftershave smelled of incense.

'Maybe you upset someone who hired the Serbians to take you out?' said one of the other detectives, in a tone of voice that suggested such a course of action would have been entirely understandable, even forgivable. His name was Furnish, and he and Parker had crossed paths before. Parker didn't think highly of him, and the feeling was entirely mutual.

'I could make a list,' said Parker, 'but who has that kind of time?'

'This is serious,' said Macy. 'With the nails and pellets thrown into the mix, that bomb was designed for maximum damage.'

Parker stared at her and spread his arms, as if to ask what more he could offer.

'If you're holding back on us,' said Macy, 'and I find out—'

'I'm telling you the truth,' said Parker. 'I don't think I even know any Serbians, and nothing I'm working on right now would attract that kind of attention.'

'What about an older case?' asked the third detective, whose name was Elkin. 'Could someone be holding a grudge against you from a previous investigation?'

'I think you'll find they're all dead,' said Furnish.

'Shut the fuck up, Furnish,' said Macy. 'Jesus.'

'I'll ruminate on it,' said Parker, ignoring Furnish.

'Do that,' said Macy, 'because who's to say they won't try again? The Fulcis won't always be ready to come to the rescue with a tire iron and a bear head.'

The three detectives departed, leaving Parker alone at the table. He waited until he was sure they were gone before co-opting Dave Evans's private office to call Louis.

'Two Serbian button men just tried to blow up my car,' he said, when Louis answered.

'Tried?'

'Tony Fulci busted the skull of one of them with a tire iron. Paulie attacked the other with a bear head, then he and Tony beat the shit out of him.'

'A bear head?' said Louis.

'It was the first weapon that came to hand,' said Parker. 'Also, this is Paulie we're talking about. He'd probably been contemplating using that bear head for a while.'

'Are the Serbs talking?'

'After what the Fulcis did to them, they're likely to be incommunicado for some time, but I don't see how this one is on me.'

'The Vuksans?'

'They could be trying to get at you through me, which means they know who you are. How close are you to finishing this thing?'

'Getting there.'

'You think maybe you could speed it up? That bomb was packed with nails and shotgun pellets. It could have done some serious damage to Dave's bar.'

'Yikes,' said Louis.

'Yeah,' said Parker, '"Yikes" about covers it. My previous offer stands: If you need company, you only have to ask.'

'I appreciate that, but when it comes to finding people, we've learned from the best. And you.'

'Very funny. Sharon Macy just left here. She wasn't laughing, though.'

'Does she still have the hots for you?'

'She never had the hots for me,' said Parker.

'So she only went out with you because the check cleared? Come on.'

'Well, perhaps she did have the hots a little, but not any longer. And she wasn't minded to believe that some random Eastern Europeans took it into their heads to blow up a stranger, not even for old times' sake.'

'It was a dumb move by the Vuksans,' said Louis.

'Only because it failed.'

'Yeah,' said Louis. 'Unfortunately, they don't always fail. I've been meaning to call you, but events got in the way. Hendricksen is dead.'

Under other circumstances, and with any other person, Parker might have been upset at the failure to share such information before now, or with the manner of its imparting, but this was Louis. The less Louis said, the more he felt.

'How?'

'He was attacked in his hotel room. They hurt him badly, and he must have talked before he died, because who wouldn't?'

'Yeah, who wouldn't?' Parker added another name to the list of the lost. He had not met Hendricksen, and knew of him only through Louis, but the Dutchman had stepped up to help when called upon, and both Angel and Louis had respected him. That was enough to make his loss personal. 'I'm sorry.'

'I think that's how the Vuksans came after you,' said Louis. 'They connected the dots.'

'A hit on me,' said Parker, 'which would bring you back here and give them breathing space.'

'Leaving no evidence that they were involved, your ledger being heavily in the black when it comes to enemies.'

Parker could now breathe a little easier. The Vuksans had shown their hand and been beaten. They could try to kill half of Portland and it would not dissuade Louis from hunting them. Instead, it would only encourage him.

'So what now?' he said.

'We have a hook buried in the lawyer,' said Louis. 'We're about to test it.'

'Don't be gentle on my account.'

'We won't. Tell Moxie I said hello.'

'He'll be thrilled,' said Parker. 'Not. And Louis?'

'Yes?'

'Step carefully, okay?'

'Always do,' said Louis, 'occasionally on other people.'

Parker put down his cell phone, closed his eyes, and took a long, deep breath. He didn't like to think how near he'd come to being torn apart by an IED. It was enough to make a man fearful of leaving the house. When he opened his eyes again, Sharon Macy was standing in the doorway of the office.

'Can I ask who you just called?' she said.

'My mom,' said Parker. 'She worries.'

'Even from the next world? That must be some phone you have. Try again.'

Parker considered telling Macy to mind her own business, but common sense prevailed. A bomb couldn't simply be dismissed, and Macy would be required to provide answers and assurances, both to the city and to her superiors.

'What happened today wasn't about me,' said Parker. 'It was supposed to divert someone's attention and force him to return here, but it failed. Worse, it's just made him more focused.'

'You wouldn't be referring to one of your friends from New York, would you?'

'That may be more detail than I'm willing to share.'

'Look at you, all secretive.'

'It means there won't be any more trouble, or not of the bomb kind.'

She smiled at him. It wasn't a sad smile exactly, but sadness was somewhere in the mix.

'But there'll be another kind of trouble along soon enough, right?'

'Trouble follows me,' said Parker. 'I think that was the title of a book.'

'It follows you like a dog,' said Macy, 'because you keep feeding it. Speaking of which, have you eaten?'

Parker looked at his watch. He hadn't realized how late it was, but he wasn't very hungry. The IED had served to deprive him of his appetite.

Then he looked at Macy and thought again.

'Were you thinking of getting something?'

'Maybe Boda.'

'You buying?'

'Sure,' she said, 'why not?'

*

Later, as she lay sleeping beside him, Parker watched the stars defy the darkness. She would leave in the morning. Perhaps they would do this again, but it did not matter. It was enough to connect, enough to touch and be touched, if only for a night.

Enough, briefly, to defy the darkness.

Chapter LXX

From where he sat, Radovan Vuksan could see no stars, only darkness. The drapes were closed, and the bedroom was dim. The chair was an antique, akin to a throne. It gave him the aspect of a judge, one forced to pass a sentence with which he did not entirely agree, but to whom the option of clemency had been denied.

He had not slept well that night. He had not slept well in a long time. Radovan was worn out by bloodshed, even at one remove. It seemed that he had known little else since before Tito passed away in a Ljubljana hospital in 1980, the room fetid with the stink of gangrene. Tito's Croat wife, Jovanka Broz, had been permitted to remain at liberty only for long enough to wave his coffin into the House of Flowers before she was incarcerated in a rotting Belgrade villa. There she had remained hidden for decades without a passport or identity card, lest any reminder of her late husband's existence should interfere with the process of dismantling his precious Yugoslav republic.

Because even then Radovan and his brother had been aware of what was coming. Their father, Sergej, had warned of it for years. The country was an artificial construct, six republics bound together by the iron will of Tito, like six thorny stems held in awkward proximity by barbed wire. As soon as Tito died, they would fall apart, and the resulting frictions would lead to a conflagration.

Sergej Vuksan had been a senior official in UDBA, the Yugoslav secret service, with special responsibility for monitoring the activities of dissidents abroad, particularly Croatians. Sergej's own sympathies, carefully concealed, lay with the Serbian nationalists. Like many Serbs, he had no love for Tito, an ethnic Croat raised as a Catholic, even as he helped to secure the dictator's rule. He had raised his sons in the expectation that, when the inevitable conflict commenced, they would do their duty to further the cause of Serbian independence. Each, in his way, had obliged, Spiridon by shedding the blood of Turks and Croats, and Radovan by ensuring that the resources were available for him to do so. Whether Sergej, had he lived, would have approved of his sons' subsequent transition to mundane, self-interested criminality was another matter, but dementia and mortality had negated the necessity of such an awkward conversation.

Now Serbia was an independent nation once again, if still something of a pariah in Europe, but the Udbasi had not gone away. Instead they had integrated themselves into the structures of the new republics according to their political or national loyalties, principally in order to feather their own nests. Within Serbia, powerful elements had recognized the usefulness of employing UDBA tactics against their enemies, which now included the Vuksans. This, Radovan knew, was what Spiridon failed to recognize: The Vuksans were engaged in a battle not only with ambitious men like Matija Kiš and Simo Stajić but also with the entire apparatus of the Serbian state. It was a fight that the brothers were destined to lose.

So Radovan sat in his chair, watching the dawn come too slowly. Shortly after 10 a.m., he made the call.

Radovan was taking a chance, of course, one of which his brother would not approve, but perhaps the Vuksans were still owed a favor or two, if only out of respect for their late father. The Serbian consulate in Vienna was situated on Ölzeltgasse. Radovan dialed the number and asked to be put through to the liaison officer for the head of mission to the Organization for Security and Co-operation in Europe. When he was informed that Ms Ćirić was not available, he asked that she be contacted as a matter of urgency, and left a number and the contact name Vrana. Five minutes later, the phone rang.

'Tell me you're not actually in Vienna,' said Teodora Ćirić.

'I have never lied to you,' Radovan answered. 'I don't intend to start now.'

'What do you want?'

'To meet, to talk.'

'You have a price on your head.'

'I'm aware of that. I wish to find a way to avoid the shedding of more blood, including my own.'

'You should have thought of that before you and your brother opened a butcher's shop on the Herengracht.'

'Teo, for old times' sake—'

There was silence, then: 'Burggasse Twenty-Four. It's a clothing store, but there is a café on the ground floor. It's not the kind of place where we are likely to attract attention. I can be there in an hour.'

'Thank you,' said Radovan, before adding, 'I'm trusting you.'

'That you should mention it indicates doubt. Given your situation, though, I'm inclined to forgive it. But Radovan?'

'Yes?'

'If we are seen together, and questions are asked, I will have to act. You understand?'

'I do.'

'One hour. Don't be late.'

In the event, Radovan arrived early at the meeting place. Burggasse 24 was a two-story vintage emporium in the 7th District, with a casual café at the back that extended across two rooms. The clientele was young and chic, and made Radovan feel like the interloper that he was. He took a seat in the main section, from which he could see the street and the open area to the left around Sankt-Ulrichs-Platz. Somewhere out there, he knew, Teodora Ćirić would be watching. He might have been early, but she would have been earlier still.

Radovan ordered a slice of tart with his coffee, and tried to keep his breathing calm as he stirred in the sugar. One call: that was all it would take for Ćirić to summon a pair of vehicles, probably a van and an escort car, and pull him from the street. An interrogation would follow, and, in all probability, a handover to the Austrian police prior to his extradition to the Netherlands, a sacrificial offering on the altar of prospective EU membership.

Then again, his compatriots might decide to deal with him themselves. It depended on how much influence Matija Kiš had already accrued and how badly Simo Stajić wanted to make an example of the Vuksans. It was only six hours by road from Vienna to Belgrade, plenty of time for Stajić to prepare a basement and gather his tools. Radovan's only consolation was that he had managed to enter Burggasse 24 unimpeded. It would have been easiest for Ćirić to seize him before he got to the meeting place.

And now here was the woman herself, a few more lines to her face, her hair entirely gray, although the color suggested that she had decided to finish for herself what nature had started. It would be typical of the Teodora he remembered, a woman disinclined to do things by half measures. Were she to have received a terminal diagnosis from a physician, she would have poured herself a glass of Prokupac before eating her gun.

Radovan stood to greet her, and they hugged awkwardly while exchanging a single, fleeting kiss on the cheek. Her perfume smelled expensive and her coat looked like it might have come from one of the more exclusive racks in Burggasse 24 itself, or be destined for them once it had ceased to delight her. She ordered mint tea and sat with her back to the wall.

'You've grown old,' she said, although she was older than he by almost a decade.

'It has a certain inevitability.'

'Isn't it supposed to be accompanied by wisdom?'

'Only in the most fortunate,' said Radovan. 'I find that resignation is often mistaken for it.'

'Yet you appear to be neither wise – because you're still laboring in the shadow of your brother – nor resigned, or else you would not be here.'

'I'm hoping to find a third path.'

'And what would that be?'

'To survive, and let others survive also.'

Her tea arrived. He pushed the plate of tart in her direction, inviting her to share it. She declined.

'Diabetes,' she said. 'I seem to be the first in my family to have developed it. I blame my exposure to the excesses of the new Europe.'

'Such invisible ailments aside,' said Radovan, 'the new Europe appears to be agreeing with you. You look well.'

And she did, even as he remembered a younger Teo, and an on-off love affair that had spanned nearly fifteen years behind her first husband's back before she traded him in for a richer, more handsome replacement, and before the Vuksan name became a byword for criminal excess. Her *vrana*, Teo had called Radovan, her crow, because he was so dark and clever. She had trained under Radovan's father, who regarded her as his most gifted protegée. Now she was one of the hidden Udbasi, with a title and position that gave her access to secrets and license to roam.

She permitted him a smile, like the flash of an old camera briefly capturing a moment from the past.

'It's kind of you to say.'

'How is your husband?'

'Thriving. He likes Vienna, although he complains about the prices.'

'Give him my regards.'

'I don't think so,' said Ćirić. 'What is it you want me to do for you, Radovan?'

'I need to know if there is a way out of this.'

'For you, or for Spiridon?'

'For both of us.'

'That's not possible.'

'You haven't asked me what might be regarded as an acceptable compromise.'

'Because there is none,' said Ćirić, 'or none that involves a return to his homeland for your brother. He is an unstable element, an agent of chaos. Even if he were somehow to be controlled, I don't believe it would be possible to hide from Interpol the fact of his presence in Serbia. If we were discovered giving him sanctuary after what happened in Amsterdam, it would be used against us in the ongoing accession negotiations. But I was led to believe that you had convinced Spiridon to leave Europe.'

'Where did you hear that?'

'Your lawyer has been making certain approaches.'

Radovan sipped coffee to hide his unhappiness. Somehow, Ćirić

320

had already learned that Frend was trying to buy new passports for the Vuksans. That information could only have come from Kauffmann or one of the embassies with which she was dealing: Radovan suspected the former. Kauffmann was testing the ground, covering herself, trying to balance her greed against the Vuksans' current and future toxicity. God preserve us, Radovan prayed, from the amorality of lawyers.

'Distancing ourselves from Europe remains the preferred option,' he said.

'Do I detect a hint of ambivalence?'

'Only regret that exile should have been forced upon us.'

'By personal misjudgment,' said Ćirić.

'And the ambitions of others,' Radovan added. 'We were not responsible for separating Nikola Musulin's head from his body.'

'Your expression suggests that I might have been.'

'Not at all, but his murder was sanctioned by Belgrade, and you, Teo, also take your orders from Belgrade. Collective responsibility did not end with the death of Josip Broz. Kiš and Stajić would not have engaged in such a public act of violence had it not been cleared from above, and if it did not serve the ambitions of the state.'

'And how,' said Ćirić, 'would such an assassination aid us in our pursuit of accession? The last time I checked, the EU continued to display an aversion to bombings in tourist areas, regardless of the identity of the target.'

'If a section of a rockface is likely to give way,' said Radovan, 'one tackles it with a controlled explosion rather than waiting for it to tumble of its own accord, or allow a fear of the threat represented by it to spread; a small sacrifice in return for a larger benefit. Nikola Musulin was soft. Had Spiridon been permitted to return to Serbia, you were concerned he might try to exert influence over Nikola, perhaps even usurp him, regardless of any assurances to the contrary – and that was before Spiridon's revenge on De Jaager and his people. Were I an advisor to Belgrade, I might have sent word to our European neighbors, perhaps through our most influential representative to the Organization for Security and Co-operation in Europe – which would be you, Teo, in all but title – advising them that it would be better if odd rumors about Nikola Musulin's death were ignored, and it was accepted that a gas leak had caused his demise.'

'Bravo, *vrana*,' said Ćirić. 'You know, your father was also a good storyteller. He even managed to convince Josip Broz that he was a loyalist, right to the end.'

'I notice you're not denying the truth of anything I've said.'

'Because whether it is true or false makes no difference.'

'It does to me,' said Radovan. 'Call off Kiš and Stajić. Giving them free rein will not serve you well.'

'Why is that?'

'Because Stajić is an animal, and Kiš is secretly frightened of him. Were you aware that they presented our lawyer with Nikola Musulin's head in a Belgrade restaurant?'

Ćirić blanched, less at the image of the handover than the temerity of the gesture.

'I was not,' she said.

'They are reckless,' said Radovan. 'Even if they were to succeed in killing us, they would leave a trail of evidence that a child could follow. If they were to fail – and if I were you, I would not underestimate our capacities – Spiridon would retaliate, and he would do so without any concern for the optics of EU membership.'

Ćirić finished her tea in silence, and Radovan did not interrupt her thoughts. Finally, she spoke.

'You have to guarantee that Spiridon will never again inconvenience us,' she said.

'You have my word, but I require something more in return.'

'You're already asking a great deal.'

'Nevertheless,' said Radovan.

'Well?'

'Some of our accounts have been frozen, probably as a prelude to a larger sequestration of physical assets back home: businesses, property. We can't leave without the resources required to pay our way, and we cannot subsist on fresh air once we reach our final destination. We need that money.'

'You're not seriously trying to tell me that you don't have funds hidden away,' said Ćirić. 'That would be unlike you.'

'I have some, but not enough to satisfy Spiridon.'

Ćirić considered the request.

'You've caused a lot of bother,' she said. 'Some form of restitution is to be expected.'

'How much?'

'Fifty percent.'

'That's unacceptable.'

'You're not in a position to negotiate.'

In truth, it was a less savage cut than Radovan had feared, but
he still pantomimed unhappiness before agreeing.

'As you say,' he conceded, 'I am not in a position to negotiate.'

'Good,' said Ćirić. 'So now you can both vanish, and I hope
this will be the last time we ever meet.'

'What else would we have to say to each other?'

'Nothing.' Ćirić began rebuttoning her coat, which she had not
removed. 'But this solves only one of your problems. From what
I hear, Kiš and Stajić are not the only ones baying for your blood.'

'All hunters tire in the end,' said Radovan, 'which means they
either give up or become vulnerable to their prey.'

'I admire your optimism. I give you a year, maybe less.'

'Then in a year I shall send you a postcard, just to prove you
wrong.'

'I look forward to receiving it,' said Ćirić, 'should it ever materialize.'

'And how long do you give Simo Stajić?' Radovan asked.

Ćirić shrugged. 'As you say, he's reckless. Men like him drive
too fast, drink too much, sleep with the wrong women, take the
wrong drugs. Their days are always numbered. Perhaps even you
may live long enough to read his obituary. Goodbye, *vrana*.'

They hugged and kissed once more, this time with more feeling.
Radovan watched her depart, his face wistful. He left cash to
cover the check, and walked through the main store to the front
window. He saw Ćirić get into the passenger seat of a large black
Audi with two men in the back before the driver pulled out and
drove down Burggasse toward the MuseumsQuartier. No van,
then. Perhaps, had the meeting with Ćirić gone badly, he would
have been consigned to the trunk of the car. Still, he waited for

a while before leaving, just to be sure he was safe. He browsed the men's section of the boutique, and bought himself a vintage scarf in celebration. The scarf was black and gold, but more the former than the latter, which Radovan thought was appropriate.

For the bloodshed, he knew, was not yet over.

Chapter LXXI

Zorya was once again by the Zollamtsbrücke, watching the water run beneath. Spiridon's friends in the United States had failed in their attempt to kill the dead girl's father, which put Zorya in a very dangerous position. The Vuksans were being hunted in this realm, but Zorya moved between worlds, which potentially left her at the mercy of human elements in one and Jennifer Parker in the other. The Vuksans' time was coming to an end, and Zorya thought she might sleep once they were gone. She did not want Jennifer to pursue her while she was at rest. A compromise had to be reached.

Slowly Zorya crossed the bridge, and Vienna faded from sight. In its place lay a gray landscape and a vast lake. A bench stood on the shore, but it was unoccupied. A fog hung over the water, a cloud of the dead seeking to lose itself in the great expanse.

'You shouldn't have come back here.'

The voice came from behind her. Zorya turned, and Jennifer was waiting.

'*I wanted to talk to you,*' said Zorya. She sounded different here, fainter. *The dead owned this place, and their utterances held precedence. Zorya was more like them than most, but she continued to cling to some semblance of life.*

'You tried to hurt my father. You tried to kill him.'

The girl spoke softly, but there was no mistaking the rage in her voice, or the threat.

'*That was not my doing,*' said Zorya.

'You're a liar!'

Jennifer slashed at her with her right hand. Zorya felt the nails tear into her left cheek, but when she touched the skin, she could find no wounds. There was only pain.

'*Stop!*' said Zorya. '*This won't help anything.*'

Jennifer relented, and peered at her curiously.

'How old are you?' she said.

'*I don't know,*' said Zorya, and she was telling the truth. '*I don't look old, and I don't feel old, but I remember so much.*'

Jennifer sniffed the fingers of her right hand.

'You smell bad,' she said. 'Like you're rotting.'

'*I'm weary,*' said Zorya. '*I need to sleep.*'

'Then sleep.'

'*I can't, not while I know you're looking for me.*'

'You should have thought of that before you set out to harm my father,' said Jennifer. 'Do you know what I think? You were hoping that if he was killed, you'd isolate me; that if he was dead, my connection to his world would come to an end, and he and I would be just like the rest.'

She gestured to the water, at the ones who would soon forget what they once had been.

'*Was I mistaken?*' said Zorya.

Jennifer did not reply, but her eyes gave her away. Jennifer Parker was not as old as Zorya, and had not yet learned to hide her feelings. Zorya had been right: the father was the key.

'You shouldn't have tried,' said Jennifer.

'*I agree,*' said Zorya. '*I should not have sown the idea in their heads. I want to make up for it. I can give the Vuksans to the ones who are hunting them.*'

'They'll find them with or without your help.'

'*Possibly, but I won't stand in their way, and I won't warn the Vuksans of their approach.*'

Jennifer was staring at Zorya's hands.

'You have very sharp nails,' she said, 'much sharper than mine, and your fingers are very long.'

Zorya tried to hide them by folding them into her fists, and felt the fingernails digging into her palms. She pressed down harder, welcoming the sting. It reminded her that she was not yet entirely as this girl was.

'How many people have you hurt with them?' Jennifer continued. 'That's what you sometimes do, isn't it? You tear at them with your nails. Perhaps a long time ago, so long ago that you've almost forgotten the details, someone hurt you, and now you hurt others in return.'

Zorya twitched, as though to shake off the buzzing of a fly.

'*No one hurt me,*' said Zorya.

'I don't believe you,' said Jennifer, 'but you still have to be stopped.'

Jennifer was very fast, so fast that Zorya didn't even see her hand move. Her right index finger cut a line across Zorya's chin. This time, Zorya felt the skin open, and the wound began to bleed.

'Why don't you stay awhile?' said Jennifer, and her eyes were entirely black. 'We can play a hurting game.'

But Zorya was already retreating across the bridge. Vienna reappeared around her, the city emerging as though waking from a dream of itself, and her chin was red with blood.

Chapter LXXII

Angel killed the call with Frend and detached the little CV-C voice changer from the cell phone. He could have used an app, but he preferred the CV-C because he knew for certain that it worked. He was of a generation that trusted the physical, and he regarded as deranged anyone who kept their most valuable personal information as data on a mobile device. Angel didn't even like people knowing his name.

His conversation with Frend had been relayed to Louis over the speaker. They'd been forced to give the lawyer time to come back to them with the information they required, because Frend claimed not to know the location of the Vuksans' hiding place. He had, he said, elected not to be privy to such knowledge in order to shield himself and his family. It was an arrangement that also suited the Vuksans as it placed an additional layer of separation between Frend and themselves. It was all about protection, Frend said.

'This can end happily for the Vuksans or for you,' Angel had told him, 'but not for both. It's a simple choice: Who do you care about more, your clients or your daughter?'

'You know the answer,' the lawyer replied. 'Don't harm her.'

'Are you ordering me?'

'No, I'm asking you, as a father. Please don't hurt her.'

'That's out of my hands. She's being held in England by our colleagues, while we're a lot closer to you. If you go to the police, she dies. If you try to fuck us over, she dies. If the Vuksans kill us before we kill them, she dies. There are a great many outcomes that can end badly for her, but only one that ends well.'

'I understand,' said Frend.

'I hope you do, because it won't be quick for her. They'll take their time, and they'll record as they go, so you'll have a permanent record of the event.'

'I'll do all that you ask,' said Frend. 'I promise.'

According to Frend, he had provided the Vuksans with a list of discreet and expensive rental properties looked after by agents who specialized in selective blindness, one of its symptoms being that they could see only the color of money. With Frend as a reference, the Vuksans would have experienced no difficulty in securing accommodations.

'I need to make some calls,' said Frend. 'Some of the agents will be difficult to contact after hours. I may not be able to talk to them until morning.'

'You have until noon tomorrow.'

'That might not be sufficient.'

'It will be,' said Angel. 'I have faith in the depth of your paternal affection.'

Louis slid a piece of paper in front of Angel. On it was written *Girl/Hendricksen?*

'How many people do the Vuksans have with them?' Angel asked Frend. 'And be careful how you answer. If you miscount, and it costs us, it'll add a very painful hour to the otherwise short span of your daughter's life.'

'One man,' said Frend, 'as far as I know.'

'"As far as I know" isn't the right answer.'

'I'm trying to be honest.'

'Try harder.'

'Yes, it's one man, just one.'

'What's his name?'

'Zivco.'

'Second name?'

'Ilić. But there's another, too.'

'You said there was just one man,' said Angel. 'Don't give me a reason to start doubting you before we've even properly begun.'

'It's not a man, but a child, a girl.'

'Name?'

'Zorya.'

'Second name?'

'I don't know. I've never heard any other used. I'm not even sure that Zorya is her real name. Spiridon found her, or she found him. It's never been entirely clear to me.'

'Where?'

'Eastern Serbia. Bor, Negotin, somewhere like that.'

'What is she to Spiridon? Is he sleeping with her?'

'It's possible, I suppose,' said Frend. 'It's not the kind of question one asks of a man.'

'Isn't it?'

'Not a man like Spiridon Vuksan.'

'If you say so. What else does she do for him?'

There was no reply. For a moment Angel was worried that the connection might have been lost.

'Mr Frend? I don't like being kept waiting.'

'I think she kills for him,' said Frend.

'You said she was a child.'

'She looks like a child – no, she *is* a child – but when you see her up close, you realize that you're mistaken. It's hard to explain without sounding foolish.'

'Go on. You're doing well – and you're helping your daughter.'

'I hope so. I really—' Frend briefly lost his train of thought. Angel thought the lawyer might have been on the verge of tears. 'I'm sorry, where was I?'

'You were talking about the girl, Zorya,' said Angel.

'Zorya, yes. It's as though someone hollowed out a child, removed its essence, and then replaced it with the soul of a creature much older. Radovan calls her his brother's witch. Spiridon consults her, and defers to her judgment. She has a condition of the spine, scoliosis. It's not very apparent, but it's there.'

'You said she'd killed.'

'She has a blade. She keeps it in her sleeve. But—'

'Yes?'

'She prefers to use her hands, or so I hear. She has sharp nails.'

Angel was about to ask if she had killed Hendricksen, just to be absolutely sure, but the question would have given Frend a small advantage. Right now, Frend couldn't be certain who had his daughter. If Angel asked about Hendricksen, he would know.

'Does she stay with Spiridon?'

'Not always. Radovan says she likes the night.'

'What does that mean?'

'She wanders when it's dark,' said Frend. 'She may even sleep rough. I wish I could tell you more, but that's all I know.'

'What about guns? Are the Vuksans armed?'

'Ilić carries a pistol. I assume Spiridon and Radovan do likewise.'

'Wait,' said Angel. 'How do you know that Ilić wears a gun?'

'He's the go-between. I haven't seen the Vuksans since they arrived in Austria, only Ilić.'

'How do you stay in contact?'

'Email.'

'Give me the address.'

Frend needed a moment to search for it, presumably on his phone or in a notebook. He then recited a Tutanota encrypted address, which Angel wrote down.

'What about phones?'

'We change the numbers regularly. Radovan has a list of my SIMs, and he sends me his new numbers by email, but he's being very sparing with them. Right now we're in transition, and I haven't yet received the latest.'

That sounded like evasion on Frend's part, but Angel didn't pursue it. Burner numbers would be of limited use to them.

'Is there a protocol?' said Angel.

'What do you mean?'

'A system. Do you email at particular times? Are there specific words to be used in the event of a problem?'

'Like a code?'

'Like an alarm.'

'No.'

'Let me warn you again about lying.'

'I'm not lying. We don't use greetings or names, but otherwise it's just straightforward communication.'

'When did you last meet Ilić?'

'At the weekend. The girl was with him.'

'Why did you meet?'

Another silence, then: 'They needed cash. I provided it.'

Angel looked at Louis, who shook his head. They had both heard the lie, but Louis made a sign indicating that Angel should let it pass.

'When will you meet him again?' said Angel.

'When the time comes to hand over the passports.'

'What passports?'

'The Vuksans have been ordered to leave Europe.'

'Who by?'

'Belgrade. I've been tasked with securing passports, under new identities.'

'How?'

'I have a source.'

'What's the name of this source?'

Frend hesitated before surrendering Hannah Kauffmann.

'Does she know who the passports are for?'

'Yes.'

'When will you receive them?'

'Within twenty-four hours, I believe.'

'How many?'

'Three: the Vuksans and Ilić.'

'Not the girl?'

'She does not wish to go with them.'

'And how does Spiridon feel about this?'

'I would assume he is unhappy, but what can he do?'

Beside Angel, Louis made a single slicing gesture: *Cut the call.*

'Keep this phone close,' Angel told Frend. 'We'll be in touch again soon.'

'Wait! I want to speak with my daughter.'

'You will, as soon as the Vuksans are dead.'

'But how do I know she's alive?' said Frend. 'How can I be sure that you haven't harmed her already?'

'Because we don't lie,' said Angel. 'We're not lawyers.'

Which was the point at which Angel had ended the conversation, leaving Louis looking impressed.

'Man, you're hard-core,' said Louis. 'I feel like I should hand over my wallet and watch before you hurt me.'

'I didn't enjoy that,' said Angel. 'It gave me no pleasure to threaten a man with the murder of his daughter, even if we have no intention of doing it.'

'That's what separates us from them,' said Louis. 'Or maybe you from them. I'm still reluctant to commit to a side.'

'You're committed. It just pains you to concede it.' But Angel was more uncertain of this than he sounded. He loved Louis, yet one could love a man and still be frightened by his capabilities. 'Me, I'm more in touch with my feelings, and my feelings tell me that holding a blade, metaphorical or otherwise, to a woman's throat is bad.'

'Do you think Anton Frend ever had to look at blood?' said Louis.

'Only if he cut himself shaving.'

'There you go. He knew how the Vuksans operated, but he kept it in the abstract. That's what men like him do. They can't function otherwise. You've just given him a long-delayed lesson in outcomes.'

Angel let it go.

'What next?' he said.

'We have the email address,' said Louis, 'but I don't trust Frend's claim that using it involves just simple messages. I wouldn't institute that kind of email contact without a protocol, and I don't believe the Vuksans would either. There's a tripwire.'

'You really think Frend would risk his daughter's life by not telling us about it?'

'Frend is shrewd – maybe not as shrewd as he thinks he is, which puts him in the same category as ninety-nine percent of humanity, but still, shrewder than most. He knows we're holding his daughter, but has only our word that we'll release her if he does as we ask. He's forfeited a lot of information to us, some of which may even be accurate, but he'll hold back enough to enable him to play us, if he has to. It's what I would do, in his position.'

'But you don't have a child,' said Angel. 'You can't be sure what a father would do to save his daughter.'

'You may be right,' said Louis, 'but I've met a lot of men like Anton Frend, and they never fail to disappoint. They become corrupted, and that corruption taints every relationship they have. He won't sacrifice everything for Pia. He'll sacrifice a lot, but not all he has. And like I said, he's also sharp. At this moment, he's figuring out the angles.'

'Which are?'

'First, go to the police or a crisis management firm: the latter's more likely than the former, given the company Frend keeps, but either would cause us problems. Second, do exactly as we say, but that's not in his nature. Third, come clean to the Vuksans, and use them to try and turn the tables on us, but that would be risky.'

'Why?'

'Because they'd view him as a liability, and probably get rid of him. He'd have to use the passports as bargaining chips – safe passage for the Vuksans in exchange for their help in securing his daughter's return – but they'd be more likely to tear out his fingernails to force the delivery of the documents.'

Angel watched Louis's expression change, which meant that he'd just spotted a fourth option.

'Or?' Angel prompted.

'Or,' said Louis, 'it could be that I have the second choice wrong. Why not just do as we say? As long as the Vuksans are alive, Frend is in danger. Even if he does obtain new identities for them, it will be assumed that he knows the names on the passports, and where the Vuksans are hiding. He'll never be able to sleep peacefully again because he and his family will always be in danger. Better to let us kill the Vuksans and put an end to the whole rotten business. But just in case we fuck up, or try to double-cross him—'

'A tripwire.'

'Yeah, but not the email, because then he has no deniability with the Vuksans. There's something else we're not seeing.'

'You know what I'd be doing in Frend's position?' said Angel. 'I'd be sharing my knowledge of the Vuksans and their latest plans with someone else, because I'd have been protecting myself all along.'

And Louis thought – not for the first time in their relationship – that, damn, the man was probably right.

Chapter LXXIII

Hannah Kauffmann contacted Frend just as he was returning to his hotel. He tried to force Pia from his mind so he could concentrate on what Kauffmann had to say.

'You'll have the passports tomorrow morning,' she said, 'but I may have underestimated the price.'

'That is very unlike you,' said Frend.

'Your clients' prospective new home is a peaceful Caribbean nation with a low international profile, and would like to stay that way. Unfortunately, its sugar industry is also in need of investment. Somewhere between those two competing pressures lies a way forward for you, but the risk factor requires payment of a premium to a new Sustainable Education Fund.'

'And who is being educated,' said Frend, 'or is it impolite of me to ask?'

'The children of the man who will sign off on the passports. He believes his offspring might benefit from studying in Switzerland. They want to learn to ski.'

'How much?'

'A quarter of a million euros per passport,' said Kauffmann. 'If it helps, that includes my fee.'

How, Frend wondered, would the world function without greed? Nothing would ever get done, or nothing worth doing.

'It won't be a problem,' he said.

'You're certain? There might be repercussions if payment is not immediately forthcoming.'

'Is that a threat, Hannah?'

'All I'm saying is that it would be out of my hands, Anton. I'm simply the intermediary. This is a delicate system on which a small number of very powerful individuals have come to depend, some of them in the same line of work as your clients. Complicating factors push up costs for all concerned, as well as attracting the kind of attention that leads to temporary restrictions on the flow of documents. There is a reason you approached me and not one of the more, um—'

'Scrupulous firms?' suggested Frend.

'I prefer the term "established".'

'You would. Where will we meet?'

'Do you really have to ask?'

'Let me guess,' said Frend. 'Among the nameless ones.'

'Exactly. I'll see you there at six a.m. Try not to be late.'

She hung up. Frend immediately emailed Radovan Vuksan, asking for a call back on his most recent number. It came within minutes.

'I'll be collecting the documents early tomorrow morning,' said Frend.

'Where?' said Radovan.

'Outside the city, but the price has gone up.'

'How much?'

'One million euros for all three passports, including the agent's fee.'

The lie came easily to Frend, as all lies did, but he would have need of more money soon. Kauffmann had been right after all, for Frend's time in Vienna was drawing to a close. Soon he might well have cause to seek her services for himself, and it would be for him to choose a sanctuary in which to live out the rest of his days.

'Zivco will bring the money,' said Radovan. 'I'd also like him to be in attendance for the handover.'

This was a complication Frend would have preferred to avoid. With Zivco Ilić present, Frend's deceit might be revealed. His intention had been to collect the cash from Ilić, skim the excess, and deliver the rest to Kauffmann as agreed. He couldn't very well do that with Ilić hovering over him.

'Why?' said Frend.

'While you may be a very good lawyer,' said Radovan, 'your experience as a cash-in-transit security guard is limited. This money was difficult to amass, as you're surely aware, and will be impossible to replace should it be lost or stolen. Plus, Zivco can do the lifting. I don't know if you've ever seen one million euros in fifties, but it equates to almost twenty kilos in a twenty-liter bag.'

Frend couldn't row back now. He would have to call Kauffmann and inform her that she would be receiving more money than anticipated, some of which was his. If he was lucky, she might only impose a handling charge, or perhaps she might be convinced to take it in lieu of a fee for securing one further passport at a small discount.

'Does this mean you've convinced your brother to leave?'

'Spiridon's future does not lie in Europe,' said Radovan.

'That's all very well to say.'

'Soon,' said Radovan, 'he'll understand.'

Frend poured himself a drink from the minibar before making a call of his own. He was forced to leave a message, as always, but he made it clear that he wasn't prepared to wait long for a reply or there would be repercussions. His phone rang just as he was making a second drink.

'I'm not sure that I liked your tone,' said Teodora Ćirić.

Unbeknownst to the Vuksans, the channel of communication between their lawyer and the Serbian liaison officer in Vienna had been open for years, but the benefits to Frend had been minimal – unless one counted staying out of jail, which was, he had to admit, an undeniable boon. Back in 2006, Ćirić had presented him with documentary evidence of activities upon which the Austrian authorities might have looked askance, all of them connected to the Vuksans. In return for her silence, Frend was required only to offer occasional updates on the Vuksans' activities and plans. They were small betrayals, and had not damaged his clients, or so Frend had told himself. But they had accumulated until finally, he now believed, they might have led to the death of Nikola Musulin and the Vuksans' relegation to the status of quarry.

'I don't care if my tone gave you hives,' said Frend. 'I've been trying to get in touch with you for twenty-four hours. Your actions have endangered my safety. You never told me you were planning to seize the Vuksans' funds.'

'If I had, what would you have done? Tried to move some of them, probably, which would have defeated the purpose of the exercise.'

'I thought we both wanted the same outcome,' said Frend, 'which is a peaceful resolution of this crisis. That requires money.'

'We may both want a resolution,' said Ćirić, 'but I'll take permanent over peaceful.'

'What about Belgrade? I barely escaped from the city with my life.'

'Who do you think warned your driver? Don't be naïve, Anton. I looked after you, just as I've always done.'

Frend wasn't so sure of this. Teodora Ćirić looked after herself first, and everyone below her survived on whatever scraps she saw fit to scatter. Frend suspected that his share was particularly lean, but common sense dictated that he should hold his tongue.

'I apologize,' said Frend.

'And I accept,' said Ćirić. 'Now, what do you want?'

'The passports are on the way. The Vuksans will be leaving Europe.'

'I know all that. I met with Radovan.'

'You *what*?'

'He made the approach, and I agreed to talk.'

Frend recovered himself.

'What did he ask for?'

'Money: the unfreezing of assets.'

Which was the same reason Frend had called her. He had to be sure that the funds were available for the passports. Depending on how he chose to handle the threat to Pia, they might never be used, but a wise man prepared for all eventualities.

'And?'

'It's being facilitated.'

Some of the tension eased from Frend.

'Good,' he said.

'Was that all?'

As this piece of the puzzle clicked into place, the larger picture became clearer to Frend, and the best plan of action became manifest – for him and his daughter, if not for the Vuksans.

'I have one more question,' he said.

'I'm listening.'

'Who else knows about our relationship?'

'You make us sound like lovers,' said Ćirić.

God preserve me, Frend thought, *that I should ever be so desperate.*

'Our agreement, then.'

'Only you and I, although some in Belgrade may have their suspicions.'

'When this is over—'

'You want me to destroy those documents relating to your past transgressions, right? You dislike having a sword hanging over your head.'

'I'd prefer you to hand them over to me,' said Frend.

'I can do that. With the Vuksans gone, what use will we be to each other?'

'Exactly my reasoning.'

'That would seem to conclude our business,' said Ćirić, 'although I'll leave you with one question of my own.'

Frend waited.

'With the Vuksans gone, Anton,' she said, 'what use will you be to anyone at all?'

Chapter LXXIV

Like Frend, Louis was also being forced to resort to bluntness in order to reopen a dialogue. He left a message for the spook, Harris, shortly after 2 p.m., this one more forceful and specific than previous attempts to resume contact. He had considered calling Ross, but didn't feel that the latter would have unconditionally welcomed the ensuing conversation. In any case, Ross – had he consented to become involved – would only have been forced to get in touch with Harris himself, and Louis preferred, whenever possible, to cut out the middleman. Harris returned his call after allowing a respectable lacuna.

'Well, well,' said Harris, and his voice contained a suspicious electronic echo that did little to make Louis feel better about dealing with intelligencers, whatever the status of their retirement. 'If it isn't the Grim Reaper. That's quite the trail of fucking carnage you're leaving.'

'I've no idea what you're talking about,' said Louis.

'This is a secure line.'

'I don't know what that means. I'm just a patriotic US citizen seeking to pass on information that may be of value to my country.'

'I detect a severe lack of trust on your part.'

'I don't know what trust is, either.'

'That I can believe,' said Harris.

'I note that you've been remiss in returning my calls.'

'We're not your valet service. We did you some favors, including wiping your slate clean with the French. We're even.'

'Not even close,' said Louis. 'But I plan to cheat on my taxes to make up for it.'

'I hope we got that on tape. You said you had something useful for us?'

'A cell phone number.'

'Whose number would that be?'

'He calls himself Rafi. He says he wants blood money from the Vuksans for what happened in Paris, but it's more likely that he just wants blood and the money would be a bonus.'

'Describe him,' said Harris.

'I can do better than that,' said Louis. 'I can send you a photo.'

'And being a patriotic citizen, you're only offering us this information out of a sense of duty, right?'

'Sure, and while I'm at it, why don't I give you the access codes to my Bitcoin accounts, and maybe you'd like to sleep with my sister, too?'

'I don't believe you have a sister,' said Harris, 'and if you do, I don't want to meet her. What's the price?'

'Rafi travels with a chaperone. I have a picture of him, too. I want them out of the way. I need a clear run at the Vuksans.'

'The Vuksans are no longer a concern for us. They're coasting on fumes.'

'But they remain a concern for me,' said Louis. 'And Rafi smells bad. It would be a shame if his people blew up a Christmas market and word got out that you'd passed on the chance to take him down.'

'And how would that word get out?'

'Do you want me to play back the recording of this call so far?'

Harris laughed.

'You really ought to look up "trust" in the dictionary,' he said. 'It could transform your life. All right, assuming we can trace Rafi, it'll take time to assemble a team in Vienna.'

Louis hadn't told Harris where he was calling from.

'If you can trace this call so quickly,' said Louis, 'you can also find Rafi.'

'It's not just about finding him, but also removing him – and those around him, because I bet he didn't arrive with just one other guy in tow.'

'So hire a bigger van.'

'In addition,' Harris continued, as though Louis had not spoken, 'wherever that cell phone is, you can be sure this Rafi, whatever his real identity, will be nowhere near it.'

'Nevertheless,' said Louis, 'it's the point of contact. Once you've targeted that phone, you'll have a location, and someone there will use it to get in touch with Rafi. And if you can capture the phone, you'll have access to emails, too. Hell, you'll even be able to listen in when they go to the bathroom.'

'Okay,' said Harris, 'give me the number and send on the images. I'll see what can be done.'

'The Vuksans are about to turn to smoke,' said Louis. 'They have clean passports on the way. I might have a day left before they run, two at most.'

'Jesus, you really want them dead, don't you?'

'I have no idea what you mean,' said Louis.

'You know, I'm not entirely happy to have made your acquaintance.'

'I hear that a lot from people.'

'I'll bet you do,' said Harris. 'Probably just before you shoot them in the head.'

Chapter LXXV

B ob Johnston had sent Angel another video of Pia Lackner. She
was holding a copy of that morning's *Guardian* in front of
her, the date clearly visible. Her eyes were red and puffy from
crying. Either Rosanna Bellingham was a gifted makeup artist or
the strain was beginning to get to Lackner. Whatever the reason,
it added to the authenticity of the footage. Angel had already
ditched the SIM card used for the earlier contact with Frend and
used a new SIM to forward the latest video to him, along with a
message that read *Five Minutes*. Five minutes and five seconds
later, Angel called Frend from the crowds by the Kunsthistorisches
Museum, where his was just one more phone among many.

'See,' said Angel, his voice once again distorted, 'your daughter
is safe and well.'

'She's not safe, and she doesn't look well,' said Frend. 'What
have you been doing to her?'

'Maybe we've been telling her stories about the company you
keep. You're a grave disappointment to her, but then, you probably
already knew that.'

'I'm doing my best to make up for it now,' said Frend.

'I'm sure that will be a source of solace to her – if she lives.'

Angel heard Frend draw a deep breath, but otherwise the
lawyer's voice displayed no signs of stress. Angel almost admired
his equanimity, even as it caused him to suspect that Louis was
probably right, and something deep inside Frend had been
corrupted to the point of near-extinction.

'The passports are ready,' said Frend. 'The handover takes place
tomorrow morning.'

'Where?'

'The Cemetery of the Nameless, at Simmering.'

'When?'

'Six a.m.'

'Will the Vuksans be present?'

'No, only Zivco Ilić and me. Ilić is bringing the money.'

'How much?'

'One million euros.'

'That's a lot for, what, two or three passports?'

'Three. There was a surcharge for rapid turnover, as well as the problematical legal status of the beneficiaries.' Not to mention his cut, which Frend didn't.

'That's a very polite way of describing a trio of murderers.'

'And what words would a kidnapper prefer to use?'

'That's very clever,' said Angel. 'I'll ask my friends to consult your daughter and see what she advises.'

'I withdraw the question,' said Frend.

'I thought you might,' said Angel. 'How are you getting to the cemetery?'

'By rental car from my hotel. Ilić will meet me there.'

'Why are you staying at a hotel when you have a house and an apartment in the city?' Angel asked.

'Because your people were following me,' said Frend.

Angel thought on his feet. 'You wouldn't have seen my people. Give me the name of the hotel, and tell me what these others looked like.'

Frend's description wasn't detailed, but it didn't have to be. Angel immediately identified them as Mr Rafi and his protector, which wasn't much of a surprise.

'They worry me,' said Frend.

'They should, but we'll take care of them. Consider it a good-will gesture – or proof of our seriousness. Whichever makes you more comfortable.'

'To be honest,' said Frend, 'neither does.'

'To be honest,' said Angel, 'I don't care.'

Angel and Louis met for dinner at China Kitchen No. 27 on Linke Wienzeile, in what passed for Vienna's Chinatown. Both of them had eaten enough Austrian food for the time being, and Sichuan appealed. The spiciness was enough to make Angel sweat, which was always a good sign. They were one of only two Western couples in the restaurant, the other being a pair of young Scandinavian tourists who spent their time taking photos of their food and conversing in what sounded like Danish. The rest of the tables appeared to be occupied entirely by noisy Chinese family groups. It meant that Louis and Angel could converse without the Austrian police listening in, unless the force had a vast resource of elderly Chinese operatives or Instagram-obsessed Danes upon which to draw. Anyway, Angel thought that the police had largely lost interest in him for the present. Some of the detectives might have entertained doubts about aspects of his story, but not enough to justify trailing him around Vienna.

They ordered double-cooked pork belly and peppery Dan Dan noodles, and stuck to beer for the main courses, with green tea to follow. The pot of tea had just arrived at their table when Louis received a call with a Virginia area code. He stepped outside to take it.

'We think that's a throwaway phone Rafi is using,' said Harris.

'Duh,' said Louis. 'If that's the kind of expertise my tax dollars are buying back home, I may have to relocate to North Korea.'

'We also believe it's been reserved solely for contact with you. It's only been used once in the last five days, in Salzburg, and then for a call that wasn't answered.'

'A test.'

'Most likely,' said Harris.

Either Rafi was very confident of hearing from him, Louis thought, or that phone was just one of a bunch sitting on a table somewhere, plugged into a mass of power outlets, while bored men with beards took turns monitoring them for incoming calls. Some or all of those calls might not even be answered, but would be used solely to instigate a callback, in all likelihood from another location entirely.

'So I use the number Rafi gave me, and you track the returned call?' said Louis.

'That's how it works,' said Harris. 'These people try to be smart when it comes to communication, but they have a fatal flaw:

345

they're addicted to their cell phones. If they weren't, half of them would still be breathing God's air instead of sitting in hell wondering where all the virgins are at. But you'll need to have a story prepared, something that doesn't set off his alarm bells.'

'Who is he?' asked Louis. 'If his name really is Rafi, I'm going to be frustrated by his lack of ingenuity.'

'Majid Ali al-Shihri. He's a Saudi, but hasn't made it into our Big Book of Bad Boys until now. The male model he travels with is Mohsin al-Adahi. He's Yemeni, but served time in prisons in Kuwait and Jordan. Him we know about, although just as a cog in the wheel. As for al-Shihri, he could be new to the game, but I'm leaning toward established and cagey. Whatever device he's using, it's not a smartphone, so there's a limit to the information we can glean from its use.'

'He's not new,' said Louis. 'He's killed, and he's enjoyed it. He has a dead light in his eyes, like he's lit up inside by swamp gas.'

'Well, his illuminated head is above the parapet now. Even allowing for precautions, he's taken a chance by contacting you directly. Our assumption would be that he had overall responsibility for ensuring those two operatives arrived safely in Paris. When they were killed at Gare de Lyon, the blame stopped at his door. If he doesn't get compensation from the Vuksans – which, as you pointed out, would certainly involve blood as well as money – he'll either end up with his throat cut or be strapped into an explosive vest and dropped off at the nearest mall.'

'But you'd like him alive and in custody,' said Louis.

'Alive would be preferable,' said Harris, 'but dead will also do.'

'You mess this up, and they may come after me.'

'They may come after you anyway, but I think we can make it seem as though whatever happens to Rafi is just bad luck or the will of Allah. Still, it'll be tight. We'll have a location on him as soon as he calls you back, but if he's covering his tracks, he'll ditch the SIM immediately after the call has ended. You'll have to find a way to draw him and his people out, so we can be sure where to find them.'

'I can use Frend as bait,' said Louis. 'I know where he's staying.'

346

'They might take a run at him before we're ready.'

'I'll give them something, but not enough. When do I make the call?'

'Ready when you are. We're all set up.'

'Give me ten minutes,' said Louis. 'I want to have my green tea.'

Chapter LXXVI

Anton Frend's wife called him as he was drinking a glass of whisky in his hotel room. She hadn't heard from their daughter in two days and was starting to worry. She and Pia usually spoke once a day, sometimes even more. When Frend's wife was annoyed with him – an increasingly frequent occurrence as their marriage endured its slow death – she had conducted the early parts of these conversations within earshot, just in case he needed to be reminded that she still had a relationship with their child while he did not. Now Frend enjoyed a frisson of pleasure at being privy to knowledge about their daughter that was denied his wife, even as he realized that he couldn't have her going to the police with her concerns. He managed to talk her down, assuring her that he would use his contacts in England to make inquiries if she had still not heard from Pia by close of business the next day. By then, Frend felt certain, Zivco Ilić would have led those responsible straight to the Vuksans, and his daughter would be released.

He was convinced of this for a number of reasons. The first was that he believed he now knew the identity of at least one of those involved in his daughter's abduction: it was the man named Louis, the hunter believed by the Vuksans to be seeking revenge for the killings in Amsterdam. If Frend was right – and it was, he admitted, a calculated gamble – Louis was an individual with something approaching a conscience, and would therefore be unwilling to add the death of an innocent young woman. Actually, Frend's fears for his daughter's safety had also been alleviated slightly by the newspaper in the video. The *Guardian* might have represented many of the liberal values that Frend disdained, but he did not think it would be the first choice of journal for someone intent on torturing and killing a kidnap victim, even if it were only to be used as a prop. Had Pia been pictured holding one of the more salacious British tabloids, Frend might have felt less confident in his reasoning.

He heard a couple arguing in the next room and turned up the TV to drown out the noise. He also emptied another bottle from the minibar. He knew he was drinking more than he should, but sometimes life left a man with little option. Frend was experiencing a sense of regret at what would soon befall Radovan Vuksan, although not enough to warn Radovan that Louis was near. Frend had always enjoyed Radovan's company, and had benefited in many ways from their relationship, both personally and financially. But Radovan's complicity in the Amsterdam killings had rendered him toxic, and he had contaminated his legal advisor by association. Radovan's death, however much it might pain Frend, was the necessary equivalent of amputating a necrotized limb lest the body entire should succumb to fatal infection. If only Radovan had been ruthless enough to take the same steps with his brother. Had the positions been reversed, Frend believed Spiridon would not have allowed fraternal loyalty to stand in the way of his own continuance.

Frend raised a glass to his reflection.

'*Zum Überleben*,' he said.

To survival.

Chapter LXXVII

O nce Louis had drained the last of his green tea, he called the number given to him by Mr Rafi. As he listened to it ringing, he mused on the chain of events that had led him to this juncture: a man who had spent most of his adult life avoiding the attention of authorities in any number of countries, now exposing himself to the highest possible level of surveillance. Much of this was Charlie Parker's fault. It was just lucky for all involved that Louis was fond of him.

His call, as anticipated, wasn't answered, and was terminated after four rings without redirection to a message service. Seconds later, Louis's phone vibrated with an incoming call from a withheld source. Louis hit the green button, and Rafi's voice said, 'I wondered if you'd get in touch, but I'm glad you did.'

Louis thought that Mr Rafi was probably being sincere, if for purely homicidal reasons. Rafi's life was in peril, and it had forced him to take chances he would have preferred to avoid. By establishing a means of communication, he risked betrayal, but he was relying on the threat of reprisal to keep Louis in line.

Except Louis knew that Rafi was damaged goods. One more false step, and his own people would cut him loose.

'I needed some time to run the numbers,' said Louis.

'On what?'

'On my chances of hitting the Vuksans and getting away clean, against yours.'

'What did you decide?'

'That it doesn't much matter who kills them, as long as someone does,' said Louis. 'If you fail, and get shot by the Vuksans or the Austrians, the world will be a better place, and I'll come at the Vuksans again when the opportunity arises. If you succeed, and get shot by the Austrians after, the world will be an even better place. It's a win-win situation for the world and me. Only a sap wouldn't let another sap do his dirty work for him.'

'That's very admirably unidealistic of you. So, what do you have for me?'

'The lawyer, Frend, is staying at a hotel in the city. You spooked him by hanging around outside his office. You should have been less conspicuous.'

'Which hotel, and what name is he using?'

'I don't know the alias,' said Louis, 'just the hotel. I imagine it's the kind of place that prides itself on its discretion. Frend used to take his mistress there to fuck her, because a fifty-euro note was enough to ensure that the desk didn't ask for ID.'

'We can't search every room,' said Rafi, not unreasonably.

'You won't have to. Frend will be leaving the hotel at five a.m. tomorrow for a business meeting.' Louis had decided it was better if Mr Rafi didn't know that the meeting would involve the exchange of a million euros, and had been arranged for the ultimate benefit of the Vuksans. 'You can take him when he leaves. After that, it's up to you how you persuade him to tell you where the Vuksans are holed up.'

'And how do you know about this meeting?'

'Frend told us.'

'Why would he do that?'

'Because,' said Louis, 'my colleagues are holding his daughter hostage.'

When the call was ended, Louis put away his cell phone and rejoined Angel in the restaurant. A text message, from a Virginia number, arrived as he was settling the check. It read: *Found him*.

Chapter LXXVIII

The original call made by Louis was traced to a recipient device in a rented apartment located above an electronic repair store on Jurekgasse in Rudolfsheim-Fünfhaus. The return call from Mr Rafi also came from Rudolfsheim-Fünfhaus, this time from a Turkish restaurant on Preysinggasse, on the other side of the maze of railway tracks leading to and from the adjacent Westbahnhof station. Within the hour both locations were under surveillance, and efforts were being made to obtain and access footage from nearby security cameras. Three men and one woman, all believed to be from the same Turkish family, were found to be renting the apartment on Jurekgasse. As anticipated, none of them matched the description of Mr Rafi or his aide. The Turkish restaurant did not have a security system on the premises, and was not over-looked by any cameras nearby, which was almost certainly the reason Mr Rafi had chosen to contact Louis from there.

But the hook had been baited, and now they would just have to wait. There was no question of alerting Frend to the danger he might be facing because the lawyer would be nervous enough already. If the operation went according to plan, he would never even know he had been in peril. Just in case Mr Rafi attempted to access the hotel that night, two teams were placed outside, and a third team checked in as a married couple and requested one of two rooms on the third floor 'for old times' sake', which left them with a view of Frend's door. As an added precaution, a mini motion sensor barely an inch in height and half an inch in width was placed next to a power outlet between Frend's room and the hallway leading to the stairs and elevator. If it was activated, an alert would be sent to the team in the room. Before he went to bed, Louis obtained a cast-iron guarantee from Harris: once the targets were in custody or neutralized, Harris's people would not attempt to interfere with Louis's plans for the Vuksans, and Frend would be allowed to proceed unimpeded to the meeting place. That night, Angel stayed with Louis, and a wake-up call was set for 3:30 a.m.

They barely slept, but lay awake and watched the dark settle.

Chapter LXXIX

U nder more favorable conditions – in a more familiar city, and without his own head being on the block – Mr Rafi might have been less vulnerable to surveillance, but he needed the lawyer and, as Louis had already surmised, was banking on fear outweighing any temptation to engage in a double-cross. In this, of course, Mr Rafi was guilty of a profound error of judgment.

The American team had flown into Vienna on a Gulfstream jet from a regional airport in eastern Poland, where the CIA had maintained a base for rendition purposes since the start of the War on Terror. It was not, therefore, the unit's first day at the office. They were already watching when, at 3 a.m., two cars took up positions within sight of the main and rear doors of the hotel, the first of the vehicles having initially circled the block three times. They counted four men, two in each car, although none was Mr Rafi.

The operatives in the hotel had taken turns to rest, but only a trio of drunks returning to their rooms in the early hours had disturbed the calm of the hallway, triggering the motion sensor. When Frend emerged from his room at 4:50 a.m., he shared the elevator with the female half of the team, who smiled at him but did not receive a smile in return, and was watched by the male half of the team, who was prowling the lobby with a coffee as Frend walked to the separate garage elevator.

A third man, unknown to Harris's people, and wearing the livery of a limousine driver, was looking at his phone in an easy chair, just as he had been since arriving at the hotel shortly before 4 a.m. He looked up when Frend appeared, put his phone in his pocket, and got to his feet. As he prepared to follow the lawyer, the man with the coffee moved in, narrowly avoiding spilling his hot drink on the driver. The man apologized in German, by which point the woman was directly behind the driver, who felt a gun in his back at the same moment that the operative in front of him produced another pistol.

Meanwhile, the oblivious Frend descended to the basement parking lot. It took him just under five minutes to get to his rental, arrange his bag and coat, and exit the facility. By then the four men waiting outside had already been disabled, one of them fatally, having made the mistake of instinctively reaching for the gun by his side as the vehicle was being surrounded. He was killed with a bullet from a suppressed Beretta carrying a seventeen-round sand-resistant magazine, a throwback to its owner's military service in the deserts of Afghanistan and Iraq.

This unfortunate incident took place at the front of the hotel, while Frend left from the rear, so he remained unaware of the details of what had occurred. On the other hand, he did see two figures on the ground beside a nondescript Nissan parked near the garage door as he drove off, six armed and masked men surrounding them, and two cars blocking one lane of the street. He thought he spotted the Austrian flag on the sleeve of a nearby figure dressed in full operational gear, with a combat shotgun held at port arms. Frend briefly slowed down, taken by surprise, before resuming his progress and doing his best to ignore whatever was happening. It might have been something to do with him, but then again, it might not. These were, after all, troubled times. Yet he was not entirely surprised when his phone rang moments later, and the by now familiar distorted voice said, 'You see? I told you we'd take care of you.'

Frend checked his rearview mirror. There were cars behind him, but he could not tell if they had followed him from his lodgings. He heard sirens in the distance.

'Who were they?' said Frend.

'The men on the ground? We'll have to wait and see, but I'm guessing they could point you toward Mecca without a compass.'

Even as he listened, Frend was recalibrating. What he had witnessed was probably at least partly the work of the Einsatzkommando Cobra, the Austrian police's tactical unit, given

the presence of an Austrian flag at the scene. The Austrian authorities did not give unrestricted access to foreign operatives on the
streets of their capital, which meant they had either conducted
the operation or cooperated with it. More than ever, Frend was
convinced that his daughter was not in any real danger, but how
could he square the involvement of Austrian law enforcement,
however peripherally, with the targeting of the Vuksans' people
by the hunter named Louis? Whatever the answer, it was now
more important than ever that the Vuksans were apprehended –
or better still, killed. If they were caught, they might implicate
Frend, but his cooperation would buy him some goodwill. If they
died, they could say nothing, and Frend was convinced that, if he
had to, he could bluff his way through any awkward questions
that might follow.

But if he could not, there was Kauffmann. He had messaged
her from his room the previous night to inform her that he had
reconsidered his position, and a new start might be in order. He
wanted a passport, to be supplied within twenty-four hours. She
had messaged back €150K and he had agreed. Really, he had
expected nothing less of her, not after he had informed her about
the extra €250,000 that would be in the bag that she was to
receive from Zivco Ilić. He supposed that she might have charged
him more, given what the Vuksans were paying, but she was
probably giving him the colleagues' discount.

Here was how it would unfold. At the cemetery, Ilić would
hand over the money to Kauffmann in return for the passports.
Ilić would leave, leading Louis and his people to the Vuksans.
Frend had no doubt Louis would kill them, and Ilić, too, securing
his daughter's release. Finally, Frend would soon be in possession
of a new passport under a new name, and on his way to a new
life in a new country. With a little luck, he might never have to
speak to another Serb for as long as he lived. They could all go
to hell: the Vuksans, Ilić, the freakish child Zorya, Kiš, Stajić.

And that bitch Ćirić. Yes, she could go to hell too.

Kauffmann was already at the Friedhof der Namenlosen when
Frend arrived. As usual, she was smoking a cigarette. The woman

really was incorrigible. It was a wonder she had lived so long, Frend thought. Her lungs must have been little more than sacks of tar.

Kauffmann frowned as he descended the steps from the chapel to the graveyard.

'You're traveling light for a man who is supposed to be holding a million euros in cash,' she said.

'A subordinate is bringing it,' said Frend. 'My clients felt that a lawyer shouldn't be carrying so much hard currency. They were fretful that someone might try to steal it.'

'You, probably. I wouldn't trust you with my small change.'

'Likewise.'

'But then, I am not attempting to swindle my clients.'

'My clients are murderers,' said Frend. 'Forgive me if relieving them of excess funds does not inspire deep feelings of regret.'

'Perhaps you ought to be more cautious,' said Kauffmann, 'particularly around murderers.'

'The time for caution has already passed, don't you think? And lest we forget, you also are now complicit. What about my passport?'

'It's just waiting for the details to be filled in. That will be done as soon as the money has been handed over.'

Kauffmann puffed at the cigarette and checked her watch.

'Where is this lackey of yours?' she said.

'It's just ten to,' said Frend. 'He'll be here. The Vuksans want the passports. May I?'

Kauffmann produced a small brown envelope from the inside pocket of her coat and handed it to Frend. He examined the documents inside. They looked good to him. He was no expert, but he had faith in Kauffmann in this regard. She might have been mired in duplicity, but money kept her honest.

He returned the envelope to her.

'Did you notice that the chapel gate appears to be open?' he said.

She looked past him and saw that the metal gate was indeed unlocked.

'That's odd,' she said. 'Is there anyone inside?'

'Not that I could see in passing.'

'Kids, perhaps,' she said. 'I'll report it after we leave, just in case.'

'Good. It would be a shame were it to be desecrated.'

'I didn't take you for a religious man,' said Kauffmann.

'I'm not,' he replied. 'I just like old places.'

'Even this one?'

'I would not care to rest here when I die, but that does not mean I wish to see it defiled.'

Kauffmann regarded him with puzzlement.

'You are a strange individual, Anton. Occasionally an admirable quality rises to the surface, only to submerge itself again when it glimpses the world you inhabit.'

'And you?' said Frend. 'What is left inside you?'

'An appreciation of music,' said Kauffmann. 'It's what passes for my soul.'

They heard footsteps behind them, and turned in unison. Zivco Ilić stood at the top of the steps, the chapel behind him. In his right hand he carried a large black canvas bag. He put the bag on the ground and stretched his shoulders.

'If I carry it down the stairs,' said Ilić, 'someone will just have to carry it all the way back up again, and it won't be me.'

'This is the associate I mentioned,' Frend told Kauffmann.

'Yes, I recognize his face from the new passport,' she replied quietly, as they ascended to meet Ilić. 'His picture flatters him.'

Despite the circumstances, Frend managed a smile.

'You have the documents?' said Ilić as they reached him.

'Yes,' said Kauffmann.

'What name have I been given?'

'Thomas Rusin.'

Ilić repeated the name aloud. 'I like it,' he concluded.

'That's of no consequence,' said Kauffmann, 'not unless you intend to spend a lot of money changing it again.'

'Show them to me.'

Kauffmann withdrew the envelope for the second time, tipped out the passports, and displayed for Ilić the relevant page on each, but did not hand them over. When she had finished, Ilić stepped back from the bag and invited her to examine its contents. Kauffmann knelt and unzipped it, revealing only a bundle of used copies of *Der Standard*. She looked up.

'What is this?' she said.

And Zivco Ilić shot her in the face.

Chapter LXXX

From the passenger seat of a van parked a block and a half from the hotel, Majid Ali al-Shihri, aka Mr Rafi, had watched his attempt to capture the lawyer Frend fall apart. Next to him sat the scarred man, Mohsin al-Adahi, the worst of his disfigurement hidden by a cap. More police cars passed, followed by an ambulance, although it was traveling without sirens or lights. Whoever it was coming for had either suffered only minor injuries or was already dead.

Mr Rafi tapped al-Adahi on the shoulder.

'Time to go,' he said.

Louis had betrayed them. There could be no other reason for what had occurred. The result had left Mr Rafi a walking corpse. He had lost two people in Paris and now more operatives here, in Vienna. In the eyes of his superiors, he would be adjudged desperately unlucky, fatally inefficient, or secretly working against jihad. None of these judgments was conducive to a long life. If he was fortunate, he might be permitted to reveal Louis's perfidy before he died, and would go to Paradise knowing he had doomed the American.

Beside him, al-Adahi turned to him as though to ask a question. Mr Rafi felt a sudden coldness at his throat, followed by a burning pain. He raised his right hand as a spray of bright arterial blood obscured his view through the windshield. He was only vaguely aware of the driver's door opening and closing as Mohsin al-Adahi walked away, the blade making a sound that was almost musical as it hit the road.

The darkness came for Mr Rafi. He fought against it as best he could, but in the end, as it always must, the darkness won.

Chapter LXXXI

F rend looked down at Kauffmann's body. Her eyes were closed and her features contorted, as though she had survived just long enough to register the pain of the bullet's passage. It had left a small hole in the bridge of her nose, but very little blood.

'Help me get her into the chapel,' said Zivco Ilić. He grabbed her left leg, but Frend did not move. He supposed he was in shock, but he was also thinking about his future, because as of that moment he no longer seemed to have one. He needed the passport, but the passport had died with Kauffmann.

'Why did you do that?' he said, once he'd found his voice. 'Why didn't you just pay her the money as agreed?'

But Ilić was too busy dragging Kauffmann into the dimness of the chapel to reply. Frend, realizing that the only thing worse than what had already happened might be someone coming across the body, awkwardly lifted Kauffmann by the arms. He lost his grip and her head banged against the chapel floor, but by then she was out of sight. Ilić finished the job unaided, dumping her against the wall. He picked up the fallen envelope and placed it in his jacket pocket before tossing the bag on top of the body. He then pulled the doors closed behind him, followed by the metal gates.

'The money,' said Frend. 'Where is it?'

'Don't you understand?' said Ilić. 'There is no money! Radovan said that he'd found a way to get it, but the funds never came through. It's of no consequence now. We have the passports, and by the time they find the body, we'll be gone.'

'You'll be gone,' said Frend. 'What about me?'

'You can talk your way out of trouble. That's all you lawyers are good for, talking. Anyway, what have you done that's so bad? You moved some cash around, nothing more. Your banking system launders millions for the Russians and your prosecutors don't even blink, so what do you think they'll do to you? You'll barely feel the slap on the wrist.'

'And Kauffmann?'

By now Frend was trailing Ilić as he walked quickly to the parking lot.

'What of her?' said Ilić. 'She's dead.'

'She didn't work in isolation. What if she told her contact at the embassy who those passports were for? What if she identified me as the mediator?'

Ilić waved a hand in dismissal. 'If she did, they'll keep their mouths shut. You think they'll want to be implicated? You worry too much.'

Ilić took out his car keys and deactivated the alarm, but Frend grabbed his arm as he moved to open the car door.

'Don't you understand?' said Frend. 'Kauffmann was protected. She had value. By killing her, you've damned me.'

Ilić spun. The punch wasn't hard, and caught Frend only a glancing blow, but he was off-balance and fell awkwardly. He felt something give in his left wrist, and he let out a yelp. Ilić showed him the gun.

'Are you in a hurry to join her?' he said. 'Because I'll put a bullet in your fucking head and all your troubles will be over. Is that what you want?'

Frend didn't reply. He was as close to weeping as he had ever come in his adult life. Ilić and the Vuksans had their documents. They could vanish, but he could not. Kauffmann's death would be investigated, and not only by the authorities. The trail would lead back to him. He was sure of it. He would become a marked man.

Frend managed to get to his feet, cradling his injured arm with his right hand. As he did so, the rage on Ilić's face disappeared, to be replaced by what Frend initially mistook for pity, until he realized that whatever the Serb was feeling was directed not at Frend but himself.

'You're not the only one who is damned,' said Ilić. 'We were all cursed from the moment we stood with the Vuksans. You think these are going to save any of us?' He showed Frend the envelope containing the passports. 'They won't. They're only going to postpone the inevitable. You know what you should do? You should go back to that graveyard, dig a hole for yourself with your bare hands, and pull the dirt down on top of you. Words won't save you. Documents won't save you. Money won't save you. You're cursed, just as I am. The only difference is that I'm resigned to it and you're not.'

'Then why don't you just give up?' said Frend.

Ilić took a moment to reply.

'Because I'm a fool,' he said, at last, 'and the dirt is in no hurry to accept another fool.'

He got in his car and drove away without giving Anton Frend another glance. Miserably, Frend walked toward his own vehicle and minutes later was leaving behind the quiet ranks of the nameless.

For the present.

On the silos overlooking the graves, flocks of small birds settled for a time before rising, forming patterns in the sky like dreams drawn from the mind of God. Only one did not join them. It was squatter and heavier than the rest, and stood on four legs, not two. The drone's propellers activated and it ascended slowly, its camera following the departure first of Zivco Ilić, then Anton Frend. It stayed in the air for a while longer before its battery gave out and it dropped back to the roof of the silo, there to join the corpses of two pigeons in their own little cemetery of the lost.

Chapter LXXXII

Radovan killed the call.

'Zivco has the passports,' he told his brother.

Spiridon was in his usual seat by the window, looking out over trees and green grass. If he concentrated only on the vegetation, he believed he could convince himself that he was gazing at the Pannonian Plain of his youth.

'Then you can go,' said Spiridon, 'and take Zivco with you.'

'What about you?'

'I'll accept the passport, because it might prove useful, but I won't use it to flee. I told you, I'm going back.'

Radovan rubbed his eyes and marveled at the depths of his brother's obstinacy. He had promised Ćirić that he would talk Spiridon around in return for the release of funds to pay for the passports, but she had reneged on the deal. Perhaps it had not been her decision. He thought, even hoped, that this might be so. Ćirić answered to Belgrade, and Belgrade was determined to trap the Vuksans in a kill box.

But they had defied Belgrade's will, because Zivco had the passports.

'You'll die if you return,' said Radovan.

'Not before I make them sorry they ever heard my name.'

'Why? It's over. If we leave, they'll forget about us. Soon Kiš and Stajić will become a more pressing problem for Belgrade, and the fact of our continued existence will be forgotten. We won't be worth the trouble of killing.'

Spiridon's face reddened. He pushed himself up from his chair and stood face-to-face with his brother.

'I *want* to be worth the trouble of killing!' he shouted, and Radovan thought how strange it was to hear his brother's voice raised in this way. He knew then that Spiridon was beyond reason.

'I *want* them to remember me! Why did I fight for all those years, if not for that? I waged wars to bring my country back from the dead. I fought the Croats and the Turks, and when the fighting was over, I sent money from Amsterdam to rebuild houses, churches, schools. I will not be forgotten. I will not end my days hiding from my enemies while *pičke* like Kiš and Stajić dismiss me as a coward. I will show them how a real man faces the world, how a real man dies. You can run. You were never a fighter. Go! Go with my blessing, but I will not leave.'

'Spiridon,' said Radovan, 'if you do this, all those who knew us, all those who called us "cousin", "friend", "comrade", will be at risk. *I* will be at risk. They will avenge themselves on everyone.'

Spiridon placed his hands on his brother's shoulders.

'I have no choice,' said Spiridon, all anger gone now. 'I cannot be other than how God made me.'

'God did not make you like this,' said Radovan. 'You are all your own work.'

'I give the devil some credit, too.'

'Then you have made him very proud.' Radovan stepped away. 'Where is Zorya?'

'I don't know,' said Spiridon. 'I have spoken with her of this, and she has confirmed that she also wishes to go home. With her by my side, maybe I will prove even harder to kill.'

Radovan went to the desk in which he stored his papers and unlocked a drawer.

'I have kept some cash in reserve,' he said. 'Euros, dollars, dinars. Not much, but what little there is might help.'

'I'll take the dinars,' said Spiridon. 'You can keep the rest.'

'Actually,' said Radovan, 'I'm going to keep it all.'

The first shot, muffled by the suppressor but still loud, took Spiridon in the chest. He stayed on his feet, supporting himself with one hand on the back of his chair, so Radovan shot him again, and this time Spiridon went down, taking the chair with him. He was still breathing, although exhaling blood. Radovan knelt and took Spiridon's right hand in his. He squeezed it hard, and felt Spiridon's grip tighten in response. They stayed that way, unspeaking, until Spiridon's hold on his brother, and this world, came at last to an end.

Chapter LXXXIII

Zivco Ilić parked the car in front of the house and walked to the door, the key in his right hand. Low walls separated the building from the properties on either side, both of which were Airbnb rentals, although only one had been in use since the Vuksans had taken up occupancy of the middle property. He entered the house, closed the door behind him, and took the stairs to the top floor. The door was slightly ajar, but he knocked before entering, as he always did.

'Come in.'

It was Radovan's voice. Ilić stepped into the room and saw Spiridon's body on the floor. Radovan was sitting in the chair by his desk, a gun in his right hand. The gun was not pointing at Ilić, but that, he knew, could quickly change.

'What happened?' said Ilić.

'A disagreement,' said Radovan, 'a conflict of interests. You have our documents?'

'Yes.'

'And your own?'

'Yes. They gave me the name Rusin, Thomas Rusin.'

'And how do you feel about that?'

Zivco Ilić had enjoyed only the most rudimentary and fleeting of experiences with the educational system. He read poorly and held the barest grasp of history, geography, and the sciences, but he possessed a certain mathematical acumen. He was currently calculating the odds against his survival, and decided that the right answer to the last question might aid him in improving them considerably.

'I think I would like the opportunity to explore this new identity,' he said.

Ilić heard Radovan Vuksan sigh deeply, and thought he might have chosen the incorrect response. His own gun felt both very near and very far from his hand, until Radovan tossed an envelope at his feet and said:

'It's just two thousand dollars, but it'll have to do for now. There are other assets, which I need to find a safe way to liquidate. When I do, you'll be looked after. Check the email address regularly. I'll be in touch.'

'Where will you go, Radovan?'

'I don't know. Not to the Caribbean. Maybe the Far East. And you?'

'Somewhere in Europe. They say Portugal is cheap, but I don't speak the language, and I will never learn now.' Ilić picked up the envelope of cash. 'Zorya told me I would die soon, so it is not important anyway.'

'Pay no attention to her,' said Radovan. 'She may look like a child, but she is a woman to the bone. They manipulate us, all of them.'

Ilić smiled sadly. 'She did not tell me anything that I did not already know.'

He took the passports from his pocket, selected his own, and handed the others to Radovan.

'I saw your new name briefly,' said Ilić, 'but I have forgotten it already.'

They shook hands, and Radovan walked to the door.

'What will I do with Spiridon?' asked Ilić.

'Spiridon is gone,' said Radovan. 'That's just meat.'

Ilić shifted uneasily. He had few redeeming qualities, but he still retained his faith.

'I will wrap him in a sheet, if you don't mind,' he said. 'It would make me feel better about leaving him here.'

Radovan nodded. 'We never liked each other, did we, Zivco?'

'No, we did not.'

'For what it's worth, I like you better now.'

Ilić did not reply in kind. He was beyond lying now.

'Goodbye, Radovan,' he said, and went to deal with the body.

*

Ilić took a clean white bedsheet from the bedroom closet, laid it on the floor, and rolled Spiridon's corpse across it once, twice, until the sheet wrapped him like a shroud. By then the material was no longer white but red. Ilić could see the contours of Spiridon's face against it. His mouth was open, and Ilić would not have been surprised had an inhalation sucked the sheet against the maw as Spiridon, or some revenant version of him, returned to this world. Ilić came from Majdanpek, and had spent his childhood living in fear of wraiths. To him, they were as real as his own mother and father.

He hated Radovan for what he had done to Spiridon, just as he hated himself for not avenging the murder, although he knew that Radovan would have shot him before he laid a hand on his gun. Who could have known that Radovan had it in him to take the life of his own brother? Perhaps Zivco Ilić had been frightened of the wrong Vuksan for all these years.

Ilić went to Radovan's bedroom and searched it before moving on to the private bathroom. He inspected the sink and discovered three nail clippings. He retrieved the fragments from around the drain and carried them back to the corpse. Ilić had a vague knowledge of the processes of autopsy from watching TV shows. He knew that Spiridon's body would be thoroughly cleaned and examined, and the contents of its stomach emptied. Using the blade of his pocketknife, he cut the clippings into nine smaller pieces. Some he lodged in Spiridon's throat, others deep in his ears and nose, aided by a cotton swab. The final one he pushed deep beneath Spiridon's foreskin. Then he prayed that at least one would remain unfound and go to the grave with his master. In that way, Radovan would soon also join the dead.

Ilić became aware of a presence behind him, and thought for a moment that Radovan had returned. He reacted a fraction too late, because when he turned, the muzzle was already in his face.

'I know who you are,' said Ilić.

'And I know who you are,' said Louis, removing Ilić's gun from its holster. 'Who's under the sheet?'

'Spiridon.'

'Did you kill him?'

'His brother did.'

'Can't trust anybody these days,' said Louis. 'Who else is here?'

'No one, only me.'

Another man entered the room, this one smaller and older. He looked to Ilić like a mongrel, with no purity to his bloodline. This, Ilić guessed, was Angel, the hunter's partner. Ilić was disgusted by his enforced proximity to these *peškiri*.

'Check the other rooms,' said Louis, and Angel moved past him. He returned shortly after to announce that they were clear.

'Where is Radovan?' said Louis.

'Gone,' said Ilić. He did not know how Radovan had avoided these men. As the old saying went: don't measure the wolf's tail until he is dead.

'Gone where?'

'Go fuck yourself,' said Ilić, because one devil did not scratch out another devil's eyes. He might have wanted to punish Radovan for what he had done to Spiridon, but he would not give this man the satisfaction of taking Radovan's life.

'And the girl?'

Ilić was not surprised that they knew of Zorya. Images of her, all partial or blurred, had made their way into media reports on the deaths of the Turk, Hasanović, and the Dutchman, Hendricksen.

'Also gone.' Ilić heard the sadness in his own voice. He didn't blame Zorya for leaving, but still he felt abandoned by her.

'I don't suppose you know where she is either?' said Louis.

'No.'

'Then what good are you to me?'

'No good at all,' said Ilić, 'unless you want to hear how your Dutch friends died.'

'Not really,' said Louis, and he pulled the trigger.

Angel and Louis left the house not long after, having first searched it for any further information about Radovan Vuksan or the girl. All they found was Ilić's new passport, but at least they now knew the nationality under which Radovan was probably traveling, unless the dead woman, Kauffmann, had sourced passports from more than one country, which seemed unlikely.

Before they departed, they poured the contents of the liquor cabinet over the two bodies. The bottles contained mostly cheap whisky with a high alcohol content, and the liquid ignited easily. They were gone from the area before the first trails of smoke began to slip through the gaps in the windows, and were already at the airport as the fire seized the house.

By the time the blaze was under control, they had left Austria forever.

Chapter LXXXIV

Pia Lackner watched Rosanna Bellingham lock the door of the cottage and place the key under the mat for the landlord. Bob Johnston was already behind the wheel of the Galaxy, the motor running. They would be back in London before dark.

Angel had called Rosanna's phone the previous night, asking to speak with Lackner.

'It's over,' he had told her. 'Or your part in it, at least.'

'And my father?'

'Alive, and still at liberty.'

Despite her hatred for her father, Pia felt a sense of relief, although she thought it might have been as much for the sake of her own conscience as anything else.

'And the others?'

'One got away.'

'What about the rest?'

Angel's silence had been answer enough. Lackner had decided not to pursue the matter, again for the sake of her conscience.

She had reluctantly surrendered her Samsung Galaxy smartphone to Rosanna upon leaving the city in order to prevent the device being traced. It had now been returned to her, along with her previous existence. As she followed Rosanna to the car, the phone rang, and she saw her father's name on the screen.

Lackner stopped. Rosanna looked back at her.

'It's him,' said Lackner.

'You can answer it if you wish,' said Rosanna. 'It's your decision.'

Lackner accepted the call.

'Pia?' said Frend. 'Are you safe?'

'Yes. Thank you,' she added, although she was not sure why. Old habits of politeness, perhaps.

'I am glad,' said Frend, 'if unsurprised. Did you collude in this?'

'Yes,' she said.

'Why?' He sounded genuinely puzzled.

Lackner paused before replying.

'Because,' she said, 'I am my father's child.'

And she hung up to the sound of his laughter.

Chapter LXXXV

For a while all was quiet, and the hunt entered a period of stasis.

Radovan Vuksan had used his new passport to travel to Malaysia, where he vanished. Inquiries unearthed rumors of a man fitting his description living for a time in Malacca, in an apartment not far from St. Paul's Church, but by the time these tales reached New York, the individual in question had already left the country, and under yet another name.

But Louis was patient, and had favors to call in. Too many people were searching for Radovan Vuksan. He could not entirely disappear. And Zivco Ilić, by his final act, had condemned Radovan to death, for Spiridon's charred body had eventually been brought back to Serbia and interred in a family plot, the keratinous fragments of Radovan's nails now inseparably a part of his brother's remains.

At night, Radovan would wake to the sound of Spiridon's voice calling to him, and a room filled with the stink of burned flesh.

At the Cemetery of the Nameless, an attendant arrived to check on the graves and clear away the trash. The discovery of a woman's body in the chapel some weeks earlier had, for a time, drawn the wrong kind of people – television cameras, reporters, gawkers – to this place that he tended so lovingly, but he had faith in the capacity of the living to forget. Only the dead remembered.

As he took the path to the cemetery, his eye was drawn to a shape lying amid the leaves and fallen trees on the waste ground to his right. It resembled a bundle of discarded clothing, but the attendant had spent too long in the company of the deceased to mistake it for anything other than what it was.

Slowly, he descended to the corpse. Its hands and head had been removed, and its feet were bare. What remained was dressed in a suit that looked expensive, and a once-white shirt set off by a silk tie that was still knotted, a flamboyant gold tie pin holding it in place. The attendant crossed himself, before reluctantly taking his cell phone from the pocket of his overalls. All those terrible reporters would now return, and his realm would again be temporarily devoid of peace, but what else could he do? An effort would have to be made to identify this man, if only for the sake of his family, but should that effort fail, a place would be found for him, and a cross set above it. He could rest assured of that, and he would not want for company.

After all, were not all men destined at last to join the ranks of the nameless ones?

Chapter LXXXVI

The two-bedroom apartment was part of a new residential development in Woodstock, the oldest suburb of Cape Town. It rented for about nine thousand rand a month, and was within walking distance of the stores, restaurants, and neighborhood market at the Old Biscuit Mill. This area of Cape Town had slipped through the cracks when the apartheid-era Group Areas Act was being implemented, and so was more racially diverse and multicultural than most of the city's suburbs, although rising prices and gentrification now looked set to achieve what segregationists had failed to do.

A businessman – superficially friendly, but generally reclusive – lived in the apartment. His name was Oscar Frey, and he held a newly acquired South African passport, although those sensitive to accents thought he might have been of Eastern European origin. Frey had been resident in Woodstock for about three months, and operated a consultancy firm offering financial and logistical support and advice to small businesses wishing to expand their access to European markets, although he also claimed some knowledge of Latin America and the Caribbean. His was a one-man operation, working from the Woodstock apartment and a small office on Albert Road, and he was therefore restricted in the number of clients he could accept. Inquiries about engaging his services were often, if not always, met with an apology. He was already stretched to the limit of his resources, he would explain, and would not wish to provide a substandard service.

His client base was entirely Eastern European.

Some were Montenegrin.

Most were Serbian.

The Serbs had insinuated themselves into South African society during the early years of the new century, attracted by the low cost of living, the climate, the endemic corruption, the ease of shielding themselves from the attention of international law enforcement, and the difficulty of extraditing them should they ultimately fall under such scrutiny. Among this influx of Serbian immigrants were assorted war criminals, thieves, drug traffickers, and racketeers. They formed intricate support networks and set about founding legitimate and illegal businesses, including establishing Cape Town as a transit point for cocaine making its way from South America to Europe. Occasionally rivals took to killing one another in Cape Town and Gauteng, but for the most part the Serbians and Montenegrins behaved themselves. It was better for business that way.

Divided loyalties over the death of Nikola Musulin in Belgrade, and the subsequent ascent of Matija Kiš and Simo Stajić, had initially caused problems for the Serbs in South Africa. A couple of drive-by shootings had occurred, with one fatality in Johannesburg, but the country's importance to the Serbian cocaine trade meant that a truce was quickly brokered. Nobody, least of all the Serbs enjoying a pleasant, profitable life in South Africa, wished to screw up a good thing.

Oscar Frey's arrival in Cape Town had briefly threatened to reignite hostilities, until a message from the House of the National Assembly on Belgrade's Nikola Pašić Square advised that Frey was to be allowed to live and work unimpeded, just as long as he remained in South Africa. To celebrate, Frey hosted a dinner on a wine farm in Constantia, where the guests ate and drank until the small hours, and shared tales of war and empire.

It was, all would later declare, a night to remember.

Oscar Frey entered his apartment and set down a box of wine and a bag of groceries from Woolworths on Adderley Street. He went to the bathroom, washed his hands, and began unpacking the bag. He thought about opening one of the bottles of chenin blanc, but they were warm from the car. It would not kill him to wait a while, and he had business to which to attend in the meantime. He took off his shirt, leaving only a vest and shorts, and turned on the A/C.

It was then that a hand covered his mouth and his right arm was wrenched painfully behind him. Before he could even think about fighting back, he had been rendered harmless: had he attempted to struggle, his arm would have been dislocated from its socket. The hand on his face was gloved, but enough of the skin was revealed to enable Frey to determine that the intruder was black. Frey kept a revolver in the apartment, but carried it only if he was driving at night. He was familiar with the stories about how dangerous certain parts of Cape Town could be, but so far had endured nothing more unpleasant than one or two unusually persistent beggars. It had never occurred to him that he might become a victim of crime in his own home, and during daylight hours.

'Down,' said a male voice in his left ear.

The voice was unusually calm. Frey lowered himself to the floor, motivated by the pressure on his right arm. When his knees touched the carpet, his arm was released, and the hand was removed from his mouth. Frey considered crying out for help, but the same voice warned him not to, and it brooked no argument. Neither did it contain any hint of a South African accent. It sounded American.

His assailant shifted position to stand before him, drawing a gun from his belt as he moved. Frey took barely a moment to recognize the intruder. After all, he had watched this man enter a house in the suburbs of Vienna, a house in which lay a body not yet grown cold, and set it aflame.

'Oscar Frey,' said Louis. 'You pick that name yourself?'

'He was an old tutor of mine,' said Radovan Vuksan. 'He taught me German. Why are you here?'

'Why do you think?'

'Spiridon is dead. So are all the others who killed your friends.'

'But you're still alive.'

'I have killed only one person in my life, and that was my own brother. I saved you the bother of doing it. You have no quarrel with me.'

'Don't I?' said Louis. 'You were there when De Jaager and the others died. You permitted the girl to torture Hendricksen.'

'I could not have stopped it.'

'You could have tried.'

'I advised against all of it.'

'I'm not sure that counts for a lot.'

Radovan stared at the gun in Louis's hand.

'I have money,' he said.

'I don't need money,' said Louis, 'but I do need information.'

Radovan's eyes suddenly shone with hope.

'What kind of information?'

'I want to know about the girl.'

'Her name is Zorya.'

'That I'm already aware of. Where is she now?'

'Back in Serbia.'

'Where in Serbia? Does she have family, friends?'

'She has none of those things. If she ever did, they're long dead.'

'The question stands: Where in Serbia?'

Radovan hesitated.

'Are you an honorable man?' he said.

'More honorable than you.'

'Even so, why would I tell you anything? How will it aid me?'

'If you tell me where the girl can be found,' said Louis, 'I won't shoot you. You have my word.'

'Why should I believe you?'

'Because if you don't tell me, I *will* shoot you. Your scope for compromise is limited.'

Radovan nodded.

'Ask after her in Bor or Negotin. Talk to the Vlachs. They'll know where she's hiding.'

'Okay, then,' said Louis. He put away the gun and produced a wire garrote with wooden handles. 'Let's get this done.'

'No, you promised—'

'You ought to listen better.'

Louis was fast, so very fast. A kick left Radovan flat on the floor, and then the garrote was being looped around his neck. Radovan managed to get the fingertips of his left hand under the

378

wire, but it sliced them off before tightening on his throat. Louis's knee was in his back, and the wire was cutting, severing. Radovan felt his skin give way, and the flesh succumbed.

Blood flowed, blood fountained.

Life ceased.

Angel was waiting for Louis at a table in the Test Kitchen, almost within sight of Oscar Frey's now redundant office. The Test Kitchen figured in every list of the world's best restaurants, and Angel and Louis had decided to try the place while they were in town. They'd booked the table weeks in advance, just as soon as Oscar Frey's true identity had been confirmed. Louis was wearing a fresh jacket and shirt. His earlier attire couldn't be saved, and was now burning in a barrel on waste ground. Louis didn't mind. The jacket was three seasons old and had never fitted quite as well as it should have.

A bottle of Charles Fox Cipher Brut sat in an ice bucket beside the table. A waiter materialized to pour Louis a glass.

'Well?' said Angel.

Louis sipped the wine.

'I reunited him with his brother.'

'Good,' said Angel. 'Nothing's more important than family.'

Chapter LXXXVII

It was late spring when Angel and Louis finally flew into Belgrade. As the only black passenger on the flight, Louis had to endure a thorough baggage search, even though he was also the best-dressed person on board. Their driver was waiting for them in the arrival hall. His name was Željko, and he came highly recommended by Most's Serbian contacts, which was as close to a guarantee of quality as one could get in an uncertain world. He spoke perfect English, and drove a black Lexus hybrid.

They had booked a suite for one night at the Townhouse 27 Hotel in the center of the city, and ate dinner that evening at Ambar, accompanied by Željko. There they consumed Balkan food, drank Serbian wine, and spoke of the Vlach.

Early the following morning, Željko drove them east to the Bor District, which bordered the Danube and Romania at its eastern extremes. At the Bukovo Monastery, they sheltered from icy fog as a monk fed them red wine from the monastery's vineyards and said that, yes, he had heard stories of a creature that had taken the form of a young girl, but there were many such legends in these lands. Some said she was one of the *rusalki*, female entities that stayed eternally youthful, formed from the souls of young women who had drowned. The Romanians of his acquaintance claimed she was the restless spirit of a witch.

But what did *he* think, Louis asked, and waited for Željko to translate. The monk took his time before answering.

'He thinks,' said Željko, 'that she's the reason the monastery has a lock on its gate.'

The monk provided them with the name of Johain, a man in the village of Kobišnica, and offered to make a telephone call to let

380

him know they were coming. Johain met them by the village's two war memorials, where the local dogs emerged to sniff the newcomers curiously. Johain's English was almost as good as Željko's, and he admitted that only the intervention of the monk had caused him to agree to meet with them.

The village had just a few stores, and the streets were empty of cars and people. Like so many other such communities, it had been decimated by emigration. But Kobišnica, Johain explained, was also a Vlach settlement and had, for two centuries, been locked in a state of feud with the neighboring hamlet of Bukovče.

'Because you're Vlach?' said Louis.

'No,' Johain replied, 'because one day someone decided that he didn't want to live in Bukovče anymore.'

Which sounded to Louis like as good a reason as any to leave a place.

'The monk said you were looking for a certain girl,' said Johain.

'That's right.'

'Why?'

'She killed a friend of ours.'

'Tell me what happened.'

Louis did, leaving out only his own involvement in any subsequent deaths. 'There was a rumor she might be Vlach,' he finished.

'She is not,' said Johain.

'Then what is she?'

'She is *strigoi*, maybe, come from below the ground. The French were mining in Bor, digging for copper and gold. They dug too deep. The *strigoi* was sleeping, and they woke her. If she has returned here, she is sleeping again.'

'Where?'

'A dark place where she won't be disturbed, probably close to where she was first woken.'

'What if we were to go to Bor and ask there?'

'You can ask,' said Johain, 'but no one will tell you, even if they know.'

'Why?'

'In case she hears.'

Louis looked at Željko, who shrugged. 'I just drive,' he said.

'What will you do if you find her?' said Johain.

'Kill her,' said Louis.

'You can't kill her.'

'Well,' said Angel, 'that's just fucking great.'

'But,' said Johain, 'you can destroy her.'

They spent the night at a hotel in Negotin, where they waited for Johain to call. He contacted them shortly after 7 a.m., as the sky filled with light. He asked if they had brought good boots and they told him they had. When they picked him up in Kobišnica, he was holding a hand-drawn map.

'I think I know where she is,' he said, as he got into the car and gave Željko directions in Serbian.

'I thought you told us people were afraid she'd hear,' said Angel.

'They whispered.'

'I hate this place,' said Angel.

'Also, if you fail, they believe she'll probably come after you, not them,' said Johain. 'And if you succeed, you'll have done them a service.'

'What about you?'

'Oh, she'll come after me, too, which is why I'm going with you to make sure you don't fail.'

Angel supposed there was a kind of logic to this, but trying to figure out what it might be made his head hurt, so he stopped.

'I must make an observation,' said Johain. 'You are very accepting of all this strangeness.'

Angel and Louis exchanged a glance, and thought of Parker.

'Man,' said Angel, 'you don't even know from strange.'

They drove to Lazar's Canyon, six miles from Bor. Lazar's Canyon, Johain explained, was the deepest, most inhospitable chasm in the country, more than three miles long and carved by the Lazar River from limestone reefs dating from the Jurassic period. It descended to nearly a quarter of a mile at its deepest point, and was twelve feet across at its narrowest, the floor strewn with boulders and sown with rock towers, the steep slopes drenched by waterfalls, marred by rockslides, and pitted with caves and caverns.

'She sleeps in there,' said Johain, pointing into the shadows of the canyon, the sunlight seeming almost to shirk from exploring its reaches.

'Did I say I hate this place?' said Angel.

'You did,' said Johain.

'Did I also mention that I'm recovering from cancer?'

'You can stay with the car, if you prefer.'

Angel turned to Željko. 'What are you going to do?'

'I also would prefer to stay with the car,' he said, 'but he' – Željko pointed at Louis – 'told me I wasn't being paid to sit on my fucking ass. Excuse me, but those were his exact words. Also, someone has to carry the hammer.'

'The hammer?' said Angel.

'The hammer,' said Johain.

'Why do we need a hammer?' said Angel. 'Actually, don't tell me.'

His gaze moved between the Audi and the canyon.

'And I thought Jersey was wild,' he said. 'Okay, fine. I'm coming too.'

They headed into the canyon. The day was already cold, but the canyon's depths were colder still. They tried their best to stay in what little sun there was, yet even that was sparse. Angel walked more slowly than the others, but not by much: the boulders on the canyon floor forced frequent detours, and sometimes they were obliged to clamber over rockslides that had blocked the way entirely. They would break a sweat only for it to cool upon them once the obstacle was cleared. It was misery for Angel, although he did not complain. He had not tested his body in this way since the surgery, and it was standing up to the ordeal. This was why he had endured the pain of the operation and the subsequent misery of chemotherapy: to feel pain and know that he could beat it.

At last they came to a small waterfall that fed into a stream. To the right of the waterfall were three holes in the rock, one larger than the rest. The cliff face looked unscalable at first, but from an angle it was possible to spot depressions that might serve as handholds and footholds.

'There,' said Johain.

'You're sure?' said Louis.

'Would I have brought you here otherwise?'

'I sure hope not.'

Angel sat on a boulder. 'There's no way I can get up there.'

'I can make it,' said Željko.

'Yeah, I reckon I can too,' said Louis. He turned to Johain. 'What about you?'

'I will stay here, with Angel.'

'Afraid?' said Louis.

'Very,' said Johain.

The climb was easier than it looked, but the largest of the caves, when Louis and Željko entered it, narrowed significantly beyond its mouth. The two men had flashlights, but were forced to crouch as they ventured deeper, until finally Louis was convinced that they might have to crawl if they were to progress farther. This he had no desire to do. He did not suffer particularly from claustrophobia, but something primal in him rebelled against the prospect of enclosure.

Then, just as it seemed crawling would indeed be forced upon them, the cave widened again, and they found themselves in a small chamber in which they could almost stand upright. In an alcove lay the exsiccated remains of a small human being, like a skeleton wrapped in old paper. The body was curled into the fetal position, the hands folded beneath the head as though to cushion it in sleep.

'Is it her?' said Željko.

The chin was pointed, and the skull slightly rounded, which suggested the remains were female. Louis focused his attention on the spine. The scoliosis of which Frend had spoken was plain to see.

'It's her,' said Louis. 'Hand me the sack.'

Željko produced a woven sack from his pack and held it open while Louis shifted the cadaver into it, the skin tearing and the bones separating in the process. They then retraced their steps, Željko leading, until they reemerged into the canyon. Louis tied off the top of the sack and dropped it to where Angel and Johain waited. He and Željko climbed back down without incident, and the four men stood around the body, the bones poking against the material, the hemisphere of the skull rising from the heart of them.

'Give me the hammer,' said Louis.

Željko handed it over, and Louis broke the bones, striking at them over and over until they were reduced to fragments. Angel then took a turn, followed by Željko, until the fragments became little more than shards and dust. Johain did not offer to help. When they were done, Louis opened the sack and tipped the contents into the stream. He turned to Johain.

'Are you sure that'll do it?'

'Can't you feel it?' said Johain. 'She's gone.'

Zorya opened her eyes. Jennifer Parker was standing before her. Behind Jennifer, the dead immersed themselves in still waters.

'You were right,' said Zorya. 'I wanted to hurt them, just as they once hurt me. Men, women, all of them.' Zorya's voice sounded clearer to her than before. She was of this place now. 'Are you going to hurt me as well?'

'We're beyond that,' said Jennifer.

'Are we?'

'It would serve no purpose. And I understand you. You see, I also want to inflict punishment. A man tore me apart. He cut off my face and punctured my eyes.'

'I'm sorry,' said Zorya.

'I know you are. I want revenge for what was done to me.'

Zorya looked beyond Jennifer to where the dead lost themselves.

'Must I go with them?' said Zorya.

'Not if you don't want to.'

'What else can I do?'

'You can be like me,' said Jennifer, as worlds burned in her eyes. 'You can wait.'

ACKNOWLEDGMENTS

It was my good fortune, during the research for this book, to cross paths with my fellow writer Robert Pimm (www.robert pimm.com) in Vienna. It was Robert – and his partner, Gözde Eren – who suggested I visit the Friedhof der Namenlosen, the Cemetery of the Nameless, while I was in the city, which gave this novel both its title and one of its central scenes. For their kindness, hospitality, and advice I am deeply grateful. *Only in Vienna* by Duncan J. D. Smith (Brandstätter, 2005), another of Robert's recommendations, proved a useful and informative guide to Vienna's more obscure sights. My thanks also go to the staff at Literaturhaus Wien, and especially its curator, Dr Anne Zauner, for giving such a warm welcome to a stranger.

While the villains in this novel may be Serbian, I experienced only unconditional assistance and immense goodwill during my time in that country. I would particularly like to thank my driver, Željko Rajkovic, who also stepped in to interpret for me at crucial moments; all at www.exclusiveserbia.com, including general manager Zoran Zupanc; and the staff at Townhouse 27 Hotel in Belgrade, for organizing everything from drivers to shoe repair. In Negotin, I was blessed to meet the wonderful Emila Petrović – author, ethnoanthropologist, and curator of the town's very fine Krajina Museum – who was helpfulness personified. Emila in turn introduced me to Ivan Gudojević, who patiently explained to me something of the history and culture of the Vlach people during a chilly afternoon in Kobišnica.

While I spent a lot of time reading about the Balkan conflict, two works of fiction particularly resonated: *As If I Am Not There* (aka *S: A Novel About the Balkans*) by Slavenka Drakulić (Hachette, 2013), and *The Hotel Tito* by Ivana Bodrožić (Seven

Stories Press, 2018). Some of the information on the sale of passports and the 'identity management' industry came from articles by John Arlidge, including 'Citizenship for Sale' (*The Sunday Times*, March 24, 2019) and 'Business Executives Are Buying Second Nationalities. Here's Why.' (*Robb Report*, August 5, 2019). Hannah Kauffmann, I should add, bears no relation to any lawyer, Viennese or otherwise, living or dead. 'The Mystery of Vlach Magic in the Rural Areas of 21st Century Serbia,' by Andjelija Ivkov-Džigurski, Vedrana Babić, Aleksandra Dragin, Kristina Košić, and Ivana Blešić (*Eastern European Countryside*, January 2012), provided a fascinating short introduction to many aspects of Vlach culture and beliefs.

I remain indebted to everyone at my British publishers, Hodder & Stoughton, including my editor, Sue Fletcher, as well as Swati Gamble, Carolyn Mays, Rebecca Mundy, Myrto Kalavrezou, Alice Morley, Catherine Worsley, Dominic Smith, Alasdair Oliver, and all the sales team. At Atria/Emily Bestler Books, my editor Emily Bestler continues to provide a welcome home for my work, aided by Lara Jones, David Brown, Gena Lanzi, and Milena Brown. Huge thanks to you all. My agent, Darley Anderson, and his crew remain steadfast as always. With the aid of my non- English-language publishers, of whom I am immensely fond, they have brought my books to readers around the world.

Dominick Montalto has, for many years, done his utmost as copy-editor to save my blushes, as has Sarah Wright. Any errors that persist do so only because my frailties know no bounds. I would also be lost without Ellen Clair Lamb, who looks after so much author-related business for me; my son Cameron Ridyard, who has designed, and maintains, my website; his brother, Alistair, who keeps me endlessly amused; and Jennie, who keeps me sane, mostly. Jennie, Clair, and Cliona O'Neill additionally read this manuscript in an effort to make the task of copy-editing a little easier.

Finally, thanks to you, the reader, for continuing to support my work, and to the booksellers and librarians who give my books a place on their shelves. Long may you all sail.

John Connolly, 2021

THRILLINGLY GOOD BOOKS
FROM CRIMINALLY
GOOD WRITERS

CRIME FILES BRINGS YOU THE LATEST RELEASES FROM
TOP CRIME AND THRILLER AUTHORS.

SIGN UP ONLINE FOR OUR MONTHLY NEWSLETTER AND BE THE FIRST
TO KNOW ABOUT OUR COMPETITIONS, NEW BOOKS AND MORE.

VISIT OUR WEBSITE: WWW.CRIMEFILES.CO.UK
LIKE US ON FACEBOOK: FACEBOOK.COM/CRIMEFILES
FOLLOW US ON TWITTER: @CRIMEFILESBOOKS